Llyfrgelloedd Caerdydd
www.caerdydd.gov.uk/llyfrgelloedd
Cardiff Libraries
www.cardiff.gov.uk/libraries

'Masterful – a far-reaching tapestry of a novel. Nuanced and whip-smart, *Act of Grace* is a work of profound empathy – a book of and for our times. As the narrative unfolds with precise muscularity, Krien's inhabitation of each character approaches the divine.'
—**Peggy Frew**

'Krien has taken a huge leap of creative faith, and from the very first page to the last I was ready to follow her anywhere.'
—**Ceridwen Dovey**

'Krien makes riveting the sweep of history and the lived price of war; at the same time she reveals, with great insight, the intimacies of daily love and tiny, splintering acts of violence in families. She is both wide-angle and close-up, and there is redemption in every line.'
—**Anna Funder**

'Krien's first novel is a high-wire performance. With its vast historical rigging, epic scope, ethical complexity and kaleidoscopic view, *Act of Grace* is enormously ambitious. The reader watches, breath held, as the novel unspools, but Krien's step is sure, and she does not fall.'
—***Australian Book Review***

'An ambitious and compelling study of trauma and how it's transferred and inherited … a nuanced consideration of the different forms and ethics of activism.'
—***Books+Publishing***

'The wisdom and balance of Krien's writing captivates.'
—***Daily Telegraph***

Also by Anna Krien

The Long Goodbye: Coal, Coral and Australia's
Climate Deadlock (2016)

Booze Territory (2015)

Night Games: Sex, Power and Sport (2013)

Us and Them: On the Importance of Animals (2012)

Into the Woods: The Battle for Tasmania's Forests (2010)

Act of Grace

Anna Krien

—

First published in Great Britain in 2020 by
Serpent's Tail
an imprint of Profile Books Ltd
29 Cloth Fair
London
ECIA 7JQ
www.serpentstail.com

First published in Australia by
Black Inc.,
an imprint of Schwartz Books Pty Ltd

Text design and typesetting by Akiko Chan

This project has been assisted by the Australian Government through the
Australia Council for the Arts, its arts funding and advisory body.

1 3 5 7 9 10 8 6 4 2

Printed and bound in Great Britain by
Clays Ltd, Elcograf S.p.A.

A CIP catalogue record for this book is available from the British Library.

ISBN 978 1 78816 421 4
eISBN 978 1 78283 649 0

Act of Grace

—

The Mouse Plague

Toohey hadn't been one of the rock-throwers, but that didn't mean he hadn't wanted to. A couple of times he'd even grabbed one of the stones Jolley piled up on the floor of the Bushmaster and taken aim as they drove through a pre-teen ambush, homing in on a kid, his hair grey with dust and bare feet hopping angrily as he dodged the soldiers' counterattack. With black caterpillar eyebrows and dark oily eyes, these kids were targets more real than the shadowy enemy.

At the start of the tour, the children had flocked around the men – it was a hazard, but the soldiers only half-heartedly shooed them away. The kids cheered, stretching out their arms for gifts. The men had footballs to give, the Aussie flag printed on fake leather. The footies had been flat-packed, and they had to pump up about twenty each, a bag of them crammed under the cage where the gunner's legs dangled. Whole thing was awkward as fuck, and they joked that some PR princess back home was getting a promotion for this. Still, the gunners enjoyed the rare safe moments when they could handball footies from the tops of their armoured vehicles. It made them feel good – the kids with their impish smiles, clamouring to high-five them. 'No, no, that's American,' they'd say. 'In Australia we do this,' giving the kids a thumbs-up and an 'oi, oi, oi!' Soon children were running at them with both arms straight out like zombies, thumbs up. Made them laugh. 'What a bunch of spazzes,' Jolley said.

Most of the kids were good kicks, and the men couldn't help but compare them to their own sullen drips, who hid behind their mothers whenever the unit returned from a tour. The kids here practically lit up, flinging aside whatever they were doing, bolting out of houses, often wearing no shoes but sprinting over rocks and thistles. Their children back home didn't come close to interested, except when a present from duty-free was dangled in front of them. Iraqi kids, they made it all worth it, the soldiers often said, as if this was the reason they'd signed up in the first place, to protect the children, oh, and the women – women and children – but shit, most of them didn't have a reason for signing up when they did, only that school was finishing and the future lay empty ahead.

Then the kids started throwing rocks. At first it was just one or two of them. 'Go home,' they'd shout, their faces hard, 'you fucking war criminals!' Words they didn't know the meaning of, had just heard from the ever-larger groups of young men who stood watching, training their eyes on the convoys. The kids' pronunciation was never right, and for a while this helped them laugh it off, especially when other children shushed the hecklers. The hecklers often ended up putting their hands out for stuff anyway, and the soldiers took pleasure in looking the other way. But after a month or so, more kids were yelling things. They'd put out their hands, take their pick of the presents, *then* start in. The soldiers began to see deflated footballs everywhere: on the side of the road, stuck up the spindly trees, in the middle of fucking nowhere. Soon they were being treated as potential IEDs and the men were ordered to stop giving them away. Some PR princess back home was getting fired for this.

It all went to shit halfway through the second tour, after a long day spent escorting a food truck through the province. A group of kids came out of a cluster of houses on the outskirts. It was dusk and the unit was tired, wary of pushing the day's luck, so the convoy only slowed, the gunners squatting to grab textas and sweets to lob. But when they came back up, rocks cracked against their helmets. For a second the unit thought it was an ambush, and the gunners swung their turrets, trying to get a bead. Then more rocks clipped the vehicles, and it clicked. The kids' voices rose up over the engines. 'Fuck off, fuck off, fuck off,' they were screaming, some coughing with the effort – croup they hadn't been able to shake since the sanctions. Their faces were twisted with hate; a few even had tears streaking down their cheeks, snot bubbling from their noses. They stared at the men accusingly, their eyes raw and red. They threw all the rocks they had and scrounged in the dirt for more, still yelling, 'Fuck off, fuck off.' The unit just gaped. Some recognised kids from earlier in the day, who'd been sweet as pie as they collected their family's rations. Eventually an order broke the spell and they accelerated in unison, leaving the children behind, ghostly in the dust, a final rock making a humiliating plonk against the rear vehicle.

Heading back, the men were mostly silent. The commander had changed the route at the last minute. If they had followed the plan, they could have taken the glow of aid back to base, but they had gone a different way and rocks had been thrown.

It kept happening after that, and the unit dropped any guise of parade, of selfless heroism. No more thumbs-up. No more 'Good kick!' They knuckled down. For the best, their corporal reckoned. Back to muscle and bone, eyes scanning the horizon. Counterinsurgency was pissing in the wind. The only skin that mattered now was one another's. Fuck the Iraqis, fuck the politics, fuck the diplomacy.

What happened next was hard to explain. None of the men could say who started it or how, but they began fighting back. Some collected rocks before heading out, piling them on the rubber mats in their vehicles. The first time they did it, the Iraqi kids were taken by surprise. In such a short time, they'd absorbed the American spin that children were sacred, that they would be protected, no matter what. They stood in the open, not bothering to hide or cover their faces, so when the unit's return fire hit, most didn't move, their mouths open, catching flies. Only when a few were struck did they start to scatter, leaping behind walls and mounds of dirt.

'Fuck you, you midget terrorists,' yelled the soldiers, whooping over their radios as the kids screamed, red-faced and furious. Most soldiers aimed to skim the kids' legs, to get a yelp and a hop out of them, but as the rock war intensified and the real war got murkier, a few of the guys started a competition: *one rock, how many children?* They'd aim for an angle: an elbow, a shoulder, a cheekbone if they were feeling real nasty, ricocheting a rock off one kid to the next. Record was four kids, one rock. Even soldiers dead against the business had to admit that hit by Wedge was pretty amazing. A good hit is all about the rock, was his theory, and he had his ammunition down to an art. He divided the desert rubble into types: the 'cluster fuck' was a chunky nugget that crumbled on impact, the 'ninja star' a sharp jagged quarry stone, and a 'skimmer' a thin, oval-shaped river rock. Wedge had flicked the skimmers at the kids like frisbees. He'd set his record with one, and so they became sought after.

*

A skimmer was what Toohey was looking for now. He was in a different desert, one with red dirt that bruised to purple at dusk, where the highway was bloated with kangaroo corpses, cattle too, belly-up, hit by road trains. None a potential IED. A different rock supply, but skimmers, Toohey figured, were universal. Jean was behind him crying, standing at the edge of the bitumen, and the night was pressing in on them. In front of him, the scrub rippled like a huge fish turning.

There was a scurrying on the ground and Toohey saw a mouse dart across his boot. A lone straggler – the plague had petered out hours back. And then he saw it: oval-shaped, flat. He knelt to pick it up. It fit the curve of his index finger perfectly, and with his thumb he rubbed the surface smooth, scanning the bush for Gerry.

*

Two days earlier, the mice had made them happy. They spilled like marbles over the highway, scampering forwards and then backwards as Toohey fishtailed the car in their direction. 'There!' Gerry would scream, leaning forward from the back seat, his arm stretched. 'There!' Pointing through the windscreen at the little grey bundles. 'You got it!' he would cheer, turning around to glimpse the carnage while Jean made a show of covering her eyes in mock-horror – a performance, because in truth squashing the mice was bringing them together. The flattened strips of fur on the bitumen, guts coming out the mouth and arse like sauce, it was making them feel like a family. The killing relaxed Toohey, and when the cheering got quieter, he sipped slowly on his cigarette, still aiming for the mice but in a graceful kind of way, and the lull, the dance of the car, got everyone dreaming.

Jean lifted herself off the seat to unstick her dress from her thighs. It was hot. The air rushing through the open windows was clammy. She took a tube of moisturiser from her handbag and, propping her feet on the dash, rubbed the cream into her calves. Before they left the bungalow in Kalgoorlie, Jean had shaved her legs and painted her toenails with peach varnish. She felt Toohey glance over at her appreciatively, one hand steady on the wheel. She caught his eye and smiled. She was happy to be going home, though careful not to show it. He'd figure she made it happen, made it all go to shit. He'd twist everything – the pinballing from Melbourne to Perth, briefly bumping inland to Kalgoorlie – until it was all her doing.

In the back, Gerry stared out his window, fingers on the glass. He'd conjured up a cowboy and could see him, riding a chestnut mare in the red dirt alongside the road. There was a fence coming up, a long, dog-proof fence, and Gerry's heart hammered like hooves. *Up*, he thought, *up*, and the cowboy cinched in his heels of his boots, pressing into the horse's belly, and up she leapt, over the fence, the cowboy holding his hat, and Gerry could barely breathe, the galloping felt so real.

It was Miss Munro who'd got him into this. She'd bring all these travel brochures into class for the kids to flick through and cut out pictures to make collages. There were lions, great big turtles floating in blue water, Maasai people wearing bright tartan robes, and so many places to stay: houseboats on old brown rivers, fancy hotel rooms with fridges and minibars, thatched huts on islands. Gerry got hooked on the brochures with cowboy tours in them: Golden Horseshoe ranches and cattle-branding experiences and bandy-legged men with stubble that flecked orange in sunsets. He would go through the box looking for these brochures and sneak them into his schoolbag, rescuing them from the scissors. At night, while his parents watched TV, he'd look at the pictures, carefully stashing the pages under the bed before falling asleep. 'It's not just cowboys in America,' Miss Munro tried to explain to Gerry, when she noticed how he coveted the Midwest brochures. 'There's cities with famous buildings and celebrities. Hollywood.' Gerry nodded, but he didn't care about those things, and while cop shows blared from the television in the living room, sirens and gunshots and men yelling 'Get down, get down!', he'd close his eyes, listening to the *clop-clop-clop* of horses in his head.

Toohey stopped the car suddenly and the cowboy almost got thrown as the mare skidded to a halt. Confused, Gerry and Jean looked at Toohey as he reversed expertly, using just the heel of his palm on the wheel. When he touched the brakes again, they were at the mouth of a small sandy road coming off the highway.

'Holy shit,' Toohey said, shaking his head. 'I wasn't sure I'd recognise it.' He stared down the track, then nodded. 'Yep, this is definitely it.' He put the car into gear, the tyres loose on the sand, and drove inland. 'You've got to see this,' he said to Jean and Gerry, his eyes narrowing.

Slowly the scrub thinned into solitary shrubs, brittle and white against the red sand. The mice petered out too, preferring to stay close to the highway. It made Jean nervous, this unexpected turn, and she balled her hands into tight fists. She kept glancing at Toohey, checking his mood. But his cheeks were flushed, his lips curled up at the corners. 'I wasn't sure I'd be able to remember it,' he kept saying, and she realised he'd been planning this, scanning the highway for a sign, timing it from the dog-proof fence.

'You sure this is a good idea?' Jean asked, as the road kept yawning out in front of them, the car bouncing over the corrugations.

Toohey sniffed. 'It's a fucking great idea.'

They drove past refrigerators and rusted husks of cars. They passed dead foxes strung up on a fence line, their tails like fiery brushstrokes, and a silver caravan with a satellite dish flattening itself like an ear to the sky. In the side mirror, Jean tried to glimpse Gerry, send him a smile, but his eyes avoided hers. She snuck her arm around the seat and gave his leg a squeeze. Several times the road forked into two and Toohey stopped, thinking, before accelerating again. He seemed to see markers that the other two couldn't, until finally he let out a low whistle. 'There it is.'

It was an eerie sight, a rural village in southern Iraq growing out of the Australian desert. Shacks, shops, even a small mosque with a dome-shaped roof made from pressed earth, and there were black electricity cables woven between wooden poles, pulled so tight that the poles leaned in towards each other. A cyclone fence ran the perimeter, and as they drove closer Jean could see the street signs with Arabic script. Toohey stopped the car at a metal gate on sliding tracks and stared. He shook his head as if impressed. 'Me and the boys thought we'd won the lottery when we saw this place,' he said. 'It was a damn sight better than Kandahar.' Toohey's unit had trained here for their second stint in the Middle East, Jean remembered. There'd been a controversy in the papers, she recalled that too, when it got out that Iraqis on temporary visas were being bussed to a secret location to participate in an army training exercise.

Toohey cracked open his door, dust pooling in the hull of the car. He got out and stretched, beckoning to them to follow. He walked past a sign warning against trespass and found a loose part of the fence, lifting it. Gerry was first, crawling under as thistles stuck to his shorts. Jean hung back. She searched Toohey's face. She pointed at the sign. 'Maybe we shouldn't?'

'C'mon. I'm not gonna hold this forever.'

Jean got down on her hands and knees, ducking her head. As she went under, Toohey playfully kicked her bum. She yelped, crawling faster and laughing as she tried to swipe him away. On the other side, she stood up, brushing the orange dirt off her knees, and shyly held the fence up for him, but Toohey spidered his fingers through the metal diamonds and climbed over, his arms flexing, muscles bulging.

Jean watched and felt an instant wetness between her thighs as he landed beside her. She got a flash of how beautiful he'd been when he came back from his first posting. His eyes had been clear, no demons, at least not of the Iraq kind. His body had been supple and brown. He'd been ripped. All the guys in his unit were. Toohey used to talk about how after training in the mornings most of them mixed up protein drinks in cocktail shakers, keeping a plastic keg of powder beside their beds. It was a point of pride that he didn't touch the stuff.

'The whole thing was a joke,' she remembered him telling her brother-in-law when they were living in Melbourne. Toohey and Stuart had been getting along for once. 'It was as if all we needed was weight, bulk, to crush Iraq,' he had said. 'But they ran rings around us. You couldn't predict a fucking thing about them, and let me tell you, those bastards never had a fucking protein shake in their life.' Stuart had laughed and laughed.

But this knowledge didn't deter Toohey from continuing to work out, Jean noticed. For ninety minutes each day he'd lift weights, puffing out his cheeks, neck taut, long spidery veins rising on his arms like welts. He'd adjust the discs on his barbell, skip for twenty and drop his dumbbells onto the carpet when he was done with a routine thud. He did the same regime he had followed when he was enlisted – same lifts, same weight, he boasted. His core strength hadn't changed. But his enthusiasm had gone. When he was younger, still part of his unit, Jean remembered how he'd approach each exercise session with bravado, often issuing himself an extra challenge. But now, Toohey did his weights like it was a sentence. On the odd occasion she'd been able to observe him, she saw a grim expression on his face as he went through his sets, his body inflating and hardening as if he were filling with cement. Still, he was beautiful.

Jean reached out to Toohey as he walked purposefully towards the village. He paused, letting her drift her hand down his arm before catching her wrist. He smiled, pulling her close. 'Come on,' he said, nodding at Gerry. The first street they entered was narrow and adorned with Arabic signs, sun-bleached billboards for Coca-Cola and Baghdad cigarettes. Toohey spun round. 'It's exactly the same!' There were rubber thongs and Velcro sandals left outside hobbit-sized doorways, and shops stacked with pretend boxes of biscuits and salted crackers, watches, belt buckles, refillable cigarette lighters and snow globes. Another stall had bolts, nuts and washers neatly laid out on a yellowed lace tablecloth alongside old tools that looked like they'd been found in a dig. There were trestle tables piled with books, rugs, hookah pipes, copper bowls, bronze pitchers and lanterns, baskets of spices and polystyrene fruit, the surface pocked by bugs. Gerry ran ahead, yelling excitedly: 'This shop has toys!' His voice had that hopeful whine Toohey hated so much. Jean checked to see if he'd noticed but Toohey was looking around, his eyes shining. 'Still think we shouldn't have come in?' Jean shook her head.

Toohey led them through the tight streets, pointing out sniper holes in the walls where the pretend enemy had rested their pretend gun barrels. They looked inside low buildings, stooping to pass through the doorways. Tattered curtains fluttered like cobwebs over the window frames. There were stained floral mattresses and lumpy couches, rickety chairs pulled up alongside. The rooms stank of piss and time.

Painted on the front of an official-looking building was a portrait of Saddam Hussein, while pasted along its side were posters of the dictator's eldest son, Uday.

'That caused a fuss with the Iraqis,' Toohey said, pointing at Uday. He explained that Saddam's eldest son had been, among other things, chairman of the Iraq Football Association. He was known for torturing the athletes if they missed a penalty kick. 'Every day the Iraqis would come past here and spit on him.' He stopped at a poster and picked at the edges, carefully peeling it off the wall. 'They'd never spit on Saddam, though,' he said. 'Most were too scared to even walk past it. We reckoned the painter had done the bastard's eyes like Mona Lisa's on purpose – he was always watching you.' Rolling up the poster of Uday, he passed it to Jean. 'Souvenir.'

As he stopped to light a cigarette, Toohey spotted a greasy blue diesel generator on the outskirts of the village. 'Let's see if this has any kick left in it,' he said, tucking the smoke in the corner of his lips as he knelt to fiddle with the switches. There was a short, wet splutter, and Toohey beamed. 'Fuck me!' he said. He tried again: nothing. Over and over he flicked the switch, but couldn't get anything beyond that small rise. Toohey stared at it, thinking and smoking. Then he winked at Gerry. 'This might do the trick.' He tossed the cigarette butt and prised the lid off a cloudy-white plastic container sitting among the tubes in the generator, bending it back so it wouldn't close. He undid his pants and took his penis out, ignoring Jean, who had let out a small gasp. Carefully he aimed at the hole, shooting forth a stream of piss. 'Radiator fluid,' he said when he'd finished, giving his dick a little shake.

Gerry's eyes were popping out of his head; he already had his shorts down and half-ran, half-hopped over. 'Can I have a go?'

'No!' Jean shrieked, just as Toohey nodded and moved aside so that Gerry could get closer to the container. Already Gerry was pee-ing, squeezing his small penis between his fingers and spraying urine over the generator.

'Jesus, kid,' said Toohey. 'You need to learn some control.'

Gerry reddened and attempted to slow his stream down, getting a trickle in the container. Jean hid a smile, shaking her head, but she had her sister's voice in her head. 'Seriously?' she imagined Bron say-ing. 'You seriously think that's a good idea?'

'Gerard needs a role model,' her sister had said to her once, 'not a fucking idiot.' Words spoken in the heat of an argument – at least that's what Bron said later, but it was just her doing the arguing. Jean had sat, head bowed, waiting for the tongue-lashing to end.

'It's because you're so similar,' Jean had said timidly at one point. It was true, to a degree. Bron and Toohey were both headstrong.

Bron was furious. 'Don't pop-psychology me,' she said viciously. 'Next you'll tell me it's because our star signs aren't compatible.'

Jean had blushed, and in the desert she blushed again, remem-bering it. She tried to switch to a different memory, thinking of the time in her sister's backyard when they had left the men to it and brought in the washing. The sweet-smelling sheets were cool against their faces as they reached up to unpeg them. Cabbage moths fluttered out of the long grass, the sisters performing a kind of waltz as they folded the sheets, stepping towards each other and out again. Jean had replayed the scene so many times in her head in the past six months that she had almost succeeded in erasing their fight and the dinner that caused it.

*

It had been their last meal together before they left for Perth. Military security systems, Toohey had explained to Jean about the job an old army mate had lined up for him. He was going to be in charge of data. Vital work, he'd impressed upon her, possibly more important than being on the ground.

Jean hadn't wanted to hold the farewell dinner at their flat, a dreary blond-brick building in Brunswick West. Usually they went to Bron and Stuart's for a barbie. Those two were good at it. They would have nothing organised and be so relaxed, putting out a platter of cheese, nuts rummaged from the pantry, figs from their tree split open with their fingers. Plus their backyard was huge, with a trampoline and a sandpit, so the kids could run around. But Toohey had insisted they come to the flat. 'It's Jean's turn to cook,' he said.

She was unable to eat that day from nerves, while Gerry was wriggling out of his skin with excitement. For hours he had worked on transforming his bedroom into the Midwest, using blocks to make rocks jutting from low plains, setting up torches as campfires and plastic cowboys surveying the land. He placed his animals in miniature scenes: horses drinking from pretend lakes, buffalo migrating in herds, Red Indians climbing out of drawers and fighting for territory.

When there was a shuffling on the step, he opened the door before the guests even had a chance to ring the bell, ready to grab his cousins and drag them into his room. But only his aunt and uncle stood there. Bron gathered him in a hug. 'We got a babysitter,' she said airily to Jean, who had prepared mini sausage rolls and cupcakes for the kids. 'It would be too hard to keep them entertained in such a small space!' She added confidingly, 'They're such monsters.'

Gerry was stricken, and it was left to Jean to coax him to show his uncle his bedroom. For a while Stuart played, picking up the plastic Red Indians and making them do a war dance that Gerry didn't like. Then he said he needed to go to the toilet but instead headed to the kitchen to talk with the other adults. Gerry, alone in his room, turned the campfire torch on and off in the dark.

'So,' Bron said, smiling at Stuart as he joined them, 'there was this woman in class this week.' Bron was standing on one leg, her right foot tucked neatly into the small of her back, wearing a tight black top, scooped at the neck and ruffled around her pregnant belly, and light blue leggings with elephants printed on them. Toohey was sitting at the laminate table watching her, his hand curled around a beer while Jean fussed at the stovetop.

'Oh my god, she was so annoying. She complained about every pose.' Bron twisted her right hand behind her to hold her ankle. '*I can't do it, it's too hard,*' she mimicked in a whiny voice. 'She said it for every pose, she didn't even *try*.'

Then, in a supple move, to demonstrate just how easy it was, she stretched her leg up so that her foot curled behind her head. She lifted her left arm to the ceiling. It was startling, and the others held their breath as she pitched forward, her top stretching so tight over her belly that Jean thought she could see the outline of the baby's feet.

'Should you be doing that?' Jean asked nervously. 'With the baby?'

Bron snorted and unfolded herself, slipping her foot back into the canvas shoe on the floor. 'Of course I should, Jean – if anything, being pregnant is all the more reason to do it. Healthy mum, healthy baby.'

Jean reddened, looking across at Toohey, but he was gazing at her sister.

Stuart grinned. 'Tell them what you said, Bron.'

Bron smiled secretively and sat back down, eyes glowing. 'Well, I got sick of it, didn't I? Everyone did. You could feel it in the room. So towards the end of the class, when she complained about the easiest pose, I couldn't help myself.'

'Oh no,' murmured Jean.

Bron grinned. 'I turned around and said to her, "You know, if we were in a hostage situation, you'd be the first to be shot."'

There was a beat, then Toohey roared with laughter, and Stuart joined in, the two exchanging looks of admiration for Bron, while she humbly cupped her glass of soda water in her hands. Jean cracked open the oven door, welcoming the whoosh of heat in her face.

'Let me guess,' Toohey said. 'Everyone avoided you afterwards like the plague.'

'Yes!' Bron said, putting her palm down on the table emphatically. 'How did you know?'

'Because no one likes the truth,' Toohey said, shifting in his chair. 'Even if every fucker in the room was thinking the same thing, no one wants to say it straight up. God forbid you hurt someone's feelings.'

Bron nodded avidly. 'It's true,' she said. 'People's feelings have a lot to answer for.'

Toohey rolled his eyes. 'Tell me about it. Man, the shit we were told not to do in Iraq because it was "cultural".' He clawed his fingers in the air like quotation marks. 'Shit like don't expect a straight-up no if you ask an Iraqi whether they can do something and they can't.

Instead you have to play this dumb-arse game of "Can you?" and they say, "I will see," then three weeks later you say, "Can you?" and they say, "I will see." You play it for months before finally, you get it: the fucker is useless. Apparently that's cultural.'

Bron sat back, her shoulders stiff. 'I don't think it's the same thing,' she said, her voice tightening.

Toohey cocked his head at her. 'No?' he said. 'Why not?'

'Well, you're talking about an ancient Islamic culture and I'm talking about a bunch of Westerners doing yoga.'

Jean started to set the table, slotting plates and cutlery between Toohey's and Bron's elbows. Taking her lead, Stuart went to have a closer look at a small painting on the wall. 'What's this of?' he asked, to change the subject.

Toohey stared at Bron, then looked at the painting, a strip of blue flanked by reeds and hills. 'It's a reproduction,' he said proudly. 'The Euphrates River.'

'I didn't know you went that way,' Stuart said.

Toohey laughed. 'I didn't.' Ignoring the expression on Jean's face, he added slyly, 'Got it from some Iraqi guy's apartment.' Bron recoiled. 'Don't worry, he *gave* it to me. Was a joke me and the guys had going, from the same army handbook that told us not to expect honesty because, as you know, Bron, Iraq is an ancient Islamic culture.'

Jean couldn't bear it. She went to the kitchen door to call Gerry to the table.

'The handbook,' Toohey continued, 'went on about how when we were in an Iraqi's home we were not to go overboard praising one of their possessions, because they'll feel obliged to give it to you.' He paused, then added, 'Red rag to a bull, don't you reckon?'

An icy silence. 'So we started to praise the shit out of the dumbest things – soap dishes, you name it. One guy even walked out of one place with a fucking kitchen chair!'

'Gerry!' Jean called again.

'And this?' asked Stuart.

Gerry trotted in.

'I don't know how I ended up getting *that*,' Toohey said. 'I was praising the shit out of an orange cushion and the idiot gave me the painting!' He was laughing and Stuart gave a polite laugh too as Gerry pulled his chair out and sat down, peering at the food. Through the steam of the peas, roasted chicken and potatoes, Jean smiled at her son.

'Maybe there was something inside the cushion,' the boy said.

The adults' eyebrows lifted in surprise. Stuart waved his fork at Gerry. 'Not bad,' he said, nodding at him. Jean felt a buzz of pride. Stuart was a schoolteacher.

Toohey scowled. 'I doubt it, kid.'

Gerry looked down at his plate.

'I would've smelt it,' Toohey said, glancing at Bron with a hint of aggression. 'Their money stank. I mean, like, literally, it stank of shit.'

Later, when Jean asked Toohey why he'd baited her sister, he told her he hadn't, that she was an idiot for thinking it; then he admitted he'd done it because of the way Bron had spoken to her. '*Healthy mum, healthy baby*,' he mimicked. Jean was surprised he even remembered her sister saying that, recalling how he'd been gazing at Bron as she stretched.

Jean sensed that for Toohey, the dinner only got better. Bron and Stuart weren't getting along, so Toohey kept bringing it back to Iraq – it was his specialty, where his word was irrefutable. Bron's hands were flat on the table, her voice strained as she looked at Stuart. 'I was just saying that Saddam was secular and now look at Iraq, it's —'

'Jesus, Bron,' interrupted Stuart, 'get your facts straight. Saddam was far from secular. He was a Muslim, for Christ's sake.'

'Yes, but the government was secular,' Bron said.

Stuart snorted. 'You can hardly call his regime secular – the enforced worship of one brute of a man seems pretty religious to me.'

Toohey chuckled, leaning across to clink his stubby with Stuart's wine glass. Then he looked at Jean. 'Tell them about the woman we saw at the beach.'

Jean stupidly lit up. She'd fallen into a funk, trying to follow what the others were saying, and was feeling thick-headed. Now, with Toohey's attention, she rallied. 'It was horrible. The woman, she was wearing the whole bit, you know, black gown, veil, covering everything but her eyes, and her husband —'

Bron cut in. 'How do you know it was her husband?'

Jean stopped, looking at Toohey.

'I guess,' he said slowly, 'we're *assuming* it was her husband. Keep going, Jean.'

'Well, he, he was practically naked, a tiny pair of swimming shorts, while she walked behind him completely covered. It made me so angry. How dare a man —'

Again Bron interrupted. 'I think you've made some fairly big assumptions there, Jean. Who are you to say what she should be wearing? Doesn't that make you just as bad as him? Maybe it was her choice to wear the niqab? Was it a niqab, Jean? Or a chador? A hijab?'

Jean fell silent. Their mother did the same thing to their dad, she thought, made him feel like an idiot, never let him finish a story, always pulling the rug out if he ever started to feel at ease.

'So what was it, Jean – a niqab? A hijab?' Bron's eyes narrowed and she pointed her fork as she spoke.

Jean started to stammer. 'I don't know ... I – it was one where just the eyes are showing.'

'A niqab,' Bron said. 'It's called a niqab.' She raised her eyebrows. 'And let me guess, Jean, all the other women on the beach were wearing bathers and bikinis and you were looking at them too and judging them. *Oh my god, that woman is too fat to be wearing a bikini!* Right?'

Jean blushed. They had been doing those things. She and Toohey had had such a fun time. He'd been in a good mood, had taken the day off and suggested they go to the beach. They'd gotten ice-creams and spoken about bringing back Gerry at the weekend. When they looked at the women stranded on their towels or bobbing in the water like dugongs, Toohey puffed out his cheeks and Jean tried to stifle her laughter, pressing her mouth against his arm, tasting the salt on his skin. But it hadn't been like that with the woman wearing the hood over her face and the long black cloak, whatever its name was. It wasn't like that. Sure, she'd liked agreeing with Toohey, seeing his face harden, the anger in his voice. *Women are not animals*, he'd said, and she loved him for saying it, god, she loved him. But women *are* animals, she knew this, and probably the shadow did too, the column of heat tracking down the beach, little kicks of sand coming off the dark gown as she shuffled slowly so as not to trip, the man wading in the sea ahead of her, trailing his fingers in the water. It felt so suddenly precarious. It was up to them, she realised, up to the man in the water and up to Toohey. It was they who would decide how it should be for her and the woman in the black body bag. Goose pimples had puckered her arms and she'd looked up to see if a cloud was blocking the sun.

In the kitchen, Bron was looking at Toohey with contempt. 'You men,' she said, 'are so good at believing your own bullshit.' Agitated, she stood and started to rub the right side of her belly. Jean recalled doing the same when she was pregnant with Gerry. She stood too and began to clear the table.

Toohey reached for his cigarettes.

Bron cleared her throat. 'I'd rather you didn't.'

Jean opened the freezer. She'd bought a selection of ice-creams, thinking it would be fun for everyone to choose their own, maybe even argue over flavours, but now she couldn't imagine anything sillier than the four of them sitting around the table with sticks in their hands. She tapped Gerry on the head. 'Choose one, Gerry. Then you can watch a couple of shows.' At once he was happy, picking out a Splice and going to turn on the television.

Toohey sat back, leaving his cigarettes on the table. 'Tell me, Bron. What is it you think I believe?'

'You believe the bullshit that by getting a woman to take off her veil or niqab you're giving her freedom, rescuing her from a cage. But really, you're just uncovering her for your own reasons.'

Toohey flared, a rush of red that began at his ears. 'That's pretty low, Bron. You think I just want to perve on her?'

'I didn't say that,' she said, now calm in his anger. 'I'm not saying I agree with women being covered up against their wishes, if that's the case, but the whole "Western men rescuing them by undressing them" story? Bullshit. Men just want to uncover them so they can reflect his glorious image back at him, like everyone else does.' Bron flicked a finger at Jean. 'You don't want a woman, you want a mirror.'

'Bron,' Stuart said, trying to interrupt, but she held up her hand.

'Let me finish. You tell me, Toohey, what if she does take off the niqab and you don't like what you see? I don't mean she's ugly or anything stupid like that, but what if she rejects you? If she doesn't make you feel special? Worst-case scenario – she doesn't *respect* you, Toohey? What then?'

Toohey was stony-faced.

'I'll tell you what then,' Bron continued. 'You'd advocate for her to be sent back, to Iraq or wherever, to her so-called cage. You'd say she wasn't assimilating.'

Jean sat down. Slumped, really. Toohey leaned forward, taking out a cigarette, not lighting it but cartwheeling it between his fingers, tapping each end on the table.

It was Stuart who spoke. Jean realised he was drunk, his eyes unfocused, lips stained pink from the wine he'd brought. 'You know what I think?' he said.

Bron looked at him. 'What?' she asked dryly.

'I just wish they'd admit it. Always going on about how it's about modesty, wearing the veil, that it's for God, or Allah, whatever. But *that's the bullshit.* It's just something kinky. No big deal, just a thing between a man and a wife trying to keep the passion alive. The whole modesty thing makes everyone else feel like they're being judged, but it's really about sex, and if they admitted it I reckon this whole debate would be over.' Stuart's eyes glistened unsteadily as he looked around the table. 'Don't you reckon?' he said.

Toohey began to laugh again. He grabbed his lighter and flamed the cigarette. Bron stepped back, pushing in her chair, which teetered before settling. She cupped her hands around her belly protectively. 'You're a fucking idiot, Stuart,' she spat and walked out. The front door slammed.

After a beat, Stuart stood awkwardly, swaying a little. 'Hormones,' he said, giving an embarrassed shrug, and rushed out after her.

Jean tried to say sorry afterwards, sending Bron five long text messages to zero response, each one making her feel more stupid. To call it a bad dinner would, she supposed, be an understatement.

*

Screw her, Jean thought. *The whole 'blood is thicker' bit – it's bullshit. Blood only makes things more disappointing.*

'A niqab, it's called a niqab,' her sister had said in her condescending tone, and Jean had wanted to scream, 'So you know the name, so fucking what?'

She looked at Toohey bending over the generator, twisting things with his Swiss Army knife, flicking the switch. The sky was laced pink and orange now, just on dusk, and the splutter became a roar. Behind them the village lit up. Coloured fairy lights twinkled around the shop fronts, a whir of fans suddenly buffeted the worn curtains: the earthen houses glowed like oil burners, single bulbs dangling inside. Arabic music began playing. Toohey picked up Gerry and swung the kid around and Jean thought, *So fucking what.* She loved him. She ran to Toohey, putting her arms around him. Screw Bron and her perfect family. Toohey was more man than Stuart would ever be. She remembered how Bron's front door was always clicking open, nearly impossible to keep shut. Bron had been nagging Stuart to fix it, worried that the boys could get out onto the street. He'd given her some idiotic reason why it couldn't be done – it was structural, he said, the house had changed shape – and Toohey had fixed it in ten minutes.

Toohey was grinning like a kid. He caught her lips with his, kissing her. Jean plunged her fingers into his hair. Embarrassed, Gerry looked away. He took a step towards the village again, urging them to follow.

Along the tiny streets, Toohey peered inside each stall, marvelling at how not a single radio dial had been fiddled with, all still set on Radio Arabic. At a stall laden with jewellery – strings of beads, amulets and charms – he picked out a headdress made from silver, threaded with coins and bells. Smoothing back Jean's hair, he fastened it over her hairline, the coins settling on her brow. The headdress rustled as she moved, the silver electric on her skin, sending tiny thrills down her spine. Jean took Gerry's hand at one point, dancing to the music, urging him along until they fell apart laughing.

They went out the same way, first Gerry under the fence, then Jean, and Toohey last, over the top. The music finished playing and a DJ spoke in Arabic. Then, as they were about to get into the car, a melancholy voice came through the speakers, singing a song that seemed to stretch and roll, echoing as the voice inflated, subsided and pressed on a single note. Toohey turned in surprise. 'It's the call to prayer.'

As if under a spell, Gerry returned to the fence and threaded his fingers in the wire diamonds. The village was glowing in the night now, the daisy-chain lights blinking. Stars like press-studs in the sky.

'It's beautiful,' Jean said, turning to Toohey, but he was looking down, cupping a cigarette with his hand as he tried to light it. It caught and he sucked in, the stalk glowing red in his mouth. Then he snorted, blowing smoke out his nostrils. 'I can't fucking stand it, sounds like a pig being gutted.' He snapped his fingers at Gerry. 'Get in,' he ordered.

When they were all in, Toohey put the car into reverse, swinging it around before turning the headlights on, and for a second they faced the darkness of the desert, while behind them the dozen Panasonic minarets called them to prayer.

*

'What the brass don't tell you,' an older veteran had said before Toohey's unit left for their first tour, flicking his head to the officers at the back of the room, 'is that home don't exist anymore.' The army had brought in veterans to talk to the soldiers about adjustment, and the men had, for the most part, tuned out. But now, getting the sense that this guy was going off-script, they sat up.

He was mostly bone, skin like worn leather. His name was Victor. The tattoos on his arms were faded blue threads, sprawling like capillaries. 'So, you're out there in Vietnam, Rwanda or Timor, or wherever you lucky bastards are heading, and you think about home all the time, it's embarrassing how much you think about it, and about the girl you're with and the things you're going to do when you get home, not just to her' – the men laughed – 'but other stuff too, like learning carpentry or another language, being nice to your mum' – the men laughed again –'and what they don't tell you is that it's gone. You're so fucking excited to be on the flying kangaroo going home, but then you get off the plane, and this place,' the veteran waved at the window, 'it may as well be the fucking moon.'

The men followed the veteran's hand, looking out at the ti-tree. In flower, the tiny white blooms were so numerous they looked like sprinkled snow.

By now an officer had made his way to the front of the room and cleared his throat. The veteran looked at him but kept talking. 'You'll readjust – don't worry about that, boys, course you will. A stint of drinking, losing your shit at the missus or blobbing out in front of the telly, and then you'll settle, get a routine going, sign up for the gym. Might even make dinner for the kids every now and then.'

The officer motioned with his hand to wrap it up.

The veteran smiled. 'But home,' he said, 'that's fucking gone.' He leaned back in his chair, satisfied, knowing he'd never be asked back. And the men laughed.

It was Wedge who'd said later, 'Someone ought to buy the bastard a pair of red slippers so he can return to Kansas,' and the guys loved it so much they ordered a pair of red sequined ballet shoes and sent them off to the veteran, the officer happy to help with his address.

The veteran was followed by a doctor. 'The risk is,' said the doctor, 'with all this media beat-up about PTSD, some of you may start to assume that you'll return damaged.' The men looked down sheepishly. 'But only ten per cent of you will truly experience PTSD,' he continued, and they stole glances at one another, wondering who it would be. Watching this, the doctor smiled. 'It's not really like that, boys,' he said. 'It's not a disease you can foresee in the genes.' He paused, before adding, 'If it was, it would be part of your screening process.'

*

That night, after visiting the old training base, Jean and Toohey sat on the edge of the kidney-shaped swimming pool at the motel, their feet dangling in the water, Gerry asleep on the single in their room. Toohey had carried him in from the car, the dozing boy's arms dangling and then cautiously curling around his father's neck.

Jean lifted Toohey's hand and kissed it. She wanted to ask about money. She'd watched him through the car window as he stood at the motel reception, saw the slow, regretful way he pulled his wallet out of his pocket and passed the woman his bankcard. She knew not to ask, but also knew if, when, the money did run out, she'd cop it for not asking. She looked at his neck instead for answers, the scattering of lumps that seemed to shape-shift every few days. In the heat they grew red and swollen, and when things were bad in Toohey's head they seemed to know it, the lumps opening like swollen mouths, beads of clear jelly oozing out. But this evening they looked calm, like the pocked surface of the moon. She reached over, touching them. Toohey flinched, but he didn't pull away.

Later, as they lay in bed, Jean touched them again, her fingers fanning over his skin. 'Do they hurt?' she whispered.

'No,' said Toohey. Then, 'Yes.'

'Sometimes?'

'Yeah. Sometimes they hurt.'

Jean drew him in close, the sheets ruffling around them, and started to kiss the lumps, her lips like a small animal nuzzling into his neck. She's brave in the dark, remembered Toohey, as she ran her hands down his arms and held him by his wrists, pinning him, and lowered herself on top of him, her body pulling him towards her. She came almost as soon as Toohey put his dick in her, shuddering down on him. Like a teenage boy, they joked, as he flipped her over and slipped inside her from behind. Since his last tour, he'd always fucked Jean like this. It felt safer for some reason, not being able to see her face. He came quickly, with a boyish moan.

Jean slept easy after that, the smell of Toohey on her, in her. But in the morning, when she opened her eyes dreamily, the sheet coiled around her thighs, he wasn't beside her.

She sat up and spotted him through the window, in the car park, talking to a man in workpants and a fluoro orange top. They were both smoking, sucking on the cigarettes like oxygen sticks. When they were finished, they ground the butts into the bitumen with their boots and shook hands.

Jean wrapped the sheet around her. She saw the silver headdress on the bedside table and hid it in her handbag on the floor beside her, scared that Toohey would see it and tell her to get rid of it. But he smiled when he entered. He nodded out to the car park. 'Bloke out there called Mac says he can get me a few days' work.' He looked around the room, eyes settling on the car keys. 'I'm going to follow him out there now.'

Jean swung her feet out of the bed and yawned, letting the sheet drop away. Toohey grinned and went over to her. He put his hand on her breast and the other in her messy hair, threading his fingers in the knots. He tilted her face up to him. They kissed, and Jean tried to tease him back to bed, her tongue searching his mouth. Toohey laughed and pushed her away. 'Tell reception to book us in for two extra nights and I'll pay them when I get back.'

Jean nodded. 'Love you,' she said as he left. Toohey waved. She watched him through the window, getting into the car. Then she looked across at Gerry and saw that he was awake. She wriggled over and pulled the sheet up, patting the mattress beside her. 'Come snuggle,' she said, reaching for the remote on the bedside table, the sheet slipping again and revealing a naked breast hanging like a bell jar. 'We can watch cartoons.'

*

Happyland Hens, said the sign. Toohey drove through the gate, parked on a strip of gravel and walked over to Mac, who was waiting for him. Five tin sheds cast shadows over a dirt paddock, their windows boarded up with old planks. 'So this is Happyland, eh?' Toohey said wryly.

Mac laughed. 'Yep, mate. You should be paying me.' He bent his head in the direction of a small portable. 'Boss sits in there. I'll introduce you.'

'I gotta piss first,' said Toohey.

'Do it up along the fence line,' came the reply. 'Keeps the foxes away.'

Toohey undid the button on his pants as he walked, breathing in the fresh air. It felt good to be up and at it early, the ground crisp with dew and the sun just beginning to warm. As he pissed through the wire fence, into the long grass on the other side, he settled back on his heels, satisfied. He could still feel Jean and smell that soapy, sugary scent of hers. The leaves on the gumtrees were a faded pea-green and his stream scared the crickets up out of the grass. He smiled, thinking of the training camp they'd visited. *Fuck*, he thought. The things he'd seen, the things he'd survived, the man he'd been – shit, the man he was – while these dickheads had been feeding chickens.

He closed his eyes, tapping out the last few drops, and then smelt it: orange blossom. Toohey snapped his eyes open, whirling around, dick still out. He scanned the property, the sides of the sheds, around the portable. Not a fucking orange blossom to be seen. Why? Why did it fucking do this? Toohey's chest tightened, then his neck, his whole body, his blood thumping.

'Mate?' A voice broke through. Toohey looked down to where Mac was yelling, hand cupped around his mouth. 'You coming or what, mate?'

'Yeah!' Toohey shouted, pushing his tackle in, still tingling with adrenaline. Zipping it all up. 'Something fucking bit me,' he called as he walked back. 'Stung like hell.'

Mac tilted his head to study Toohey. 'Must have been a fire ant.' He pointed to the open door of the portable. 'Bob's in there. I told him you were coming. Come and meet me in the first shed after you and him sort out the numbers.'

In the flimsy fibro, a fan was already going full-blast. Behind a desk was a man eating chicken nuggets, a can of Coke keeping a pile of his papers from blowing away. Bob was enormous. He looked as though he had been poured into his chair like a soft-serve ice-cream into a cone. Toohey watched as he examined a nugget, turning it over as if it were gold, before putting it in his mouth.

Toohey stepped forward and offered his hand. 'Hi, mate. Toohey.'

Bob waved it away, lifting the Coke so he could leaf through the paperwork on his desk. 'How long did you say you wanted?'

'Three days,' replied Toohey. 'Five days max. We're just passing through.'

Bob squinted at him. 'Reckon you could pick up some night shifts too?'

'Depends what you're offering.'

Bob put another nugget in his mouth, chewing it meditatively. He swallowed. 'I can do eighty cash for the day, fifty for the nights.'

Toohey put his hands in his pockets to hide his clenched fists. He had no fucking choice.

*

For his third deployment, Toohey's unit had been posted to Baghdad, and while none of the men would admit it, the location didn't suit them. They felt hemmed in, missing the sprawl of the south. They even missed the Iraqi soldiers they'd been in charge of, pathetic as they were, scattering like cats at first contact and leaving their gear behind for the insurgents to take. Here, the unit were little more than glorified taxi drivers, escorting diplomats who barely looked up from their paperwork. There was an excess of briefings and officers, one superior replying coolly, 'You're in Baghdad now,' when Jolley offered an opinion without being asked, as if they'd been frolicking in the meadows their last two deployments.

Red was the only soldier in their unit who thrived. 'This,' he said as they drove down the fortified streets, his face still flushed from talking to yet another VIP, 'is the nerve centre.' The others started to hate him and began banging on the dunny door when he was having a shit.

Truth was, the Green Zone was too big a pond, and the boys were feeling lost in it. 'Hearts and minds,' they muttered, as they nudged cars off the road with their vehicles, flipping the bird at the Iraqis who got out to shake their fists. They kept an eye out for sticky bombs, magnetic devices stuck to the undersides of vehicles, and to other units they talked up the superiority of the daisy-chain detonations they'd been used to.

'Bush good,' some Iraqis kept repeating at the checkpoints, as if it was still just after the invasion. 'We love America!' When they discovered the soldiers were Australian, they'd make a hopping motion, their grown men's hands bent like paws. 'Kang-ga-roo?' It pissed the unit off. Their luck had to run out soon, that's what everyone kept saying. With civvies back home getting their knickers in a knot over WMDs, and after an operational blackout that meant another Aussie had been wounded, their newsfeeds filled with articles calling for the troops to be withdrawn, as if they were a bunch of pansies.

'I'd rather die out here than in a fucking nursing home,' Jolley growled.

Then, four months in, a suicide bomber swerved into Toohey's ASLAV. It was a bit of a fizzer, but Toohey was taken to the medic while the others skull-dragged the vehicle back to base. The American doctor said it wasn't essential to remove the shrapnel; it could do more harm than good. Best to let it make its way out in its own time. He dressed Toohey's neck with a bandage after heaping on a stinging antiseptic. 'It'll hurt like hell for a while,' he said, giving Toohey a strip of painkillers and a handful of tiny tubes of cream, as if they'd only been provided with samples. Some guys liked to think of their shrapnel as souvenirs, the doctor said. Better than herpes, he added.

When Toohey got back to base, Jolley was talking about how they found the bomber's foot lodged under the ASLAV. 'He was wearing Adidas socks with sandals,' he said. 'No wonder the fucker wanted to die.' They laughed, Red too. It was as if a boil had been lanced.

Toohey got twenty-four hours off, the padre checking in, their commander too, everyone wanting to know about his mental health. 'We're happy to bring your rest period forward if you'd like,' offered the commander, but no way did Toohey want this. He felt fine – great, actually, like he'd licked death. He felt lighter than he had in ages going out to do checkpoint that evening, cracking gags as they set up, sorting out snipers in the buildings, paper-scissors-rock for foot patrol. The breeze was sweet with orange blossom.

Toohey was with Jolley and Red and they'd almost sauntered, forgetting the weight of their gear. Later, it was written up that Toohey was in a state of shock from the previous blow-up – but in reality he was happy. It was almost lazy, the way he hoisted his gun and fired when the street suddenly lit up with headlights. He said in his army interview that he could've sworn he'd already heard someone fire off a warning shot and the car had kept coming. It was effortless, his aim. He nailed it, the car swinging around and coming to a stop, the nose facing the other way. And then the wailing started up and men got out, their faces anguished. '*Li-yesh?*' they kept saying, pulling their hair. '*Li-yesh?*' Why?'

The unit was separated for interviews after that. A bunch of bureaucrats were flown in from Canberra to make a report, and Toohey was put in a stuffy empty room and told to write up the night. He had to ask for a new sheet of paper because he kept starting at the end, with the woman and the blossom of blood on her blouse. When he finally got it down right, they ran through his version of events three times, to see if it lined up with the other accounts, before getting him to sign off.

At the barracks, everyone rallied around him. The car didn't fucking stop, that's what they said. He did what he'd been trained to do. But still Toohey got paranoid, got the sense he was being carved out of the unit. When he learned the commander had gotten some of them to convoy back to the neighbourhood to deliver an act of grace payment to the woman, he felt like they'd stabbed him in the back. But he sucked it up. Put his head down, did his job.

*

'Hope you ain't scared of mice,' Mac said with a grin as he led Toohey through the shed. 'We got a fucking plague.'

The stink was unreal, and the place was swarming. The chickens were chasing after the mice, feathery necks bobbing. They struck with their beaks, leaving a shallow imprint in the dirt and then a lump in their throat as they swallowed the grey rodents whole. 'You'd think the buggers would steer clear,' said Mac. 'But they just come back tenfold.' Behind him, mice ran up the walls – whole sections of the corrugated tin were carpeted with them – and out along the wooden beams, they looped in and out of the white plastic pipes that refilled the chickens' drinking supply. 'It's like a fucking horror film.'

Toohey bristled. 'You haven't been to Iraq, mate. That's a horror film.'

Mac looked at him with interest. 'Yeah?' Then he tilted his head. 'You see any action? Kill anyone?' He looked at Toohey the same way most civvies did when they found out he'd been to Iraq, eyeing him for an anecdote. Toohey felt his stomach slide. Civvies made him sick. Most weren't even hungry for these stories, they were just something to chew on, same way the Americans chewed gum, jaws going even when they were yelling the fuck out of the Iraqi soldiers.

'Course I did,' Toohey said roughly. 'That's the point.'

Mac looked sheepish and Toohey stared at him, not saying anything, just holding the stare, and watching with enjoyment as a blotch of embarrassment crept up Mac's neck. 'You can tell the strength of a man in how he handles silence,' a US corporal had said to him once. 'You don't even need to lay a finger on most fuckers.'

Sure enough, Mac was soon in a state, stammering about how he'd always been for going into Iraq, that the city wankers who had protested knew nothing about nukes, until finally Toohey looked away and Mac sagged in relief.

Toohey walked around the shed like he was just there to inspect it, the dust thickening each time the chickens got into a flap. Nothing free-range about this operation – turned out 'Happyland' was code for 10,000 chickens crammed into a tin box, a pecking free-for-all.

Mac ran him through the day. 'Normally you'll do all the jobs for this shed, but Sonny's already fed them this morning so you only have to do that at the end of your shift.' Mac showed him how to change the water, where the cleaning equipment was and how to shovel the shit into plastic bags for manure. Then he led him through the flock, demonstrating how to mark the birds ready for harvesting. 'They're all tagged, but you'll be here for the rest of your life if you're picking every bird up to check when it was hatched.' He grabbed a hefty red hen. 'You want the birds that look like this.' He held his hands over its wings and tipped it over so Toohey could read the tag on its leg. 'Should be about eight or nine weeks.'

Toohey calculated. 'Yep, just on nine.'

'Perfect,' Mac said. 'Can you grab that wheelbarrow and bring it here?' Toohey walked to the far end of the shed and wheeled it back, birds squawking out of his way, the wheelbarrow carving out a channel like a boat through water. Mac held the bird up. 'You know how to kill a chicken?'

'Got a gun?'

Mac laughed. Then he gripped the bird's legs with one hand and dangled it upside down. He cupped the head with his other hand. The bird was surprisingly still. 'You put your index and middle fingers here,' he said, pressing into the bird's neck, 'just where it connects to the head. Then at the same time, you just yank the head down and lift the legs up.' Mac tugged the chicken sharply at both ends. 'Easy. You should feel a pop.'

Now that it was dead, the bird began to flutter, as if it had only realised after the fact that it was in trouble. Mac tossed it into the wheelbarrow, its wings flapping and legs kicking in a frenzy, only settling when Mac thumped another carcass on top of it. 'When the barrow is full, you take it to the bone shed, the last one on your right.'

'Got it. Should I keep count?'

'Nah,' said Mac. 'The ladies will do that.' Mac surveyed their surroundings. 'There should be about two thousand, two thousand five hundred, in here ready to be slaughtered.'

Toohey looked around. 'Jesus, all today?'

'Nah, two, maybe three days.'

Mac also showed him how to pick out the sick-looking birds to toss into the tubs outside. 'Pet food,' he explained, watching as Toohey killed one bird with an ugly growth under its wing. 'You can kill them if you want,' Mac said, shrugging, 'but it's quicker if you don't.'

So all morning, Toohey snapped necks and threw birds. By the time the bell rang for lunch, he had tossed about a hundred in the tub and killed about double that. It was automatic after a while, though the mice gave him the creeps, skittling around the shed and gathering in clumps.

*

Kill anyone? The only time Toohey had ever answered the question properly was back in Melbourne, at a pub on Melville Road. It was late and he didn't want to go home, so he propped up at the bar next to an old guy who looked like he'd been parked there for a long time.

'You got a feather duster?' Toohey had asked the girl behind the bar, nodding at the man. 'I reckon this fella needs a bit of a dusting.'

The old man grinned, his watery eyes like a flounder's. 'Kill any-one?' he'd asked when they got to talking and he learned that Toohey had been in Afghanistan and Iraq. Toohey had almost flipped him off, like everyone else, when he stopped himself, sizing up the shrunken man, and figured what the fuck – what was the harm in telling an old wino? He said he had, of course he had, that was the point, but he went on, talked about the fog of war.

'You know that saying?'

The old man nodded, his fish eyes sliding into the bone of his nose.

'Well, they never spoke to us about that when we were training, like they thought it was too smart an idea for us grunts. They got vets in to talk about coming home, how queueing up for chicken and chips would give you the shits, but fog of war, nothing. And there's another thing I bet you never heard of. It ain't in *Apocalypse Now* or *Saving Private Ryan* or fucking anything. You listening?'

The man nodded.

'Act of grace. You heard of it?'

The man shook his head.

'Nope,' said Toohey. It felt good, like finding a fleshy hole and talking into it, knowing that the words would stay right there. He got to thinking that maybe confession would be a good thing if the priests could guarantee they'd be drunk and not remember a thing. He told the old wino about the incident, set it up like a riddle, asking questions along the way, checking to see if the wino was still on his side, and when he got to the punchline – because it was a punchline, a fucking king-hit – when he got to the car that lay sideways across the street and the bit where he was looking in at the woman in the back seat, her blouse blossomed with blood, her mouth open, and he thought, *how can she be screaming if she's dead?*, and then he saw it wasn't her who was dead, it was the bundle in her arms, a little meat-works of his own making.

The wino didn't blink; his flounder eyes took it all in, down into the sandy bottom of the bay. When the girl called last drinks, Toohey felt cleansed. He paid the wino's tab, shook his hand and felt the old man's pulse, there but weak. It was perfect. The night was clear, and for the first time he noticed people's gardens, their homes, a lone bat flying overhead.

*

The veteran had been right: it was embarrassing how much Toohey had thought about Jean, and towards the end of each tour the dreams would get so vivid, he'd wake up feeling the shape of her, his body curved around hers. But when his last tour wound up, a creature clambered onto the plane with him. A few of the other guys felt it too, brushing past their legs, but when they looked, nothing. Yet if there was a lull in their talking, it would be there, slick. It crept behind them and touched their shoulders. So the men kept talking. They talked over one another, getting louder, yelling down the aisles, honking with laughter when Wedge gestured at one of the air hostesses and whispered, keeping his back flat against the window so she had to lean over the others to hear him, her shirt gaping open.

At one point word spread that the defence minister might be waiting at the airport to greet them. 'What is this,' one of them scoffed, 'a fucking pony show?' They laughed and neighed. But when the plane touched down and the minister was nowhere to be seen, something was sucked out of them; the bravado faltered. No one looked at Toohey, but he felt them thinking, *It's because of you. No brass wants to know us because of you.*

In duty-free they milled around. 'What're you getting your boy?' Red asked kindly, probably just for something to say, and Toohey growled, 'I'm the fucking present, mate.'

When customs waved them through, the soldiers frowned and made a show of unzipping their bags, talking loudly about security. But still, it was happening too quickly. The unit reached the sliding-glass doors and the guys at the front peered through. 'Shit,' they said, and the soldiers took a collective step back. It took a nudge from an elderly couple wheeling their bags to force them forward.

'Well, it's back to being useless pricks again,' Jolley yelled, copping a look from the older lady.

'Fat fucks, here we come!' rallied Wedge, as the doors slid open.

There was cheering when they appeared. Homemade placards flopped like the heavy heads of sunflowers. *You're my hero, Daddy*, one read. None of them knew about the act of grace. It was all under wraps. Toohey hadn't even told Jean, and never planned to. People held their phones above the crowd to take photos, and some of the nervier soldiers flinched, shielding their heads with their arms. More than a few looked back longingly as the doors shut behind them.

Almost immediately, Toohey spotted Jean and Gerry leaning over the railing. She was calling his name; the boy's big eyes were staring at the blur of khaki.

'Toohey, honey!'

Toohey did something strange. He pretended not to see them. A wild, unhinged thought ran through his head – he could tell her that he had forgotten something, that he had to return to customs, that he'd be back in a sec, and keep going, arrange a ticket, get on a plane, go, go, go. He tried to slow down but the men behind propelled him on.

Up ahead, they were being released into the throng, their backpacks on the floor, arms around girlfriends and wives, kids hoisted onto shoulders – as if the men hadn't carried enough – hands already clutching greedily at their presents. He should have gotten the kid a present, something to hold out, to put between him and them. *How can I even look at the kid?* Toohey stopped and stepped to the side. *Oh fuck.* He flattened his palm on the wall to steady himself. He could see Jean wending her way to the front of the crowd, pulling the boy's hand.

'You okay, Toohey?' It was Red. He was peering at Toohey with a concerned look. Toohey could see Red's family, his girlfriend, at the railing waiting for him.

'Yeah,' Toohey croaked. 'I'm fine.' He pointed at the girlfriend. 'Go on.'

Red nodded but didn't move, still considering him.

'Toohey!' It was Jean. Toohey didn't look.

Red put his hand out and Toohey shook it. It took every bit of control he had left to let go.

*

It was just on four when Mac stuck his head into the shed and said it was time to do the feed. 'You want me to help?' he offered, but Toohey waved him off.

The feed was in a small airless room towards the front, and Toohey held his breath going in so as not to breathe in the stink. He opened

the blue plastic barrels and mice poured from under the lids, running up his hands and arms, some leaping from his shoulders to the
walls, grey legs outstretched like sugar gliders. Others skidded down
his jeans to the floor. Toohey didn't flinch even though the room was
writhing with the fuckers. Then, as Mac had shown him, he mixed up
the feed and filled ten buckets, picking up five in each fist and kicking the door open. As it swung back, a couple of mice got squashed
along the hinges.

He wasn't even thinking when he re-entered the holding pen.
You don't think, Sarge had told them, *you keep your mind clean, like
your weapon.* But then the entire fucking shed came to life. Thousands
of chickens rushed at him. Some were just skeleton and skin like
chooks in the supermarket, feathers already pulled out. They came
out of the walls, from under machinery, from clumps of hay, these
prehistoric birds, tufts growing out of their claws, sinewy necks bobbing, black beady eyes on him. Even the ones lying in the mesh came
to life, scrambling, their legs caught in the wire. They threw their
flimsy bodies at him and Toohey screamed. Not once on tour did he
scream and now, in a chicken shed, he was screaming his head off.
Dropping the buckets, he started to kick the birds away, spinning
wildly in circles as they came at him, his steel-cap boots snapping
their heads back so their necks dangled loose. Feathers, dust and mites
floated around him, but still they came at him, pecking till there was
not a grain left, and only then did the remaining chickens scurry away.
A ring of dead and almost dead chickens surrounded Toohey. His
boots were smeared with blood and feathers. The other workers had
gathered in the doorway, staring.

Then the mice moved in. With tiny teeth bared, they began to
fight over the carcasses, sniffing out the blood, tracing it back to the
source and finding their way inside the skin, past the bones. As a sea
of grey fur washed over the carnage, the remaining chickens came

back, pecking and swallowing up mice. Toohey bent over and vomited. He pushed his way out of the shed, past the other guys, past fat
Bob in the yard, who was moving as fast as he could, wobbling towards
him. 'What's going on?' Bob shouted, and Toohey kept walking, got
in his car and got the fuck out of there.

*

In the motel room, Gerry was watching TV, lying on the double bed.
His mother was in the shower. He wasn't really thinking, doing that
thing where you get sucked into the program, the rest of you switching off – which was stupid because when the door snapped open, he
wasn't prepared. Not like normal, when he was alert to his dad's
return, listening for the car. On hearing it park he'd curl up wherever he was, often surrounded by Lego, shut his eyes and pretend to
be asleep. It was something he'd started doing before they left
Melbourne. He would listen to the key in the door, for his father's
voice – 'Where's Gerry?' – and then the footfall, Gerry feeling his
dad's gaze on him, the room filling with a muddy feeling, and he'd
try to detect the meaning of the static in the air. Back in Melbourne,
if it felt calm, he'd open his eyes, pretending to be sleepily surprised
to see his dad. Toohey would come over and look at what he was
building. But later, in the new city, when his dad's job fell through,
Gerry didn't do that, even if it felt safe. He kept his eyes shut, sometimes falling asleep for real, because the static, it could change too
quickly, too unpredictably.

'Get up, you lazy shit!' The motel door rebounded off the wall
and his father punched it back open, his face jagged with rage. Gerry
tried to move, but he was frozen. 'Up, you shit, up!' His father shoved
him off the bed and onto the floor, and then walked around to where
he lay and scooped him up, throwing him against the wall. 'Up, you
shit! Up!'

'Toohey?' Jean stood in the doorway of the bathroom, her wet hair dribbling down into her breasts, a towel held tight around her torso. An outline of steam poured out around her and briefly enveloped Toohey as he put his face in hers. Jean whimpered and Toohey shoved her with force. 'No fucking way,' he snapped. He pointed his finger in her face. 'Don't you dare fucking cry.' Jean nodded, trying to stop trembling. Toohey spun back around, grabbing the suitcase off the floor. 'Get dressed,' he said. 'We're going.' When neither of them moved, he swung around again. 'Get fucking dressed,' he snarled, and it was enough to make Jean and Gerry start in fear, the distortion of his features, the way Toohey's eyes were almost entirely black, his blue-grey irises sucked into the pupils.

Gerry held his arms out like a doll, letting his mum help him get dressed. She frantically yanked his swimmers off and put on his shorts, while he risked a glimpse at his father's neck. They were moving. The way rice shivers in a jar when it has weevils in it. At the last school – the one in Cannington – he and the other kids had watched when some men with a digger came to get a car wreck out of the oval. Somehow, overnight, it had risen from the earth. The lumps were mysterious like that. A bunch of times since his dad got back that final time, he'd called Gerry into the bathroom to show him a piece of metal the size of a sesame seed that had worked its way up and out of his skin. After examining it, he put it in a jar with the rest of the shrapnel that had come out. Once, there was a piece of glass. 'I reckon that's from Red's specs,' Toohey had said. Another time, a fleck of green lacquer. When he presented it to Gerry, he said, 'I was right. It was a green Volvo. The bastards kept telling me it was blue, but look.'

Gerry was dressed and on his knees looking for his sneakers when he saw Toohey grab his backpack, and before it even happened he knew they were going to fall out. Knew he hadn't done the zip up properly. The travel brochures he had hoarded from Miss Munro's class fell onto the unmade motel bed, fanning out as if in a commercial. Toohey stopped and stared, his anger momentarily stilled. 'What's this?' he said, and Jean, who was waiting at the door, looked over. 'What's what?' she asked nervously.

'This,' Toohey said. He picked one up and began to flick through the glossy pages. Gerry pitched forward. His heart had been racing before but now it was going too slow. It was hard to breathe, his palms sweaty. His dad was looking at the brochure with Horseshoe Ranch on the front and he knew – again – that his father would stop on a page towards the back. It was like Gerry had been here before, had dreamt it, because sure enough Toohey did pause.

It was the page where the tours were listed. Gerry had circled the three-week tour, which involved sleeping out with cowboys and riding alongside them. 'Four thousand three hundred and twenty dollars,' Toohey said slowly. 'Plus taxes.' He looked at Gerry. 'Who gave you this?'

'It was for school,' Gerry said, stammering slightly.

'And you think you're going to go? Leave your mother and me while I work and pay for you to have a good time?' Gerry shook his head. He was going to pay for it. He was going to find a job and save. He started to cry. Jean tried to go to him, but Toohey blocked her way.

'You reckon you could earn this kind of money, Gerry? You think it's easy? What can you do, Gerry?'

Gerry squeezed his eyes shut.

'No, really, Gerry,' Toohey said in a hard voice. 'I want to know. What do you think you can do? Answer me, Gerry. What. Can. You. Do?'

Gerry sobbed, his eyes still shut. He tried to picture the cowboy again, the one who had ridden alongside them on the drive. But the vision wouldn't come. 'Toohey,' Jean said, her voice faraway. 'Please Toohey, he's just a kid.'

'Exactly,' Toohey said viciously. He flung the brochure across the motel room. Gerry quickly opened his eyes and Toohey caught his gaze. 'Exactly,' he said again. 'Get in the car.' And just with his eyes, Toohey made the boy stand up and walk around him, skittish as a horse, into the car park.

*

For dinner they stopped at a roadhouse, *CHEAP BURGERS* flashing in neon outside. They sat out the back, where white plastic tables and chairs were set up under a tin roof, beside a play area with a slide and a sandpit. There was a boy there, carefully transferring sand into a dump truck and tipping it onto the surrounding fake grass. Wary of him, Gerry climbed up the slide's ladder and sat at the top, watching. In the quiet, the boy hummed to himself.

Then, out the front, there was the wheeze of air brakes. A bus. Gerry slid down and sat next to his mother as within minutes the roadhouse filled with tourists. The play area became crowded with children. Their voices bounced off the tin, the place deafening.

Toohey became agitated, looking around furiously for the waitress. 'Where's our food?' he said, when he spotted the teenager with lurid cherry-red hair rushing past with a handful of plastic menus.

'I'll check,' she called, as she handed out the menus to the new arrivals. Then, as she made for the kitchen, a table of six people stopped her and started asking questions.

Toohey pushed his chair back, about to get up and go find out for himself, when a hoarse voice rang out from the sandpit. 'Get out! Get the fuck out!'

The outdoor area fell silent as everyone looked at the boy who had been there first and was now waving his red plastic spade at the other kids. 'Get the fuck out!'

The children stared at him and then looked to their parents.

The boy started to flick sand at those close to him with his spade. 'I said, *get out!*'

The tourists looked around, raising their eyebrows at one another, waiting for the boy's parents to intervene. The waitress disappeared inside.

'Get the fuck out!' the boy screamed again and filled his spade with sand, throwing it in a girl's face. A woman leapt out of her chair and ran over to pick up the crying girl.

Gerry, along with the other children, was in awe. The adults all looked shocked – except for Toohey, who'd forgotten about the food, and was watching the scene with a strange smile. His grin broadened when a short, sunburnt man stood up and walked over to the sandpit.

'Give me the spade, mate,' the man said, putting out his hand.

The waitress returned with plates of food. People started to look away, making room for their meals. Jean and Gerry quickly began to eat. Toohey had said in the car they were to be in and out of the roadhouse. No fucking around, he'd said pointedly to Gerry. But now Toohey barely looked down as the waitress slid his burger and chips in front of him.

The kid stared at the man. 'Fuck you, arsehole.' He scooped up more sand and flicked it in the man's face.

Again, the food was forgotten. People stopped mid-chew to stare as the man clutched at his eyes. 'Argh!' he yelped. 'You little bastard!' He drew himself up so that the boy had to lean back to look at him. 'Where are your parents?' he asked, and glanced around, his eyes finding Toohey.

Toohey cocked his head in reply as if he were a friendly dog, before cupping his hand around his lips like a megaphone. 'Not me, *mate!*'

There was a flicker of confusion from the man at Toohey's response, but then the boy moved to throw more sand in his face.

The man flushed furiously. 'Give me the spade,' he said. 'I'm warning you. This sandpit is for everyone to enjoy.' He waved at the other families, looking around for support. No one said anything.

The boy tipped his head back so that he could look the man in the eye. 'Fuck off, you're not the boss of me,' he said, and Toohey whooped with delight.

The man went a deeper shade of pink. 'Give it to me,' he said, and this time he grabbed the spade. The boy started to scream, pulling on the handle and spitting at the man.

'I'm warning you. I'm warning you, son,' the man repeated, and gave a final tug. The boy lost his grip and let go, falling back into the sand.

'You arsehole! You arsehole!' he screamed. He started to punch the sand, sending fistfuls of it into the air.

Neither Gerry nor Jean had noticed Toohey stand up, but he was there, beside the sandpit, the entire bulk of him flexing. 'Give me the spade,' Toohey said, and the man sagged with relief, handing it over, glad to be released from the situation.

'Thanks, mate, I just —' he said, but Toohey cut him off.

'Now fuck off.'

The man's eyes bulged. 'What? Now listen, if this is your son, then —'

'He's not my son.' Toohey stepped closer to the man, standing over him just as the man had done to the boy.

The man glanced around for help, but no one met his gaze. He held up his hands and stepped out of the sandpit. 'Alright, alright. Take it easy, mate,' he said as he backed away, heading over to his wife and kids. He pulled out his chair to sit down.

'No,' Toohey said. 'Get the fuck out of here.'

The man stopped, his mouth round with surprise, and looked around desperately. His wife leaned over to gather up their things from the floor, her hair hanging over her blushing face. She bustled the kids out of their seats. He put his hand out to stop her, but she glared at him and pushed past. A moment later, he scurried to follow and they disappeared inside the building.

The waitress reappeared with more food and people looked down at their plates, appetites diminished. Only Gerry and Jean dared to watch when Toohey bent down to give the spade back to the boy. As he put his hand on the kid's head, the boy's eyes briefly closed. He pushed his head up into Toohey's palm like a cat does for pats. Gerry briefly shut his eyes, imagining he was the boy. When he opened them, his hair was tingling.

*

In the bathroom at a service station, a stuffy cubicle down the side of the building, Toohey was pacing while Jean and Gerry waited in the car. He couldn't stand being near them: he'd driven a hundred kilometres with Jean too scared to speak and he fucking hated her.

They weren't far from Melbourne now – four, maybe five hours. Houses had started to appear more frequently by the side of the road. They seemed to rise up out of the ground like teeth. In front yards, lemon trees were bloated with gall wasp.

As they'd drawn closer to the city, Toohey had begun to sweat, his chest hammering. It had been a bad idea to go through the desert, and an even worse idea to come out of it. But there was no place, really; everywhere was simply an idea that disappeared as soon as he reached it.

His neck was throbbing. The cubicle was wet, as though it had been hosed down. The toilet seat was saturated, the roll of loo paper wrinkled like feet left too long in a bath. The mirror was flecked with dark spots, and Toohey arched his neck, leaning close to look. With his fingers, he pressed on both sides of the inflamed lump, coaxing it, feeling the sting of it, and a pop. The stink of pus. He wiped away the blood, touching the hard, jagged speck. He rolled it carefully between his fingertips and washed it under the tap, pinching it tight. He put it in the centre of his palm. It was about the size of a match-head, yellowing and smooth on one side, pocked like coral on the other. His hands trembled.

He was in the bathroom at the service station. Jean and Gerry were outside, waiting in the car. The key to the bathroom, it had to go back to the guy at the counter. These were the things he kept telling himself to hold it together.

Because: it was bone.

It was bone.

It was bone.

*

Jean was surprised when Toohey let her drive, saying that he needed to sleep. Gerry was to sit up front. For a while Toohey chain-smoked in the back. Puffs of smoke unfurled out the window, ghosts snatched by the wind. Then he closed his eyes and lay on his side, curled up like a baby.

At first, his dreams were banal – a lot of driving, trying to light cigarettes that refused to light. Outside, the night thickened around them. Every now and then the car lifted at corrugations, and there was a whir as Jean drifted over the painted line into the emergency lane. Gerry fell asleep too, his face pressed against the glass, father and son twitching as if a dream were passing between them. There was dirt on Toohey's hands and he was pulling bodies from the ground; he dug deeper, clumps of earth collapsing into the hole, and then black chadors came flapping out of it, crows with human faces. He put his hands up to protect himself, but beaks suddenly grew from the faces, pecking him, and all over his body there were holes, tiny pricked holes that had a strange quality of opening and closing. Eyes, he realised; he was covered in eyes.

When his own eyes snapped open, the beaks receded, but the feeling of holes in his skin stayed. He sat up. The car had stopped. They were at an intersection, on the edge of the desert. The lights were green, but Jean wasn't moving. There was a car in front of them, he saw, its hazard lights on.

'C'mon, you idiot,' Jean muttered under her breath. He leaned forward and made out the U-shape of a powerline that had fallen across the intersection. It hung low, the black cable whispering above the bitumen. Jean made an impatient sound. 'Bloody hell,' she said, turning the steering wheel so they could go around the car.

Toohey sprang forward, and Jean screamed as he grabbed the wheel, swerving them into the lane on the opposite side of the highway. 'You want to get us fucking electrocuted?' he yelled. She was still screaming as he pulled the handbrake up. He began to punch her in the head to stop the sound of her cries. *The niqabs*, he thought, oddly recalling the argument he'd had with Jean's bitch of a sister. *The men make the women wear them because they're tired.* 'You stupid bitches, you stupid bitches,' he shouted. Jean tried to protect herself with her arms, and the door on the other side opened as Gerry scrambled out, his sneakers hitting the gravel, disappearing into the scrub.

'Is everything okay?' It was the driver of the other car. The man had got out, leaving his engine idling. They could see his outline in the orange flashing lights. Toohey stopped hitting Jean and opened the door, muscles triggering, burning. The man stepped back, uncertain. Toohey started to run towards the car, haunches rolling like a dog sprinting at speed, and the man got back in, jamming his gears and driving off the road and into a ditch, then careening around the powerline to the other side. The wheels got stuck briefly in the dirt before heaving back onto the bitumen.

Toohey turned back to Jean. She was out of the car now, crying and cowering. The headlights cast two long beams into the scrub. 'Gerry,' she said, pleading. 'He's out there. Please, Toohey.'

Toohey stared hard at the darkness in front of him, and slowly the landscape took shape. 'Gerry!' Jean screamed. 'Please, Gerry, please!' and Toohey felt a sharp pain in his head, a white flashing in his vision, the taste of metal at the back of his throat. Her voice, all their voices, the high pitch – they were everywhere now, on the radio, even on the fucking football. He couldn't stand it. Always some pathetically suppressed emotion, edging towards hysteria and laced with bitterness. At least in Iraq they weren't on the airwaves, voices coiling in your ears like tapeworms. But still, they were always wailing. *Shut up!* he had yelled once at a group of women after an explosion at a checkpoint, but they kept on wailing, ignoring him, flapping their black ponchos. How useless the training had been – they'd always had nothing but mechanical noise to work through, not this screaming, these women's mouths open, and he thought of a bath draining when he heard them, the way they sucked the sound in. Toohey thought war would have almost been peaceful if it weren't for their screaming.

'For fuck's sake, Jean, shut up!' he yelled and, unlike the foreign birds, she did. For that, he loved her. A solitary grey mouse came out of the scrub, sniffing his boots. Toohey looked down and was about to stomp on it when, just in front of him, he saw the skimmer. He crouched to pick it up, and rubbed it between his fingers. Then he spotted the kid staring back at him from behind a bush. From experience he knew it was moments like this when strange realisations struck. Like the time his unit came to a settlement and saw a group of women helping their children climb over a rock wall and the shift of shadows in the shacks and he realised he was training his sights on the women while the rest of his unit were aiming at the shadows in the shacks. *Something is wrong*, he had thought, ever so briefly, *with me*. Or when the green Volvo ignored their warning shot and he thought, *What hope do we have in this piece-of-shit place when you can't even trust a Volvo?* And so, when he moved to clock Gerry, he thought, *The kid, he was never asleep.*

Turning Off the Lights

Robbie started seeing Nik, short for Nikita, in Year Ten. He'd been one of the more unremarkable kids in her class, a bit of a nerd: the teachers were always calling on him to answer their questions, and he played the violin. But then he started selling dope and acid and suddenly he was beautiful. Pale and thin, with long, straight brown hair that fell over his eyes.

Robbie began to watch him. At lunchtimes he made his way across the schoolyard, his hand in and out of his pocket, placing parcels in students' palms still smeared with tomato sauce and pastry flakes from sausage rolls. With less grace, they'd slip him money. Nik was like a cat the way he worked the yard: with everyone trying to catch his eye, he'd skirt most, always calculating who to stop at, who to sell to. Someone started calling him the Messiah, someone smart enough to see how everyone seemed to lean into Nik, wanting to be blessed by him, and it caught on. Even the older kids said it.

It was first term when things started between Robbie and Nik. Robbie was sitting with Tash, their backs warm against the bricks, Robbie's long bare legs folded, dress hitched up to her thighs. Nik was talking to a guy near them and Robbie put it in her eyes, her interest, not moving a muscle in his direction. He became alert to her. He was about to walk over, she could see it, but the guy he was speaking to raised a fist to bump against Nik's. Reluctantly Nik held his fist up, but just as the guy was following through, he changed his mind, dropping his hand, and the guy hit air. Robbie laughed and Nik grinned, showing his sharp teeth. It was difficult to know who was reeling in who.

When he sat next to her, their arms touching, he didn't look at her; instead he followed her gaze across the yard. 'When will this end?' he said, as they took in the groups dotted around the stunted trees, a Year Eight inflating his empty juice box and laying it on the ground, creating a loud *pop* as he stamped his foot on it, briefly stunning the mingling bored. It was a holding pen, high school. There'd been a short-lived spurt of enthusiasm in Year Seven, repeating itself briefly each year after – they showed up in January with their books covered in contact, margins ruled for at least sixty pages. They all had the same thought – *New year, clean slate* – though each sought a different out-come: *I'm going to be popular, I'm going to be taken seriously, I'm going to get straight As.* But before Term One had even wound up, they were all back in their old skins: class idiots, loners, sluts and so on. And for the most part, they stayed stuck, dutiful in their banal personas. Except the Messiah, of course.

Robbie looked at her wrist, as if checking a watch. 'Two years and nine months,' she replied.

A week later, he kissed her in the vacant block behind the school. They skipped sixth period and squeezed through a gap in the fence, sneaking down a laneway, to where he'd stashed a bong in a clump of grass. It was a regular hangout for the Year Elevens and Twelves, and a bunch of flattened cardboard VB boxes had been laid out as makeshift seats, around a midden of lighters, bottlecaps, empty chip packets and cigarette butts. Robbie watched as Nik took a wooden bowl and a pair of scissors from his schoolbag and transferred a mix of tobacco and dope into the bowl, pumping the scissors into the grain.

His sleeves were rolled up and Robbie saw an ace of diamonds inked on the inside of his wrist, a home job, the blue blotched where someone had blown the ink too hard. He packed a cone and flicked his eyes – blue like the ring of a gas flame – up at Robbie, and her heart kicked so hard she had to look away.

He passed the bong, producing a lighter and handing it over like it was a knife, safe end first, and Robbie dipped her head over the glass vase, angling the lighter. The cone crackled as smoke unfurled upwards into her mouth like fog off a small black pond. She closed her eyes, feeling it stack inside her chest and move out, flooding her body. After Nik did a cone, he leaned across and kissed her on the neck. No one had ever started there before.

*

In the nursing home, Robbie's father turned off the lights. The nurses let him do it before bed. They said it relaxed him, made him more manageable. 'Off he goes,' a nurse said to Robbie and her mother and brother one night, all of them watching as he flicked the switches, a kind of collapsing darkness following him. The nurses turned the lights back on after he passed by, and once he was in bed, they pulled up the sides of the cot, latching them, so he couldn't get out and do it all over again.

Danny was forty-eight when he got dementia; Robbie was ten and Otis, seven. The doctor said he was too young for dementia, but he got it anyway. Danny had been a small-time boxer back when he and their mum met, but he would not let her say anything about it to the doctor. He said the doc would judge him, and she agreed. 'Of course he will. It's a stupid thing to do.'

They'd still teased each other back then, had a laugh. But nothing would make their father trust the 'system' – that was how he described it. The system was basically everything: hospitals, cops, schools, the government. He said if Claire, their mum, hadn't been there at his first medical appointment, he would have been made to do a breathalyser test. He'd always been like that, a bit paranoid. When Otis broke his arm coming off the neighbour's trampoline, Danny wouldn't let Claire take him to the hospital. He claimed they'd work out who he was – 'or what', he said contemptuously – and next thing, Human Services would be at the door. But the swelling didn't go down, and when Otis got a temperature, Claire drove him to Emergency. Robbie stayed home with Danny, watching her father pace, the townhouse heavy with a sick, scared feeling.

Before the illness, Danny had been a caretaker at a private boys' school in Hawthorn. They liked his being Aboriginal. Fancied they were doing their bit, hiring him. 'Half-Aborigine,' he pointed out to a teacher there who prided herself on including the Dreamtime in her religion classes. 'Maybe less. And only in blood,' he added. She gave him a lecture on the 'all-encompassing spirit of Aboriginality', that he ought to be '100 per cent proud' of who he was. Her name was Mrs Eckersley.

Mrs Fucking Eckersley. There were still times when those three words popped into Robbie's head, the focus of a rage she couldn't let go of, as if in her mind she'd decided *Mrs Fucking Eckersley* had made her father sick.

At home the family had gotten to know her – at least they imagined they did. Danny would fill them in on what Mrs Eckersley had said during the day and their mother would act it out, popping a grape or a cherry tomato in each cheek, making up how the religion teacher spoke (an odd mix of posh and squirrel-like) and how she walked. Robbie's dad would snort, laughing at her mum, but also in relief. It became a ritual.

'And she said, "Aborigines are very good at football, aren't they?"' Danny reported one night to the three of them. Otis frowned, too young to understand, worried this might affect his basketball ambitions.

'You're joking?' Claire said, her face incredulous.

'Nope,' Danny replied, shaking his head. He explained that she'd sung it out to him when she was on yard duty and a group of students were walking past, bouncing a footy.

Claire laughed, telling Robbie and Otis their father couldn't kick a goal to save himself. 'You,' she said, pointing to Otis, 'take after my side of the family.'

'What about Dad's boxing?' Robbie said defensively, keenly aware that she did not take after her mother's side of the family in this respect.

Claire smiled at Danny, a teasing look on her face. 'I never said your father was a *good* boxer.' Danny narrowed his eyes in mock anger. 'Your father's only talent in the ring,' Claire continued, 'was getting out of the way.' To demonstrate, she wriggled her arms and legs like the tentacles of an octopus, wobbling around the kitchen until Danny grabbed her, pulling her close.

'You, on the other hand …' he said gruffly, as she snuggled into him. Then, looking at Otis, he nodded. 'Your mother's right, you take after her side. You've got talent.' Otis beamed.

It was clear to Robbie that her father loved Otis best. No, that wasn't quite right: it was more that when he looked at Robbie, he saw something of himself, and didn't like it. Otis resembled Claire – his skin fair, his eyes blue and his hair a rusty brown – while Robbie was darker, her eyes owlish like his. When Danny looked at his son, he had hope, a buoying sense that his kin would get through the system unimpeded. Robbie couldn't articulate this, but she intuited it, the same way she understood that she gave her father a sinking feeling, an unshakeable sadness, a miserly sense of history repeating. Claire could see it too, and tried to counter it, gathering Robbie into a hug when Danny reached for Otis. But Robbie never held it against her father. She held it against the world. Against Mrs Fucking Eckersley.

*

The Messiah's townhouse was red brick with a split-level roof. A panel of yellow dimpled glass beside the front door shone at night when the hallway light was on. The street was one-sided, the houses lined up in a row, facing a large concrete wall buffering a highway on the other side. The first time Robbie visited, Nik let himself in with a key he kept around his neck and led her up the stairs. His bedroom was dark and smoky, with the curtains drawn. It took a while for her eyes to adjust, making out the posters of fluorescent fractals on the wall and the various decks and amplifiers from which tiny blue lights glowed. The screensaver on his computer was a vortex of shapes and lines, constantly transforming.

Then, as night drew in, people appeared in his room, like apparitions. Nik, his skin transparent and otherworldly like an axolotl's, greeted them, measuring out grams on kitchen scales, wrapping buds in al-foil, hair in his eyes. The bong was passed around and the doorbell rang again, and it was only later that Robbie wondered how they all got in. But for a time, as in a dream, she did not question it.

In a lull of people making their communion, Nik took out two plastic ziplock bags, one filled with white pills, the other with perforated paper. 'Mitsubishis,' he said, taking out a pill and breaking it in two, putting one half in Robbie's mouth, another in his. 'One of the best batches I've had.' He slid open the other bag and carefully ripped a tiny square off along the dots. 'Purple ohms,' he said, cutting it in half with nail scissors, licking the thin blades afterward. 'Try and keep it on your tongue for as long as possible.'

The candyflip was good, coming on in waves. As people visited, Nik looked after them and even gave out gear on tick, while Robbie talked, her voice rushing out. She trailed her finger along the inside of people's arms and felt the approving glances of Nik's friends. 'So *you're*

Robbie O'Farrell,' one of them said, and she understood he'd been aware of her for a long time, perhaps longer than she of him. Robbie had a reputation; she knew this. She and Tash were known for their wildness and their aloof, tenuous connections to the machinations of school life. For a stint the two of them regularly chromed, a couple of times wandering around the schoolyard with silver paint splattered around their mouths, and the year before Robbie had been suspended for a week when she revealed her art project, two mirrors titled 'Go Fuck Yourself', one with a padded hole at crotch level, the other with an erect rubber dildo sticking out. Had she done it for attention? Her teachers said she had, but Robbie didn't think so. For the most part, she'd wanted just that, for everyone to go fuck themselves.

But with the pill and acid, the anger slipped a bit. It didn't disappear, more drifted, gave her some space. In Nik's bedroom, someone put on some trance and she danced next to the speakers. She shared cigarettes, cradling and cupping them like lit candles, and when everyone was gone, she put her head in Nik's lap and slipped her hands inside his T-shirt sleeves, pulling him lower. His upside-down lips on hers; the two of them tasting each other for the longest time, fingers electric. And then a pulse between their pelvises, as though they were magnetised. Robbie had had sex before – if that's what you call a fifteen-year-old lying on top of you in a playground at night, his body jerking towards a sticky ending. But this was different: the two of them moving so slowly that Robbie kept forgetting where she was, so she became less a body and more a meandering feeling, until, without warning, she and Nik seemed to align. *Oh my god*, Robbie heard herself saying over and over, *oh my god*, like the pleasure was splintering, coming out of her in a multitude of ways, an explosion of pink.

Later, when they were lying naked in Nik's single bed, Robbie sat up and opened his curtains. The night was almost done. She propped Nik's window open with a cricket bat. In the yard next door, a black-and-white cat was knotted in sleep. Nik stayed in the shadow, rolling a joint, while Robbie watched light slowly pour into people's gardens, the outlines of chairs, plants and a swimming pool filling with colour.

*

Before Danny got sick, Robbie and Otis used to walk to his work after school. It was about six blocks, and Otis would dribble his basketball the whole way. He was so constant, so persistent, that Robbie would worry when he skipped a bounce and turn to check. They passed the 7-Eleven, slowing down to stare wistfully at the kids buying Slurpees. Sometimes, on really hot days, they'd get money to buy their own, and Robbie would discreetly wander the aisle with her cup, filling it with chocolate bars or sherbert sticks – once a pair of sunglasses, good ones – before returning to the Slurpee machine to cover the stolen merch with the icy drink. It scared the shit out of Otis, the poor kid trembling at the counter when she paid for their drinks. *Don't tell Dad*, Robbie would warn afterwards, and Otis never did. It had been a triumph, nicking those sunnies. A victory over the system.

They had to wait a long time at the fancy iron school gates for him. A couple of the buildings were old and solemn-looking, with arches, towers and turrets like out of a *Dungeons & Dragons* book, while on the other side of the oval was a dome-shaped building made from multicoloured bricks and gold-tinted glass. It shimmered in the light like spilt petrol. Her dad said it was the gym. 'When I turn the lights out in that building,' he told her, pointing to another modern building, 'I'm almost done.' And so, every afternoon after school, Robbie would watch the building while Otis practised his dribbling up and down the footpath. The windows were not like normal windows, in neat rows; they were clustered together in groups, each group making the shape of a fish, and when Danny turned the lights off, it was like the fish were diving down, following one another into the deep.

Some afternoons a school bus would park at the kerb and the students would pile onto the footpath, lacrosse sticks poking from their enormous bags, socks crimping down their calves. They were loud and smelled kind of pungent, and Otis would stop bouncing his basketball, moving in close to Robbie, the two of them watching as cars – mostly silver or black 4WDs, the odd bullet-shaped sports-car – slid in, the mums winding down the passenger windows and leaning over, glossy-lipped. 'Hi Nathan, hi Cory, hi Thomas,' the women would chime, the boys chorusing back, 'Hi Mrs Button,' or 'Hi Mrs Carrier,' or 'Hi Mrs Horton,' while one of them would get in the car, his ears burning as he slipped down in his seat. Robbie caught sight of Otis once, his mouth open in the same way it was when they watched TV, like the screws on his jaw had been loosened, and she realised she probably looked like that too. From then on she made a point of not staring, jabbing Otis in the ribs with her elbow to stop him too.

Occasionally, if Danny was in a good mood when he finished his shift, he'd bring them biscuits from the janitors' room and then shadowbox on the way home, pretending to try to pummel Robbie's and Otis's shadows with his fists. They'd run and squeal, Robbie slow-ing down hopefully, taking her father's embrace when she could get it.

A few times, though, Danny was in an inscrutable rage when he met them at the gate. Once, he appeared carrying two plastic super-market bags filled with books. He barely looked at the two of them. 'Let's go,' he said curtly.

When halfway down the street the handles on one bag tore, the bottom thumping on the footpath, he swung his boot back, about to kick it, but stopped himself. He gathered the bag up, holding it from underneath, while Robbie and Otis stole nervous glances at each other.

In a moment of absentmindedness Otis bounced the basketball and they both froze, expecting their father to turn on them, but he didn't. Just kept walking.

At home, Danny waited till Claire arrived before spilling the contents of the bags onto the table. Curious, Robbie looked at them. There were about a dozen books, with titles like *Finding Your Path in the Dreamtime*, *The Rainbow Spirit in Creation*, *The Aboriginal Gift*, *Totem Animal Spirit Journey*. Mrs Eckersley ('Call me Susan, Danny') had left them in his cleaning closet. Claire gaped at them and started to laugh.

'It's not funny!' Danny snapped. He rubbed his eyes, kneading his fingers into his sockets. 'It's like, it's like – I don't know. It's like sexual harassment or something.'

Claire put her hand over her mouth, trying to stop. 'I'm sorry, hon, seriously I am,' she managed to splutter. Danny sighed. He began to pack the books back into the bags, snatching *Aboriginal Awakening* out of Robbie's hands, while in the courtyard the backboard vibrated repeatedly as Otis practised his shots.

Later that evening, over dinner, Danny told them that Mrs Eckersley had asked him to speak to her Year Nines about 'his culture' and the Dreamtime. 'They are very interested,' she'd said.

'I told her I didn't know anything about the Dreamtime,' he said. 'Next thing I know there's those bloody books in my cupboard.'

'Maybe you should complain?' Claire said.

'What do I say?' he asked. 'I can't say, "Hey, this woman is discriminating against me," can I?'

She shook her head. 'I guess not.'

'I can't say she's a racist, can I?' he continued.

She shook her head again.

Danny banged the table with his fist. 'Jesus Christ, Claire, I'm fucking damned if I do and damned if I don't.' Robbie lit up inside at that word, *fucking*; she played with it silently, turning it over in her mouth. She didn't often hear her dad swear.

Claire gave her a sharp look, before turning back to Danny. 'But it doesn't matter, does it? It doesn't matter what other people think?'

Once or twice at Robbie's school there had been a special assembly where the principal would talk about bullying, how words *can* hurt, that sticks and stones isn't accurate, that kind of thing. But Robbie had never needed that lesson. She had her father, and she could practically see the welts and dints that words left in his skin. It was possible she saw it better than anyone, even her mother. For Danny reared up when Claire said that, his eyes flaring. 'Doesn't it?' He pointed to the plastic bags on the floor. 'Did you have to carry these books home? Do you have your own little spirit guide at work?'

Claire reached across the table for his hands but he withdrew them. 'I'm not saying it's easy, but —'

'No, it's not fucking easy!' Danny stood up. He was big suddenly, towering over the table, the three of them. 'It's not fucking easy! Everywhere I go, it turns into something. I don't see anyone else being told to get in touch with their inner fucking leprechaun. Do you?' The three of them shook their heads as one, and Danny dropped back, recognising the obedience he was demanding, the fear he was instilling. He put his hand over his face.

'It's okay, my love,' said Claire, reaching out again, but he warded her off with his other hand, shaking his head.

'I just need some space,' he said, his voice muffled, and he walked through the house, out the front door.

An hour later he came back, carrying four icypoles. They all sat on the front step eating them, and quietly Claire said that maybe he *should* talk to the Year Nines about his culture. 'You could tell them about Christmas Day with Grace and Greg,' she said. Danny smiled.

'Huh?' Robbie said. 'Tell *me* about Christmas Day with Grace and ... who?'

'Greg,' Danny responded. 'Remember? My dad – not my real dad, but the dad I knew.'

'Remember, Rob?' Claire said, looking at her and Otis. 'We told you two about Dad's parents, how they weren't his real parents but they brought him up.'

Robbie nodded. 'Oh yeah.' She sat there thinking, licking the icypole from the bottom up. Then the last chunk of Otis's fell off the stick and into the dirt. 'Fuck*ing*,' he said, testing it out. Robbie glanced quickly at their parents but they'd looked away. They didn't say anything, but their bodies were shaking and Robbie knew they were laughing.

*

It was Nik's mother who opened the door to his visitors. She was a small woman with a worn-out look, her shoulders always wrapped in shawls that may have been beautiful once but were now dull. She spoke little English. At least that's what Nik said. When Robbie asked him what his mum thought of all of them coming and going, he grinned. 'She thinks I'm really popular,' he said, after doing a cone. 'She doesn't mind.' He said it confidently, like he'd discussed it with her. 'I'm still playing the violin,' he added.

He played for Robbie in his bathroom sometimes, where the tiles made for the best acoustics. They'd lock the door and Robbie would lie in the empty tub listening to him. Though it was also the Babushka's bathroom, she never gave that too much thought.

It wasn't that Robbie, or any of Nik's friends, treated her outright badly – they politely chimed, 'Hello, Mrs Kowalski' when she opened the door, took their shoes off at the foot of the stairs, said, 'May I speak to Nik, please?' when they called on the landline – it was just that they didn't give her any thought at all. Everything they had been taught about adults, about rules in other people's houses, none of it seemed to apply to the Babushka. That's what Robbie took to calling her, and like 'the Messiah', it caught on. Even so, Robbie wasn't deluded like Nik's friend Pete. 'Nik's mum is awesome,' he'd enthuse to the mates he kept bringing to meet the Messiah, his dreadlocks tinkling with the tiny pixie bells his girlfriend had threaded in. 'She's totally cool with everything.'

Pete was a dickhead. The Babushka was clearly far from awesome. But still, when Robbie locked the bathroom door, she never thought, *what if Mrs Kowalski needs to come in?* When she undressed and lay naked in the tub, listening to Nik play the violin, the pads of his fingers pressing on the frets, the horsehair bending in low, svelte notes, and she beckoned him to join her in the tub afterwards, where the two of them fucked, their thighs rubbing against the porcelain, she never considered, *what if Mrs Kowalski needs to pee?*

*

Robbie was in Grade Six when things started to go wrong for Danny. It was the hottest February on record, and at school the ceiling fans were on full bore. Whenever a teacher stepped out of the room, the class threw dusters at the spinning blades, shrieking as clouds of chalk billowed down, dusters spasming against the walls. They'd had enough. At recess and lunch, they hung around the fence, as close to the edges as possible, talking to strangers walking past, learning how to lure them in. Robbie was sent home with several notes, but Danny signed them without appearing to care. At first it was cool, but there were other things that weren't so cool. He kept hiding stuff – his wallet and Claire's purse, his work keys, both sets of house keys. There were times they couldn't go anywhere because they couldn't find them, turning everything in the house upside down, inside out. Nothing.

Often Danny tried to help with the search, but he got agitated. He kept hitting the side of his head. 'I can't remember what they look like,' he'd say. 'Is that strange?' He'd stare at Claire, scared. He wanted her to say it was normal, but she didn't. She was scared too. Otis would usually be the one who found the keys and the wallets; once Danny had placed them carefully inside the fuse box and no one except Otis had thought to look in such an unlikely spot.

It would happen in spells and then Danny would be normal again, but each spell lasted a little longer.

It was around this time Robbie started to want the older kids at Danny's school to notice her. She'd stretch her legs out on the concrete steps, hitching up her dress so the hem was just a breadth from the pouch of her undies. She'd begun to shave, using her mother's razor, and rubbed in olive oil to make her legs shine. More often than not the boys would just trip over her, their boxy bags banging her on the head. Sometimes the mothers scowled at her from their cars – 'Hi Benjamin, hi Michael, hi James,' they sang, electric windows sliding down – but Robbie kept doing it, fuelled by the odd blush and mumbled 'sorry', into which she read all manner of destinies.

In winter she changed tack. She sat huddled on the step, rubbing her hands together dramatically for warmth, like the little match girl. The plan was for one of them to feel sorry for her, and then to fall in love. Previously she'd ignored Otis, pretending not to know him when he came past dribbling his basketball, but now she called to him in a motherly way, hoping to indicate to whomever was watching that they were two orphan children. The boys continued to trip over her. It had never occurred to Robbie that she might be ugly to them, or at least weird-looking. Her teeth were too big for her face, her dark hair flat on top with squiggly curls at the bottom, like a kid's drawing.

Then one afternoon a teacher clicked through the gates towards her and Otis. Bony and primped, she walked like a hen, her neck bobbing, high heels splayed. Her nails were painted mauve. Her eyes turned bright when she found out who they were. 'Danny's kids,' she said.

She motioned for them to follow her, taking them inside the school and up two sets of stairs to the staffroom. On the table was a tray of biscuits. 'Go on,' she said, and Robbie took one, Otis three. Robbie scowled at him, but Otis ignored her. The woman looked at them appraisingly as they ate. 'You're skinny as strays.' She shook her head, clicked her tongue. 'Poor Danny.'

Robbie choked, crumbs flying out of her mouth. What did she mean, *poor Danny*? The woman darted over to pat Robbie on the back. 'You eat like a stray too,' she chided.

It's Mrs Eckersley, Robbie realised. *It's Mrs Fucking Eckersley.* She started to panic as Mrs Fucking Eckersley rubbed her back. She couldn't control her coughing.

'I'll get you some milk,' Mrs Fucking Eckersley said.

'No, thank y—' Robbie tried to say, while Otis nodded happily.

'Don't be silly.' The teacher was at the fridge already, pouring milk into two glasses. She set both down in front of them. 'Here, drink up.' Robbie glanced at her face. It was thick with make-up, wrinkles cracking the clay-like surface around her puckered mouth. Her eyes were small, lashes gooped together with purple mascara. She pulled out the chair and sat down. Robbie could feel her staring. Then Mrs Eckersley leapt up. 'I've an idea,' she said. 'I'll be back in a minute.'

She disappeared out the door. 'Otis,' Robbie hissed, 'it's Mrs Eckersley.' Otis stared back at her blankly, his mouth full of biscuit. 'She's Mrs Eckersley,' Robbie hissed again. 'Dad is going to kill us.'

Then the woman was back, pushing the door open with her hip, carrying a basket of clothes. 'Lost property,' she said, winking at them. 'You need proper coats.' She put the basket on the floor and went through it, pulling out a couple of dark blue jackets. 'These are very good,' she said, rolling up a sleeve to show them the fleece inside. 'Very warm. Waterproof, too.' She pulled out a few more and checked their labels, shaking them out so she could get a good look. 'Try these ones on.' She indicated to Robbie to stand up, and it was as if the woman had cast a spell, Robbie holding out her arms as Mrs Eckersley started to thread the sleeves over her wrists.

When the teacher paused, peering at the inside of her left arm, it took Robbie a while to realise what Mrs Eckersley was thinking. At school Robbie and Tash had been doing smileys on each other using a lighter Robbie had nicked. They'd burn the flame for a minute and then quickly press the hot metal to their skin, holding it there for as long as they could take before lifting it off to reveal a smiley face. She had about seven of them on the inside of her arm, welts varying in size and redness. 'Is everything okay at home, dear?' Mrs Eckersley said carefully, eyes like searchlights.

It was one of those mismatched moments – tears sprang to Robbie's eyes from the fury of being examined so closely and yet so desperately misunderstood. Mrs Eckersley returned the jacket to the pile and pulled a chair in close. 'It's okay,' she said gently, as Robbie gasped for air and clarity.

'Our dad,' she stammered. 'He might be finished. He might be trying to find us.'

'Of course,' Mrs Eckersley said. 'I'll go fetch him, if you two feel okay with that?'

Why wouldn't we be okay with that? Robbie wanted to retort, but instead she nodded feebly. Mrs Eckersley stood, still looking at Robbie. 'Try these on,' she continued, pointing to the jackets on the table.

When she left, all Robbie could think of was their father's face as Mrs Eckersley clicked her way to him. *Mrs Fucking Eckersley*. Otis understood by then, and was staring at Robbie for a plan. *We could run*, thought Robbie, *or hide*. She looked around the staffroom, but neither the brown vinyl chairs nor the long table was really an option, so instead she just stared at the door, waiting for it to open. Otis got off his chair and stood beside her, his hand hovering near hers, not taking it, and he too watched the door.

When it opened, Danny came in first. 'Here they are,' Mrs Eckersley said breathily behind him, and for a moment the teacher receded, barely existed, as she locked eyes with her father. A tremor came off Danny's skin, a barely perceptible fury. Then Mrs Eckersley clicked in front and waved at the jackets still on the table. 'You haven't tried them on yet?'

Robbie shook her head, staring at her father. Otis looked at the carpet.

'It's cold outside, Danny,' Mrs Eckersley said. 'Your daughter doesn't have a proper coat. I thought she could have one of these.' She held up a jacket.

Danny shook his head. 'No, thank you, Mrs Eckersley. Robbie has lots of coats, she just refuses to wear them.'

Robbie nodded her head vigorously. 'It's true.'

Danny gestured to them. 'We have to get going, you two. Your mother will be getting worried. Say thank you to Mrs Eckersley.'

'Thank you, Mrs Eckersley,' chimed Otis, but something came over Robbie. She was scared, yes, of her father's anger, knew the walk home would be awful – but there was no way she was going to thank Mrs Fucking Eckersley. She looked at her sneakers, lilac fake Converse, her fists clenched.

'Robbie?' Danny said.

She was silent.

'Robbie,' he said again. 'I said, "Say thank you."'

She stared harder at her sneakers, stared so hard her shoelaces blurred and came to life – she could see every speck of dirt on them.

'Robbie.'

'It's okay, Danny,' Mrs Eckersley said. 'She's shy. I understand.'

Robbie snapped her head up then, furious, but Danny stopped her with a look. 'C'mon,' he said, and they followed him, down the stairs, out the gate, up the street and around the corner, where he turned and whacked Robbie on the head.

Otis tried to defend his sister. 'We didn't do anything,' he said. 'She just came out and got us.'

But Danny and Robbie looked at each other, both knowing that there'd been a deception, a trick of pity and skin. Finally Danny spoke, and it was a warning. 'Don't you do that ever again,' he said.

*

After that, they waited for Danny at the park across the road. From the swing, Robbie could see the lights turn off at the end of his shift. She liked to hang upside down, her hair brushing against the tanbark, watching each window gasp into the dark. *Goodnight, rich fish*, she'd think. Sometimes she'd help Otis practise his passes, but mostly he'd just bounce his basketball off the play equipment by himself, while Robbie hung on the swing, blood rushing to her head.

It was nice at the playground. For a stint, they got to be young again. After the lights were all out, Danny would come and push Robbie on the swing. He'd play defence against Otis, crouched and crab-like, and on the way home he'd put his fingers in Robbie's hair and pick out the bits of bark.

But the forgetting kept happening. He'd have his arms around them, firm and knowing, and then suddenly he'd go limp. Halfway into the hug, he'd forget who they were. There were times when Claire put dinner on the table and he'd thank her formally, as though she were a waitress. They went to doctors and then the hospital for tests, Otis and Robbie exploring the corridors, following the coloured lines, seeing broken bodies and faces they couldn't un-see, hearing shrieks and moans they couldn't un-hear. The doctors put him on medication and for a time it worked, but then it wore off, like sticky tape that lost its adhesive.

One evening at the playground, Robbie and Otis were waiting for the lights to be turned off when Danny appeared, and walked right past them.

It was strange to watch your father see you and not register. Otis ran to catch up with him. 'Dad!' he yelled, and Robbie didn't move from the swing, only watched as Danny stopped and stared at Otis, not comprehending. She always felt bad about that, not rescuing Otis from that moment, for she'd heard the collapse of her little brother's voice. 'Dad? Daddy? Dad?' Seen his hands grabbing and Danny recoiling. Robbie could sense him flicking desperately through the files in his head, trying to find a match for this kid with imploring eyes.

He was put on indefinite leave a week after that. The principal of the school phoned Claire to say they were very sorry and hoped Danny could come back soon. Mrs Eckersley, they learned, had been instrumental in convincing the school to keep Danny on as long as they had.

Grade Six finished, and at assembly they threw their legionnaires hats into the air, and for a time the doctors seemed to work out the right dose of medication and Danny's symptoms eased. The four of them spent the last few days of the summer holidays at Half Moon Bay in Black Rock, Danny and Robbie swimming out to the wreck of the *Cerberus*. Looking down from the rusted hulk, they could see a carpet of stingrays lying flat on the bottom of the bay.

Danny pried a limpet off the wreck and tossed it towards a ray, startling it. Both of them watched as the ray lifted its fleshy wings and swam low, over the others, to a spare patch of bay. Robbie gazed, already drawing them in her head so she could sketch them at home in her special drawing book.

'Hey, Robbie?' Danny said, breaking her lines. She looked over at him. He was sitting on the metal, resting his elbows on his knees. He was thin from all the drugs but still the dad she recognised, tall and gangly, which Robbie thought was gorgeous in a man – less so in a girl, like her. Water ran down his hair and chest, and gathered at the hems of his boardshorts, dripping diamonds.

'Yeah, Dad?'

'I love you,' he said. 'You know that, don't you?'

Robbie nodded. She sat next to him and put her head on his arm, careful not to look him in the eyes for fear he would stop talking.

'I know I'm hard on you,' he continued, 'harder than I am on Otis. But I have my reasons, Robbie. Don't tell your mother I said this.' He paused. 'But it's none of people's business, okay?'

Robbie stole a look at him. He was staring out at the water, his eyes dark. 'What isn't?'

He put his arm next to Robbie's. Glistening with seawater, they both shone brown. 'If anyone asks, tell them you're Italian.'

It was a funny feeling, the way her insides tilted when he said that. He could see it, too. 'It's not worth it, Robbie. Trust me.'

Robbie stared at their arms, side by side, then gave him a little nod.

Danny kissed the top of her head. 'I can't believe you're going to high school. You nervous?'

'I don't think so,' Robbie said with a shrug. 'Maybe a little.'

'You'll be fine. You're ready, I reckon, Robbie.' He sat back so he could look at her properly, tilting her face towards his, his hand under her chin. 'I'm sorry about this,' he said, tapping his head, 'this trouble in here. I keep thinking that if I didn't box, this wouldn't be happening – but then if I didn't box, I wouldn't have met your mother and we wouldn't have had you and Otis. But I'll beat it, okay? I won't forget you, I promise.'

On the shore, Claire was waving them in, Otis holding a parcel of fish and chips high above his head for them to see. The sun was going down and the cliffs behind them were a burnt orange, as if on fire. Danny grinned. 'Let's go,' he said, giving Robbie a squeeze. Together they perched on the edge of the wreck. 'One, two, three!'

Robbie held her nose and jumped, Danny pausing to make sure she landed okay, then following. Beneath them, the rays startled, lifting their grey wings, undulating, and flew a little to the right.

But he did forget them. The medication stopped working. The doctors changed it, but they couldn't stop the decline – that's what they called it. It got so bad that Claire had to start locking him inside. Too many times they'd be distracted for twenty minutes, half an hour, and he'd be gone. The three of them would set out to find him and eventually they would spot him, walking with a kind of ragged purpose, crossing streets without looking for cars. Robbie couldn't stop thinking about the time she found the neighbour's cat on the nature strip one morning, rigid and wet with dew. It got in her head that the same would happen to Danny, that he'd be hit and left on the side of the road for his owners to find.

Finally Claire organised for him to go into a home. But the guilt ate away at her. She began to drink, especially after the visits. Once, in his ward, they found a nurse with her hands on Danny's shoulders, holding him down in bed. She was on her tiptoes, putting all her weight on him as he struggled to get free. 'It's quiet time,' she said sternly, and when she saw them in the doorway, she simply repeated it. 'It's quiet time, Daniel.'

Claire went wild. She yelled at the nurse that Danny was young. He needed to move around. Couldn't she tell? 'He's fucking sprightly in comparison to the others,' Claire snapped, looking around at the residents, all of them white and skinny like albino stick insects. Otis began to cry and Robbie only watched her little brother. She wanted to hug him but couldn't. It felt like they'd all turned into islands, where once they were joined.

Back at home, the smell of boiled vegetables and urine seemed to stay with them, in their clothes and their hair. Robbie had visions of all those purple legs encased in pressure socks and of the woman who always stood next to the window, wrapping and unwrapping herself in the curtain, turning around and around.

*

A year into this new order, Claire's work friend Ruth urged her to start dating and signed her up to eHarmony. They'd sit in the study giggling, wine glasses in their laps, heads together over the computer as Claire scrolled through all the men. 'Ooh, now there's a silver fox,' Ruth would shriek, and reach out, clicking to message him before Claire could stop her.

Neither Robbie nor Otis liked Ruth – she was bossy, always telling them to help their mother and lecturing Claire to edit her profile so she'd get more matches. 'Do you want to meet someone or not? If you do,' she'd say, 'you need to keep changing your algorithm.' When Robbie went past the study once, Ruth called out to her. 'Your mum's a sucker,' she said. 'Always stopping at the ones with cats and dogs in their photos. See, look!' Robbie came over and peered at the screen, showing a man in a grey T-shirt sitting on a couch with a dog. 'Borrowed,' Ruth said knowingly.

Robbie couldn't stand it. A couple of times she'd logged in when her mother wasn't around, looking through the 'available' men. There were guys with pot bellies, bald blokes with tattooed chests and peroxided beards, men in military uniforms. None looked like her father. They all seemed to leer. Even those posing with a kid, usually with some sort of disclaimer at the bottom: *Not my son – my nephew!* Robbie had a sick feeling that maybe their mother had posted photos of her and Otis, so she looked at her profile. She hadn't. Instead she'd put up two photos Danny had taken of her when they spent the Christmas holidays in Rye a few years ago. She was smiling, a sarong patterned with hibiscus flowers tied over her bathers, a cluster of freckles sprinkled on her shoulders. In one photo she was wearing her straw hat and looking at the camera from under its brim, straight at what Robbie knew was Danny, her eyes shining. Her profile read, *I love summer, the beach, fish and chips, men who know how to change a tyre. I've got a son obsessed with basketball and a sassy 15-year-old daughter going on 18 (help!)*

Robbie read and reread the paragraph. Then she waited for her mother to get home.

Claire's face was drawn when she got in, plastic supermarket bags pinching her wrists. 'Can you help me with these, Rob?' she said as she passed the study.

'No.'

Claire stopped and frowned. 'Robbie,' she began curtly, but Robbie cut her off.

'What the fuck is this, Mum?' she demanded, pointing at the computer.

Claire's frown deepened, peering at the screen. 'That's private.'

'Private, sure,' Robbie snapped. 'It's on there for the whole world to see. "Going on eighteen"? What the fuck is that?' Then, prissily, '"*Help*"? What the fuck is *that?*'

Claire sighed, easing the bags from her arms and onto the floor. She shrugged off her work blazer, leaving it on top of the printer. 'Honey,' she said tiredly, walking towards Robbie.

'Don't "honey" me!' Robbie felt a fury building inside her. She snatched the paperweight that had been on the desk forever, a lump of resin encasing a Christmas beetle, and hurled it at her mother.

Claire reeled as the weight caught the corner of her eyebrow. 'Ow!' she screamed, covering her face with her hands. 'Oh my fucking god, Robbie!' She moved a hand away, peering at her palm. Blood was spurting from a gash and running down her cheek. She pressed her hand back over the wound, smearing blood into her hair.

Robbie was instantly regretful. 'Mum, oh Mum, I'm sorry, I'm sorry.'

Otis ran out from his room and halted when he saw the blood. 'What happened? Robbie, what happened?'

'I'm sorry, I'm sorry,' Robbie kept saying, trying to press her hand to the gash, but Claire pushed her away, hurrying to the bathroom. Robbie followed, standing outside the closed door. 'I'm sorry, Mum,' she called, and then in a rush of anger, 'Fuck, Mum, I apologised!'

Otis stared at her. 'What did you do, Robbie? Why did you hit Mum?'

After that, a silence crept out over the three of them; a distance grew that they couldn't fix. Even after Robbie and Claire talked it out, there was still something between them, a wall that kept growing.

*

'IS EVERYBODY READY?'

The MC's voice boomed, the enormous wooden shed atop the old shipping pier rattling. Thousands of arms went up, spun with glow bracelets and tattoos, spindly in the flashing lights.

'IS EVERYBODY READY TO GO HARD?' Pictures kaleidoscoped over the roof, the walls, skin, patterns breaking into shapes and spinning outwards.

'I SAID,' the MC boomed again, 'IS EVERYBODY READY?' People began to cheer and stamp their feet. If you were high, which everyone was, the sound was like a perfect wave, lifting the human hordes up in its crescent.

'ALRIGHT!'

A single beat whistled over the crowd.

'LET'S GO,' the MC yelled as the beat dropped, the wave crashing as everyone threw themselves forward, launching into the dance, sweat arcing in the air, and if Robbie's father was forgetting everything, she had every intention of remembering everything, kicking up talcum powder on the floor, her arms unfolding like wings. She had conversations with her father out here, his voice as clear in her head as her own. *We're made up of winners and losers*, she heard him say, *our blood, our bones* – and she felt it, the blood running in her veins like creeks, her bones beach-bleached sticks. *So what do you do?* her father's voice hummed deeply with the bass. She knew what he would say. *You back the winners, that's what you do.* But as the shed popped with beats and bursts of light, as people unfurled into the sound, Robbie felt her world realign. *No*, she always thought, at the peak of the night. *No, I'll back all of me.*

*

Robbie had been with Nik for almost two years when she learned that things had changed with her mum. School was edging to a finish, but she pretty much only went for art classes anyway, scraping through the other subjects. She and Nik were almost living together: nights were spent at his place, but she'd go back to the townhouse for a few hours alone, usually in the afternoon.

It was during one of those visits that Claire came home early. There was a guy with her.

'Don't worry,' Robbie said. 'I'm going.'

Claire shook her head, grabbing her daughter's hand. 'No, I'm happy to see you.' She glanced at her backpack. 'I want to talk to you. Do you think you could stay for a bit?'

Robbie shrugged. She let her bag slip off her shoulder as Claire motioned to the guy to come closer. He was wearing a denim shirt, buttoned all the way up, brown pants and polished shoes. He was plain-looking, with brown hair, his head slightly too big for the rest of his body. 'This is Nathan,' Claire said, smiling at him.

'Hi,' Robbie said dully, hefting the bag back onto her shoulder, but Claire reached out to stop her.

'No, I'd like to talk to you,' she said, and then, looking at him, 'with Nathan.'

They sat on the couch. Robbie perched on the edge, looking at her hands.

'So,' Claire started nervously, 'I met Nathan ... at a church.' Robbie looked up. 'Sunnyside,' Claire added.

Robbie groaned and put her head on her knees.

'Robbie,' Claire pleaded. 'Don't be so judgemental.'

Nathan started to laugh. It was a deep, bell-like sound. Robbie turned so she could see him, resting her cheek on her thigh. Claire turned to him too. 'What are you laughing at?' she said sharply.

'Well, she is funny, you said so yourself.'

Claire snorted. 'Yes, but not in a very nice way.'

At that moment Otis came in, tossing his bag in the doorway. He stopped, surprised to see Robbie. 'Hey Mum, hey Nathan,' he said, then looked uneasily at Robbie. 'Hey Rob.'

Robbie looked at Otis, then back at Claire. 'Please don't tell me you've got Otis involved.'

Claire tossed her head. 'Look, Robbie, it's not a cult, I'm not going to make you join. Or Otis,' she said, and added, 'Oh god, Robbie, please don't even think of joining!' Robbie smiled despite herself and Claire put her hand on Robbie's hair, stroking it. 'I just wanted you to know. That I'm happy. Look at me – I haven't had a drink in eight weeks.'

She did look good: her eyes were clear. But she seemed older. Her hair had silver in it. Along her eyebrow there was a scar, notched like the starred head of a screwdriver, from the paperweight.

'What about Dad?' Robbie said defensively. It had been months since she'd been to the home, just letting the time between visits drag out until it was no longer time between but since. 'Does he know about Dad?' She nodded in Nathan's direction.

'Oh, honey, he's met Dad. Nathan's been coming with me twice a week to help.'

Tears shot into Robbie's eyes. She looked away. 'That's nice,' she said, shifting her gaze to the wall. She stood up, bag in hand. 'I've got to go.'

Claire put her hand out, held Robbie's wrist. 'Can't you stay? Have dinner with us?'

Robbie shook her head, avoiding her mother's concern. She glanced over at Nathan instead. 'Nice to meet you.'

He nodded. 'Same.'

'See ya, Otis.'

'Bye, Rob.'

On the bus to Nik's, Robbie plugged in her headphones. She tried to catch the beats, swim into them, letting one wave go, riding the next. But the repetitiveness annoyed her. Scrolling through her albums, she settled on The Church, one of her father's favourite bands. She thought about how he used to say the lyrics, not sing them. He'd look at her and Otis in the rear-view mirror, his eyes intense. Fingers furious on the wheel. '*Our documents are useless,*' and he'd practically spit the words out, '*Page forty-seven is unsigned, I need it by this evening.*' Did he miss them? In the nursing home, did he ever remember them? Robbie's heart hurt. She missed him so fucking much.

It was raining when she got off the bus. Cars streaked past, slurries of water coming from their tyres, their headlights bleeding into the night. At Nik's, the Babushka opened the door. She was wearing those fleece slippers they sell at the supermarket, with the sticky grip on the soles. Robbie could hear them squeak as they peeled off the lino when she walked back into her kitchen.

Nik was on the phone when she entered. He nodded at her, pushing the mix her way, and she packed a cone, sucked it down and packed another. When he ended the call, Robbie sat on his lap, straddling him. Nik looked up at Robbie, bringing his lips close to kiss her.

Suddenly, she wanted to hurt him. She pushed his face away, forcing him flat on the bed, and tugged his tracksuit pants down, keeping her other hand on his neck so he couldn't get up. Then she wriggled out of her jeans and undies. She could feel something turning in her, a dark shape, about to reveal itself.

Nik tried to kiss her again but she wouldn't let him, instead working his penis into semi-hardness with her mouth, viciously nipping at the edges of his skin. Nik flinched. 'Ow, Robbie,' he said, attempting to shift away. She sat up, straddling him again. She forced Nik's chin away, the heel of her hand on his throat so he couldn't see her. 'Robbie,' he said again, trying to push her hand off. She ignored him, putting her weight on him, hand still on his throat, grinding with her pelvis.

'Robbie,' Nik said in a strained voice, 'I can't fucking breathe.' Dully, she released her hand a little. She closed her eyes, concentrating. It was there, a small flare in the dark, a weak pulse of heat. She chased it down.

A jagged snarl caught in her throat when she came. The heat throbbed and bloomed all the way up to her neck.

She rolled off Nik and he sat up, rubbing his neck, looking at her strangely. Then there was a knock on the bedroom door and he sprang up, pulling his pants on. Robbie slid under the doona and faced the wall. 'Hey, bro,' she heard a voice say. Pete. *Awesome, man*, Robbie mimicked in her head.

It was the regular Thursday-night boom for Nik. Robbie put a pillow over her head but could still hear people coming in and out, slapping palms like they were all ghetto. She could feel Nik shifting bags of stuff from under the bed, others unwrapping their foils, adding to the mix bowl; she heard the warm-up of scissors, the sucking, bubbling, exhaling. There was the nervous laughter of new girls, girls who smelt of sweet musk and probably took itsy-bitsy tokes. 'Pure THC,' Nik said to one of them, and the girl asked a question and Nik laughed. 'Nah, no bad trips, I promise.'

Robbie sat up, and a few people jumped. 'Shit, Robbie,' Pete said. 'I didn't even know you were there.'

'Well, it's the fucking room of surprises then, isn't it?' she snapped, and the doorbell rang again. Robbie looked at Nik. 'Why don't you answer the door for a change?'

He stared back, trying to work her out. Then he laughed, returning to mixing.

'No, I'm serious, Ni-*kit*-a. Why don't you answer the door?'

'Shut the fuck up, Robbie,' he said quietly.

Robbie looked at Pete. 'What about you? You're pretty much always here these days. Why don't you go answer the door?'

Pete blushed, looking to Nik for help.

'Why don't you, Robbie?' Nik said, louder this time. 'Why don't you fucking open the door, if you care so much?'

'Great idea,' she said, swinging her legs out from under the doona, still naked from the waist down. A couple of the girls sniggered as Robbie stepped around them, finding her jeans. 'I'll give your slave, sorry, *your mother*, your regards,' Robbie called to Nik as she shut the bedroom door, getting dressed in the corridor.

On her way down the stairs, she recognised a couple of girls from her English class coming up. 'Hey, Robbie,' one said, as they stopped to let her pass. Robbie didn't answer. She saw the back of the Babushka as the woman shuffled down the hallway to the kitchen.

Through the yellow glass beside the front door, a shape came up the footpath and the doorbell rang again. Robbie answered it. A guy whose name she could never remember was standing on the doormat with his arm around his girlfriend in her midriff top, showing off her pierced belly button. Robbie rolled her eyes, stepping back so they could come in, then slammed the door, making the girl jump.

When Robbie turned around, the Babushka was staring at her. A low lamp on a side table gave her the look of someone holding a torch under their chin, the underside of her lips, her nostrils, her eyelashes and the protruding centre of her forehead lit up in the dark. 'I thought I'd give you a break,' Robbie said, as the couple went up the stairs.

The Babushka didn't say anything.

'I mean, you must get sick of it?'

The woman shrugged, then slowly turned to walk back to the kitchen. Her slippers squeaked. Robbie decided to follow her and the woman's back stiffened, sensing this.

It was bright in the kitchen, with its blond timber cupboards and fluorescent light. A Big W catalogue was open on the shiny pine table, a mug of tea beside it. The Babushka went to the far side of the room, as if putting the table between them. Robbie had never really seen her in the light before, and it was like seeing a ghost inside a ghost. She could see Nik's eyes and lips. But she couldn't imagine this woman being his mother and doing motherly things, like reading to a young Nik in bed, kissing his head, tickling him. Not like she and Otis had with their mum and dad.

Robbie's eyes blurred. She looked around the kitchen for a way to halt the tears. 'I was wondering if, maybe, I could make a cup of tea?' she asked awkwardly.

The Babushka hurried to the sink to fill the kettle.

'No, don't you do it!' Robbie said, too loudly. The Babushka jumped and moved quickly back to where she had been standing. Robbie went over and picked up the kettle, filling it and clicking it back on its stand. Then she opened the cupboards, looking for mugs. 'Would you like one too?' Robbie said when she found them, choosing a mug featuring a Jack Russell. The Babushka shook her head and glanced out to the hallway.

'I've only been in here a few times before, isn't that crazy?' Robbie said. She was feeling funny, a rising nausea in her throat. 'I've been going out with Nik for two years' – the Babushka was staring at her – 'and I haven't been in here more than a couple times, isn't that crazy?' She kept talking, trying to keep the sick feeling at bay. The Babushka said nothing and Robbie opened the cupboards again, looking for teabags. 'Do you and Nik ever have dinner together? I mean,' she continued, 'does Nik even eat?' She saw a jar of loose tea and reached up to grab it. She was starting to panic. What was she doing in here? She put the jar on the bench. The leaves were moving, like it was filled with bugs. Fuck. She was wasted. Fuck.

Then, as Robbie was trying to open the jar, it slipped and fell, shattering on the floor. Next thing the Babushka was on her knees with a brush and dustpan, moving around Robbie. Robbie lifted her feet and stepped back, leaving two imprints in the leaves. Glass shards had scattered far across the floor. Robbie looked down at the Babushka, bent over on her knees. Her hands were shaking as she swept. Another feeling came over Robbie then, same as she'd felt upstairs with Nik, of wanting to hurt him. She felt a twitch in her foot, an impulse to kick. The want was so strong, the woman just kneeling there, that Robbie's mind went dark.

Did she do it? For years, Robbie would pretend that she didn't know. But there was a yelp, a sound like she imagined a dog would make if you kicked it just so in the ribs, and it stayed with her.

Out on the footpath, Robbie ran. Cars passed her, headlights flaring, wipers going. At one point Robbie stopped to catch her breath, then ran again. She ended up at Danny's old school. Robbie wrapped her hands around the iron gates and recalled how she'd sat on the step, pretending to be the little match girl. She banged her head against the metal. *Fucking idiot, fucking idiot.*

Grabbing hold of the wet bars, she climbed over and onto the school grounds. She was soaked, her hair dripping down her neck. She walked past the gothic architecture to the building where her father used to turn the lights out. She remembered standing in the staffroom with Otis, watching the door, and her father's face when he came in. He'd been scared, she realised. In his head he'd probably played it out – Mrs Eckersley's word against his – and he had figured she'd win. If she decided he wasn't fit to look after them, well, they could be taken away. It had always only been the four of them, and Robbie had never questioned why. It was lonely at times, but she'd just figured they were close-knit. Now she thought their father had not trusted to share them. Not even with Grace and Gregory, his foster parents – or maybe especially with them. Maybe he'd thought if they could be complicit in that with him, what would stop them doing it again? Danny had the three of them, that was all he had. And now? What did he have now? A nurse pinning him down saying, *it's quiet time, it's quiet time.*

Robbie saw the lockers lining the forecourt and went over, trying each handle until one banged open. Inside was a pencil case and some textbooks. She rifled through the pencil case and found a black Sharpie. She took it out and was about to close the locker when she saw, on the top shelf, a jacket just like the ones Mrs Eckersley had wanted her and Otis to try on. Robbie tugged it out. It was navy blue, with the gold insignia of the school on the breast. *Annuit Cœptis.* Robbie put it on. Mrs Eckersley was right; the fleece was warm on her skin. She flicked the hood up.

Robbie went back to the building with the fish windows and found a dry section under an eave. She started to write in big thick letters on the brickwork, and when she finished, she stepped back to admire her work:

MRS FUCKING ECKERSLEY

On the street, a security car stopped in front of the iron gate and a man with a torch got out. Holding an umbrella, he unlocked the gate as Robbie flattened herself against the bitumen. On the school grounds, he shone the light over the buildings and the oval. The beam swept over her. Robbie kept still. She waited until he walked around a corner. Then she ran, hunched down – made for the open gate, and heard a yell behind her, saw a ball of light dance about her sneakers. She kept running, down the street, past the 7-Eleven where she had stolen the sunglasses, and as she ran, the fancy school coat swishing, the rain coming off it in sheets, she thought of her father, his eyes in the rear-view mirror as he drove, looking straight at her. She knew what he was thinking. The system: it would come for her.

Saddam's Horses

She'd gone to bed fully dressed the night they came. It was almost a relief when she heard them break down the door, but when they entered her bedroom, black hoods over their heads, Nasim wished to return to the waiting. They hauled her out of bed by her hair and dragged her to the kitchen, muttering hadiths while one put the plug in the sink, turning the tap on. When the basin filled, someone put his hand on Nasim's head and shoved her down, into the water. Everything went blue, red, pink, and then the back of her head cracked against the tap as she was pulled up, guttural sounds coming from her mouth. One of the men put his phone close to her face, yelling at her to look. At first she couldn't see, couldn't make sense of the image on the screen, but finally it began to take shape. They weren't her girls, that was her first thought.

A few drops of water fell from her face onto the screen. The man yelled at her, taking the phone away, wiping it on his shirt. *Allahu Akbar*, you whore, he shouted, and the others said it too. He thrust the phone in her face again. Nasim identified a few of them this time, girls she'd worked with in the past, wrists she'd twisted, fingers she'd unpeeled from her own and bodies she'd shoved into cars. They were in a shower, six or maybe seven of them, the ones on the bottom with their legs sticking out, the others thrown on top, tight T-shirts and capri pants tugged the wrong ways, grazed knees, straps of flesh around their bellies, fingerprint bruises pressed into their thighs, a spill of breast over the tops of their bras. Blood pooled around the bodies on the tiles, leaking along the grout towards the drain.

The men pressed on Nasim, wrenching her head back, making her kneel and then stand, pushing her between them. In the other room she could see one of them smashing her piano, grunting as he swung his hammer, as though he had been harbouring resentment towards this hulking instrument all his life. He put his whole body into it, shoulderblades stretching and folding under his shirt, bringing the hammer down, then down again, keys flying off like exploding teeth. A couple of the men joined him, sinking their boots into the wood, and Nasim focused on the notes, saying goodbye as they detonated. *Goodbye, F minor*, she thought, *Goodbye, B major*.

The sound muffled as one of them pushed her under the water again, her face pressing against the gritty specks of food stuck on the bottom of the basin. The firm hand on the back of Nasim's head was almost reassuring as her legs began to kick out from under her. It was then Nasim belatedly recognised one of the dead girls in the photo – something about the swanlike flop of the neck, the shade of her dyed hair. It was Sabeen.

Nasim couldn't hold her breath any longer. She opened her mouth, sucking in water. The burning in her chest suddenly felt very faraway and her hair, swirling like tentacles, created a pleasant sensation. It was almost done. Then the grip on her head was released and she fell backwards onto the floor, vomiting water and bile, as the shadows inexplicably receded out the door.

For a time Nasim lay there, studying the thickness of her ankles in a daze. She turned her head to look at the bits of smashed piano strewn across the other room. Some keys were loose and scattered, others were hanging in strips like ammunition. She lifted her fingers, one at a time, and tapped out a slow trembling tune to steady her breathing. *Sabeen*, she remembered. The woman's story had been convoluted; many of the girls' stories were, and Nasim had not believed it at first, but when Sabeen had showed her a letter outlining a compensation payment, the paperwork with its strange insignia of a kangaroo and tall, leggy bird, Nasim had noted this with interest. She'd watched Sabeen carefully refold the letter, before returning it furtively to her small bag of belongings. The woman treasured that document from the Australian embassy, as if it were her only proof of a life she no longer had. Nasim sat up, her fingers now drumming purposively. She began to plan. She had a talent for this, this surviving.

*

Nasim's mother had played the piano. Nhour couldn't read music and had always regretted it, compensating by arranging lessons for her daughter. Nasim took to it like breathing: her mother attributed this to the lessons, but Nasim knew it was the hours she had watched Nhour play, memorising how she felt her way along the keys, gently forming sounds into chords and wincing when she hit an off note. Her melodies went unrecorded, fleeting as clouds but engraved on Nasim's bones.

Nhour Amin was a celebrated poet. She was called a 'true' Iraqi, commended for stripping the British influence from her poetry, for her love of country and her revolutionary spirit. A modern woman, Nhour was often out at meetings and readings, openings and lectures, salons and dinner parties, while Nasim's father stayed home in the evenings to look after Nasim. When her mother was home, it was mostly to work in her study or to bask in the company of many guests, including visitors from other countries, who brought Nasim gifts and sang her songs in curious languages, until she was bustled to bed while

Nhour held the guests in thrall. It was often said that Nhour Amin's poetry was like rain to a desert, but in conversation she spoke plainly and with a delicious humour that few dared. People both feared and loved her honesty.

Nhour despised the black abayas worn by the Shi'a women. 'They are like garbage bags,' she had sneered to Nasim once, as they walked behind a flock of them on the street. And at the parties her parents held, her mother would laugh at someone's half-hearted case for modesty. 'Modesty?' she would say. 'Modesty? Look at them in the market – they're the pushiest, rudest women there.'

Once Nhour imitated a goose to illustrate her point. She pushed her chin out, puckering her lips, shouldering everyone out of her way as she grabbed cakes from the table and clutched them to her chest, a wet hiss issuing from her lips. Everyone laughed in recognition. 'For their husbands!' someone called out.

At this, Nhour stopped and looked over at her husband, a Shi'a man, and smiled sweetly. 'Forgive me, my dear,' she said, picking up a throw and dropping it over her head, arms outstretched as she made howling sounds, blindly searching for him. 'My darling husband!' she called, 'it is me, your modest, stupid wife!'

Chuckling, he ran around the room as she tried to catch him, until the guests caught him for her and she embraced him clumsily, still howling like a ghost.

Her mother would apologise later, Nasim watching as she whispered in her father's ear, seeing his smile as he put his arms around her, but she was merciless. 'I'm sure your mother was a wonderful slave,' Nhour added loudly.

Many ventured that Nhour had Bedouin blood. It was a compelling thought, for her eyes were the copper of sand vipers, and her oval face was rugged with freckles. But it was more than that. She had an unyielding quality that reminded her admirers of the much-romanticised desert Arab – something unbending, a streak that would not, could not, adapt.

At the time, Nhour Amin's piano-playing was an afterthought; it was something she did in private, like prayer. But then everything changed.

It happened after Nasim's tenth birthday. She was in bed, her father having tucked her in, and she lay awake listening to the dinner party downstairs. She was in the habit of holding her breath so the sound of her breathing would not get in the way of her mother's voice, which flowed into song as the night thickened, joined by the twang of her father on the oud. The doorbell rang. It often did, but this time after the door was opened there was a strange hush, followed by movement as chairs were dragged across the floor, and then a frenzied popping of corks and clinking of glasses. Nasim got out of bed and propped her door ajar to listen. The laughter and the music had resumed, her mother's voice still bell-like, but there was something new: an unease in her tone.

Nasim, in her white nightdress with pink ribbon threaded through the bosom, tiptoed to the top of the stairs, peering down between the banisters. At first, she did not see anything beyond the flurry of guests, but then, in an opening of bodies, she saw him. He was sitting in their best armchair. Handsome, he looked just as he did on the posters: dark eyes kind and interested, eyebrows bushy and brooding. On television, Nasim's favourite part was when he rode his horse, an Arabian mare, Al-Awra, named after the Prophet Mohammed's favoured horse, meaning 'the one-eyed mare'.

Her mother liked him too. This Nasim knew because she had heard her defending him once. 'He's bringing Iraq into the twentieth century,' she said, when a guest voiced disapproval of his harsh methods. And now, he was here. In their home, listening avidly to her mother. Nasim was so excited she felt her chest might burst. She flew back to her bedroom and sat on her mattress, hugging her knees and holding her breath, listening for the voice of Saddam.

*

It had been a wonderful time. He told Nasim to call him 'Uncle', and when she shyly asked after his horses, he immediately organised a convoy of cars to take her to his palace. At the stables, Uncle lifted Nasim onto Husam, a mottled silver and white stallion, showing her where to hold the reins, putting her feet in the gilded stirrups. As he spoke to the stablehands, she put her arms around the horse's neck, her face in his mane, and closed her eyes, the earthy scent filling her. Quietly, so no one could hear, she told Husam that she loved him, whispering into a velvet ear. The horse nickered, a wet warmth coming from his nostrils. Seeing this, Uncle laughed. 'He likes you.'

He ordered a stableboy to lead Husam outside slowly, reminding Nasim to hold the reins. She nodded and pressed her thighs against the horse, weighting the balls of her boots on the stirrups. Then, with her ankles, she gave the stallion a flick. Without knowing, she had instructed Husam to gallop. He took off as the boy lurched to the side, and behind her she heard the startled shouts, and forgot to pull back on the reins as Uncle had showed her. Instead she sat low, the leather straps and the horse's mane threaded in her fingers, sky and earth blurring as Husam kicked up clods of grass and shot across the field.

Suddenly, Saddam was beside her, on a beautiful black horse he hadn't saddled, just flung himself onto. He pulled his animal close to hers, yelling, 'Oif!' and grabbing her reins, bringing Husam down to a trot with his. Nasim sat up and smiled.

Saddam began to laugh. 'You are happy?' he said. 'You smile instead of feel fear?' He laughed and laughed.

Later, when they rode back to the others, he told her parents, 'I thought she'd be in tears, but your girl was smiling. She is a natural.' And she was.

Nasim took to riding much like she'd taken to the piano, but this time, in contrast to her father's high praise of her piano-playing and her mother's insistence that she practise daily, her parents said nothing. When she tried to talk about the horses on the chauffeur-driven journeys home ('Which car would you like?' asked Uncle, and when her parents deferred to him he would say to her mother, 'This one, it matches your lovely dress'), they would not answer.

'I love them all, but I love Husam the best,' Nasim would say breathlessly, and to her mother, 'Which one do you like best?'

Once her mother had snapped, 'None of them, none,' and her father put his hand on her knee, jerking his chin at the driver. Her mother frowned and stared out the window again. Confused, Nasim also fell silent.

*

At parties in his Baghdad palace, Saddam's daughters would lead Nasim up the spiral staircase and into an enormous dressing room filled with gowns and shoes and jewellery and perfume. They were older than Nasim, and would undress and dress her like a doll, frowning expertly as they made up her face, applying lipstick, dusting her skin with a gold-flecked powder while Nasim squeezed her eyes shut. Armed with dryers, curling irons and bottles of hairspray, Saddam's daughters would do her hair, getting the scissors out to 'straighten' her fringe. Nasim would sit still, thinking of the horses, understanding this was a game she must play. They put her feet in too-big high heels, showing her how to strut as if on a catwalk.

Finally they would lead her downstairs to perform a fashion show for the guests. Nasim stared ahead as she walked the prescribed length – 'Here,' one of them said, standing at one end of a long ornate rug – and struck a pose, hands on hips and freezing for one, two, three seconds, then swivelling around to totter back up the stairs, delighting the guests.

Often the daughters fought over her. 'I'll dress her,' the older one would say, pulling Nasim's arms. 'You can do her hair.' Nasim would not say anything, knowing not to state a preference, simply waiting for them to tire of her so she could run to the stables, rubbing the make-up off her face with her sleeve. There, she'd go to each of the horses and whisper in their ears, which flickered with her breath. At home, she played the piano and thought of the horses, imagined calling their names as they cantered towards her. She pressed her body against the piano as she played, just as she did against the horses' flanks.

*

Presents kept arriving: a large freezer that would only fit in the living room; a doll's house; a brass lamp of a ballerina, her hand outstretched as she held aloft a lightbulb; a tiger skin. Each time something arrived, Nasim hopped around excitedly, helping to unwrap, impatient with her parents, who seemed reluctant to find out what new treasure they'd been sent. Nasim's mother recoiled when she revealed the tiger skin, pushing it down in its box. It was her father who reached in, drawing it out and draping it over the rug in the living room.

'No,' Nhour said and tried to remove it, but her husband's face was grim.

'We have to, Nhour.'

Their parties continued, but there were more guests now, different guests, and more food, more popping of corks. There was still laughing and singing, dancing too, but it was louder, foot-thumping, frenzied. Often Uncle stood at the bottom of the stairs and called

Nasim down to join them. She couldn't believe her luck – but then, one night as she ran down in her nightdress, she caught sight of Nhour watching. Her mother's face was taut, furious. Then Uncle picked Nasim up and spun her around, the guests applauding. When she looked back at her mother, Nhour was clapping too, a smile on her face.

After this, Nasim started to pay more attention. There were times when her parents had gone to bed and the doorbell rang. She listened as they quickly got up, whispering as they put their clothes on and opened the front door with what seemed like false cheer.

Other times, during the day, a car would arrive. Nhour, seeing it through the window, would stiffen. Before she left, she would tell Nasim to stay inside, that her father would be home soon. When her father came home and heard of the palace car, his face would darken. In the beginning Nasim thought her mother was having an affair with Uncle, a notion that brought mixed feelings. She was sad, yes, for her father, but also wildly excited for her mother. But one day, Nasim summoned up the courage to ask where Nhour went when the palace car came to collect her, and her mother replied, through gritted teeth, 'To advise Uncle on his poetry.'

Saddam had taken to writing poems, and when Nasim's mother returned from these sessions, she would not speak, retreating instead to the piano, her playing frustrated and violent. The first few times her father went in, to try to comfort her, but Nhour was not one to be soothed. She'd slap his hands, pushing him away. 'Leave!' she'd demand, as the piano raged.

Nhour stopped writing. Instead she spent her days playing the piano. Nasim and her father began to move through the house to the music of her mother's moods; they emerged from their rooms, Nasim her bedroom, her father his study, like soldier crabs, with a scuttle, trying to avoid the other's gaze. At times the piano-playing was so raw, so sad, that Nasim felt they might all crack open. She could not understand why her mother did not love Uncle, and there were times when Nasim loathed her. How could she be so mean? She hoped Uncle was not hurt by her mother's cruelty.

Their house continued to fill with guests, but Nasim knew now that they had not been invited. Her mother let them hold her hand, eyes glazing as they quoted her poetry, or asked her to sign one of her chapbooks. Only Nasim and her father could detect the contemptuous flourish of her pen as Nhour inscribed her name. When the guests asked her to recite a poem, she would defer to Saddam; when they asked if she would play the piano, she said she could not play, that she just picked at the keys as if at a plate of leftovers. She instructed Nasim, often dressed in the satin Chinese pyjamas Uncle had sent her, to play instead, and soon guests were clamouring, calling out requests, framing her still childish face with their hands, kissing her cheeks.

In the early hours of the morning, when the guests left, floor and tiger skin covered in party debris, Nasim and her father would go to bed, but the house would fill with their mother's mournful, restless playing and they would not sleep. Once, Nasim looked through her window and saw people had gathered in the street to listen. Not the guests – they'd been satiated by Nasim's playing – but others: street cleaners, early-rising chai sellers, those who were too scared to sleep. They swayed to her mother's sad song, their eyes filled with something Nhour no longer believed in, a true love of country.

Then, a few years later, when it became clear that Nasim was well on her way to becoming a successful pianist, her mother stopped playing. Uncle did not call on them as often, poetry no longer a priority. His attention was elsewhere, but a car would still arrive every now and then for Nasim, to come ride his horses.

*

'You like this one, don't you?'

Nasim froze. She'd been brushing Husam, and the horse nudged her hand with his muzzle, snorting at her to keep brushing. She did not move, staring at the man who had spoken, his frame filling the archway of the stable. At the palace parties where she'd played her part in his sisters' fashion parades, he had never spoken to her, not even when he stood beside his father and shook her parents' hands. He had been gangly then, with thick brown hair and a toothy grin, slouching over to greet dignitaries, most of whom stood on their toes to bestow kisses on him. His eyes were dark, intense, and Nasim had the feeling he'd been watching her all along.

He stepped into the stable, brushing against her as he put his hand on the horse's neck. Husam showed his teeth. Uday laughed. 'Seems he only wants you,' he said, and Nasim blushed.

'It is Nasim, yes?' She nodded. 'The pianist, yes?' She nodded again. 'As well as horse rider, daughter of the wind?' Uday grinned, his eyes dancing, and Nasim blushed again, not sure if he was making fun of her. He put his hand out and cupped her chin in his palm. She jumped, his touch electric. He laughed again and put his face close to hers, his dark eyes turning serious. 'Will you play for me one day?' Aware that she had not yet said a word, Nasim tried to think of a response, but failed and simply nodded again. Uday smiled, letting his hand drop, his fingers floating downwards against her skin. Nasim had a glimpse of a future then, of being a princess, a princess with a silver horse.

Many years later, people whispered that Uday Hussein could read your thoughts. It seemed to Nasim at this moment that he could read them because he made you think them. His fingers kept moving until they were on her dress and inching up her hem.

Then, outside, there was a commotion as several cars pulled up. The empty stable filled with grooms, smoothing their uniforms.

Nasim could hear their solemn greetings. It was Saddam.

Uday smiled as he stepped away from her and put his finger to his lips. Then he reached for Husam, pulling hard on the bridle so the stallion had to lower his head and splay his front legs to steady. The horse whinnied. 'I would like to give you this horse,' Uday said quietly. Nasim looked at him, confused. 'He is yours.' He was watching her, waiting for her to say something, when Saddam appeared in the doorway, stopping as he saw the two of them together. Uday loosened his grip on Husam, not taking his eyes off Nasim.

'Thank you,' she said finally, and he nodded, going to greet his father. Nasim watched as Uday kissed his father's cheeks, her dress pinched in her fingers as always, ready to curtsey, before Saddam dismissed the gesture with a wave and instead put his arms out for an embrace. But this time Uncle didn't look at her, not once. From then on, palace cars no longer arrived to take Nasim to the stables.

When her father noticed, he looked at her carefully at breakfast one morning and asked if something had happened. She shook her head, not looking up from her baked eggs. Alone, playing the piano, she cried, the felt-tipped hammers echoing the ache in her chest. Sometimes she imagined she was on Husam, riding the silver horse so fast her breath caught, her fingers tangled in his mane. Sometimes she imagined she was playing for Uday, as he had requested.

Three months later, Nasim's father was arrested. The men who took him from his bed, not letting him change out of his pyjamas, said he was to be charged for speaking against the regime in his faculty. He was gone for six months, and when he returned he was missing three fingers. He never played his oud again. After that they lived in a kind of muted fear, their house still decorated with Saddam's gifts.

*

It was a fellow poet that sped Nasim's mother to her inevitable end. He was a friend of hers, Jacob Bekhor, a Baghdadi Jew who had refused to join his family in the vast exodus to Israel in the 1950s. Zionism, he had claimed at the time, was for European Jews, not Iraqi Jews. He declared publicly that his loyalty to his nation took precedence over his faith, though in more private moments with Nasim's parents he admitted it was his poetic sensibilities, his connection to place, that kept him there.

The poets' friendship ran deep – and Nasim, who was born long after Jacob was eventually forced to leave, often wondered, hearing the way her mother spoke of him, if they had once been lovers. Nhour told Nasim that Jacob had held on in Baghdad, his love of country far exceeding that of 'many Arabs'. He had lost his teaching post, and was forced to carry a yellow card marking him out as Jewish, but still he would not leave. When she begged him to flee, he would reply, 'But without Iraq, who am I?'

Then the Republican Guard turned its gaze on Jacob, accusing him of spying for Israel and encoding secret messages in his poetry. At last he had to concede defeat. By then Radio Baghdad was regularly broadcasting calls to celebrate the execution of Israeli spies, most infamously the bodies of nine Jews left hanging in Liberation Square. Carrying a bag of his notebooks, Jacob left Iraq. But, Nhour always added, he refused to seek sanctuary in Israel, blaming it for turning his country against him. Instead he found refuge in New York, marrying a German Jewish widow who had a faded blue tattoo on her arm. 'He is not stupid, though,' Nhour said firmly to Nasim. 'He knows he is living in the cradle of the enemy.'

Nhour often spoke to Nasim like this. Nasim's own life – her days at the conservatorium, visiting the ice-cream parlour with her friends, listening to pop music – was of no interest to her. 'Come to me when you have lived,' Nhour once said, when Nasim complained of not being selected to represent the academy in a special 'Arab unity' tour. Nasim figured Nhour would give her a sign when she had lived enough to be taken seriously. That her mother would not live long enough herself – this had not occurred to her.

The two poets, Nhour and Jacob, wrote letters and exchanged poems. In 1976, Nhour sent news of Nasim's birth and Jacob managed to send a fancy American-made stroller, which drew much attention, even in increasingly modern Baghdad. When Nhour stopped writing poetry, many years later, he continued to send his work to her, and she edited it for him, annotating the margins with notes and scrawls. These edits, Jacob said, were invaluable. Now he wanted to thank her in person on his way home from a book tour through Europe.

It was a bad idea. Nasim's father knew it, as did Nasim, who was old enough to know such things by now. But her mother's eyes lit up at the poet's suggestion, and it was like seeing daylight after the longest night.

When the time came, her father insisted the visit be kept secret, as if such a thing were possible, and bundled them into the car, driving to a lakeside town. A stern-looking woman gave them a key to a cottage, and they carried in their things, including a basket with cheese, dates, coffee and bread, and waited in tense silence.

Two hours later, there was a knock on the door. Nhour opened it. It was Jacob and his wife, Anke, relieved they had found the right cottage. After they waved their taxi away, there was much hugging and crying as Nasim's mother pressed her face to Jacob and then Anke, closing her eyes. Somewhat dramatically, Jacob presented Nhour with his book. It was a thin object, dark green, with a photo of a burning pyre on the front. He nodded, as if to say 'Read on,' and she opened it, Nasim's father peering over her shoulder, his eyes widening. Jacob had dedicated the collection to her: *For Nhour Amin, the true Iraqi poet*. Nhour started to cry. Nasim's father was also crying. He kissed his wife and kissed Jacob too. He disappeared to the kitchen and returned with wine and glasses.

Their spirits lifted as Jacob read aloud from his book, Nasim's mother clapping at turns of phrase, while Anke cuddled up with Nasim, asking her about boyfriends and admirers. They had less than twenty-four hours together, and it became clear that Nhour and Jacob intended to waste none of them on sleep. Nasim curled up on the couch next to her mother, who was threading her fingers in and out of her hair, basking in her mother's happy voice, her touch, resisting her father's attempts to shoo her to bed.

At one point in the night, as Jacob read aloud, Nasim's father, who had been lounging in a cane chair, eyes shut as if snoozing, sat up straight. His face was alert. 'Read that again,' he ordered. Jacob and Nhour exchanged a look. Nasim sat up sleepily, pawing at her mother's lap like a kitten, trying to soften it again, but her mother had turned to stone.

'If you won't read it, pass it to me,' Nasim's father ordered. To Jacob, he held out his two-fingered hand.

Nhour nodded at Jacob. 'You read it,' she said.

Jacob cleared his throat. Nasim listened as well. At first it was just words. Poetry, she sometimes thought, is mere rope. Something you tugged at until finally, if you were lucky, a pail of water was hauled to the surface.

Tonight the dark well seemed unending. But then, the words slipped into her veins and her heart started to race.

'*In Tikrit*,' Jacob read, '*the watermelons are fat with blood.*'

Nasim looked at her father. He was staring at Nhour, his eyebrow twitching as it did when he was angry. Jacob continued:

> '*The boats
> they send down the Tigris
> are made of skin.*

In the hulls
are the innards
of foolish slights.
Tongues still twitching.
The river is black with ink
A common carp surfaces
gills muddy with massacre,
round silver eye on you.
He is a taxi driver,
a cigarette tout
He is glass in your shoe,
the man who twisted
your mother's nipple
until her milk soured.
Iraq's true son.'

Jacob paused.

'But if he is a poet, then poetry is dead.'

The cottage was silent. Jacob looked over at Nhour. Finally he said, 'You didn't tell him?'

Nhour did not look at him, her eyes locked with her husband's. She shook her head. 'No,' she said quietly but resolutely, sparking her husband into rage. He leapt up, knocking the book of poems out of Jacob's hands and onto the floor.

'You have killed us,' he yelled, kicking the book. He kept yelling, kept kicking it, until Nasim started to cry, begging her father to stop. At last he lowered his voice. 'You,' he said to Nhour, 'have killed our daughter for a poem.'

It was the only time Nasim ever saw her mother waver. A tremor crossed her face. Then her mettle returned. 'We were already dead,' Nhour said.

*

The next morning, they walked around the lake. The town had the acrid scent of orange peel and spiced fish. The group was silent and withdrawn. Nhour walked in front, with Jacob behind her; then came Nasim with Anke, their worrying hands entangled; and her father, carrying a long stick he'd found, smooth, white as bone, holding it like a staff.

They returned to the cottage, saying little as they prepared the table for lunch. Once the food had been laid out and they had sat down, there was a knock. Everyone stiffened, staring at the wooden door as if trying to see through it.

When the knock came again, Nasim's father answered it. The man standing on the doorstep nodded at him, and then, as if he was expected, stepped inside. He was dressed casually in jeans, a white shirt and leather slippers.

There was a beat, and then everyone swung into action, making a fuss over him, asking his name, if he had travelled far, setting an extra place at the table. They resisted glancing at one another, instead focusing on the uninvited guest, asking him questions. Anke praised the Baghdad airport, the condition of the roads. 'American roads,' she said with a practised grimace, 'are in terrible condition.'

But the uninvited guest was an expert. As Nhour served the fish and the rice, he asked her, 'Have you written much lately?' She reddened, saying she had not, at which he expressed dismay. He proceeded to steer the conversation to Nhour and Jacob. What was their relationship? Why had he returned? What did he think of the changes in Iraq? He had lived here for a time, yes? He reeled off the address where Jacob had lived, the faculty in which he'd lectured, even the number of his office. And the poetry of their leader, had he read it? Had Nhour provided him with the president's poems? Was it true he had just published a book? Did he have a copy here?

Jacob's replies were sound, and for a time each man batted the other's words back across the table. The lunch drew to a close and Nasim's father announced that their visitors had a plane to catch. But then the uninvited guest began to talk about the Holocaust, what a great fiction it was. Was Jacob familiar with the hoax? Jacob sat forward in his chair, ignoring Anke's hand on his arm. 'Such a success, this fiction,' the guest continued, 'but it is not finished, no?' He looked at Nhour, then at Jacob. 'You are not yet satisfied, no?' He gave a sweet, open-faced smile to Anke, who had largely avoided his gaze until now. 'You Jews are never satisfied.'

Jacob bit. Blood rushed to his face as he rolled up Anke's sleeve and thrust her arm over the plates and into the uninvited guest's face. Anke cried out, trying to pull it back. For a moment they struggled, she wincing in pain as Jacob gripped her arm. Nasim put her hand over her mouth. She'd seen tattoos before – most memorably the three dark blue dots on Saddam's wrist – but something about the crudely etched numbers on her new friend's arm startled her.

Jacob was a deep shade of plum now, spit forming at the corners of his mouth. He jabbed at the tattoo with his finger. It was a frozen tableau around the table as Anke hung her head, Nhour stared at the wall and Nasim's father hovered over his chair. The uninvited guest gazed down at Anke's arm, as if committing the numbers to memory. 'This,' Jacob said, still jabbing at the tattoo with his finger, '*this* is your fiction.' He pointed at the numbers. 'This,' he added, 'is your great Uncle's poetry.'

The guest glanced sharply at Jacob. Then, as if dealing with a child, he wagged his finger at him sternly. He pushed his chair back, looking at his watch. 'I believe you two have a plane to catch.' Anke nodded feebly, not looking up. The guest picked up the volume of Jacob's poetry on the coffee table. He looked at the cover before slipping it in his pocket. Then he turned to Nhour and thanked her for lunch, gathering his coat from beside the door.

When he left, the stillness collapsed. Anke started to hit her husband with her fists. 'You idiot, you idiot,' she said, pummelling him until Nhour put a hand on her arm. 'Stop, Anke, stop. We must go now, or you will be late.'

In the car Jacob begged for them to come into the airport with him, to fly to Beirut, told them that he would organise the rest – promised it as if his little book of poems could achieve this. But Nasim's parents shook their heads, knowing they would not be allowed to fly. They returned home and waited.

It took a long time. None of them knew why it took so long.

*

There was champagne and ice-cream in the foyer beforehand, and Nasim wore a pretty yellow dress. She and her father were sitting in a row close to the front, next to the other music students. The ceiling of the theatre was a swirl of painted pink roses, an enormous golden eagle perched in each corner. Nhour had stayed home, unable to let go of her vigil of dread. Above the stage was a portrait of Saddam, his expression benevolent yet stern.

There was an excited hush as the lights dimmed and the velvet curtains parted to reveal a black grand piano. Beatrice Ohanessian strode onto the stage, stately and elegant, with a flowing pale blue veil over her hair. She silenced the applause by sitting and playing a single shimmering note. Nasim leaned forward, along with everyone else. Her face shone, her heart pressing against her dress.

As the notes unfurled, it was not like people said, that time stopped: rather, it felt to Nasim as if time unravelled. With each swelling sound, she could see time as it was, ribboning into the future and into the past, less like dying and living than an infinite dive into the sea.

So enthralled was Nasim that she did not see the man walk slowly down the aisle, flicking his lighter, a tiny flame jumping in and out of the darkness. She only noticed when he paused at the row in which she and her father were seated. He turned sideways so he could make his way across, everyone shuffling to let him pass. He held up his lighter, flicking it on and off, while onstage Ohanessian fumbled, sensing the disturbance.

Then he stopped in front of Nasim, his legs crushing hers, and peered up at the dress circle. He held up his lighter, flicked it on. The flame, she realised, was a question. Nasim and her father turned to look, seeing only the faint outlines of people sitting high up in the dark. But then there was a solitary flame, a lighter held aloft in the darkness. The man looked back down at Nasim, his eyes coolly sweeping over her. He put his lighter in his pocket, nodded at her, then returned to the aisle, brushing everyone's knees the other way as he passed. As he reached the exit, the audience resettled, turning their attention again to the stage, and Ohanessian regained composure. But Nasim sat gasping. The famous pianist's tone was tinny now, as if coming from a transistor.

She clutched her chest and remembered one of her mother's most famous poems. It had extolled the Bedouin method of slaughter: how the desert herders would make a small slit in a goat's chest before reaching inside with their hands, feeling for the creature's heart. As they squeezed it, the goat would writhe in their arms, before sliding into death. A true Arab does his own murder, had been her mother's point; a true Arab knows the importance of another creature's heart. Nasim felt a draft on her chest, even checked to see the front of her dress had not been cut open. She began to shake, and her father's two-fingered hand sprang out to hold hers. Above them, the eagles had opened their eyes.

When the curtains fell and the lights came up, Nasim and her father did not move. No one looked at them as the audience stood and stretched, gathering handbags and coats, pushing towards the exit. Then the theatre was empty, except for Nasim and her father and the entourage waiting at the door.

*

Two men led her out of the theatre to a black car with tinted windows and a golden eagle on the bonnet. One put his hand on the back of her head, tightening his grip when she tried to turn around to see her father. Her last memory of him was face down on the marble floor, arms twisted behind his back, and his muffled, 'Please, I beg you, please.'

They drove through the streets of the city, the driver on the horn, traffic quickly pulling over to let them pass. Nasim asked what was going to happen to her father, and when the men said nothing, her voice rose: could they take her home so she could tell her mother? 'Please? We could just stop there, I can run in and come back out.' One of the men looked at her in the rear-view mirror and smirked. 'Please?' she said again, but they said nothing. 'Please!' Nasim felt herself unhinge, and started to punch the backs of their seats. 'Say something!' she screamed, her face wet with tears. The man who'd smirked turned then, thrusting a gun at her forehead. Nasim scrambled back, pressing against the door, her arms over her head.

'That's better, darling,' he said.

They turned into the royal drive, with its statue of Saddam, and passed the Swords of Qādisīyah, the arch made from the melted weapons of the Iraqi war dead. The two massive fists coming out of the ground holding the swords were said to be sculpted in the image of Saddam's own hands. At the huge roundabout, the driver turned right and crossed the long bridge with undulating arches. Across the water, she could see Saddam's palace; it was lit up for the evening, green lights reflecting on the lake. Nasim pressed her face against the glass, willing the car to turn back, to go there instead. But they kept driving over the bridge, towards the island palace of Uday Hussein.

'Out,' the man with the gun said, before reaching into the back and pulling her from the car. He led her into the palace, past a formation of guards, across the huge foyer with two sweeping marble staircases that met in the centre and a tiered golden chandelier. Except for the sound of their shoes, it was eerily quiet. Nasim followed as the foyer opened onto a ballroom, the tiled ceiling billowing like silk. They cut across to another archway and into a bar clad entirely in mirrors. A disco ball spun over the empty dance floor, sending diamonds of light cascading over Nasim's naked arms.

The man walked behind the bar and returned with a glass, a long stick in his other hand. 'Drink,' he said, then there was a *whoosh* as he whipped the stick through the air.

Nasim peered into the glass. 'What is it?' she said, and he whipped the cane across her legs, the pain searing.

'Drink, you silly bitch.'

Nasim drank. It was overly sweet, and less like swallowing a liquid than a gas, the feeling of it rolling down her throat, leaving a burning sensation in its wake. 'Faster,' he said. *Whoosh.* When she had drained the glass, Nasim gave it back to him and stood very still, watching her hands, as if waiting for her body to do something. 'Stay,' the man ordered. He left her on the edge of the dance floor.

Music started to play. She recognised it immediately: Beethoven's Moonlight Sonata. When she was thirteen, she had practised every day for a month so as to play it perfectly. Proudly, she had asked her mother to come listen, finishing the piece with a flourish, bringing her hands up before setting them down on the keys again, like she'd seen famous pianists do. She looked to her mother for praise, but Nhour was making a face as if Nasim had done something disgusting.

'Don't do that, Nasim,' she scolded, mimicking the flourish. Then she sat beside her on the stool and told her to play it again. Nasim felt a flare of anger but set her jaw and played while her mother adjusted with her hands and her shoulders and her legs. She flicked at Nasim's calf and said, 'Don't press the pedal so hard,' and lifted Nasim's palms: 'Don't flatten them. Make them curved, fingers like spiders' legs.' She was right – it was the same thing her teacher had told her – but Nasim flattened them again.

'Be delicate, humble,' her mother urged, and Nasim suddenly slammed her hands flat on the notes, making a loud, ugly sound.

'What would you know?' she said, tapping on the sheet music. 'How would you know how this is meant to be played?'

Her mother's face hardened. 'I know music that is felt, Nasim Amin,' she said, her copper eyes remote. 'Your playing is soulless.'

Her mother was cruel, Nasim realised now, standing in this garish bar. Her truth was unyielding.

But the sonata tinkled over Nasim and there was a loosening in her bones, as if the drink had somehow gotten between each joint, and when Uday came into the room she did a strange thing. She smiled. He was wearing a white silk shirt, flowing black pants and jewel-encrusted slippers. He grinned as though they'd been planning to meet here and held out his hands. Nasim pretended to hesitate before putting hers in his. He leaned in and kissed her cheek, then the other, running his hands down the length of her yellow dress. Then he pulled a barstool out, gesturing to her to sit, watching as her dress gathered around her thighs as she drew herself up. He walked around to the other side of the bar and poured out two glasses of scotch, a can of Coke shared between them.

'I trust my men were kind to you,' he said, and it was then that

Nasim made a leap, felt herself in the air, imagining a gulf beneath her. She looked down at her hands and put them around her glass as a child would.

Uday looked at her, alert. 'No?' he said. She kept her eyes downcast and he leaned over the counter to put his hand under her chin. 'You can trust me,' he said, lifting her face so that she gazed back at him. Nasim gave a small frown as if grappling with a dilemma. He nodded at her and she took a deep breath.

'The man, the one who brought me in here.' She stopped.

'Tell me,' Uday encouraged, and she looked at her hands again. 'He touched me.'

She listened as Uday sucked in his breath, a startlingly vicious sound. 'Where?' he demanded. His face twisted with fury.

Nasim pointed slowly to her breasts. 'Here,' she whispered.

Uday's eyes flashed. 'Drink,' he said, tapping her glass. 'I'll be back.'

She watched as he left, his body alert with anger. Then she lifted the glass to her lips, staring at her reflection in the mirror. She could hear him now, yelling; there was the sound of a stick, a familiar *whoosh*, and a voice pleading. More voices now, loud and excited, the pleading not involving words anymore, just a series of screams, and Nasim smiled, her image smiling back at her, slightly in awe. This was a wisdom all her own.

When Uday returned, his greeting was cooler, but still he smiled. He mixed another drink and Nasim accepted it, then another and another. He took her hand and led her to the dance floor, where he taught her how to dance sexily, how to lower herself practically to the floor without curving her back, writhing back up and catching the crook of her crotch on his knee as he ground into her. He showed her the cowboy-style gun in his waistband and said he'd used it to kill the man who touched her.

'Feel,' he said, placing her hand on the barrel. 'It's still warm.'

Uday put his hand over Nasim's so she could not pull away. It had an effect then, the gun, the drinks, the shards of light from the spinning disco ball. Nasim felt woozy, her eyes hot with tears, and it was in an almost fatherly manner that Uday picked her up and carried her to a bedroom. The gold and white bedframe, grandiose and gaudy, rippled like an enormous meringue, draped in pink silk sheets and dotted with red satin heart-shaped pillows. From the ceiling a salmon-coloured velvet curtain hung down behind the bedhead, drapes tied open with tasselled sashes, revealing a length of cream silk behind it. It was here, with Nasim almost smothered against a satin heart, that Uday fucked her.

*

As with the piano and the horses, Nasim learned quickly. She learned to deflect his violence and learned when she could not, turning over sections of her body to him. She was lucky (yes, she was) in that Uday had not yet fully realised his sadism, was still in the experimental phase, satisfied with using Cuban cigars to burn circles on the inside of her thigh and penetrating her with one of the hundreds of trophies his teachers had been forced to give him. He had a dressing room filled with women's clothes and shoes, and, like his sisters, he dressed and undressed her. He fucked her on top of a cage filled with screeching golden tamarin monkeys. In another room she fell asleep on a different bed, and when she woke he was sprawled on top of her, snoring. She gasped when he kicked her, his eyes still closed, in the stomach, and kicked her again until he'd pushed her off the bed.

When he woke, he was hard again. He found her on the carpet and pulled her over to the window, pushing her hands to the glass, fucking her from behind, and then it was more drinks. At one point Nasim tried to work out how long it had been since she'd left the concert hall, for it seemed that it was always night when she surfaced, as if Uday had even that under his control. But then it was daylight. Nasim came to in the ballroom. The marble floor was cold and she was shivering, her hair matted with lumps of her vomit. The palace was quiet.

She stood unsteadily, tugging down on the tiny black skirt and red corset Uday had put on her, and pressed herself against the walls, feeling her way to a bathroom. There she stood under a jet of hot water, patches of red rising up on her skin. In the dressing room afterwards, she chose a simple cream dress with gold embroidery and sat at the mirror framed with lightbulbs to comb her hair before braiding and coiling it into a bun. It was still quiet when she finished. She waited.

He returned at night, accompanied by a group, the women in tight dresses, the men in suits. He called her down and in front of them gave her 400,000 dinars. Counted it out into her hand while the others snickered. Uday waited. Finally, Nasim looked up. 'Thank you,' she said.

*

Later, she would see Uday at parties, walking around as people sang and danced, clapping their hands in time as he held a bottle in one hand, pouring bourbon into a cup before handing it to someone, smiling, always smiling. The women drank from the very beginning, without protest, because women are quick to learn. But there was always a man, a silly goofy man, who'd peer into the cup and shake his head, smiling too widely. *No, no*, he'd mime and try to give the cup back, and Uday would nod *Yes*, pushing the cup back, and the man would touch his chest, as if to say *I am weak*, and there'd be another man on hand, gliding through the party like a shadow to give Uday his gun, and he'd shoot it above the man's head, smiling, and the man would drink.

Later still, after the assassination attempt, Uday would sit brood-ing on his own as people milled around him. He'd signal and a bodyguard would step forward, handing him his shotgun and a mag-azine clip. Uday would load it, take a pair of earplugs out of his pocket and put them in. Then fire off a round. There'd be a scream, and every-one's hands would shield their ears, but the Iraqis were well trained by then, the band barely missing a beat as the party-goers quickly recovered, their dancing becoming frenzied, faking enthusiasm as Uday remained seated, grinning.

'We are at the mercy of a child,' Salima once confided to Nasim, a sign of their increasing closeness. Salima had been among the group at Uday's palace who had watched in amusement when he paid Nasim 400,000 dinars and sent her on her way. That evening Salima had approached Uday and he'd generously told her the girl's name. A good sign. There'd been times when he'd snapped ferociously, 'Let her rot,' ensuring that the girl would meet a grislier fate than Salima, a sheikha of some standing, could provide.

Salima went to Nasim's neighbourhood straight from the party in the early morning and found the girl pacing her street, listless and looking absurd in the same dress she'd left the palace wearing. A man stood on the step of what Salima assumed had been the girl's home, his arms folded. Salima could see the neighbours in their windows watching the girl, not one of them coming to help. '*Ya kalb*,' she spat at the man as she stepped onto the footpath. Her driver, Alby, a Sudanese, chuckled, his canines gold-capped. The man on the step said nothing, staring at Salima and her sleek black car. Salima turned to look at the girl, waving her hand at the house and the man and the faces pressed against glass, her wrist jangling with bracelets. 'All of them, *ya kalb*,' she said. 'Dogs.'

Nasim did not recognise her from the palace; she'd been too humiliated to look directly at anyone. Now she stared at Salima, who was wearing a head-to-toe skin-tight black chador with roses on it, decorated with sequins.

'C'mon, honey,' Salima said, nodding towards her car as Alby leaned out his window to grin at Nasim, tapping his fingers against the door to a beat.

In reply Nasim wrapped her arms around herself, wanting to howl like a child.

Salima came closer, a cherry-red lock of hair revealing itself from under her hood, and mimed shooing Nasim towards the car. 'C'mon, sweetie,' she said softly. 'You're not a rosebud anymore.'

*

'Is that even halal?' This, Nasim learned, was what Salima said when she had a new girl to show the men, summoning her from behind the curtain, getting her to twirl – *is that even halal?* – and then leaning over and winking at the men before nodding at her to sit in a lap.

When Nasim made her first appearance, wearing a ruby red gown, Salima drew her close, pretending to take a bite out of her. 'Delicious,' she said, the men roaring approval.

Salima's club was called Nostalgia. She only kept Iraqi girls – no gypsies or Filipinos – and dressed them traditionally, in delicately embroidered gowns, each specially tailored with revealing slits and plunging necklines. Curiously, Salima required her girls to wear veils at a time when most sheikhas were doing the opposite.

It was the first time for Nasim. 'You take it off when you are alone with a client,' said Lana, one of the older girls, as she showed Nasim how to put the veil on properly and how to take it off so that her hair uncoiled like a length of silk. 'This,' Lana said, mimicking Salima's coarse voice and touching Nasim's hair, 'is more profitable than this,' pointing between her own legs. They both laughed.

It felt like years since Nasim had leaned breathlessly forward in the theatre, listening to Beatrice Ohanessian; since her father had been shoved to the floor, one of Uday's men standing on his neck, as he yelled to Nasim that he loved her, and she'd been unable to reply, fear like ice in her throat. In fact, it had been how long – a week, maybe two?

Yet oddly enough, Nasim felt a peculiar relief in this unassuming art-deco building just beyond the wealthy Al-A'amiriya district. She felt a sense of reprieve, her fate no longer unspooling out of her control. Unlike many of the other girls, she did not fear being found by a family who wished her dead to regain their honour; nor did she any longer feel the breath of the regime on the back of her neck. And so she let Lana and the other girls soften her fall, let them dress her for the big night ahead. *Oh, will this being dressed by others ever stop?* she thought with a wan smile, as Lana fitted an ornate headpiece over Nasim's veil, its gold charms tinkling over her brow.

When she had been introduced, twirling and bitten into like an apple by Salima, Nasim settled onto the lap the sheikha had pointed out to her earlier from behind the curtain, and made herself Omar's firm favourite. He was a mid-level Ba'athist bureaucrat, Nasim learned, as well as the club's guarantor. A tall man with a chink of silver in his hair, he'd fought in the Iran War as a special forces commander. For a time Nasim would discover a new scar each time she undressed him: a circle of disfigured flesh covering a plastic kneecap, a raw dip in his armpit where a bullet remained lodged, a spray of shrapnel in his calf. It became a ritual, hearing a story for each scar, satisfying his pride, although the former commander was not without humour. When she hovered over one nasty scar on his thigh, kissing it passionately, he sighed, closing his eyes as if returning to a disturbing memory. 'Now this,' he began, 'was perhaps the fiercest battle I fought.' He paused. 'It was with a rake, in an orchard.' Nasim laughed and kissed the man tenderly. She almost liked him.

On learning that Nasim played the piano, Salima arranged for one to be delivered to the club. Nasim played folk songs, taking requests from the men while the other girls danced and led men into bedrooms, and for a time Nostalgia was special – not in the sense that it was above its primary purpose, but it exuded a warmth. Yes, the girls were prostitutes, but they were also Arab, proudly so. There was fondness among them, and blissful times between business hours when they sat on the couches in leggings and T-shirts painting their nails, the heady fumes making them silly. It was the girls who eased Nasim's grief when she received her mother's body, their soft incantations willing her to the surface of her despair. By this time, she'd become more like a mistress to Omar, and it was through his intercession that she was allowed to receive the body and arrange a plot, with a small plaque, in which to bury her.

Salima permitted Lana to help Nasim bathe and prepare the body, both girls taking in its nail-less fingers and toes, its scorched genitalia. When Nasim put her hands on her mother's face to dab the grimy skin with soapy water, her fingers slipped inside Nhour's mouth, and she jerked them out in horror. They had cut out her tongue. *Come to me when you have lived.* It was a relief to put her mother's body in the ground and cover it with earth. It was a relief to return to Nostalgia.

*

'Pretty at a distance but stinks like something rotten up close,' Alby said to Nasim and Salima, as they sat in the back seat and discussed a rival club that had opened up, Flamingo's Garden. 'They stand in their own shit,' the Sudanese driver explained of the birds in his homeland, and the women were delighted.

Flamingo's Garden was a luxurious villa decorated with plastic palm trees and plastic birds perched in blocks of green polystyrene.

The dance floor was a pattern of cubes that lit up in different colours, and the ceiling was pocked with enthusiastic gunshots. It was 1996, well into the sanctions. By now Nasim was an old hand, proving a cool head with business, and Salima no longer made a decision without the girl's input. The two women had invited themselves into Flamingo's Garden one evening on the ruse of selling a girl to the madam, Farrah, but in truth they wanted to see what made the club so special, for it seemed everyone was getting favours from the regime except Salima.

After seeing the club, Nasim and Salima paid their new guarantor a visit. He was an insipid, overweight man in the information ministry who'd made himself indispensable after Omar disappeared, offering to sign the lease when their landlord became aware the women were on their own. In his office, with a portrait of Saddam looking down on them, he waved dismissively when Salima started to describe Flamingo's Garden. 'No need,' he said. 'I've been there myself. Splendid place. Made me wonder why Nostalgia is so behind the times.'

A tremor of anger went through Salima. 'I think you know why,' she said carefully, their guarantor feigning ignorance.

'No,' he said. 'Why?'

Salima opened her mouth to reply, but Nasim shot out a hand, putting it on her sheikha's arm.

Their guarantor's eyes glinted as he took his time to fill the silence. 'Now, I understand times are tough – Iraq is being cruelly punished – but Farrah has been particularly helpful in these hard times. It is only right that she is rewarded.'

The women glanced at each other, hearts sinking. Inside the club they'd watched as Farrah excused herself from their negotiations to take the arms of new arrivals, men who paid no attention to the women on the dance floor or at the bar. She led them to a guarded door at the back of the room, opening and closing it swiftly.

Children, Salima and Nasim had thought, and now, listening to their Ba'athist man, his voice rich with a new knowledge, a new pleasure, they were certain of it. They weren't fools: they'd seen the widows on the streets with tattooed faces, wearing black abayas largely out of poverty, not devotion, children clinging to them like kittens on dried-up teats. It would not cost the madams much, a few thousand dinar perhaps, to pry loose those mewling children.

Saddam was everywhere now. There was a tradition – many said it was born in his home village near Tikrit – for girls and women to be abducted from the families of regime opponents and raped for weeks. They were often returned home accompanied by videotapes of the rapes. 'Breaking the eyes', it was called. And now, as their guarantor continued to speak of the merits of Farrah's new club, Salima and Nasim looked at their laps, not meeting his gaze, for it was all in the eyes.

*

Evenings at Nostalgia became increasingly strained. Their clients, whose needs Salima had been able to intuit for so long, had become inscrutable. They began to dismiss Salima and the girls abruptly, leaving early, sometimes in the middle of a dance, complaining about the girls' hair, their lacklustre eyes, that they were bony and didn't smile enough, and that when they did their breath stank.

Once, Nasim ventured that they were hungry and drew a vicious look from the men. 'No one in Iraq goes hungry,' one of them said, his eyes menacing.

It had been a long time since Nasim had been asked to play the piano. Instead they started to bring in videotapes, Western pornography, and the content got harder over time, increasingly cruel, the situation made all the more bizarre when they demanded that Arab pop music be played on the CD player at the same time.

It was around this time that Salima became sick, her handkerchief stained with blood and yellow matter as her body was wracked by coughs. Nasim took charge, and it was under her helpless watch that the clients replaced the flagons of wine with American bourbon and increasingly her girls were hurt, Nasim unsure how to approach the men for money to pay for their injuries. On Salima's sickbed instruction, she told the older girls, including Lana, to leave, and began selling some of the younger ones, including Sabeen, trading three for a girl whose hips had not yet filled out. It was no relief when news came that Farrah had been executed as part of Saddam's Faith campaign, her severed head now on display outside Flamingo's Garden.

On hearing this, Salima spat into a bowl. 'So, they'll fuck us by night and kill us by day,' she said, dropping her head back on the pillow. They moved the club into an apartment and Salima's sickbed into the kitchen, and it was here they learned, along with the rest of Iraq, of America's designs on Saddam. He is a man, the Americans wrote in the pamphlets they dropped over Baghdad, who cannot go to sleep at night without killing someone. *The coalition forces are committed fully to the liberation and the wellbeing of the Iraqi people*, the pamphlets said in Arabic – and Nasim and the girls, for a moment, considered what such a liberation might bring.

Salima set them straight, the stink from her bedclothes rank. 'More cock, that's all it'll bring,' she said, and the women laughed, for even the hipless child was now a woman, and they looked to the horizon, for General Tommy Franks and his platoon of cock, the 'open and pale-faced infidels', as Uday described them on the radio, exhorting Iraqis to rise up against the Western pestilence. 'Sacrifice yourselves, even the children,' he said, a sentiment his father later echoed on television.

Their guarantor paid them a visit, flanked by two men, and ransacked the apartment for what was left of their earnings, Salima spitting at him from her corner of the kitchen while Nasim discreetly disappeared a dirty roll of dinars inside her vagina.

*

In the beginning, the fighting was against the Americans. The Ba'athists handed out rifles. Median strips were dug up and filled with oil. Soldiers hid behind stacks of boxes, the barrels of their guns pointing out like crabs' eyes, waiting for General Franks to drive over the horizon, for the explosions, the red tracer and magnesium flares, the whistle of faraway missiles, to become real. As the Americans drew closer, the call to prayer became constant, the amplified *Allahu Akbar* a soulful accompaniment to the scattering of unexploded cluster bombs that went off in children's hands. Visitations from the sky saw buildings stripped of their cladding like bodies of their clothes, and the levels of various concrete headquarters concertinaed to the ground.

When the Americans finally drove into Baghdad on the six-lane highway, tossing the wrappers of their MRE breakfasts from the tops of their tanks, the Iraqis greeted them and danced. '*Al kalb* to the end,' Salima muttered, her own days numbered.

The screens on their television sets flickered and died. It was done.

*

Nasim was standing in a narrow street that twisted through Baghdad like smoke. People were running, cheering as they pushed wheelbarrows loaded up with Persian rugs, kitchen sinks, gaudy ornaments, even IV drips attached to their metal stands. There were old women standing in their doorways, with sour expressions like Salima's, already wearing the muted colours of mourning. They knew how it was going to play out, Nasim realised later, but at the time she hated them, their wrung-out faces, their deadness, while inside she stoked a tiny flame of hope. Would they be released, now, from all the consequences of times past? Could she go back, pick up where she left off – the girl in Chinese pyjamas, playing the piano for an appreciative audience other than whores and whores' lovers?

Someone ran past with an oud, twanging the strings with his fingers, and Nasim smiled, watching him disappear. She had an image of her father, dancing as he strummed, his footfalls soft and gentle, and of her mother playing the piano, one naked foot on a pedal, releasing it slowly, like a clutch, conjuring the melody of hooves.

Then she smelt them: the sweaty flanks, the hot yellow dust, the tang of salt and flint. Nasim turned as they rounded the corner, a group of men chasing, trying to corral them. She did not move. Instead she imagined she was a tree, a rock, a streetlight even, and she felt their breath, the warm whip of their hair, as the horses, Saddam's horses, spilled around her like a bolt of velvet.

The Eel Trap

When Bindi Noon came barrelling out the front door, the others weren't paying attention. It was close to midnight and Robbie was coming up the stairs with Sophie. Robbie had her hand in her bag, feeling around for the key. Sophie was talking, as usual. They didn't think when this skinny black woman came out of their flat; they just pressed their bodies against the wall so she could pass. She was carrying two plastic bags, and it was only when a bag brushed Robbie's leg that they woke up. Robbie yelled, and the woman started to run. Robbie leapt down seven steps to the next level, and Sophie followed, all of them skidding to the bottom of the stairwell. The woman disappeared around the corner and Robbie chased her, only to find her on the ground, vomiting up foamy spit. The bags were strewn around her, with Robbie's laptop, Sophie's camera and a heap of their CDs spilling out. The two flatmates stood there, not sure what to do, listening to her retch. Then Sophie started to pick up their things, pulling the bags away almost apologetically.

Finally, the vomiting stopped. It was quiet, except for the flap of leathery wings as a bat dipped low, then up into a palm tree. The woman flattened her hands on the concrete to steady herself, and they saw she was wearing Sophie's rings – cheap silver ones from St Kilda market. Sophie opened her mouth to say something, but the woman heaved again, a flurry of slop coming out.

A light came on in one of the ground-floor flats, and there was the jiggle of their neighbour unlocking his door. 'What the fuck is going on out here?' he barked. It was the guy Robbie and Sophie hated; he'd always magically appear when they were taking out their rubbish and follow them to the bins, accusing them of dumping stuff in his. He was scowling now, arms crossed over a pair of flannel pyjamas.

'Nothing,' Robbie said, and went quickly to the woman and put her hands under her armpits to help her up. The woman's hair hung over her face, and a slag of spit lengthened from her mouth.

Robbie began to walk back to the stairs slowly with the woman leaning against her, and he turned away, disgusted. 'Any more noise and I'll call the cops,' he said. Sophie, who was behind carrying the bags, muttered 'Arsehole' after he closed his door.

At the top of the stairs, their door was wide open. There were chips of paint and wood on the doormat from the jimmied lock. The woman stopped and looked around wildly. She wriggled away and was about to head back down the stairs when she stopped and swayed, emitting a guttural sound. Sophie rushed to the kitchen, returning with a bowl and holding it under her chin as the two girls crab-walked her inside and over to the couch. She retched into the bowl, but nothing came up. 'There's spew in the kitchen, it looks like there's blood in it,' Sophie whispered, as they stared at the woman. 'Should we call an ambulance?'

'No, no,' the woman said, trying to lift her head. She rolled herself off the couch, her face thudding against the carpet. Slowly, her arms shaking with the effort, she started to crawl towards the door. For a second or so, they watched as she dipped her head, closing her eyes, willing her way across the mud-brown carpet. She was wearing cut-off denim shorts and a grey hoodie that hung heavy, like a pregnant cat's belly, around her middle. The soles of her thongs were gummed with grass tufts and price stickers and threads of chewing gum. Then, from under the collar of her jumper, Robbie's necklace slipped out, the one her mother had given her for her eighteenth. It was a long silver chain with a shamrock on it, as well as a copper eel traced and cut from a metal sheet. The way it was hammered, the copper seemed to ripple when it was worn.

'An iuk,' Claire had said when she gave it to Robbie. 'You know they built these ingenious eel traps along the river?'

'So now you're handing out totems?' Robbie responded and put it aside.

But of course, after that Robbie saw eels everywhere. Smoked and hanging in stalls at the market, plastic chunks in the windows of sushi shops, even one washed up on the beach. One night she turned on the television and watched a man in a raincoat balance on a rock as young glass eels pushed against the current of a river. He spoke of the upstream migration of these primordial creatures and how Aristotle once speculated that eels were born of the mud. Robbie's mother had put the damn things in her head even if she didn't want them, and now there was this woman, the iuk around her neck, and Robbie couldn't shake the revulsion that one had found its way here, gills choked, eyes closed, trying to feel its way free.

*

It was Nathan who got her mother into it. He had found Scottish ancestors in his family tree and bloodlines dotted all around the Arctic, down into Nunavut territory. 'Whalers,' he told the three of them, saying it reverently, as if carving off hunks of dark fibrous meat while standing ankle-deep in guts was inspirational stuff.

'So that's where you get your sense of adventure from,' Claire said, and Robbie had thought she was joking, but then she squeezed his arm and Robbie wanted to be sick. The man lived in Glen Waverley.

'So let me guess, you're also Inuit now?' Robbie asked, smelling a rat. Nathan didn't respond but started buying Inuit art online, and one day he was showing them a print of an Eskimo spearing a fish and Robbie suggested maybe he should invest in some colonial rapist artwork as well.

Claire lost it then. 'What is wrong with you?' she said, and for Robbie, it was like, *Exactly. So much is wrong with us.*

Once Nathan got Claire interested in it too, they spent days at the library and at home sitting at the computer, his hand on hers, clicking the mouse together. 'A seamstress,' her mother would say of a great-aunt, or 'A convict,' of a great-great-uncle – 'just a pickpocket', she'd mumble, a dreamy look on her face. It enraged Robbie. 'It's not hurting anyone,' Otis would say when she tried to get him riled up with her.

But it was worse when Claire got into their father's stuff. She would walk into any Aboriginal place she saw, even a medical clinic, and ask if anyone knew Danny O'Farrell's mum or her people, and sometimes someone said they did and Claire would get the phone number and call them. Robbie would hear her crying on the line as if she'd been trying to find them forever. She told them about Danny and the dementia, even organised meetings at the home so their father could meet his cousins, half-siblings, aunts. He sat in a chair, bewildered, and in rare lucid moments tried to remember them and cursed his illness when he couldn't, not understanding that they hadn't been there to begin with.

*

How the woman came back to life, Robbie didn't know. Sophie had managed to coax her to the couch, and then put a blanket over her because she was shivering. The woman held her hands between her thighs like a child. Eventually, when her shivering began to ease, she popped a hand out from under the blanket. 'Either of youse got a smoke?'

Next thing she was on their balcony, smoking Sophie's cigarettes, telling them to put on a CD. Robbie got three glasses and brought out the cask, squirting red wine to the rim of each.

She was Bindi Noon. 'It's a good name,' she said proudly. She told them about heroin and how much she loves it, how even when she's spewing her guts up on it, it feels amazing. 'Not like that,' she grimaced, gesturing below to where she'd vomited. 'Fucking awful, that is. No, no. You dream on this stuff.' She sucked hungrily on the cigarette. 'You know that feeling when you're coming in and out of sleep? It's like that.'

Robbie nodded. The early morning was her favourite time of day, when it felt like the world was still asleep, everyone just animals, limbs strewn, sheets creased like the trunks of ghost gums, the sky outside a healing bruise.

'Even breathing feels good,' Bindi continued. They were all quiet for a moment as if focusing on their breath, considering it. Then Robbie noticed Bindi Noon looking at her.

'So, who are your people then?' she asked, and Robbie felt her cheeks grow hot. She lifted her shoulders and let them drop, glancing at Sophie.

'What?' Sophie said, looking at Robbie curiously. 'You're black?'

Robbie shrugged again. 'I don't know. Sort of. Like a third.'

Sophie puffed out her chest in annoyance. 'Why didn't you tell me?'

'I don't know. It's never come up.' Robbie didn't look over, but she could feel Bindi watching.

'You ashamed?' Bindi asked.

'No,' Robbie said curtly, and took a gulp of wine. 'You?'

She snorted. 'Course not. But then,' she touched her skin, 'not like I can hide.'

'I'm not hiding.'

'Sure looks like it.'

'What the fuck would you know?' Robbie felt a jolt of rage. Now this woman who'd robbed them and spewed all over the place was having a go at *her*?

'Well, you haven't even told your friend,' Bindi said defiantly. She looked at the flatmates. 'You two lesbians?'

'No!' they said, and Robbie added, 'I'm not hiding anything. I've got nothing to hide.'

They were all silent again. Bindi reached over and squirted more wine into her glass.

'Well,' said Sophie finally, straightening in her chair, 'I'm Maltese, if anyone cares.'

Robbie stared at her. 'I knew that.'

Bindi peered at her too. 'Isn't that a fucking dog?' she said, grinning.

*

'*Ngardang?*' It had been two years since Robbie had visited her father and she'd spent a good portion of the drive in listening to her mum remind her that he would not recognise her. '*Ngardang?*' he said again, his face incredulous as he sat up in his bed and stared at Robbie, while the other residents in the ward eyed the scene warily.

Robbie looked at her mother. 'What's going on?' she whispered, thinking that perhaps this was a new quirk of her father's dementia, but Claire shook her head. She was wide-eyed. 'I don't know.'

Claire had told her to prepare for the fact that Danny had changed since Robbie had last seen him, and she'd expected that he'd be older, frailer, which he was. But he was blacker, too. She had not anticipated that. He was smaller, more crinkled, and molasses brown. 'Like a sultana,' one of the nurses said later. It was happening to Robbie too, much sooner than to him. Her face had changed, the skin around her eyes becoming even duskier, like a light in her was being dimmed. It was clever, she thought – as if, needing to survive, their genes had resorted to a slow release.

'*Ngardang!*' her father said again, impatiently. He began to fumble with the side of his cot, trying to get out.

Claire gave Robbie a push. 'Go,' she said quietly, 'go to him.'

Robbie was scared. It was hard to know of what – not of her father, exactly, but of not knowing what he needed, how to act. She went to his bedside reluctantly and he grabbed her hands, pulling her close. He tried to put his head on her chest but she was stiff – and he kept kneading her, head-butting her gently, as if trying to make her softer. Claire came over to help. 'Pretend he's an animal,' she whispered in Robbie's ear.

'He is an animal,' she replied irritably.

'You know what I mean.'

Robbie sighed shakily. She closed her eyes. As they'd walked to Danny's ward, they'd passed several glass cabinets lined up along the walls. Claire had explained that these were a new initiative from management, the cabinets to be filled with objects showing the 'individual personalities' of the residents. 'Talk about tautology,' she'd said of the phrase. Robbie had walked slowly, partly buying time but also out of curiosity. There were photos of husbands and wives, children and grandchildren, beloved pets and cars. Benign seaside watercolours and psalms printed in calligraphy. Hand-knitted footy scarves, self-published memoirs, military medals on a swathe of velvet. 'This one is my favourite,' said Claire, stopping at a shelf with a packet of Winfield Blues, a car's dipstick and a photograph of an older woman with greyish-red hair lying seductively on a chaise longue in a green silk dress, the lens soft. Robbie smiled. When they reached Wattle Ward, Robbie saw her mother had placed on her father's shelf an acrylic painting Robbie had done of Half Moon Bay: two tiny figures sitting on the *Cerebus* wreck, surrounded by stingrays on the seabed. 'Oh, Mum,' Robbie had said softly. She remembered painting it, the relief and the slight displacement of the wreck, placing it much further out to sea. How she'd hidden the figures of her mother and brother in the orange cliffs. Robbie opened her eyes and pushed her father back gently so she could unlatch the side and sit comfortably on the bed. Then she let him settle back into her arms. He nuzzled into her and, with a small, sweet smile, fell asleep.

Afterwards her mother wouldn't stop talking about it. 'He must have known her,' she kept repeating.

Robbie was resistant. 'You can't say that for sure. Do you know what the word for "mother" is in his language anyway? How do you know it's not just a sound people with dementia make?'

Still, whatever was behind it, this behaviour from Danny became a kind of euphoria for Robbie. It didn't happen every time she visited, so it was a bit like gambling: she couldn't stop recalling the wins, the happy times he folded into her. It was complete surrender. But there was always the dissonance. She would be his *ngardang*, but when she helped him out of bed to go to the toilet he'd catch sight of himself in the mirror and nod solemnly, as if at a stranger. 'Poor bastard,' he'd whisper to Robbie – and she had to agree.

Later, for an exhibition, she recreated the objects in the glass cabinets, all of them banal and victorious in their sameness, with the odd exception. Every now and then, there'd be a kind of glitch – a love letter, a telling X-ray, a court summons, an unpaid bill, mismatched birth and death certificates, a blackened teaspoon.

*

'I got a guy who says he'll look out for me,' Bindi said, jutting her chin in the direction of Barkly Street, keen for the girls to know she hadn't done that, not yet. 'You seen the bastards who drive around throwing eggs at them?'

Sophie and Robbie had seen a guy lean out his window once and splatter an egg at a woman's feet, shell sticking to her heels. They'd also seen guys in hotted-up cars pull over, wait for a girl to walk up, and screech off when she bent down to talk to them.

'You know,' Bindi said, 'I reckon it's those guys I wouldn't be able to handle. I could do the fucking and sucking and everything else.'

'Don't do it,' Robbie said, and Sophie murmured her agreement.

Bindi's head shot up. 'Easy for you to say,' she said, suddenly sneering.

Sophie and Robbie looked at each other. It was time to get her out of here, but how the hell were they supposed to do that?

'How old are you two, anyway?'

'Twenty-four,' Robbie said.

'Twenty-three,' said Sophie.

'Nineteen,' Bindi said proudly and, seeing their faces, went on the defensive again. 'You don't believe me? Well, I fucking am, and I seen more than both of you.' She was still a teenager; Robbie didn't know how she hadn't seen it before. 'I been grown up when you were still having your noses wiped.'

'Jesus,' Sophie said, holding up her palms. 'What the fuck is your problem? Remember, you're the one who was nicking our stuff.'

The girl stared at Sophie, then Robbie. She picked up her empty glass and flipped it over the balustrade, grinning at both of them before it shattered on the ground. Sophie started to scream at Bindi to get out, and Robbie agreed that needed to happen, she definitely needed to go, but it was like her arm and hand didn't agree, and neither of them noticed until it was arcing over their heads, a spur of red wine and Robbie's glass soaring through the air. They listened to it shatter. Then there was the sound of the neighbour's locks jiggling.

Sophie turned to Robbie. 'What, you two are sisters now? Fuck you both,' she said. 'I'm going to bed.' Inside, she picked up the bags. 'With our stuff,' she added.

*

Robbie's mother learned that Danny's real mother, Betsy Carol, had tried to get him back after he'd been fostered out. Several times she went to the welfare board office, in a grim sandstone building in the city, and when they refused to help she went back to the hospital where she'd had him to get a copy of his birth certificate. But they said there was no record of her or of him. They told her the birth didn't happen. When she wouldn't leave, they called the police.

It was like an old riddle of Danny's: 'If an Aboriginal kid dies in jail but no one ever told him he was black, is he black?' he'd ask, and Robbie would stare back at him, not knowing what to say. When Danny began to call her *ngardang*, Robbie asked Claire about this. It was like a strange version of 'if a tree falls in the woods'. Her mother said that when Robbie was younger, a teenager called Darren Wouters had hanged himself in a police cell. His mum was Aboriginal. A few years later, a fuss was made about whether Wouters ought to be included in the royal commission, if his was an Indigenous death in custody or not.

'Was it?' Robbie asked.

Claire shrugged. 'I guess that was the riddle.'

*

'We're not sisters,' Bindi said.

'No way,' Robbie agreed.

'I fucking hate that shit,' Bindi continued.

'Yeah, bro,' Robbie replied, and they both laughed.

*

There was a woman Claire found whom Robbie liked: Beverley. At first, they didn't even know if she was blood, but she came with the others to one of the meetings Claire organised and sat in a paisley armchair. She didn't press on Danny who she was, waving Claire away when she tried to include her in the introductions. When enough time had passed, the others hurried towards the exit in relief and she followed slowly, shaking her head.

A few days later, Robbie, Otis and Claire visited again, and they found her and Danny in the sitting room, in companionable silence. Beverley smiled at them. She had a paper tray of oysters on her lap and was shucking them with a sturdy pocketknife. Her long skirt and hands were dusty with grit, and a tower of the shells wobbled on her knee as she squeezed a quarter of lemon over one, passing it to Danny. He hadn't seen them, and they watched as he smiled at the woman, and nudged the grey mollusc into his mouth with his finger. He carefully placed the shell on top of the tower and licked his briny lips. Later, the woman told them Danny would have been her older brother, her half-brother. She did not say that he was. Robbie waited for their mother to correct her, but Claire didn't say anything. Maybe the main reason Robbie liked this woman was because Claire started to back off – she was less frantic about connecting everyone like callers on a switchboard. There was a frankness about the woman, and her visits to Danny calmed him and made everything settle for a while.

*

Bindi Noon was getting agitated again. The cask was nearly empty, and she took the bladder from the box and squeezed what was left into Sophie's glass. Sophie had taken the cigarettes with her to bed. 'Go in and get them,' Bindi said to Robbie, but she refused. Robbie asked for her necklace and Bindi took it off angrily, tossing it in Robbie's lap. She paced and said she should go. Robbie nodded in agreement, but Bindi didn't leave. Instead, she asked if they had a deck of cards.

Once Robbie dug out a pack of her parents' old playing cards, Bindi shuffled and dealt out a hand of canasta. She turned a card over to start, then stood abruptly and said she needed to go to the loo.

When she didn't come back, Robbie found the bathroom door. There was no answer. She opened it and saw Bindi bent over the toilet bowl, hair in her face. A splatter of vomit streaked with blood was on the tiles.

'Oh, shit,' Robbie said, lifting her head out of the toilet bowl, 'you've got to go to the hospital.'

Bindi wrenched her head away. 'No,' she moaned, falling sideways, 'no ambulance.'

'I can drive you,' Robbie said, wiping her mouth with a towel.

She didn't say anything, so Robbie sat her up, then ran out to get her bag and car keys. She thought she'd left the keys on the fridge, but they weren't there, so she looked in the lounge room, pulling the cushions off the couch, and went into her bedroom, then into the bathroom again to check on Bindi. She was back over the toilet, her body shaking as she retched.

'I can't find the keys,' Robbie said. 'Just let me call an ambulance.'

But Bindi shook her head, held out her hand as if to say 'wait' and retched once more. Then she wiped her mouth with her sleeve and put her hand into her front pocket and pulled out the keys. She didn't look at Robbie as she held them out, still staring deep into the bowl.

'Sorry,' she said, her voice muffled. Robbie moved closer so she could see the girl's face. Bindi's eyes lifted and she grinned.

Act of Grace

At the border the women greeted the Syrian guards warmly, introducing the girls, their pretty faces beaming in the direction of Damascus. 'Off to meet their new husbands,' one woman said, to laughter, the girls smiling uncertainly, the first prick of doubt flitting across their faces.

Standing in the queue, Nasim watched. *Many more pricks to come,* she thought. She'd recognised two of the women on the bus and they'd recognised her, but Nasim kept her distance. Inside the black chador she clutched her handbag, repeatedly dipping her hand in to check for five rolls of money, her passport, Sabeen's identity card and paperwork. It had cost Nasim a third of what she had left to get Sabeen's documents. The man who had them – he had all the dead girls' possessions, it being his flat where the prostitutes had been stacked in the shower – had no idea why Nasim wanted Sabeen's things, not buying her ruse of sentimentality for a second. He rifled through the items and stared hard at the dead prostitute's paperwork. He eventually settled on a high price but still looked haunted as Nasim bundled it all into a sports bag, no doubt fearing it would dawn on him later what she wanted so badly.

The journey to At Tanf, the US garrison in Syria, had been rife with tension. Nasim had gazed out a window, past the old, squashed-peach face of the woman next to her, trying to say goodbye to Iraq, to find something in her heart. But she could concentrate only on the driver. Everyone on the bus had been focused on him, their collective breath held for six tense hours, thinking *go faster* as they went through militia zones, *go slower* as they approached American checkpoints. The bus was jammed: whole families; the madams with their naive cargo; and boys, so many boys, sent away by their relatives to escape abduction by militia or just being shot on the street, because boys turn into men and it was best, many of the insurgents thought, to get it over with. And so no one said goodbye to Iraq, only stared at it grimly.

The border was congested with traffic, and the wait took hours. The area stank of urine; people squatted behind flimsy screens made from stakes and hessian sacks. By morning, the bus was finally waved through, everyone on board now clutching pink slips of paper. The visas have changed, a Syrian official told them: one month only now, then you apply for a new one. Same price.

Once the driver crossed the border, he pulled over and they filed off, sitting under a battered tarpaulin while he unloaded some cardboard boxes. On this side the road was also clogged, mainly with trucks, the drivers drinking tea or waiting behind shattered windshields. The madams sat near Nasim, talking rapidly and gesturing with their hands, bracelets clanging. Nasim was tempted to join in, to start negotiating, to cast out on a path she knew, but she resisted. This was her chance. She turned away to watch three Bedouin men in the distance, a scattering of goats around them.

When one man stopped, waving at the other two, she did not wonder about it, unable to stop listening to the women behind her. It was not until the boys sitting under the tarp went over to the men studying the ground, followed by the younger children, who ignored their mothers' hisses to stay still, that she became curious. She expected an ordinance of some kind – an unexploded gift from Russia perhaps – but when she pushed her way to the front, the men muttering at her, she saw a long brittle skeleton on the sand, strips of dried, knobbled skin stretched over its ribs. It looked like a giant mythical eel, its curved tail crumbling, the tip desiccated. There were two yawning holes the size of fists on the top of its skull, and the creature's long jaws were tapered, teeth intact and sharp. Then Nasim spied the four legs, the finer bones crushed like shell grit. It was a crocodile. She looked around, as the Bedouin men had done, trying to find a leak in the land that could have delivered a crocodile here, but aside from the makeshift shelters, the tea stalls, the long grey road and the trucks rippling in the heat, there was only cracked yellow earth. She looked to the sky, but it offered nothing, no clouds or spiralling birds.

Their bus started up, its engine spluttering into life. One of the Bedouin men knelt, the edges of his white robe in the dust, and began to loosen the teeth, making a pile next to the carcass as the rest of them headed back to the bus, leaving the tribesmen to their excavation.

*

Why do you fear living in or returning to the country you listed at Question 25? The young Syrian translator took a sip of the cinnamon and apple hookah, Nasim's form on the table in front of him, waiting for her answer. Since her departure from Baghdad, she'd taken to wearing black abayas, and had arrived at the café early so that she could sit facing the wall. Everywhere she looked in this part of Damascus, there were Iraqi men from the regime. Just three tables away, a group of them sat talking. She became aware of one staring at her coolly and pulled the hood closer around her, covering her mouth, leaving only an opening for her eyes.

Time was running out. They'd all felt it slipping away on the bus when they were two hours from Damascus, hearts sinking on seeing the slums rising from the ground. There were thousands of makeshift tents, sacks stitched together, hallway rugs turned into canopies. 'Syrians,' one of the madams said knowingly, 'peasants, farmers.' The road was dotted with the rural folk, and each time the wind picked up, they would stop and fold into themselves, shielding their faces from the whipping sand with their sleeves. Nasim imagined their skin pocked like pumice.

Their bus driver kept stopping for passengers, grinding his desert-dry gears, unable to resist the extra fares, and pointing to the roof, where people were already perched on the racks. When they banged on the roof with their fists, the bus stopped. The Iraqis watched as the men leapt off first, then held out their arms for the bags tossed over by the women, who climbed down in their long colourful dresses, children clinging to them, all disappearing into the vast tent city.

Every day since arriving in Damascus, Nasim had been stopped by police checking her paperwork, telling her how many days she had left. This morning she and the other Iraqis in the hostel were woken by a group of soldiers waving a piece of paper from the 'Baghdad government' – 'Free buses back to Baghdad,' they yelled, refusing to leave until someone gave in.

Now, in the café, the Syrian man sat back and looked at his phone as though accustomed to Nasim's silence at this question. 'I got a warning,' Nasim said at last. 'Leave or be killed.' He barely looked up, writing down her answer as if he'd heard it many times before.

*

What she had become was not what she was meant to become. Nasim tried to explain this, at least an edited version of this, in her interview at the Australian embassy. The Syrian translator had proved his worth, getting her an interview. She was using Sabeen's name but was not ready to give herself up entirely. She had studied under Najat Malaki, she said to the Australian official, who had been taught by the pianist Beatrice Ohanessian. 'You must know of her,' she insisted, but the interviewer shook his head. She had studied, listened to music, read the classics. 'Like you, yes?' He said nothing.

'My mother, she —' Nasim stopped. 'Are you sure you don't know Ohanessian?' she asked instead. She offered to spell it for him, but he declined. When he jotted a few words on his notepad, Nasim surrendered, reaching into her handbag and bringing out Sabeen's paperwork. She pushed a letter across the table, the interviewer's brow creasing when he saw the Australian government crest. He read it, then read it again, and left the room.

In the silence a sickness rose in Nasim's throat. Was there anything she would not do to survive?

When he returned, his face was grave. 'Why did you not tell us about this in your application?'

The sickness turned to shame, Nasim's face burning. She looked at the floor. She heard him pull out his chair, the rustle of his clothes as he sat down, and she glanced up. His eyes were soft now. 'We are glad you came to us, Sabeen,' he said. 'We will do everything we can to help you.'

Nasim closed her eyes. She remembered the day she had found Sabeen; she knew straightaway she had an earner. They were common as dogs by then, the women, mostly widows, wearing dusty black niqabs and walking among the traffic, hands out, begging. It was routine for Nasim to scrutinise them, those wretched ghouls. Alby was still driving for her, though his large black hands trembled and he could not function without the hideous rice wine he fermented in his basement bedsit. He had an instinct for nubile hips and breasts even under all that cloth, while Nasim studied the hands and eyes for lines. When Sabeen paused at Nasim's open window, Alby nodded in the rear-view mirror.

Nasim had put her hand into her purse and pulled out a single dinar. 'You can have this,' she said, placing the note in the girl's hand. Then Nasim took out a wad of notes. The girl's eyes widened. 'And if you want work,' she said, 'you can have this.' The cars around them began to rumble forward. The other widows in their black niqabs hurried back to the kerb, and the girl was torn. Nasim knew the feeling well. The cruel, false notion of choice. She opened the car door and shifted over, patting the seat beside her. 'C'mon, honey,' she said softly. 'You're not a rosebud anymore.'

Nasim was right – the girl was a good little earner – but the impressive breasts turned out to be shredded newspaper. Less than a month earlier, Sabeen revealed, she and her husband's family had been shot at in their car when approaching a checkpoint outside their neighbourhood. At first she thought she had been hit, the impact of the gunshot thrusting her against the seat. When she looked down her lap was bloody, but it wasn't her blood; it was her baby's. The girl was dead. They came past later, the soldiers – Australians, she said, showing Nasim the document the lieutenant had given her. 'If you sign, you can have this.' There was US$2500 in the envelope. Sabeen signed, and when the soldiers left, her husband's family took the envelope and threw her out. Her breast milk had not yet dried up, and the girl had stuffed her bra with shredded paper to soak it up.

*

Sabeen, Sabeen, Sabeen, Nasim repeated to herself on the flight to Australia. *Yes?* she envisioned herself answering the question. *Yes, I am Sabeen.*

She'd been scared getting onto the plane. 'What if it falls out of the sky?' she heard herself asking the man beside her. *You are like a dumb peasant*, she told herself. As a child she'd flown with her parents to Egypt and Jordan; they had even been to London once, when her mother was invited to a literature festival. She'd not felt an inkling of fear then, only excitement.

'If it falls out of the sky,' the man had responded, his tone purposely playful, as if she were a fool, 'we will be well rested.' And with that, he propped his seat back and closed his eyes; a seasoned traveller. Nasim – no, *Sabeen* – scowled at him, loathing his calm. But they made it, and Nasim was full of regret as she followed the other passengers into the terminal, shivering at the cold wind that came up through the gaps of the gangway and flinching at the crass, brassy accents. People were half-dressed and ugly, their thighs and tummies spilling out, the men thick-necked and the women sloppy. There were floor-to-ceiling posters of bikini-clad girls on surfboards, and Nasim wished she'd joined the deceitful madams with their village girls instead. Life had given her a role and she'd refused to say her lines. For what? This? *This?*

She asked herself the question again, months later, as she walked past the girls on St Kilda Road, near Carlisle Street, their left legs folded beneath them like birds as they leaned against the dark green fences. Yes, she had landed on her feet – survived – unlike the unfortunate Shi'a girl she'd bought in the Baghdad traffic and later sold, but for this?

Nasim counted the girls, as she always did. They were mostly white, hair greasy, cheeks dappled with acne, feet forced into stilettos, skin marbled blue from the cold. Two Asians. No Arabs, Nasim always noted. Not yet. Once she had looked up to see a photographer kneeling in the middle of the road as if in a combat zone, snapping as she walked past the prostitutes. For a few seconds she thought she was in his way. Then she realised it was she he was capturing, hunched against the wind in her cloak with all that flesh behind her.

When a white van pulled up at the kerb, two men flinging open their doors, Nasim spun to warn the girls, expecting them to startle and lope away in their heels. But they just smiled, lazily unfolding their legs. Nasim watched as the men waved and opened the van's back doors, revealing a large urn beside a stack of paper cups and a box of sandwiches and fruit. The girls gathered around as the men handed out coffee, helping themselves to milk and sugar, carefully blowing the steam away, chatting.

Nasim stared for so long that one of the girls noticed. She waved and held out a cup.

There was a kick of fury in the Iraqi woman's chest. She began to yell at the girls, cursing in Arabic: '*Ya zbala! Ya kalb!*' She shouted all the things she had been called and worse, not knowing why, only that this country, this country, was ridiculous.

The girl holding out the cup snarled, 'Well, fuck you then, you frigid hag!'

The others chimed in.

'Go home, ugly cow.'

'Good luck getting any wearing that, darling.'

When one of the Asian girls yelled, 'Assimilate, bitch!' there was a brief silence, and then they all erupted into laughter.

Nasim turned away, abaya flapping, hands trembling. She continued to curse them as she walked. She wanted to yank them by the hair. *Your country*, she wanted to say, *is pathetic. You are a ridiculous people.*

She had cried when they stamped her documents in Damascus. They had thought she was crying with relief, with gratitude. High on their charity, the Australian officials said they would be happy to assist with collecting her child's remains, that they could provide a plot in Australia. Nasim shook her head. The child – her child, she corrected – was home. She belonged in Iraq. Nasim did not say *with her mother*, wherever it was that Sabeen's body had been dumped. Nor did she say that there was something they could assist her with.

If they could rebuild the streets, put the music back in the radios, return the gardens to Babylon. If they could undo the borders, shred their maps. If they could let her fry kubba, almonds, cinnamon sticks and mince once more, so when men put their lips to her hair they could taste home. If it meant heaving on the ropes and pulling the statues back up to standing, so be it. If it meant putting the bodies back in Saddam's prisons and reanimating them, then that too. She felt sick with shame as the embassy's printer jerked into action and spat out inked letters. An act of grace.

*

'It's up here somewhere,' Toohey yelled, face flushed as he weaved unsteadily along the footpath, peering down another laneway. He'd put on weight, Gerry had noticed when they met at the train station; his neck was heavy. People – women in heels, men with ties loosened in preparation for the weekend – gave him a wide berth.

'Here it is!' Toohey cried, as he zigzagged into the mouth of a lane, three girls swerving out of his way. 'Merry Christmas,' he called out, turning to admire them. One scowled and carried the dirty look over to Gerry, who was lagging. He was taller than his dad. Like the weight, this had taken him by surprise.

They had met under the clocks at Flinders Street Station, had shaken hands like men. On the way there, Gerry had listened to his mix, mostly Tupac, tunes to make him feel strong. He'd carried the feeling as far as the pub his father had suggested, a depressing place with pokies and fluorescent lights, but by the time a waitress noticed them he had slipped into his old habits, mumbling his answers, wishing he had said no to meeting up.

'How's school?' Toohey had asked, thrusting each word across the table. Later Gerry wondered how his father managed to make even the simplest questions so aggressive. Of course, he blundered.

He had planned on not saying much – just filling in the gaps and getting it over with. But less than five minutes in, he'd stupidly mentioned he was studying Civics and Politics and was thinking of going on with these the following year.

'Civics?' Toohey said. 'What the hell kind of subject is that?'

Gerry looked down at his paper serviette, rolling it between his fingers. 'Democracy, diversity,' he mumbled. 'Rights, that sort of thing.'

Toohey laughed. 'Rights? You got to fucking earn them.'

Gerry looked wistfully at a waitress as she delivered a bill to another table. He was an idiot. What did he think, that listening to a bunch of Tupac tracks was going to make this any easier?

'What about the politics?' Toohey said, and Gerry blinked, looking at his father.

'Huh?'

Toohey's eyes narrowed. '*Huh?*' he mimicked. 'What are you, a chimp? Whose politics are you studying – what country?'

'Oh. America.'

'Yeah? Which president?'

'Bush,' Gerry replied. 'Senior.' Then added defiantly, 'Oil tycoon.'

Toohey bristled. 'What are you talking about?'

'He was, before he was president.'

'No, he wasn't.'

Gerry didn't say anything. He was sure, though, *sure* Bush had been.

'He was director of the CIA,' Toohey said. 'You don't know what you're talking about.'

Heat bloomed up Gerry's neck. He resisted the urge to look it up on his phone and stared at the beer his dad had ordered for him, drawing stripes with his finger in the frost on his glass. 'Same thing,' he muttered.

Toohey's face darkened. He drained his glass and leaned forward.

'Tell me, Gerry,' he said. 'What's a tycoon?'

Under the table, Gerry dug his nails into his arm, leaving a trail of red crescents as a reminder for later. He had said yes to this because he felt guilty. He had already lied twice when Toohey had asked to see him: the first time, he had too much studying to do; the second time, he was going away with a friend. 'So, you've got friends now?' his father had said on the phone – and it hadn't sounded cruel, a little wistful if anything, and Gerry almost came clean and said he wasn't really going away. Truth was, he still hadn't made any friends, just like at all the other schools. Though this time, it was a loneliness of his own making.

The community school had been Aunty Bron's suggestion. She had raved about it to Jean. She said she and Stuart would have sent their kids there if they hadn't moved. 'Down-to-earth' was how Bron described it. 'Soft' was how Gerry saw it. He had spotted this right away when he and his mum had a tour, the same way one might clock the soft and pinkish underside of a dog.

Glowing like a religious icon, the principal came out of her office to greet them. She had long brown hair, and the skin around her eyes was dusted with sparkly gold make-up. She wore a paisley shawl over a cream blouse, and a long denim skirt with red sandals. As she showed them around, students said hello, using her first name. In a courtyard with a gum tree at the centre, its roots rippling the brickwork, a group of students and a teacher watched as two boys played chess. Along the back of the science building, students in face masks spray-painted a mural, following the outline of a Chinese dragon a projector splashed onto the wall. The principal introduced them to a guy called Gomez, in a Slayer T-shirt and baggy denim shorts, with sleeve tattoos. 'Gomez is a street artist,' she explained. The students were colouring in the dragon. 'Do you like it?' she asked Gerry.

He shrugged nonchalantly. 'Sure.'

On the lawn, some senior girls were lying on a picnic blanket, legs tangled as they read textbooks, highlighters poised above the pages. A group of boys playing soccer darted around them. A guy kicked a goal as they watched and did a victory lap, taking his jersey off. He grinned as he ran past, the others catching up, all falling into a joyful stacks-on. The principal cupped her hands like a megaphone. 'Well done, Zareb!' She looked at Gerry and Jean. 'Zareb is a special boy. He's come a long way.' He'd fled Sudan with his family in 'tragic circumstances', she said, and the school had worked hard to make him feel safe and help him thrive. 'Now he is representing the north in the state league *and* excelling in his studies.'

Jean was delighted. 'This is exactly the kind of environment Gerry needs,' she gushed.

But it was too late for that kind of thriving. And so, on his first day, he walked in with a swagger, earphones in. He sat alone in class, pretending he had somewhere else he wanted to be. He mastered his father's long uncomfortable gaze if anyone asked him a question.

A few times in Term One, the principal had invited him to her office. She'd offer him tea like he was a grown-up. He'd always shake his head. 'This is a safe place,' she told Gerry, and he would suppress a smile. 'Sure,' he'd reply. 'Sure it is.' Sometimes he'd marvel at his nerve, at the distance he could maintain. It was like he'd swum into a cold part of the ocean, a dark blue shard in among all the sunlit swathes of turquoise. The principal was right. It was a safe place. A safe place to grow a new armour, test it out.

By Term Two, the principal stopped inviting Gerry to her office. His grades came in as average and sometimes even above. He wasn't slipping through the cracks. And there were others who needed tea: girls with shaved heads and shadows under their eyes, boys with violent tempers, a kid who had a meltdown if he accidentally stepped with his right foot first instead of his left. Gerry's armour was serving him well. But that night, after he'd lied on the phone about going away with a friend, he dreamt about his dad. His father's neck was weeping with pus, and then up through the tiny holes came worms, hundreds of them, their ringed bodies writhing. His father was screaming, trying to pull them out, but they kept coming. Gerry woke up, his pillow wet with sweat. He decided to see Toohey.

Now, in the pub, he felt like an idiot. His dad was fine. Unchanged. 'There are no other people in your dreams,' he remembered his Aunty Bron had said once, opining in that superior voice of hers. 'There are only projections – representations of your own feelings and fears.'

Toohey signalled for another pint. 'What's this fucking school your mother's sending you to? If I'd known it was some leftie wanker place, I would have put my foot down.'

Gerry ground his teeth. He hadn't done it in months, but they found their familiar grooves. He knew that Toohey couldn't put his foot down, not anymore, but he still hated him for thinking he could. He hated them all. He'd overheard his aunt talking about his anger. 'You need to make sure Gerry learns to manage it,' Aunty Bron had said to his mother. He had wanted to smash his aunt's face. Like he had no reason to be angry?

'Your mum is a brave woman,' Bron said to him once. 'She did this for you.' Gerry had a fleeting thought that he was from a different planet: it was the only explanation, because she knew, she had to know, it was impossible not to know – it was in his file, for god's sake – that he had been moved away and his mother had simply followed suit. No one had been brave. Except perhaps his father, the truest irony, for it had been he who pushed for Gerry to be reunited with Jean, saying the boy needed to be with his mother, and promised to stay away. His mum did nothing, except open the door for him when he arrived.

As for this evening, he'd waited for her to offer some advice, maybe 'don't talk politics', or even some support. But she just kissed him on the cheek and asked when he thought he would be home. As if he was going to see a movie.

He had asked her, when his dad started to make contact with him, why she never said anything, and she replied, 'I don't want to get in the way of your relationship with your father.'

Gerry had lost his temper. 'Well, that's fucking impossible,' he yelled, 'considering you fucked him and had me.' And she did that thing she used to do with Toohey, shrank, her eyes turning round and scared, and for a second he thought, *no wonder Dad hated you.*

*

'Here!' Toohey said, pointing at a neon sign atop a building, a neon waiter holding a neon bowl of spaghetti, yellow strands flashing.

Gerry hung back. 'Maybe we should call it a night?' he suggested, cringing as he heard his pathetic voice.

Toohey stopped and looked back. 'What?' he replied, scowling. 'Why?'

Gerry pointed to the main street. 'The trains will stop running soon.'

Toohey snorted. 'Don't be an idiot. You can stay at my place. We'll just have a couple of drinks. A nightcap. I haven't seen you in a year.'

Gerry looked down the laneway. It was crowded with bars. People were overflowing onto the footpath, laughing, exclaiming, men showing off their tattoos, raccoon-eyed girls flicking their hair, cut asymmetrical on purpose. His dad looked lost in the middle of it, with his neat blue jeans, white cross-trainers, old but clean – he put them in the washing machine, for sure – and shirt buttoned all the way up.

Out of the darkness, two skateboarders glided up, cigarettes parked on their lips, and Toohey jumped as they flanked him. Swinging his fist in a wide drunken arc, he hit air. 'Hey, ease off, old man,' the skater called and casually tacked his board away, his mate laughing. Toohey whirled again, his fists ready. He looked shaken. Gerry went to his side. 'C'mon, Dad,' he said, hand on his arm, pulling him into the stairwell. 'Let's go in.'

Inside, Toohey's eyes shone. 'It's exactly the same!' He spun around the restaurant, pointing at the laminated posters of Italy, the photographs of cheese and bread, the newspaper clippings tacked to the wall. Gerry looked around too. The place was a dive. Like one of those weird coffee shops that were fronts for something else, and inside old men sat around playing cards.

Only a few tables had diners. Some of them glanced at Toohey as he walked around, checking everything out, and they poked at their plates of half-finished dessert with little forks, and lifted their coffee cups to and from puddled saucers.

Then Gerry saw her. He looked at his dad, but Toohey was in his own world, brimming with nostalgia. She was standing at the register, holding out an eftpos machine for a customer. She looked up at Gerry, catching his eye. 'Kitchen's closed,' she called, and Gerry felt his stomach bottom out. His father looked over and recoiled. The girl, the waitress – she was wearing one of those black religious things that covered her hair and went all the way down to her ankles. Gerry didn't know the name for it, but he knew it meant trouble.

*

'Could you show me how to wear one of those?' The girl pointed at Nasim's black abaya.

That was how Nasim Amin, now Sabeen Tahir, met Robbie. They were both bringing in their bins. Nasim felt the girl looking at her, trying to catch her eye, and pretended not to notice, but then she parked her bin and they did that little dance, stepping the same way and then the other. The girl laughed. Then asked her curious question. Nasim was tempted to be offended, but something about the girl's candour vanquished the feeling. She was unusual-looking, with brown skin, dusty dark hair and eyes set deep. She was barefoot, in faded blue jeans and a worn grey T-shirt flecked with paint.

The girl inclined her head, waiting for Nasim to answer, balancing on one leg as she wiped the dirt and tiny gumnuts off the sole of her foot and onto her jeans.

'Why?' Nasim said, her voice croaking into audibility. It was the first time she had spoken in days.

The girl propped her bin on her hip. 'I thought it would be interesting to wear one for a few weeks,' she said. 'See what it's like. How people react to you.'

It was naive, Nasim thought. Rude, even.

'I mean,' the girl continued, 'have you experienced any racism wearing it?'

Racism. This country was obsessed with that word. 'Racism?' she said, thickening her accent.

The girl blushed. 'Sorry. Stupid question.'

Nasim nodded and, despite herself, smiled. The girl grinned back. Her teeth were wide and white. Nasim surprised herself. 'Come,' she said, her voice stronger now. The girl followed her up the driveway and into the stairwell.

Nasim had never had any visitors in Australia. As the girl walked behind her, she wondered if she was doing a very silly thing – what if the girl robbed her? But she was so childlike: the way she looked around the bare flat and, spying a patch of sunlight on the carpet, sat in it, crossing her legs, instantly intimate.

In the corner Nasim's single mattress was made up with a purple throw and a cheap flat pillow. On the opposite wall was a clothes rack she'd wheeled home from the second-hand shop a few weeks ago.

On it were three abayas, black and dark blue, with their matching hijabs, dangling like hanged women.

Nasim put her hand on them and felt tricked suddenly. She'd spent – what, ten years? – taking these off girls, and now this silly Australian wanted to put one on. She looked over at the girl, her silver clips keeping her dark hair out of her eyes. Nasim felt hot with anger. She didn't want to put an abaya on her; she didn't want her in here.

The girl looked up at her and smiled. 'I'm Robbie, by the way. I live in number eight.'

Nasim did not take her hand. Instead, she stiffened. 'It is not proper for you to wear an abaya,' she said, and went to the door, holding it open, waiting for the girl to leave. As the girl passed by her into the stairwell, Nasim added, 'You are very rude,' and shut the door.

She stood for a while, hands over her face, breathing hard into her palms. Then she drew the curtains and took off her abaya, her hood, and lay on the mattress, pulling the throw over her. She had been doing this lately, going to bed in the day. What she loathed in this country, the lethargy, was getting to her too. A tram rattled past, shaking the thin glass, the driver ringing the bell. *Ding, ding, ding.* She rolled onto her side and stared at the clothes rack. She had taken her most beautiful dresses with her to Damascus – a black crushed-velvet tight-fitting abaya, a long red dress with navy embroidery, and her favourite, a teal abaya with a diamante peacock on the skirt, its tail feathers fanning up and across the chest, an eye feather adorning the hood. She'd allowed herself a small fantasy, whenever she put it on in the Baghdad apartment, that she was waiting in the wings, a grand piano onstage; but her girls always interrupted, shrieking as they spilt nail polish on the couches. They were so tacky, and Nasim knew she too was tacky, the dress too showy, and there were no wings to wait in, just a crude apartment with velour drapes, heavily perfumed to cover up the stink of fucking, her only cue a knock on the door.

In Damascus, with her visa assured, she had persuaded herself that once in Australia she would take off the gloomy robes she'd donned for her final months in Baghdad and then Syria. But when she arrived in Melbourne, equipped with a new name and bureaucratic grief for a baby accidentally killed, the shops overflowing with cheap and lovely lilac jumpsuits with silk hoods, cheetah-print abayas, even swimsuits – everything she and her girls had yearned for – the black abaya stayed. Why, Nasim barely knew. Back in the Middle East, she'd used it to hide, but now it could hardly be called hiding. If anything, she stood out. What did that man yell at her from his car – that she was a Grim Reaper? But it was as though it had attached itself to her, its material fused to her skin.

As a child, she had imagined the descent into hell to be like travelling on a slide, fast and breathtaking. She had even composed a piece on the piano to mimic it, a staccato dance descending rapidly to the lowest note, where the music ended with a dramatic death rattle. Now she knew that the descent to hell is slow, never-ending, the ground always opening further. If she were to dare compose something now, which she would not, hell would be relentless. Notes would cut across one another, clash, smother, simper, until even her fingers couldn't be trusted, refusing to yield. Every now and then there'd be a drawn-out chord, flat and bone-tired.

There'd been a piano for sale at the second-hand shop where she'd bought the clothes rack. Nasim hovered near it, pretending to go through a box of linen but really inhaling the scent of wood, felt, wire and dust. While she stood, a woman in tight jeans and a singlet dragged a little boy over and lifted him onto the stool, directing him to bang on the notes while she shopped. The instrument was out of tune. When the boy tired of it, he wriggled off the stool and Nasim went over, sat down and held her hands above the keys, not touching them.

The keys were yellow, nicotine-stained teeth. Her fingers shook, and to stop them she pressed down, the piano belching in reply. Nasim recoiled, her hands jerking to her lap. She remembered how guilty she had felt when her mother stopped playing – how an awful ambitious relief had coursed through her with the knowledge that her mother had finally left the stage. The keys on their piano, Nasim recalled, had been grubby with her mother's prints. There were pencil marks, too, tiny words on bone. Nhour, unable to read music, would sometimes mark a note or a series of notes to record a sound, a chord or a melody. Much of it had been in a code only she understood, but there were also clues such as '*Daw Almadi*', last light – and when Nasim played those four notes, she could see it as well: a thread of gold over their city's skyline, a green-blue night. When her mother stopped playing, Nasim cleaned the keys with lavender oil and a handkerchief. Rubbing out her mother's markings, she had felt, briefly, as though she could rise out from under her mother's shadow. Now Nasim tried to remember her mother's notations, to map them on the piano in front of her, but the boy was back, pushing her out of the way, smashing his chubby hands against the keys.

*

'Closed?' Toohey said to the waitress, drawing himself up, taking in the length of black material gathered around her face and draped over her shoulders. 'What do you mean the kitchen is closed?'

The waitress's face hardened. She moved a step closer to the register. Gerry saw that she was wearing black lace-up Doc Martens under the long dress. In blue pen, she'd scrawled notes on her hand. 'Kitchen closes at eleven,' she said coolly, gesturing towards the clock on the wall, which read *11.02*.

Gerry felt a wave of fury come off Toohey, and a familiar stench of something on his own skin. Fear. 'I remember when this place used to be open —'

'All night,' the girl interrupted in a bored voice.

'— and used to serve wine in —'

'Coke cans,' she supplied.

Toohey glared at the waitress, and Gerry felt unsteady. He put his hand on the wall, his vision blurring. For a second or two he shut his eyes.

'Look,' he heard the waitress say, in a kinder tone. He opened his eyes to see she was looking directly at him. 'I can get you dessert and drinks, if you want. Not coffee though, we've cleaned the machine.'

Gerry looked at his father, Toohey giving a barely perceptible nod.

'You can sit there.' She pointed to a table next to the drinks fridge.

Gerry started to walk over, but his father did not follow. He spun around and went to a large table set with napkins and cutlery. 'No, thanks,' he said. 'We'll sit here.' As he sat, he pushed the cutlery to one side.

The waitress paused, then shrugged, pulling a white tub along the bench towards her and extracting a fork, polishing it with a tea towel. After Gerry sat down opposite his dad, she brought them a bottle of water and two glasses. 'The desserts are written up there,' she said, 'and can I get you some house wine or beer?'

'Thanks,' Gerry said quietly.

'We'll have a bottle of red,' Toohey said. He was staring at her in that open-faced way he had, daring her to react.

The waitress ignored him. 'Do you want to order now, or do you need some more time?' she asked, but he didn't say anything, just kept staring.

'Dad,' Gerry said, feeling his face redden.

'Why are you wearing that?' he asked finally, thrusting his chin out.

'Dad!' Gerry said again.

'You don't look like an Arab to me,' he continued.

'Well, if you knew anything about Muslims,' the waitress replied curtly, 'you'd know they're not all Arabs.'

The restaurant had gone quiet as the other diners tuned in.

'"They're?"' Toohey said. 'Don't you mean "we're"?'

The waitress gave a small smile, as if conceding him a round. 'Look, are you going to order or not?'

*

'*Ngardang?*' Nasim heard the plea as she closed the door behind her. She paused at the top of the stairs, contemplating going back inside, waiting for whoever was out there to leave.

'*Ngardang?*' It was shakier now, a man's voice. Whoever was saying it was scared. Nasim took a breath and went down the stairs.

In the car park stood a man with blotchy brown skin, hunched and gaunt. The girl from number eight, Robbie, was with him, her hand resting on his arm. '*Ngardang?*' he said again, and to Nasim's surprise the girl answered, 'I'm here. It's okay, here I am.' The man relaxed, his features loosening. He took a step, then stopped and looked wildly around, fear in his face.

Seeing Nasim, Robbie nodded at her, then turned back to the man. 'It's okay,' she said. 'Here I am.'

He gripped her hand and his eyes veered over the car park, the block of flats, the sky. Then he turned, letting go of the girl's hand, walking fast towards the street. 'I want to go home,' he said.

'Stop!' Robbie called, jogging a few steps to catch him and trying gently to pull him back. 'Dad, stop!'

He shrank from her, and Robbie froze. 'Sorry, I'm sorry, I mean Danny, stop. It's okay. We just need to make a few phone calls and then I'll get you home, I promise.' She pointed up the driveway. 'Just this way,' she said, taking him by the arm.

Nasim watched as they passed her, sad suddenly that she had ordered the girl to leave her flat that day. 'Can I help?' she asked, and Robbie looked up.

'No, it's okay,' she replied.

The old man closed his eyes, lifting his chin, his lips moving, Nasim unable to make out what he was saying as Robbie put her arms around him. 'I'm here,' she said. 'It's okay, here I am.' She led him towards the stairwell, then stopped, looking back at Nasim. 'Actually,' she said hesitantly, 'yes, you can.'

*

Danny warmed to Nasim. She bustled around the girl's kitchen, making him a cup of tea, popping in a couple of ice cubes to cool it down, talking and humming to soothe him while Robbie spoke on the phone in another room. It was a kind of hamming it up, playing an Iraqi woman, one she imagined these Australians would like. At the same time, she took in the girl's flat, revelling in its curiosities: small delicate skulls; odd ceramics with phantom animal faces; jade plants in olive-oil tins, green heart-shaped leaves cascading down the kitchen cupboards. She'd cut cellophane into feathers and covered the window over the sink with them. Nasim ran her hands through a patch of coloured sunlight.

'I know it was stupid, Mum,' she heard the girl saying on the phone. 'I know, okay? I'm sorry!' And then, more quietly, 'Okay, let's do that. Will you call the home? I'm sorry, Mum, I just thought he seemed better the last few weeks. I know. Okay.'

When the girl came back into the kitchen she looked so sheepish and sad, Nasim wished she could hug her. The girl sat next to the man and rested her forehead on the table. 'I'm such an idiot,' she

declared dramatically, and Nasim couldn't help but laugh. The man
was buoyant from Nasim's fussing, and he laughed too. The girl looked
up in surprise. She smiled at Nasim. 'He likes you,' she said.

*

'This place used to be open all night,' Toohey said again, his eyes
glazed from the wine. 'Your granddad brought me here. They served
wine in Coke cans because of the liquor laws.' Gerry nodded, silently
willing his father to finish his tiramisu. 'All the waiters used to come
here after they knocked off.' Again, Gerry nodded. They were the
only customers left.

He had been aware of the waitress the whole time, watching as
she finished polishing the cutlery, then dragged a chair to the counter
and used it to climb onto the bench. Her black dress lifted as she did,
Gerry taking in her black boots and black-and-red striped tights.
She poured Pepsi from a can onto a cloth and wiped the chalk off
the blackboard on the wall, leaving 'Specials' at the top, and climbed
down. She took a bottle of white wine out of the fridge and poured
herself a glass, then drew two uncooked sticks of spaghetti from a
container and gave one to an Indian guy in the kitchen. He grinned
and they crossed their spaghetti sticks like swords, twirling their free
hands in an upward flourish. Gerry forgot about his father as he
watched them joust, foiling one another and laughing. When the
girl's stick snapped, he felt weirdly crushed, hoping she'd draw
another.

'The history here,' his father said again. 'You listening, Gerry?
The history here!' He twisted in his seat to find the waitress. 'Do you
have any idea of the history in this restaurant?' he called out.

The girl looked at him, her expression deliberately blank. Gerry
started to panic. She was going to say something, he could tell; the
way she squared her shoulders, held her head high. Then she glanced

at Gerry, and whatever she was about to say, she didn't. She gave him a quick sympathetic smile instead.

The chef came out of the kitchen, pushing his baseball cap back on his head and leaning on the counter. 'Hey, Robbie, do the till.' The waitress nodded and went to the till, tapping the buttons until a reel of white paper started to whir out.

'No, she wouldn't know the history,' Toohey said to Gerry. 'Bloody Muslims are all about destroying history.'

Gerry glanced at the girl and saw her stiffen, her fingers pause. God, would his dad ever let him leave? He picked up his phone and checked it for messages under the table.

'What's the matter, Gerry? You embarrassed?' Toohey's eyes were bulging as he leaned over the table. 'You embarrassed of me? Want to go home to your mummy?'

Gerry slapped his phone on the table and held up his palms. 'No! Jesus, Dad! Can we just go now?'

'We're not finished,' Toohey said, pouring the dregs of the bottle into his glass.

The girl appeared, sliding a saucer between them with a bill on it.

'What kind of name is Robbie for a Muslim girl?'

The waitress didn't say anything.

'You're not Muslim,' he said then, a low menace in his voice.

From the kitchen, Gerry noticed the chef look up. The waitress stared back at Toohey. 'What's it to you what I am?' she said.

'A lot, actually,' he replied. 'We had to have a woman on our unit in Iraq just so we could search women wearing that kind of get-up. It was a liability having a female soldier with us.'

The waitress looked at him in disbelief. 'No, you didn't,' she said.

'What, you don't believe me?' Toohey laughed. 'Go on, tell her, Gerry.'

The waitress turned to look at him and Gerry nodded grimly.

Her eyes widened, then narrowed; Gerry could almost see the new information register, see its meaning settle. She was about to say something, but the chef interrupted. 'C'mon, Robbie, take that shit off.'

The girl's eyes flashed at him. 'No way. That's discrimination and you know it.'

The chef laughed. 'Not if you don't believe in it.' He came out from behind the counter. Toohey leaned back in his chair, a smile playing on his wine-stained lips. 'Sorry about this, mate,' the chef said, and Toohey shrugged. 'C'mon, take it off, Robbie. This is a restaurant, not a fucking art show.'

The girl had her hands on her hips now. 'Jesus, Louie, I can feel the loyalty. I've been here for how long, and you take this guy's side?'

Gerry watched his dad. He was drumming his fingers on the table, the happiest he'd been all night. *You are a fucking prick*, he thought. His phone beeped. *Are you coming home?* His mum. Gerry wanted to explode. He stood up, pushing his chair so hard it fell backwards.

'We're going, Dad,' he said, not looking at Toohey. He held out his card to the waitress. 'Savings,' he murmured, not looking at her either, looking at nothing, so that when his dad stood, sloppily knocking over his glass, Gerry didn't see it, only felt it. Felt his father behind him, the sensation so familiar he was relieved. This was what his dad had wanted all along – some kind of eruption where a molten truth could be spat out, a truth that could only be animated in violence. He straightened, chasing any softness from his shoulders, held his head steady, all of him ready for the blow. But nothing happened. The girl was holding an eftpos machine out to him and he focused on it, typing in the four digits. Together they waited for it to clear.

*

'You're a silly girl.' Nasim smiled as she adjusted the abaya. Robbie grinned, her face bursting outwards, her freckles standing out now that the rest of her had receded into the black material.

Nasim shook her head. 'You can't smile like that,' she said sternly. 'It is clear you are not true.'

Robbie rectified her expression, dampening her grin into a modest Mona Lisa smile. It made little difference. The girl's hair was also a problem; it kept escaping from the hood like a creeper searching for a foothold in the sun. 'You'll have to use spray,' Nasim said.

Robbie made a face. 'Yuck.'

'*Yuck*,' Nasim mimicked. She tucked a strand of Robbie's hair under the hood and stood back to look at her. 'It will not work.'

Robbie was undeterred. She went into the bathroom to see herself. 'It will!' she called out. 'It's just because you know me,' she added.

Nasim followed Robbie into the bathroom. 'How long?'

'A year,' said Robbie. 'I'll keep a diary and do some sketches. I'll get a friend to document it. He's a photographer.'

Nasim thought of the photographer crouched on the road, taking photos of her, the prostitutes lined up behind. She laughed, a little bitterly. 'A year,' she said. 'You think it is a long time, but it is not. It is not a life.'

Robbie turned to face her. 'I know that,' she said seriously. 'I do.' Then she turned back to the mirror, held up her arms and flapped them. '*Oooooooo oooooooooo*,' she sang out, 'I'm a ghost!' And as always with this girl, Nasim couldn't help it – she laughed, and the black ghost swung around and caught her in a hug.

*

'Hey!' The voice cut through the rain. 'Wait!'

Gerry stopped and looked back, unsure if the voice was directed at them. Toohey stopped as well, but he was too drunk, whirling around and bumping into the wall. He stayed there, holding onto it, blinking.

'Stop!'

It was the girl. She was running down the alley towards him, her black boots slapping in the wet, her hood sleek as a swan. When she reached him, she was puffed and had to catch her breath. Gerry stared at her, confused. Then she held out his card. He groaned, took it, mumbled thanks, and was about to turn around when she leaned in and kissed him on the cheek. Gerry was so surprised he didn't move. As she kept her lips pressed on his skin, he felt the warmth of her, felt it come off her and into him. Then she was gone. Running back along the lane, her hood falling off, hair spilling out, she disappeared up the stairs.

Gerry stared at the empty space she'd left, still feeling her lips on his cheek. When he turned back, Toohey was swaying unsteadily. His eyes were a little off-centre but still he managed to ask, 'What the fuck was that about?'

*

Robbie kept the hood off as she walked to the tram stop, enjoying the feeling of the rain on her hair. The abaya was now unremarkable, just a long, baggy dress. Her tips had diminished since she started wearing it, though; her share of this evening's offering, a handful of coins, was just enough to pay for her tram ticket. Was that racism, she wondered, or sexism? Tips aside, the hijab, the abaya, it wasn't working. Nasim had been right. As an experiment it was impossible. Her lecturer had been so excited when she told him about the project – he'd said it was edgy and brave, and, in the beginning, she agreed. To an extent, maybe it was important to experience the hostility that came off people towards her, the visceral hate that saw her even more loathed than a fat person. Shit, even fat people scowled at her. But beyond that, what was there to know? Nasim had said there were too many contradictions, that she would only be able to understand the abaya as a physical thing, when it was more, so much more. Robbie had countered that if it was spirit she was talking about, then yes, she felt smothered too. Nasim laughed. 'You cannot forget yourself,' she said, 'this is the problem. With the abaya, there is no self, no individual.'

Robbie was perplexed. 'But what about you then, Sabeen?'

'What about me?' she replied.

'Well, you're not nobody. You've got a name, a life that is yours. Even if you can't control the way things have turned out, it's still your story. Surely that can't be taken away?'

Hearing this, Nasim had almost laughed aloud at the irony. 'Yes,' she murmured instead, keeping her expression blank. 'This is true.'

Robbie neared the arcade where a bunch of kids gathered on Friday nights to breakdance, taking turns in the circle's centre, twisting like cobras on the tiles. A speaker attached to a phone thumped out the rhythm. Robbie watched for a while, some of them recognising her and waving. They were her favourite thing about working Fridays. One night, she promised herself, she would persuade Nasim to meet her at the restaurant, to walk down to the tram, and she'd show her these kids. A girl in the crew swaggered into the circle and began to dance. *I Don't Want Your Money, Honey* was scrawled in pink across her T-shirt. She was awesome and wild and free, in a Western way no doubt, but fuck, who cared.

Robbie decided she was going to stop wearing the abaya and the hood. It was a stupid project. Nasim would be happy.

At the tram stop, everyone who planned not to get blind drunk and stuck in the city till morning was waiting, necks craning as they gazed down the street, squinting through the rain for a familiar shape. Robbie stood under the shelter near the lights and began to read the newspaper someone had left behind. She was trying to finish an article when a car stopped at the red light in front of her, beats belting from it. A man in the passenger seat flopped his hand out his window, tossing an empty can of Red Bull. It clanged and rolled into the kerb, near her feet.

'You cannot forget yourself,' Nasim had said. And another time, when Robbie had a run-in with the awful neighbour, she said, 'You do not think, this is your problem. Nothing in you averts.'

But it wasn't true. She did think, and she thought of her father, how he had cleaned up after schoolboys, how they saw him coming, tossed their wrappers on the ground for him.

Robbie bent down, picked up the can and threw it back into the car.

The rest was quick. The man was out of the door and in her face, pushing her backwards until she was up against a shop window, three unseeing mannequins behind her. 'You fucking ugly bitch, what the fuck did you do that for? You ugly cunt, I'll flatten you.'

Robbie couldn't think straight – she could only see his face, and the eyes of everyone around them, sliding away. It was all so out of proportion. She had a thought that if she were to sketch this it would require no sense of scale, no squinting or lining up her pencil. He had the can in his other hand and crushed it. Then he shoved it into her stomach. It tinkled at her feet.

'You should put it in the bin,' Robbie heard herself saying, and he grabbed her abaya at the collar and made as if to headbutt her. She flinched, and he stopped.

'You stupid fucking cow,' he said instead. 'You're the ugliest thing I've ever seen.'

The car beeped. A girl was leaning over into the passenger seat, her hands on the wheel. 'Cal, come on,' she called out, 'the light's green,' and she looked at Robbie sourly. Before the man turned away, he kicked the can so it bounced against her shoes. 'You put it in the bin, bitch.'

*

The problem with killing a man is that you can only kill him once. This is what Nasim thought when she watched the execution of Saddam on her phone. They had found him in a hole not long after the invasion, and the news of his capture spread like a fever. The Americans said he had been hiding on a farm near Tikrit; that he was a crazed, bearded wild man; that they'd flushed him out like a spider. At first there were rumours that the Americans might let the Iraqis have him and tear him apart on the streets, but they put him in one of his old palaces with twelve young Marines as guards. It was said those American boys ended up falling in love with him. He was like a grandfather to us, one later told an American reporter. The Iraqis spat at their televisions with anger when they learned this. But Nasim understood the American soldiers. Everyone had loved Saddam once, if only for a day.

When Saddam was hanged, Nasim was still in Baghdad, but she could not watch the execution with her girls. Instead she disappeared to the rooftop of her apartment building and forbade them ever to speak of it. Despite everything, she had not been able to wring her heart clean of him. Now, in Melbourne, Nasim decided to watch. She had always known the footage was there, on the internet, patiently waiting like all the other grisly productions.

It was almost boring, how she'd come to the decision that evening, and she wondered if this was how most perverse choices were made. From her window she'd looked at the houses on her street, the pale blue glow as people watched television in their living rooms. In a way, it was loneliness that made her do it. She could just as easily have brought up images of the dictator in his heyday, proud and powerful. But that would have been a treachery, so she decided it was time to see him die.

When he appeared, the footage grainy, she cried out. He had a beard, and his silver-and-black hair was combed back in neat waves, revealing his wide, serious brow and solemn eyes. He was wearing a formal coat, buttoned to the collar, and polished leather shoes. Four men surrounded him, each wearing a black hood. They were dressed casually beneath: unbuttoned shirts, beige pants and bomber jackets. Nasim felt anger as the men kept swapping positions and conferring, their palms pressing on Saddam as they led him up to the gallows. Then, on the platform, there was confusion. Nasim watched closely, trying to work out what was happening. Saddam did not want to wear a hood, she realised. There was much gesturing and talking while Saddam resolutely shook his head.

'Make him,' hissed Nasim, as if it were happening in real time. But the men didn't. One of them gently looped the hood like a scarf around Saddam's neck. *What?* Nasim scoffed in the silence of her flat. *You want to protect him from rope burn?* She almost threw the phone down in frustration. But she watched on as they led him to the front of the platform, where a thick rope was hanging, the noose lying coiled over a balustrade. One man put the noose over Saddam's head and tightened it around his neck. Then, they all stepped away.

If they had hoped to show him as a man stripped of everything, they had failed. Saddam glared down at his audience as if nothing had changed. It almost seemed possible, to Nasim, that he could start calling out names, beckoning unseen henchmen waiting in the shadows to come lead them away, one by one, to be shot.

But still, the crowd was bold. They started to exclaim, praising Muqtada al-Sadr; light flashed across Saddam's face as they took photos. Nasim wanted to stop it – the footage, the yelling, the execution – but as with all things on the internet, it was too late.

Suddenly Saddam roared: 'You call this bravery?'

It was as though he could see her. *No*, she wanted to whimper, *it is not bravery*. She thought of what he would think if he could see her now, hiding in a cheap, barely furnished flat in Australia and watching his death five years after the fact on a tiny screen. Still scared.

'Go to hell!' someone in the crowd yelled, and the hatch could have opened then. But there was a pause instead, as if the executioner was curious for a reply. 'The hell that is Iraq?' Saddam said, and then, a short hadith later, the hatch opened. The rope dipped down with the man like a sparrow checking his flight, then it pulled up tight, and the deed was done.

Nasim watched this last part over and over. It was reported after the hanging that one of the Marines who'd guarded Saddam in those final years had to be held back when the hooded men undid the noose and brought out the body for people to spit on. 'It just felt wrong,' he told the reporter afterwards, and Nasim wept, remembering this, the words *the hell that is Iraq* still ringing.

There was a knock on her door and Nasim jumped. Briefly she forgot where she was, but the knocking continued, someone calling out. It was Robbie. She flung the door open, and Robbie was standing there in just her striped tights and a singlet, the abaya and hijab folded over her arm. The girl's face was blotchy, as though she had been crying.

'You were right,' Robbie said, holding out the clothes.

*

'Gotta feed Melanie,' Toohey was saying. 'Poor bitch will be freaking out.' Gerry had no idea what his dad was talking about. He had been ranting in the taxi all the way, and now Gerry had to half-drag him upstairs to his flat. 'Stole her, cunt was treating her something rotten, so I waited for him to go out and went in there.'

They were wet from the rain, but it was sweat Gerry was struggling with, his hands slipping from under his dad's arms. 'One more,' Toohey said, looking around, swaying as he pointed up the stairs to the next landing. 'Tried to bite my hand off like a fucking piranha.' He stumbled backward, Gerry stumbling with him but managing to stop the fall, pulling Toohey back to his feet. 'Was sitting in its shit. I could feel its ribs, and its heart was going so fast I thought she was having a heart attack.' *Shut up*, Gerry thought.

They came to a stop outside a neat white door. 'This is it,' Toohey said, and dug his hand into his pocket and dragged out a key. There was a light tinkling as the key went flying, tumbling down the stairwell. Toohey sat on the doormat while Gerry searched for it, yelling out instructions that made no sense.

When Gerry came back, holding the key aloft and away from his father, Toohey put his face close to his son, his hands on Gerry's shoulders. 'She was fucking ugly. Lost most of her hair and what was left was grey dreadlocks smeared with shit. Cowered every time I touched her. You wouldn't know it now.'

Gerry wriggled from his father's grip, trying to avoid his breath. 'I don't know what the fuck you're talking about, Dad,' he said, putting the key in the door, but when he opened it a tiny white dog came yapping out, jumping up on his dad's legs, pink tongue trying to reach his fingers. His father tapped his chest and the dog leapt up. He caught her, letting her lick his face, his neck. He had his eyes shut, smiling, saying, 'Hey girl, hey beautiful girl.'

Inside the flat Toohey set the dog down on a blue couch and poured out a bowl of biscuits, putting it on the floor and almost toppling over as he did. He went into the bathroom and shut the door. Gerry looked around. Aside from the couch, there was a television; in the kitchen, a bar fridge, a microwave, a table and chair. A blue camping mug upside down, next to the sink. A mattress in the bedroom, pillow with no cover, doona, clothes folded neatly in the corner.

He went back to the living room and sat on the couch next to the dog, letting it lick his hand. He rubbed the pinch of fur above the dog's temple and she relaxed, rolling onto her back, paws up, belly pink with dark blotches. Gerry had no money left for another taxi, but he could walk home. It didn't matter how long it would take. He called to his dad but got no response. Melanie sat up keenly. He got off the couch and knocked on the bathroom door.

'Dad,' he called out, 'are you okay?'

There was no answer. He listened and couldn't hear anything. *I could just go*, Gerry thought. *Not say goodbye*. But instead, he opened the door, only a crack, and saw that his dad had passed out on the toilet, his jeans and undies around his ankles, and a cigarette dangling between his fingers, a cylinder of ash on it.

'Dad?' Gerry said again. His father didn't move. The dog tried to enter and Gerry held her back with his foot. He edged around the door and closed it. It was a tiny bathroom, the sink tucked in tight next to the toilet, a sliver of soap stuck on the enamel beside the taps and a cabinet with a mirror above it. Gerry looked inside. There was a razor, a ratty toothbrush, an almost empty tube of toothpaste, a couple of band-aids. His dad's old jar was in there too, filled with specks of metal and glass. He took it out and held it for a moment, rolling it carefully, listening to the tinkle of shrapnel. Then he put it back and shut the cabinet, studying his face in the mirror. His cheek tingled as he recalled the waitress running after him in the lane. He pressed his finger to where she'd put her mouth, his dick stirring.

Just then, his father stirred too, shifting on the seat as if finding a more agreeable position. Gerry reached over and took the cigarette, dropping it between his father's legs into the toilet. He had a memory then, of his dad lying on the carpet next to him – he wasn't sure which house they were at, but he was playing with his train, and as he pushed it along the track, his dad stopped it, took the cigarette from his mouth and stuck it in the engine's funnel. 'Toot, toot,' he said, giving it a push, and the train, to Gerry's delight, had its own little purl of steam.

Sorry Rocks

So much for being in the middle of nowhere, Robbie thought as she stood to watch the flashing blue-and-red lights speed down the strip of bitumen towards them.

'They're coming,' Viv yelled to the boys staggered on the eastern slope of the massive rock, heads down, ears filled with the roar of blowtorches. The wail of the sirens saw sections of the desert light up: fancy canvas domes, tarpaulin mansions and tiny taco tents glowed. The headlamps of backpackers in their swags collided like lasers in the night. Someone had called it in, a mysterious spatter of orange sparks spilling down the side of Uluru.

Lifting his thumb from a blowtorch, Charlie pulled up his goggles. He was drenched in sweat.

'It's cool, Charlie,' Jay called. Charlie nodded slowly and pulled down his goggles. Digging out a lighter from his shorts, he relit the torch, his tongue poking from the corner of his mouth in concentration, bringing flame to metal.

*

Charlie was a big guy, shy. Seventeen years old. Past initiation age, but the elders hadn't put him through ritual yet. He hung with the younger teenagers in the community: Jay, Reg, Rose, Viv and Jez.

The kids Charlie's age were too fast – driving, having sex. Some already doing time. 'He was an alcohol baby, Charlie was,' Eileen told Robbie. 'You can hear them in the early morning: when the community is still and quiet, they start up bleating like sick lambs.' Charlie sometimes worked in the art room where Robbie was assisting Eileen, who managed the remote community's art program. 'He's a beautiful painter,' Eileen said, 'but only if you intervene in time.'

When Robbie first saw Charlie make art, she was mesmerised. He played with the paint like the younger kids played with fire and spinifex in the evenings, pulling the long grass from the dirt and lighting it, fearlessly winding it around their fingers like a cat's cradle, hands swifter than the flame. Charlie seemed to knit the hues onto the canvas just like that. Often, he'd be painting so briskly that he'd grab a second brush to use in his other hand. As though each colour were a note, he'd create a melody – from the bottom of the canvas a landscape would rise out of shadows he had already laid down. Then, after a time, Charlie would fling aside the brushes and use his fingers to push the paint around.

At this point, Eileen would get ready to slide between him and the canvas. 'That's enough now, Charlie,' she'd say in a singsong voice, and he would look at her, bewildered, as if emerging from a trance. Then he'd nod, letting her take the painting away.

Robbie had been left in charge one day when Charlie was painting, and she'd been so absorbed watching him – his large clumsy body hardened to a single focus, the painting forming like photographic paper in a chemical bath – that she forgot to step in. At first, she didn't notice his fingers start to push the paint more fiercely, only that the sky seemed to churn. Then he pressed his palms flat, making wide circles, building boulders before skidding them outwards.

'Charlie?' Robbie finally said, but it was too late. He grunted and pushed her away with his shoulder as though they were on the football field. He put his face close to the painting, peering into it, hands working harder until it was just a mess of brown, a shit-coloured storm.

'Charlie?' Robbie said, worried for him. He stopped, body heavy again, arms by his side, muddy hands dangling. He was panting, struggling to control the rise and fall of his chest. He hung his head. 'Sorry,' he said quietly. Robbie saw he had bitten his tongue, bright red pooling on pink. He looked so sad that she had to fight the urge to hug him.

But on her second day in the remote community, the cultural relations officer, Quinn, had told her that showing affection was inappropriate. 'These are traditional people, you know. An ancient desert culture, very conservative.' He had looked at her T-shirt, eyes on her breasts. 'I'd suggest a looser-fitting shirt as well.' Robbie set her jaw. Quinn was a prick. She had figured that out almost instantly.

In his office, he sat close, pulling his chair around. He told her he had a skin name given to him by the local people and had witnessed ceremonies he was not permitted to talk about.

'Then why are you telling me?' Robbie asked, and he sat back, sizing her up.

'There's hierarchy out here,' he said. 'It's best you know where you're placed.'

In hindsight Robbie wished she had walked out of his office then, told him to piss off, but she was already learning that the tyranny of distance meant having to rely on all manner of pricks.

Still, Robbie wasn't acclimatised enough to call Quinn's bluff on hugging. Instead, looking at the wrecked canvas, she said unconvincingly, 'I like it,' but Charlie was slow, not stupid. He made a muffled noise as he got up to leave, wiping his hands on his pants. Robbie thought about a couple of the babies she had seen, the ones born from briny alcoholic wombs, their limbs scrawny, chests caved in. Their constant bleating, always thirsty. Born with a hangover. She tried to imagine the ache in their heads, how the light of day glared at them. The health workers, when they flew in, focused on the alcohol babies: took their measurements, gave them shots, revised their formula, shushing them when they arched their backs, tiny furious bodies opening and closing like scissors.

She tried to imagine Charlie as a baby: shrivelled and grey, bulbous in the wrong places, thrashing in the heat. There was a gracelessness about him; he walked as if he'd made numerous adaptations to cope, one shoulder lurched forward, neck crooked, eyes on the ground. It was only when painting that he briefly found his grace.

Eileen was annoyed that Robbie hadn't intervened in time to rescue the painting. 'You have to grab it before he does this,' she said tersely as she wet a sponge, rubbing as much paint off the canvas as she could. 'He doesn't paint anywhere near as much as he needs to make a living.' Robbie nodded, watching. There was something sad about Charlie's painting being washed down the drain, even though it was mostly awful to look at.

*

'Charlie!' Reg yelled, and Charlie's head jerked up, Robbie's too, both looking to the rock where Reg was working. 'Faster, man!' Reg yelled. Charlie nodded, fumbling a little under pressure. *You can tell a novice*, Robbie's metalwork tutor had said to her class once, *by an excess amount of slag and sparks*. The night was thick with an orange storm of slag, the sparks blowing up into the boys' faces, flecking their bare arms and legs with rice-sized burns. Charlie had started at the bottom of the chain, Reg at the top, and Jay was going between them, delivering fresh butane canisters from his backpack. He also had Robbie's orange Makita speaker with him and was picking the tunes.

Two more cop cars had appeared, catching up with the first one, and when they got closer, Jay ditched the Detroit beats and fiddled with his MP3. 'Hold up, Reg!' he yelled. 'Listen up! Charlie!' The teenagers cocked their heads to listen, the girls too. There was the scratching sound of vinyl and then the beat kicked in. Jez, Rose and Viv leapt to their feet, grinning. Reg laughed and held his blowtorch up in the air, shooting a flame off into the sky.

'Right about now!' yelled Jay, and Charlie held up his arms, wagging his palms to the beat.

'Judge Dre presiding,' Charlie bellowed, a big shiny grin on his face as the girls cheered.

'Order, order, order,' Jay sang. 'Ice-Cube, take the muthafucken' stand!'

Then they all chimed in: 'FUCK THA POLICE!'

Robbie started to laugh, an awkward, gulping kind of laughter. She shouldn't be here. As soon as she realised what they planned to do she knew she was up shit creek, but by then it was too late. Now Robbie watched the six teenagers with their determined faces, full of *fuck you*. They had a plan – a *plan*, something with a past, a present and a future. Something she had most days without even realising it. Robbie wondered if it was the first time for these kids.

*

Earlier in the evening Robbie had caught Jay trying to nick her speaker. Bullant had been asleep in a cardboard box at her feet and suddenly the puppy's black ears pricked and he scrambled out to catch Jay in the act. When Robbie followed, she found Bullant licking Jay's legs and saw the other kids waiting at the open door of the arts centre, although she'd clicked it locked two hours ago.

'We'll bring it back,' Jay said, and picked up the speaker. It was paint-spattered, covered with protest stickers.

Robbie put up her hand. 'Ah, no fucking way, Jay.'

He glared at her. When he saw she wasn't going to budge, he went back to the group at the door, all of them talking in language – Pitjantjatjara probably, Robbie still couldn't tell. She pulled on her boots and a jumper while they argued, Bullant excited, clawing at her jeans. 'How about this?' she said, when she was ready. 'You can borrow it if I come with you.'

The six teenagers fell silent and stared at her. Robbie flashed Viv a smile and Viv did a small, almost secret wave, flicking her wrist out from her hips.

'No,' Reg said firmly. He was the leader, tall and lanky, a good footy player. He turned and began to walk away.

'Please?' Jay said to Robbie, staring longingly at the speaker.

She shook her head. 'Only if I come.'

Jay kicked the ground fiercely. 'Fucking gubba,' he muttered. Robbie didn't say anything, just arched an eyebrow. Viv said something in language to him. 'Sorry, Miss,' he finally mumbled, and Robbie shrugged. 'Don't worry about it.'

Jay ran off then, and caught up with Reg. Jay talked fast, gesturing. Viv split next, joining Jay, talking too and pointing at her. As they spoke, Reg studied Robbie. His gaze was intense. She knew from seeing him at the swimming pool ('No school, no pool' was the mantra) that his chest was still smooth, not yet nicked with scars. His black hair was woven into cornrows, African-American style. He wore basketball gear – a red satin singlet, baggy black shorts, high white socks stained pink by dirt, and black sneakers. His skin, like many Anangu, reminded Robbie of kelp, brown but seemingly lit orange from within. Odd, she had thought when she first arrived, to gaze at the skin of a desert people and think of the sea.

'Okay,' Reg said finally.

Jay spun around, grinning. He gestured to her and the others impatiently. 'Come on.'

Robbie hefted the speaker onto her hip and whistled to Bullant. Already the teenagers had begun to fold into the night. She rushed to catch up when they suddenly doglegged off the street and into the scrub. Robbie followed, but within seconds she'd lost them. She stared hard at the dark. A few outlines formed, waiting at the tall wire fence that stretched around the community. Most had already wriggled under it. Viv was holding the bottom of the fence up, waving at Robbie to hurry.

*

The day Robbie landed at Ayers Rock Airport and stood at the kerb waiting for her lift, a window wound down on a dusty 4WD and a young white guy in a national park uniform leaned out the driver's window. 'Robbie O'Farrell?' he asked, and she scowled. Robbie had been expecting Barry Mooney, and if not him, an Indigenous local. But instead she'd gotten possibly the whitest guy she'd ever seen. His nose and cheeks were dabbed with thick zinc. Even his ginger eyelashes were tinged with white, like he'd blinked them in zinc. His red hair was shoulder-length and tangled. 'Jack,' he said, grinning, seeming not to notice her scowl. 'Throw your stuff in the back.'

The vehicle was strewn with maps and empty water bottles. There was a wide-brimmed felt hat with a national park logo, and she purposely put one of her bags on top of it. When she climbed in the front seat, there was red sand everywhere: clumpy caterpillars of the stuff gathered in the cup holders and along the top of the radio, prints on the rubber foot mats. Robbie ran her finger along the dash and Jack laughed. 'Turns your snot red, too,' he said. Then he put his hands on the wheel. 'So how're you feeling? Mooney said to take you to see the sorry rocks first if you weren't too tired.'

Robbie looked at him sharply. 'You?' she said.

'Yeah, me,' Jack replied, 'if you're not too tired. If you are, I can take you tomorrow.'

'Why can't Mooney take me?'

It was Jack's turn to look annoyed. 'Well, first of all, he doesn't live here, he lives in Alice. But even if he did live here, he couldn't take you.'

'Why not?' Robbie demanded. 'I'd have thought a local from the community would be best suited to show me around.'

The park ranger stared at her in surprise.

'What?'

'You don't know?'

'Know what?'

'Ah, shit.' Jack looked away and tapped his teeth, thinking. 'I thought for sure you'd know. The mob, they can't touch them. They can't touch the sorry rocks.' He glanced at her as if hoping she'd remember, that she had been told after all.

Robbie shook her head, still confused.

'Well, the sorry rocks,' he said with a sigh, 'all the rocks and sand and stuff people send back here, they never say in their letters where they nicked them from, they just write "Uluru". So, they could be from a sacred site, men's business or a secret women's place.'

Robbie winced, the penny dropping. 'Fuck.' She closed her eyes and leaned back.

'Yeah,' Jack said, not sure whether to continue. 'Um. So, if some-one in the mob ends up handling a rock or something they're not supposed to —'

'They'll be breaking their own laws,' Robbie finished, opening her eyes. 'Fuck,' she said again. 'Fuck, fuck, fuck. Why the hell didn't anyone tell me that?'

Jack looked sheepish. 'I don't know. Someone should have. I mean, it's sort of why you're here, isn't it?'

Robbie didn't say anything, instead running her fingers viciously through her hair.

'So,' Jack tried again, 'what do you want to do?'

By now the car park was empty. The tourist buses had pulled out, heading into Yulara. Above them, Robbie could see a bird flying in slow, easy circles, its wings fanned.

'Well, I guess we see the sorry rocks now,' she said reluctantly. Jack nodded and started the engine. At the T-intersection, he drove in the opposite direction to that Robbie expected, away from Uluru.

She'd seen the mammoth rock from the plane. 'There it is!' a girl in the row in front of her had said, smudging the round window with the stub of her finger. 'It's blue!'

'Blue?' Robbie heard the girl's mother say as she leaned across. 'It's not supposed to be blue.' But it was, a trick of the light. It seemed to throb from the flatness of the desert, a three-dimensional bruise.

Now, in the 4WD, Robbie twisted to see the rock through the rear window.

'It's also a biosecurity issue, not just cultural,' Jack said. 'Uluru is part of a national park, so we can't just take the rocks back in. We store them out here. Great way to say sorry, hey?'

Robbie gave him a small smile. She'd been thinking the same thing ever since she got the project. She considered the senders of the sorry rocks and their apologies – first the theft, and then, via post, the return of the stolen object. Were the local people just meant to accept the apologies? She watched as jellybean-shaped hire cars, mini-buses hauling trailers, campervans and 4WDs hurtled past, towards the rock.

After a few kilometres, Jack turned onto a dusty red track, passing two sloppy-eyed cows chewing dry grass. 'They're down here,' he said. Ahead, three skinny kangaroos hopped across the track, the last a joey. When Robbie looked to see where they had gone, she saw dark bushes, burnt stumps, all mimicking the stance of a still kangaroo. The red anthills she'd seen back along the highway got taller and taller out this way, as if freed from the limitations of the bitumen.

She shot a look at Jack, wondering how old he was, if he was younger than her. He was concentrating on keeping the car in the corrugations so it didn't bump too much. 'Jack,' she said, 'Mooney reckons there are twenty thousand sorry rocks in storage. What do you think – is that true?'

Jack thought for a minute, his lips moving as if counting. Then he nodded. 'Yeah, that'll be about right. Plus there's always more coming in.'

'So,' Robbie said slowly, her anger spilling into hopeless hilarity, 'how the hell am I supposed to do a "community-involved" artwork if they're not allowed to fucking touch them?'

Jack forced a neutral expression, trying not to laugh. He didn't make eye contact.

Robbie grinned. 'Don't you dare fucking laugh, ranger.'

He snorted, the zinc on his face cracking.

Robbie was about to ask where he was from, but two shipping containers appeared in the distance, *EVERGREEN* stencilled in white on their sides.

'They're in those,' he said, and they pulled up alongside the hulks, which had rust wearing the corners. Out of the car the heat hit again, sweat immediately trickling down the backs of Robbie's legs. Jack unlocked a chain and heaved open the door of the green container, carving a semi-circle in the red dirt. Sunlight poured in and Robbie saw row upon row of clear plastic tubs, stacked to the ceiling, each filled with postage parcels, Tupperware containers and ziplock bags. Inside these were dirt, crumbly rubble and chiselled rocks – pieces of Uluru – all looking as though they had been chipped off a sunset.

'Jesus.' Robbie stepped inside, her sneakers making a dull thud.

She could see a thin, precarious path between the tubs. Then there was a beam of light as Jack shone a torch over her shoulder.

'Come on,' he said. 'I'll show you down the back.'

She moved aside so he could lead the way. They went about twelve metres and stopped, shining the torch at a wall of wooden crates stacked with big red rocks.

'The largest is thirty-two kilos,' he said. 'A couple in Adelaide said they'd lifted it into their campervan back in the eighties. Thought it would look good in their garden.'

'They posted it back?' Robbie said in amazement.

Jack laughed. 'Nah, they left it out the front of a gallery in the middle of the night with a note. No names, of course.'

He put the torch between his teeth and carefully levered a couple of tubs free, then walked back towards the sunlight with them. 'You want to have a look?' Without waiting for an answer, he prised off the lids and pulled out the contents. There were parcels from all over Australia and overseas: Berlin, London, New York, Montreal, Moscow. Robbie gazed at the foreign postmarks. Plastic bags of sand; rocks wrapped in tissue paper; notes, mostly brief, some lengthy and para-noid, but all with *I'm sorry* handwritten, some laboured over in large print letters, others in elegant cursive.

Robbie wondered how the crumbly orange rocks and red dirt had fared in the northern light. She pictured the small, grim London apartment she had lived in three years ago. She had struggled with the light there and spent much of her residency painting European landscapes, which were exact in form but mismatched in colour, light and shadow. 'Hideously so,' said one of the professors. There had been much blunt talk about her lack of skill, the immaturity of her craft. 'Naive,' said one well-known artist in a sneering tone.

Robbie had been unnerved at the time. She considered reverting to her usual forms – collage, sculpture and video art – but found she was hooked on fucking up the European light. She persisted, feeling lonelier and lonelier. Her snow was slightly yellow, like frozen piss; her lakes amber; her English oaks marbled white, red and pale green. 'Hideous' was perfect, she realised. The landscapes were lurid, sickly. She called the paintings *The Acclimatisation Series*. Now, gazing at the sorry rocks, Robbie wondered if they'd dimmed in the European light. Had they been placed on windowsills? She unfolded a letter and read aloud. '*I had such a special time at Uluru that I wanted to take a piece of it home with me. I didn't know it was wrong and I hope you can forgive me.*'

Jack sniffed. He was sitting on the ground, not minding the ants. 'How could they not have known?' he asked hotly. 'It's written all over the place – it's on the website, on the signs around the rock.'

Robbie had wondered when reading up on Uluru who had written the signage, the rangers or the Anangu people. 'The website is pretty lame, if you ask me,' she said. Jack looked at her, surprised. 'I mean, *please respect our wishes*,' Robbie continued, 'it's so, I don't know ... ' The word 'pathetic' came to mind, but she didn't say it. 'And what about the climb?' she asked instead, referring to the hundred or so metal poles two white men had jackhammered into Uluru fifty years ago, along the eastern flank, threading a chain to make a railing for tourists to hold so they could clamber to the top.

'What about the climb?' Jack said.

'Well, why don't they just shut it down?'

Jack bristled. 'It's not as easy as that,' he replied.

Robbie looked at him with disdain. '*Please don't climb Uluru. We worry about you and we worry about your family*,' she said, repeating the text on the government's Parks Australia website. 'Who wrote that?' She didn't wait for an answer. 'I mean, surely no one gives a fuck if a climber gets hurt? If anything, it would serve them right.'

Jack stood up and began to snap the lids back on the containers.

'What are they meant to write?' he asked in a flinty tone.

'I don't know,' Robbie said. 'Maybe something like, "More than 20,000 Aborigines were killed in Australia's frontier war, thousands more displaced, then displaced again, kept on the fringes of townships, starved, had their children, their children's children, taken away, their cultural links severed. Many still face inequitable hardship and poverty today. They are three per cent of the population, so democracy isn't very fucking helpful. Don't be a cunt and climb Uluru, but if you do, after reading this, we hope you fall into a crevice and die a miserable death."' Robbie took a deep breath, a satisfied look on her face. 'That could work.'

Jack stared at her, his eyes hard. 'Well, that sounds like a fun visit.'

'Who said it should be fun?' Robbie took the tubs from his hands. 'I'll do this.' She balanced the containers and carried them inside, fumbling without the help of Jack's torch. She was trying to stack them properly when she heard the clunk of the metal bolt and had a vision of the ranger locking her in there. She left the containers on the floor and hurried towards the light.

Jack's face was blank as he lifted the metal door and closed it behind her. It was hot, the sun beating down. In silence, they got back in the car. Robbie's head was beginning to ache. She felt a pinching sensation behind her eyes. She needed more water; her bottle was empty, but she refused to ask Jack if she could refill it from his cooler in the back seat. Instead she looked out the window, silently chanting at him, *fuck you, fuck you, fuck you.*

*

'It will eat you up,' Robbie's mother had warned her once, 'all this anger. It ate your father up and it will do the same to you.'

'Well, I'll go do some yoga then, shall I?' Robbie snapped, and without telling her mother, she did, and stretched impatiently for an hour in a drafty scout hall. A woman at the front told the class to focus on their breath, to be mindful, reminding them to stay in the present, as if the past and the future were just lists of things already done and things to do. It had enraged Robbie. It felt honest, her anger. Still, during a visit with her father, she appraised him, considering what her mum had said, whether his anger had eaten him up.

She remembered a time in their kitchen, before they knew he was sick, when he had set the table for dinner and un-set it, putting everything away before they'd even sat down. 'Silly duffer,' Claire said as she mashed the potatoes. Robbie's father seemed perplexed, but Claire and Robbie just laughed. So many signs – but they didn't yet know how to read them. Outside, in the courtyard where their father had rigged up a hoop for Otis, there was the repetitive, ever-present bounce of the basketball.

When they were seated that night, Otis perching his feet on the ball under the table, Robbie asked their dad if he had ever met his mother's people. She had been thinking about it, but it must have come out of the blue for their father, judging by the way his head shot up.

Danny was silent for a minute, chewing, his jaws working back and forth. 'They said I'd been "turned inside out",' he said finally, and added, 'They said I had no claim, I was only there for money, and the whole time *they* were smoking *my* cigarettes.' Claire frowned, but he didn't notice; he was staring at something behind Robbie, so intently that she turned to look, but saw nothing except last year's calendar on the wall. 'I told them to fuck off,' he finished. 'I said I'd rather be white than a black prick.'

'Danny!' Claire snapped.

He startled, realising what he'd said. 'Oh, Jesus – sorry, kids,' he said. The basketball rolled out from under the table as Otis and Robbie stared at their father. 'I'm sorry,' he said again. 'It was a long time ago. I was messed up, angry.'

It was Otis who broke the silence. 'You smoked?' he said, making Claire laugh. It was his job in the family, Robbie realised later, to pierce the tension.

Danny grinned at Otis, reaching over to pat him on the head. 'What an idiot, hey?'

Still, Otis couldn't fix everything. They should have known then that something was wrong. That Danny was losing his grip. He was like a sealed room filling with water, unable to stop his thoughts lifting from where he had set them down. Later, much later, when they knew what was happening, Robbie became scared for her father in these moments, for it was the remembering of the present that seemed to hurt him the most: it was like the yank of a hook in his mouth, his eyes clearing with the realisation that he'd lost them.

*

Jack and Robbie didn't say a word as he drove back past the airport turnoff, following the sleek bitumen road as it wrapped around Uluru and tailed off towards the remote community. They passed a large road sign that warned drivers without a permit to turn back, and then another that declared they were entering an alcohol-free area. The gate appeared, along with a cluster of large trees. Jack got out and opened the gate, drove through and stopped the car again. Robbie unhooked her seatbelt, but he exited quickly and closed it himself.

'I could have done that,' Robbie said, breaking the silence between them, when he returned.

'Plenty more opportunities,' he said, not looking at her.

The road turned to gravel and Jack drove slowly, winding down his window to wave to people in the distance. A woman in a pink

T-shirt and a sarong was hanging clothes on a line, while a child near her rode a wheeled office chair down an incline, slamming into a fence before dragging it back up again. The houses were grim, built from grey blocks, like the toilets at sports ovals. A few were painted dark green, others orange. Some windows were boarded up with plywood offcuts, and the odd wall had been done in a mural, one a landscape painted in the style of Albert Namatjira, with bluish light cast over red rocks and purple outcrops, and the long, sculpted trunks of ghost gums in the foreground.

They passed a man kneeling in a front yard, swinging a pick-axe into the dirt, and another gazing into a car engine, bonnet propped up with a broom, tools on a towel beside him. One yard had a lemon tree, while most had cars on blocks. Some of these were just metal skeletons skinned for parts, while others seemed to be waiting, for a sought-after part maybe, to make one more 800-kilometre round trip to Alice. Mattresses were laid out under trees, stripped of their linen and chunks bitten from the orange foam. Patches of dirt sparkled with glass. Plastic bags rolled and curled and clustered against metal fences. Robbie tried to suppress a feeling of panic.

She had dismissed Mooney and the board when they suggested she visit the remote community before committing to the project. She said she'd travelled widely and seen her fair share of confronting places. Robbie grimaced now, remembering how Mooney had smirked. He'd nodded, let her have her way. But she hadn't been totally naive; part of her hadn't wanted to see it first in case she got spooked.

On the road in front of them, a kid in nothing but shorts was dragging a cardboard poster. Tom Cruise as Jack Reacher stared out at her, holding a pistol. Her Jack stopped next to the boy. 'Hey, Lenny!' he said, and the kid grinned, coming closer and staring in at Robbie. 'Where'd you get that?'

'The tip!' the boy replied, whirling it around so they could get a good look. 'Cool, hey?'

Jack smiled. 'Sure is.' He turned off the ignition and pulled out the keys, taking one off and holding it out to Lenny. 'Hey, Len, this is Robbie,' he said. 'You wanna go open up the gate for her at the workers' units?'

Lenny nodded, his face serious. He took the key and ran off, the poster bumping behind him as he cut through the front yards.

'He's cute,' Robbie said, forgetting herself as she watched him scamper around car wrecks. Jack shrugged, starting the car again. Robbie saw that the street ran in a loop, spitting you out the way you came in. In the shade of a thin tree, she spied a group sitting in a circle, each with a fan of playing cards, a couple of toddlers nosing around among them.

'Normally you'd see a heap of camp dogs everywhere,' Jack said, and his voice was friendlier. Robbie felt annoyingly relieved. 'They wouldn't even move for you,' he continued. 'You'd have to drive round them. But most have been put over there.' Jack pointed to a row of metal cages back near the fence line.

'Why?' Robbie asked, leaning forward. She could see the shapes of the dogs, tails flicking at flies.

'We had a group of vets fly in last week to do a check. They marked most of them to be put down.'

'When are they going to do it?'

Jack gave a half-smile. 'That's the million-dollar question. Turns out the Territory won't cover the extra cost, so they're planning on using local shooters instead. The vets, they were pissed. Pretty gullible.' He looked at Robbie. 'Nothing in Central Australia gets euthanised.'

He stopped the car next to a group of units separated from the rest of the community by a tall metal fence. Lenny was standing, proud and antsy, next to the open gate. He ran around to Jack's side, holding out the key.

'Give it to Robbie,' Jack said. 'It's hers.'

Shyly, Lenny went back to Robbie's side and held out the key.

'Hey, thanks so much, Lenny,' she said, taking it. 'Gee, you were quick.'

Lenny grinned, looking her in the eye. 'Like a cheetah,' he said, grabbing the poster from the ground and taking off.

The units were made from the same bricks as the houses but painted white. In the sunlight, they shone like igloos, the red sand drifting up against them. She saw a dog lying on one of the shady verandahs, flanks twitching, safe inside the fence. Jack put her bags and speaker on the ground, then stood beside her, holding the hat she'd flattened and punching it back into shape.

Robbie blushed. 'Sorry about that,' she said.

The ranger smiled. 'I'm sure you didn't mean it,' he replied, poker-faced.

*

Robbie's unit was well equipped. There was air-conditioning, a television, a toaster, an electric stove, a washing machine, a microwave and a kettle. It took her half an hour to unpack. Outside the light was finally yielding, and she sat on the verandah, whistling to the dog. It was the colour of wheat, and it got up slowly, stretching before coming over. She scratched its head for a while, stopping when she heard the swing of the gate, and watched as a woman juggled an enormous ring of keys before snipping the padlock. Then, with a warm smile, the woman waved and strode towards her.

'Robbie,' she said, her jewellery tinkling like music as she walked. 'It's Eileen.' Robbie stood and smiled back. They'd already spoken on the phone. 'I've been working with desert mobs for almost two decades now,' she'd said in a raspy voice then.

She looked exactly as Robbie had imagined: mismatched and colourful, overdone with pendants, bangles and earrings. She'd pinned her hennaed hair loosely in a bun so that tendrils hung out, catching around her face, becoming stuck on her bright red lipstick. 'C'mon,' she said, 'I'll show you the arts centre.'

Robbie followed Eileen to the road and up a path leading to a tin building the size of a small aircraft hangar. It had a row of windows around the top, near the roof, covered with chicken mesh. A small building had been added on the side, adorned with paintings of emus, snakes and lizards. Again, Eileen got out her enormous keyring. When she slid open the glass door, the familiar smells of acrylics and glue and wood shavings embraced Robbie.

Eileen showed her where she stored the finished canvases, in a small locked room. 'Most of these are pretty standard,' she said, 'piece-work, mostly. More like practising the craft. But they sell. I've found it's only every few years or so that an artist out here creates something extraordinary. There's a few of those in there.' She pointed to the metal drawers. 'Clancy Mann, Riley Jones, Daisy Williams. There's a kid, too, Charlie, seventeen. Major talent; major risk, too. I'll show you when there's more time. I'm trying to find the best buyer for them.'

There was a rattle on the sliding door. 'Hey?' came a man's voice, and Eileen sighed. 'Hi, Bert,' she called, walking back to the main room. Robbie followed, seeing a thin older man at the door in brown pants, a blue shirt and a pair of massage thongs. A stockman's hat was pulled low on his brow. Eileen started pulling boxes from the shelving, sifting through stacks of canvases. 'You know I'm not allowed to do this, Bert,' she said, voice muffled as she searched.

'Hmph,' replied the man, shifting impatiently. He glanced at Robbie.

'Hi,' Robbie said nervously, and he looked away.

'Hmph,' he said again, seemingly bored by the sight of her.

'Here's one,' Eileen announced, holding up a scrappy-looking painting. She walked over to him. 'This is your signature, isn't it?' But the man didn't look; he just took the painting and very slowly walked out to where he'd parked a little beaten-up red Mazda. There was a girl in the passenger seat.

'Grumpy old bastard,' Eileen said, watching him ease into the driver's side and toss the painting into the girl's lap. She sighed and started to flick off the lights around the large room, disappearing briefly to lock the smaller rooms.

When Eileen had slid the doors shut, Robbie asked about the old man. 'Bert, bloody Bert,' the arts manager said, seeming to wrestle with whether she ought to say more. Eventually she shrugged, giving in. 'Bert has an unhealthy obsession with those camp dogs. The ones meant to be put down soon. You seen them?'

'Yeah, Jack pointed them out.'

Eileen smiled. 'Ah, Jack, he's a lovely boy. Well, every couple of days Bert shows up here asking for an old painting to sell down in Yulara and then hits up the IGA for dog food. I'm not meant to, goes against my contract, helping him panhandle paintings. Devalues the whole lot.'

They reached the street and Robbie stopped to admire the sky. The colours rippled like the pearly underside of an abalone shell. 'So why do you?' she asked. 'Help him?'

Eileen shook her head. 'I don't know. Not sure I could say no to old Bert. He's a warrior man, you know? Knows the old ways, Cathy says – you met Cathy yet?' Robbie shook her head. 'Cathy's the main nurse here, clever girl, strong, a bit stand-offish. Anyway, Cathy says Bert's got all the old scars: all the initiation nicks up his arms, on his chest. Patterns she's never seen on anyone else. You seen body markings, the desert ones?' Again, Robbie shook her head. 'Well, it looks like grains of rice arranged under the skin, and the more elaborate the pattern, the more important you are. That's what's said. Bert's might not have been that elaborate back then. But he's the only one left who had it done that way, pre-contact.'

'Pre-contact?' Robbie said doubtfully.

'Sort of,' Eileen said. 'I been told he came in as a child to Hermannsburg, the mission, but he'd often leave with his parents, go back to country. Store their mission clothes inside a tree hollow.'

'Jesus,' Robbie said.

Eileen smiled. She nodded towards Uluru. The massive rock hulked on the horizon. 'You been yet?'

'No.' It was burnt orange when they had entered the arts centre. Now it was a deep red, the sky vast and violet. 'It's beautiful,' she said.

'Uh huh,' Eileen said knowingly. They were walking along the street Jack had driven in on. Robbie stopped when they came near the cages with the dogs. 'Can we have a look?'

Eileen tilted her head. 'Sure. It's pretty stinky. Hold your nose.' They walked over the dry grass. One dog popped its head up and, seeing them, it threw itself against the fence, whining. Instantly the others did the same, emerging from car wrecks that had been chucked in there for shade, barking and nipping at one another to get in front. They pressed their snouts to the fence; mangy patches of mostly brindle hair stuck through the wire. Ribs rippled against their skin and open sores wept pus, thick with flies. Most of the bitches had heavy bellies and raw-looking teats dragging near the ground.

'What are the Xs for?' Robbie asked. Every dog had a pink X spray-painted on its side. On the drive back with Jack from the sorry rocks, there had been an upside-down cow, a bloated corpse, on the side of the road. It, too, had the sign on its side.

Eileen had her blouse over her nose. 'To mark them out from the healthy dogs,' she said in a muffled voice. Robbie pinched her nose and stared. The dogs were snarling now that they understood the women didn't have food.

'Ugh!' said Eileen, walking away, gagging. 'I can't stand it.'

Back on the street, they gulped in air. Robbie shook her head. 'That's pretty fucked up.'

Eileen snorted. 'That's an understatement. There's about fifty, sixty dogs in there. Do you know how many dogs they didn't mark? Ten. Ten measly so-called healthy dogs.'

'Where are they?'

'Hiding.'

Robbie was confused. 'Huh? What do you mean?'

Eileen started walking. 'We'd better hurry if we want to grab you some food.'

About a hundred metres away was a squat building with two petrol bowsers out front. In the doorway hung faded rubber strips to keep out the flies. A bunch of kids sat nearby, stretching jelly snakes. Robbie recognised Lenny.

'Before the vets came,' Eileen said, 'no one here, not even us at the workers' units, saw much difference between the so-called healthy dogs and the sick ones, but after, when them ten dogs got their shots, wormed and sent on their way, locals started to hate them.'

'Why?' said Robbie.

Eileen shrugged. 'I don't know. Maybe they saw a little bit of history repeating itself. You know, full-bloods go over there' – she pointed to the cages – 'and the rest go and join them' – she pointed to their units behind the fence. 'People started kicking them healthy dogs, flicking embers at them when they came sniffing around the fires, so the dogs ended up staying with us. Now the locals call them stuck-up gubba dogs.'

They reached the shop. The kids scampered around the corner and stared back at them. Robbie waved to Lenny. He beamed and whispered to his friends.

Eileen stopped at the bowsers. 'You want to have dinner at mine when you're done here? You eat meat? I can do a spaghetti bolognese.'

Robbie nodded. 'That'd be great.'

*

Over time, Robbie's father had become less agitated, more settled, accepting of his fate. He was no longer moved by Robbie; she, Otis and Claire were simply fishy shadows in the gloom of his murky world. But still, Robbie had been uneasy about leaving for three months. It was bad timing, the sorry rocks project. Claire and Nathan were also going away. They had booked a cruise two years before, and Robbie understood her mother needed the holiday. No one said it, but the truth was that her father was supposed to be dead by now. Each of the past five Christmases was meant to be his last, but the years rolled on. His face got craggier and his hair bushy and grey. Would her father only die, she wondered, when he resembled the man he was meant to be? Not the part-Italian he'd been told he was by his foster parents, not Danny, but a Wurundjeri man. Possibly Wathaurung, too.

It was Beverley who had thrown that into the mix, the Wathaurung.

'Really?' Claire said. 'What about his father? We thought he might have been white, a Scot?'

'Half,' Beverley replied. 'Maybe a third.'

Beverley hadn't been to see him for a long time. She'd been sick, her daughters said when Claire rang. It was too hard for her to travel into the city by herself now.

Otis would be around while Robbie was away. But Otis was useless, Robbie bitched to her mother. Claire didn't say anything, although Robbie could tell her mother was wavering on the holiday. 'I'll talk to Sabeen,' she offered, recalling how well her friend had gotten on with her father, right from the time they'd met.

Claire brightened. 'Yes!' she gushed. 'That would be wonderful. Danny likes her. Do you think she'd like to? We could pay her?'

*

Robbie sat with Eileen on the verandah, each balancing a bowl of spaghetti on their lap.

'I saw Bert,' Robbie said, 'and the girl, feeding the dogs.' She'd been on her way back to the units with groceries when she saw the red Mazda. She stopped and watched as the old man put a knife through the plastic bags of dried food, then dragged them over, tossing handfuls through the fence. The noise was deafening, a high-pitched barking and squealing as the dogs fought over the scraps. The girl followed, picking up bits Bert had dropped and pressing them through the fence. She had straggly hair and was wearing an extra-large hoodie as if to hide her breasts, her legs skinny as two cigarettes. Thirteen, maybe fourteen, Eileen had said, when Robbie asked how old the girl was.

'Viv,' said Eileen. 'She's his granddaughter, or great-granddaughter. Don't know which.'

Twirling the spaghetti around her fork, Robbie was quiet for a bit. A couple of stuck-up gubba dogs came over, smelling the food, and settled under their chairs. Robbie played with one's ears, feeling the burrs stuck in the fur. 'When will they do it?'

'I don't know,' said Eileen. 'Gotta be soon, though. If the vets reckoned they were bad for your health before, it'll be ten times worse now. You smelt it.' Robbie nodded. 'But it'll finish him off,' Eileen added. 'Bert. I reckon it will.' They were quiet as they considered whether sixty flea-bitten dogs was an acceptable price to pay for a man who remembered the old times. Then Eileen sighed. 'Don't feel too sorry for the bastard. I've heard he was a nasty piece of work in his time. Put a star picket through his wife's thigh. Blood-let her like a pig.'

'Serious?'

Eileen chortled, enjoying Robbie's naivety. 'Oh, honey, you'll see. You find me a woman out here with all her teeth and I'll give you a fifty.'

In the dark, down the path, the gate creaked. Over the week Robbie would meet all six workers who stayed in the units. There was Brix, the pool maintenance guy from Coober Pedy, and Brian and Pattie, husband and wife, who taught the primary-school kids and wore gold crosses on thin necklaces. Cathy, a former ICU nurse from Sydney, friendly but always busy, was up before sunrise, cooped in the stuffy health clinic all day and sometimes well into the night. She worked ten days straight and then flew out for a week or so, a replacement flying in. Robbie got the sense that Cathy partied hard on her week off; on her return there'd be a speediness to her talk and a clammy odour. And finally, there was Quinn the Prick. His job mostly seemed to be about tracking locals down for their signatures on funding applications.

It was with Quinn that Robbie reluctantly hitched a lift to Uluru. His 4WD was laced with empty cans of Sprite and he had the air-con on full blast. As he wound around the serpent of bitumen, Robbie shivered. She hugged her arms over her T-shirt, worrying that her nipples were showing.

Quinn insisted she see the cultural centre first. In the cool dark passageways he made sure she read every board and took in every film. By the time he pulled into the main car park at the base of Uluru, it was full of tourist buses and campervans. *Palya*, read a sign. Welcome.

When he undid his seatbelt as if to join her, Robbie couldn't bear it. 'No!' she yelped. Quinn looked at her, startled. 'No,' she said again.

'I'd like to do this on my own.' He pouted, and Robbie felt a stab of fury that she'd had to rely on him in the first place. 'Thanks for the lift,' she said stiffly, opening her door.

'I can pick you up here at three,' he said.

'It's okay. I don't need a lift.'

Quinn looked at her. 'How you getting back then?' he asked.

'Jack,' Robbie said, the lie coming easy. 'Jack's going to take me.'

Quinn raised his eyebrows.

'Bye,' Robbie said, slamming the door. Her water bottle was in there, she remembered, down the side of the seat, but she couldn't bear the thought of calling out to Quinn to stop. Instead she kept walking, twitching with anger that she'd gotten there so late. Flies buzzed in her face and she picked up a twig, whipping at the insects with its dry leaves. The car park was loud with chatter. A group of sweaty Japanese tourists rested in the shade of a tree; others whirred along the path on Segways, seesawing on the ridiculous machines. In front of her, at the base of Uluru, was a little wooden gate. The entrance to the climb. Robbie saw a line of people ascending the flank of the magnificent red rock, a row of ants with their shiny antennae – cameras, sunglasses, phones – glinting. She scowled at them, then turned, following the path southwards.

As she got further away from the car park, she allowed herself to look up, and the rock swept over her. It was beautiful, the mammoth orange curves sculpted like limbs, the insides of thighs carved by thousands of years of wind and rain. Stripes of black algae ran down the rock's rivulets, markings left behind from the rainy season. There were overhanging lips, and sandy shelters, while signs indicated that this was where bread was made, this was where business was conducted, and so on.

Ahead, Robbie saw tourists gathered on a metal grate over a waterhole. A woman in khaki shorts and a T-shirt lay there on her back, staring at the rock. Robbie stepped around her and leaned on the railing. Tadpoles darted in the weeds. Beside her a sign read, *Close your eyes here and feel a connection to this special place.* All Robbie could feel was her head throb. Her jaw was clenched, she realised, and sore, as though she had been chewing gum for hours.

The grate creaked as a man rounded up the tourists. 'Alright,' he said. 'Let's keep going.' And with a wink, he glanced at Robbie. 'It's all yours now.'

Robbie watched them disappear around the bend before quickly cupping handfuls of water, slurping it up. She popped three Panadol from their silver foil and swallowed, then tore the corner off a sachet of electrolyte rehydrates and poured the powder into her mouth. She emptied a ziplock bag of dried fruit and nuts into her pockets, and filled the bag from the waterhole, scooping out twitching black specks.

Refreshed, she kept walking, and eventually began to feel as though she were on her own. She started to notice small things: the flit of finches, the husks of desert lantern flowers, the boot-sized anthills on the path, with rectangle slits at the top like coin slots. A thin wire had been put around the rock to keep visitors to the left of it, only letting people peer into shady overhangs, and there were more signs, telling where seeds were ground into a flour, and so on, every piece of information seeking to convey a sense of the sacred.

But really, it was just memories, Robbie thought. Like, here we prepared dinner, here we napped in the heat of the day, here we picnicked, here we met to talk about serious issues, here the kids came to collect skinks. Here was where we hid from the big dust storm. Not as unknowable as it was made out to be. To Robbie it felt like a beautiful ghost town, happiness and sadness lingering in every fold and overhang.

She came to another waterhole and paused to lie on the grate. She let her fingers trail in the water, flicking it up, wetting her face.

The branches of a small lush tree dappled the walkway with shade. Looking to check no one was coming, she inched forward and dunked her head.

'Do the locals ever get to hang out at Uluru?' she had asked Eileen. 'It seems like it's always being used by the tourists.'

Eileen had smiled a secret smile. 'Oh, yeah. Out the back, the kids often go to the dunes, kick a footy, ride their bikes. People go after the gates are locked, too.' She laughed, adding, 'Mostly for mobile reception. Plus it doesn't happen so often now we've got the pool, but the kids sometimes nick off through the scrub and go in the back way – it's quicker than driving in – to swim in the water-hole. The dogs used to go with them too, before the vets.'

Robbie let her hair drip down her back, jealous that she couldn't slip into the water like the kids. She dangled her fingertips, tadpoles moving in for a nibble. *The race was on for them*, one sign read, *to turn into frogs before the water receded. Then they would burrow down deep into the ground, sleep until the next rain*. Feeling sleepy herself, Robbie urged her body to get up and keep walking, wondering how she would get back to the community. She decided she would try to join the kids next time she saw them heading out for a swim, learn the best way through the scrub so she wouldn't have to rely on Quinn.

On the last leg of the walk, Robbie caught up with an odd-looking man, tufts of hair sticking through the holes in his straw hat. When she encountered him, in a small clearing, he was pushing back the nose of his spectacles, held together with tape, as he busily scribbled in a notebook. Robbie saw he was drawing diagrams of sediment, layers of rock, numbering down the margin, his tiny script scrawled around the edges. When he saw her looking, he explained he was a retired geologist – used to work for a mining company, tin and nickel. 'Did you know,' he said, pointing to Uluru, 'it's like an iceberg? Most of it is underneath us.'

Robbie didn't know. She stared at the red rock. Up close, you could only see it in sections, curves and ridges. 'It's just the tip,' he explained, 'what we can see.' Robbie shook her head in wonder. She walked back the rest of the way with the geologist. He told her facts that seemed more magical than scientific. 'It's actually grey, you know,' he said, 'the rock. It's just the surface that's burnt orange – surface iron oxidisation, it's called.'

When they reached the car park, he drove her to the start of the road leading into the community, and as she waved to him she felt lighter, more in control. Walking in, a few kids caught up with her, including Lenny, who ran off and reappeared with a hot can of Coke. 'You are a cheetah,' she said as she clicked it open and gulped down the sweet fizzy drink. The sky was pink, the sand was a burst of scarlet, and the kids were wild with energy. They leapt about, and Robbie mucked around and joked with them, shrugging off her backpack at the gate. A couple of times she looked to the horizon, catching the eye of Uluru.

The park gates would be shut by now, she knew. Chairs and white-clothed tables would be set up on the outskirts, crackers, cheese and flutes of champagne ready for top-dollar tourists to watch the sunset, while others stood on the bonnets of their hire cars to take the perfect photo. But inside the gates, it was like a brief reprieve for Uluru. Robbie could have sworn she saw the rock breathe out, but later the thought occurred that it was possibly her. Her head had stopped throbbing.

That evening, the kids showed off their skills, first back-flipping off a stack of old spring mattresses, then flicking a flame into life and cascading it into the long grass, stamping it out with their feet when it flared. Sometimes an adult would call into the dark and one of the kids would leave, but return a few minutes later. Robbie asked if they'd take her the next time they swam at Uluru, ignoring a stern voice in her head – Quinn's, perhaps, maybe Mooney's – that said she should really be asking one of the elders. The children grinned and said they would.

*

Lenny was seven. He liked being called Cheetah and became useful in rallying the troops for Robbie's art classes. It was far more difficult with the teenagers. Each time she approached, they had an uncanny skill of receding, slipping behind each other, eyes downcast as they weaved backwards until she was on her own again, talking to no one. Lenny and the kids were definitely easier to inspire. They crowded around in the arts centre when she tried to teach them Photoshop and copied her, clicking the mouses with happy concentration. She showed them how to make fantastical creatures. 'See,' Robbie said, 'you can use construction cranes for legs, ocean waves for wings, a silver colander for a head.' After the first session Robbie printed their work and suggested they put it on their walls at home. The children nodded, with gappy grins, tumbling out the door. Robbie felt triumphant; she had connected.

But when she left the centre an hour later, the pictures were scattered over the street, some caught in spiky shrubs, others trodden into the dirt and covered with footprints. She'd been pissed off, bending to pick them all up, calling out the kids' names to come and help her. None of them did.

'They didn't do the pictures for them,' Eileen explained to her later, 'they did it for you. Did it to please you.' Robbie frowned, not in the mood to be soothed. Eileen grinned. 'I'm not saying it to make you feel better. What I'm saying is, think about it, Robbie: what does Photoshop mean to them? You can't be angry at them for not seeing the point.'

Robbie pressed her palms to her temples. 'I guess not,' she said. 'But, Eileen, how the hell am I meant to do the sorry rocks? The board – the fucking board – they said the community has to be involved, but no one wants a bar of me.'

'I know.' Eileen sighed. 'You're going to have to give it time. Give people time to trust you. There'll be something sooner or later, a flash-point – always is – but you've got to trust the process.'

'Mooney said I had three months.'

Eileen laughed. 'No one ever has three months. He's bullshitting you. Just wait. Give it time.'

But Robbie wasn't used to waiting. When she could, she bor-rowed Eileen's ute to go out to the containers and document what was there. She set up a table and chair in a shady spot and took pho-tos of each parcel – the letter, if there was one, and the sorry rock – later uploading it all to her computer. Often at night, she'd click through the images and stare at the rocks, bits and pieces stolen from the red landscape, poring over people's handwriting.

When I learned about the history and treatment of Aboriginal peo-ple, Emily W. wrote from Sydney, *I felt so guilty for taking a small piece of Uluru home with me.* Robbie wished the woman had been brave enough to write her full name and address. She wanted to ask Emily W. exactly what she had learned.

She grew attached to the rocks. Felt for them each time she shut the door on the shipping container, had eerie visions of them glow-ing like embers in the dark. They had, against all odds, found their way home, but whatever memories they held, wherever in the earth they belonged, too much time had passed. Even here, they were lost.

On one of these visits, a thumb-sized rock tumbled into her palm from a padded parcel containing no note or return address. One side was dimpled and burnt-orange, the other side grey, just like the geol-ogist had said. When it was time to pack up, something about that rock tugged at her. Robbie slipped it into the pocket of her shorts and carried it back to the community. This felt like a transgression, the rock hot against her skin, for she knew without asking that bringing it, tiny as it was – insignificant, really – through the national park gates would be against the elders' wishes. When she got back to her unit, she pressed it into her palm, a voice telling her to return it to a plastic tub in the darkness. But she didn't.

*

Bert was sucking on ice cubes when she approached, a mug of them on the ground beside him. He sat in the shade of a scribbly gum, leaning against the trunk, not minding the long lines of ants that traversed the outline of his check shirt.

'Hi,' said Robbie. Bert looked up. One of his eyes, she realised, had a bluish membrane, probably trachoma. His dark skin was dusted white with scales. 'My name's Robbie,' she said, urging herself to keep talking. She shifted so he didn't have to look into the sun. 'I'm living here for a while.' Bert turned his head, following her shape. 'I'm doing the sorry rocks project,' she added. She wasn't sure if he knew what she was talking about. He was thin, his clothes hanging loosely on him. His stockman's pants were dusty around the cuffs, the waist tied with a leather belt. He looked about as clean as a man could be out here. Robbie wondered who helped him, if that girl she and Eileen had seen with him did.

Robbie looked at the cages. 'Is one of those dogs yours?' she asked, and Bert's eyes followed hers. She wondered how much he could see. He smiled and shook his head, saying something, his words muddy to her ears. Robbie felt like an idiot, and although she had been getting somewhat used to that feeling, she didn't like it. She hadn't anticipated that the different languages would be so prevalent. She was no good at learning even the most rudimentary phrases, and couldn't tell the difference between dialects.

'He says it's hard to say which one,' said a voice. Robbie looked up to see the girl, with a fresh batch of ice cubes in her palm. She tipped them into Bert's mug and he smiled and spoke, the girl nodding. When he finished, she looked at Robbie. 'The dogs, they been with us since they were pups.' Bert nodded, his body rocking. 'Some things,' she said, 'they have been one way for so long, it's hard to separate them.'

Robbie gazed at the dogs. Some of them looked vicious, with battered, scarred ears, their teeth locked in permanent snarls, while others stared forlornly from the car wrecks, chins on paws. She tried to imagine them as pups, one slung under the arm of this girl when she was little.

'I'm Robbie,' she said, putting her hand out.

The girl smiled shyly. 'Viv,' she said, shaking Robbie's hand.

Bert made a noise, gesturing to his lips with his finger. Viv put her hand in the pouch of her hoodie, took out a plastic pocket and pinched a shaggy clump of tobacco. She rolled a cigarette expertly. She put the cigarette on his bottom lip and produced a lighter. Bert puffed quickly, his face lost in a swirl of smoke.

'So, I'm doing the sorry rocks project,' Robbie said again, this time to Viv. The girl shrugged, still watching Bert. Robbie tried not to be annoyed. 'Can you tell Bert?' she asked Viv. 'Tell him I'm doing the sorry rocks project?'

Bert began to cough and Viv waited for him to stop, then spoke in language, Robbie catching the words *sorry* and *rocks*. When she finished, Bert shrugged as well, and went back to staring at the dogs, puffing on his cigarette. Robbie forced herself to stay put. She glanced at the dogs. 'When do you think the shooters will come?'

Viv smiled as she said something to Bert. He laughed, a dry sound that rattled from his chest. He spoke fast, his hands moving animatedly. Viv listened, then said to Robbie, 'They did come. Early morning yesterday, but Bert wouldn't let them take the dogs. Said he'd cast a spell on their testicles.'

'Really?' Robbie said.

Viv nodded, her eyes light with laughter.

'And they believed him?'

She shook her head, snorting. 'Course not. White men. But Bert scared them off. They didn't want to start anything.'

Bert made a ring with his fingers around his neck, looking at Robbie as he spoke. 'He remembers,' Viv explained, 'when our people had shackles put around their necks and were chained together.'

Robbie tilted her head. 'Really?' she asked, trying to guess how old Bert was. 'He saw that?' Bert pointed to his eyes and nodded. He put his finger in the dirt, talking as he drew first with his fingers, then with his knuckles.

'He remembers the tracks the chained men made,' Viv said, 'how they had to shuffle, the drag of their feet, same as the track of an injured animal.'

He spoke again, and Viv stiffened.

'What?' said Robbie impatiently. 'What did he say?'

Viv's features set and she suddenly looked older, tired. 'He said they didn't chain up the women, figuring they didn't need to, that they'd just stick with the men.' She got up off her knees, shaking the dirt and ants. 'He says they were wrong. They should've chained up the women too.' She glared down at Bert and said something to him Robbie couldn't understand, but then she translated it. 'I told the old bastard he could get his own ice cubes today.'

Bert grunted as she stalked off.

Robbie stood awkwardly for a while next to Bert, listening to him crunch on an ice cube. She had planned on asking for his advice on the sorry rocks, if he had a vision for them. 'Well,' she said instead, 'see you, Bert.'

*

It was the middle of the day when the children came to get her. They called her name from outside the gate to the units, and she fumbled in the heat to unlock it, hands slick with sweat. 'C'mon, Miss Robbie!' yelled Lenny, the leader of the pack, pulling her arm.

'But it's the middle of the day,' she said lazily, sheepish about wanting to return to her cool unit.

'Yeah, yeah, it's too hot,' Lenny said, and his mate Bingo did a wheelie on his BMX.

'Pool's closed,' the kid called. 'Brix's pissed at us.'

The group collapsed in giggles. Robbie let them pull her across the street, into the scrub and through a hole in the cyclone fence. Grasshoppers sprang out of the spinifex as they ran. Robbie tried to get her bearings but soon gave up, focusing on keeping up with the kids. Lenny was at the front, wearing his footy jersey. A girl was dragging a boogie board, and it flipped up behind her. She slowed, and Robbie came level with her. 'You aren't worried about the tourists?' she asked, panting.

'Nah, Miss,' the girl said with a grin. 'It'll be too hot for them.' The pink foam board kept bumping and catching, but she didn't seem to mind. A desert skink zipped across their path and the girl swerved after it, but it disappeared down a hole. 'Tjaliri!' she yelled to the others. But they didn't stop, Lenny calling over his shoulder, 'Later! Later!' The girl frowned, kicked up the dirt and started to run again.

Uluru loomed close now, and the children tore up the wooden walkway to the waterhole. They climbed the railing and balanced on the top plank. Then they dived into the amber water, dragonflies flitting away.

Robbie stood near the railing to catch her breath. From the water, the rock curved upwards, a tiger stripe running down where the waterfall had been. 'Jump!' Lenny yelled, the others splashing and laughing. Robbie climbed up shyly, trying to gauge how deep it was.

The kids were watching her, their heads bobbing, sleek as seals. Feeling clumsy and hot, she flopped in, her T-shirt and shorts unsticking from her skin as she sank to the bottom. She opened her eyes and could see the kids' legs kicking up a storm. She swam over, grabbing their feet. 'Rah!' she yelled as she jumped out of the water. They squealed, swimming off in different directions. They played like this for a while; then the children showed Robbie how they scrambled up the rock and leapt into the water, and how they perched on the railing, backflipping on top of one another. Robbie was barely able to watch, peeking through her fingers. Eventually she swam to the bank and lay on the mud, stretching her legs in the water. Lenny sat next to her, digging into the wet earth with his hands, levering out a fat, surprised frog. He played with it, then gave it to Robbie to hold, shouting when she let it, out of sympathy, hop into the water. He swam after it and soon all of them were chasing, the waterhole churning.

Robbie lay back, not wanting to witness the frog's fate. She stared up at the blue sky and the fiery flank of Uluru.

*

She'd looked it up, the neck shackles and chains. She wanted to find out if it was possible that Bert had seen it, followed the tracks of prisoners, that it wasn't memory passed down. A photograph in 1935 showed a group of Aboriginal men in chains standing around a dead bullock, their crime. Central Australia was the location given. She came across another photograph taken in Queensland in 1942, of a lone Aboriginal man chained to a tree. In Queensland, she read, the practice was not phased out until 1960. She could not find when the same was done in the Territory. When she asked Eileen if she knew, the arts manager retorted, 'Who says it's been phased out?'

Robbie took to sitting with Bert every so often on her breaks, usually sharing a bag of chips. He spoke sometimes, Robbie struggling to follow if Viv wasn't around, but mostly they just sat in silence.

It was Viv who gave her Bullant. 'Bert's idea,' she said, calling Robbie into their house when she came past one day. It was clean, sparse, with a fridge, a table and three chairs. On the bench, a toaster and a kettle, jars of Vegemite and honey, a box of teabags. On the wall, a faded newspaper poster of the Aboriginal flag and a round clock, its soft tick filling the room. In the corner, lying on a length of foam, was one of the gubba dogs, with a litter of puppies sucking on her teats. A black pup was trying to push its way in, but the others kept kicking it away. Viv picked it up by the scruff. 'Bert reckons you should have this one,' she said, passing it over.

Robbie was confused, holding the pup in her palms, trying not to hug it to her chest, knowing she'd be lost if she did. 'I don't know, Viv,' she said. The pup started to lick her hands with its gravelly pink tongue. 'Why?'

'Well, he's not going to last in there,' Viv said, gesturing at the litter, which had settled comfortably now the runt was gone, paws kneading a teat each. 'Or out there,' she said. 'A black dog no good out here. He'll cook in the heat. Bert says you won't be here long, so you can take him back with you.'

For a second Robbie tried to make sense of this. Did Bert mean she would be leaving earlier than planned, or was he just saying that her project was not very long in the scheme of things? And was what Viv said even true: are there no black dogs in the desert?

It was a moment too long. The pup nuzzled in, licking her arm so that she instinctively drew him close, and then he was up at her neck, his paws hugging her. Robbie laughed and brought him to her face, smelling him. Viv grinned. 'He no bigger than a bullant, hey?'

*

At the waterhole, she turned on her side to watch the kids. The frog was gone and Robbie hoped he was safely snuggled in the mud. Suddenly a loud, wasp-like sound came from the sky. Robbie and the children looked up: a black thing as big as a bird was hovering above them. It was a drone, Robbie realised. It came lower, blinking two red lights, and tilted slightly as it flew over the waterhole. The kids stared, their mouths open. Then a chubby boy screamed, and they started to swim in a rush to the railing, slipping over one another as they pulled themselves up. A girl struggled in the chaos, sobbing, falling back into the pool and swallowing water. Lenny jumped in and hauled her onto the walkway. They stood in a wet huddle as the drone reversed and swung back to where Robbie was sitting. It hung above her. She could see its lens, hear it click and whirr, almost life-like in the way it peered at her.

Robbie stared back furiously. 'Fuck off!' she yelled. Then a rock smashed into its side. Lenny whooped, pumping his fist in the air. Robbie scrambled back onto the walkway as the kids flung rocks and handfuls of sand at it. The drone wobbled, and they cheered, digging around for more ammunition, their faces fierce. Robbie put her hand in the pocket of her shorts, pulled out the small sorry rock without thinking, and pinged it at the drone, striking between its red-light eyes. It tipped, and then another rock smashed into it, the drone swerving before crashing into the water. Robbie and the children froze, watching it sink.

Robbie swam in then and fetched it up from the bottom. 'Run!' she yelled when she surfaced, holding the black hexagonal shape aloft. On reflection it was childish, her telling them to run – it was silly to be scared of being told off – but in the moment they all turned heel and ran back across the scrub. Lenny laughed, clasping his sides as he ran, his cheetah legs wobbling, and soon they were all laughing, Robbie too, giggling and gasping in the hot, sticky air. They had to stop, stitches stabbing their chests. They sat on the ground, the laughing like an endless carousel. Whenever they settled, it took just one look between them to start it off again.

When the laughter finally died down, Robbie lay on her back in the dirt, her wet clothes drying. Her dripping hair wallowed in its own muddy puddle. She closed her eyes as the kids yabbered to one another, jumping up to re-enact the rock attack, the decisive blow, and then the escape. Later, back at the community, she gave the broken drone to them, watching as they pulled it apart like a pack of cockatoos. It was at night, in bed, that she remembered the sorry rock she'd thrown, now at the bottom of the waterhole.

*

Robbie was doing it again, running back over the scrub, though this time in the dark, trying to keep up with a group of teenagers, her orange speaker in one hand and Bullant nipping at her heels. She crawled under the fence that Viv held up for her. The boys had on backpacks that, as they hurried forward, clinked. Booze, Robbie figured.

Reg led the way. When they reached the empty car park, Robbie thought maybe they planned to walk to one of the caves. But Reg went to the little white gate where the climb began. He opened it and started to make his way up the eastern flank, Charlie following, then the three girls. Jay stood next to Robbie. He was wearing a backpack like the other two boys. He held out his hands for the speaker. Nervous, she gave it to him. 'What's going on, Jay?'

'You'll see,' he said, keeping the gate open with his foot. Bullant bolted in joyously, ignoring Robbie's whistle. She didn't move. She stared at the six teenagers. Reg was pulling himself up with the chain, while Charlie had sat at the bottom, next to the first metal pole, and was opening his backpack. *Fuck*, thought Robbie. *Fuck*. Charlie put on a pair of large goggles. Then he pulled out a long metal pipe with an orange tube, screwing it onto a butane canister. *Fuck*.

'Guys!' Robbie called, rushing forward. 'Hey, Charlie! Stop!'

Charlie froze.

Jay moved to block Robbie. 'You asked to come,' he said in a low, surly voice.

Robbie was panicking. 'Yeah, but,' she said, 'I didn't know —'

'What did you think? That we were planning on getting pissed and stoned?'

Robbie stepped back. She'd always thought of Jay as clownish – he often walked the community mouthing beatbox riffs – but now his face was taut with loathing. She dropped her shoulders, swallowed her pride. 'Yeah,' she replied. 'I was thinking that. I'm sorry, Jay.'

Jay looked surprised, then smiled. He reached into the pocket of his baggy shorts, producing a fat joint. 'Well,' he said, 'you were half-right.'

There was a shout. Reg had reached the top. He shot a flame above his head, lighting a small piece of sky. Charlie was doing the same thing with the blowtorch in his hands. Both boys studied their flames, twisting the dials, the flares growing, rustling as if alive, burning off yellow and orange feathers. Then they twisted the dials the other way, the flares turning sunset pink and into a long cylinder of white, greenish-blue at the base, purple at the tail. Reg crouched and held the torch to the metal pole sticking out of Uluru. Charlie did the same.

'Give this to Jez,' Jay said, without looking at Robbie, handing her the joint. Then he held onto the chain, pulling himself up towards Reg. Robbie balanced on the rock and climbed to the girls. Their eyes were big, taking in the orange slag splattering down the rock, sparks tumbling like Catherine wheels. *Shit, shit, shit*, Robbie thought.

This was fucking big. She looked out at the dark, wondering if she should walk back on her own. She touched Viv's arm. 'Viv,' Robbie said. Viv dragged her eyes away from the flames and stared at Robbie. 'Viv,' she said again, 'I shouldn't be here.' Jez and Rose looked at her too. 'Seriously, guys,' she continued, 'this is not something I should be part of. I shouldn't be here.'

Jez cackled. 'Well, you're here now.' She reached over and plucked the joint from Robbie's hand. Rose giggled. '*I shouldn't be here*,' Jez mimicked, parking the joint on her bottom lip. Rose produced a lighter and lit it. It was a kind of violence, Robbie thought, recognising the way the fourteen-year-old girl was wrenching her entire body to suck in the smoke, as if she knew no other way to receive pleasure.

Then, Jez slowly softened, her limbs loosening. She opened her eyes: warm and generous now. Lazily, she passed the joint to Rose, her slender wrist crowded with friendship bands. She smiled at Robbie and turned to face the top of Uluru. 'Woohoo!' she cheered, cupping her hands around her mouth. Jay peered over and waved. Jez leapt up, flicking her hair and doing a loose dance, rolling her hips. Jay grinned, waggling his hands in the air.

Then Reg appeared, further up. He knelt at a pole, applying the flame. He was already about six poles into the job, Robbie figured, working much faster than Charlie, who was still trying to cut through his first. When Reg straightened, Robbie could see a small orange ring, fat as a slug, at the base of the metal rod. 'Everyone ready?' he yelled and, without waiting for an answer, swung his foot and kicked the pole, snapping it at the neck. It made a dull thud as it fell, then a rattle and a clunk as the chain followed.

There was pause among the teenagers, as if the pole took a little longer to fall in their minds. Then Jay bounded over to Reg, lifting him up off the rock, the two toppling over. Jez and Rose hugged each other, and Viv climbed down to Charlie and put her arms around him. Rose nudged the joint between Robbie's fingers and joined Jez in dancing.

Robbie looked at the joint, unsure. Viv returned, flopping beside her, watching with a small smile. 'You want it?' Robbie asked, offering the joint.

Viv shook her head. 'Nah. Makes me crazy.'

The black pup scrambled onto Robbie's lap. The boys had their heads down again, working the torches. 'Fucking hell,' Robbie muttered. Viv began to laugh. Robbie took a toke, then another, and lay back, resting her head on Uluru, listening to the music.

＊

The stars seemed shinier now the joint was finished. Robbie's eyes felt sticky, like the night sky was snagging on her retinas. There was a pinkish glow directly above them. 'Is that Mars?' she asked. The girls followed the arc of her finger, but no one said anything.

Jez lit a cigarette and lay back, her hair sprawling over the rock. 'We can only say if it's in the shape of an emu,' she said dryly.

Rose elbowed her in the ribs. 'Come on, Jez,' she said, then looked over at Robbie. 'There's the emu,' she explained, tracing her finger in the air until the outline of a long-legged bird formed in Robbie's mind. 'And the Seven Sisters are over there,' she said, pointing to a cluster of extra-bright stars.

There was another clunk of the chain, this time closer to the girls, and they turned to watch the boys' progress. Reg and Charlie had done about forty poles altogether, the gap between them getting smaller. Jay was between the two, bobbing his head to the beats.

Then the flashing blue-and-red lights appeared on the horizon.

'Shit,' Robbie said quietly. Everyone stopped. The girls stood when two more sets of blue-and-red lights appeared.

The first cop car stopped at the tollbooth, the other two catching up. They could see the cops standing in their headlights, looking at the boom gates, talking into their radios. One of them pointed off to the side and they got back in their cars, swerving off the road and into the scrub.

Then, to the north, the camp dogs started howling. There was a shudder of fluorescent lights in the community houses, a movement of shapes on the verandahs. The girls stiffened. 'Mob's up,' Jez called. For a second everyone faltered; Robbie felt the teenagers waver.

'It's cool,' Reg yelled. 'Stay cool!' The rest of them looked at him. 'It's cool,' he said again.

Charlie nodded. He and Reg put their torches back to the poles they were working on, gas on, flame on. Hot metal spilled down the side of the rock. The three girls held hands and stared out at the community.

*

The sun was rising when the chain fell. It slithered down Uluru like a snake, poles ricocheting and catching on the odd ridge, Reg following and shifting them till they were loose, the chain slithering again. At the base, it lay coiled against the white picket gate, a nest of scrap metal, its power undone. The cop cars were waiting and the grown-ups, elders, some of the kids too. A line of buses, campervans and 4WDs stretched for a kilometre or so from the boom gates, rangers at the front, gesturing to them to turn around.

Robbie couldn't tell if Jack was there. She climbed down carefully with the others and was ignored, left to the side at the base as the teenagers stood in a line, their eyes downcast. The adults bustled around them, speaking loudly, shoving them in the chest with the flat of their palms. A woman slapped Viv, then did the same to Jez and Rose, and Robbie was stunned, feeling a heat in her cheek as if she too had been hit. She was about to go to them when there was a tap on her shoulder. Jack.

She braced herself, expecting him to start lecturing her, but his voice was urgent. 'Get in the car,' he said. 'You need to get your things. Your dad, he's gone missing.'

※

As Jack drove, Robbie called the nursing home. She'd thrown things in a bag and had Bullant on her lap. The director explained that Danny had gone missing in the night. The police had been there and were doing everything they could to find him.

'What do you mean he went missing?' she asked in a tight voice. 'What do you mean?'

The director spoke cautiously. Robbie knew instantly she had had advice on what to say. 'When the nurse for Mr O'Farrell's ward came in for her midnight shift, she noticed his bed was empty. Ms O'Farrell, I can assure you she raised the alarm immediately.'

Robbie exhaled sharply, covering her face with her hand.

'Ms O'Farrell?' said the director. 'Are you there? We have been trying to contact you since midnight – the police have been here and have his picture. We know this must be extraordinarily difficult for you. I can assure you —'

'I'm coming,' Robbie interrupted. 'Look, I'm at Uluru, it'll take me a few hours. I'm coming.'

The phone cut off then. Looking at the screen, she saw she had zero reception. Robbie lurched, and felt as though she was going to be sick. She flung the phone down and opened her door. Jack exclaimed as he swerved, braking. The car had barely stopped when Robbie flopped out of her seat, her knees in the gravel, and retched. There was nothing in her stomach but bile. Jack got out and came over.

He held her shoulders to stop her falling flat on her face. 'You're okay,' he said. 'You're okay.'

Robbie's hands were shaking. She felt bloodless, clammy. She couldn't breathe. Jack searched the floor of the car, coming back with a paper bag. He held it over her mouth, telling her to inhale. The bag buckled and inflated. In, out. It worked. Robbie felt the panic ease, the blood come back into her veins.

Carefully, Jack helped her to her feet and into the car. In the glove box, he pulled out a packet of jelly snakes, stuck together from the heat. He tugged one free and gave it to her, then another and another. Her hands stopped tingling; her colour returned. 'You okay?' he said. She nodded. He looked at the highway. 'Keep going?' Robbie nodded again, put her head back and closed her eyes. She listened to Jack call Bullant back in, felt the pup's warmth on her lap, wet nose in her hand, as the engine started.

'The airport won't be open,' Jack said. 'We can wait there for a couple of hours til it opens and see if we can get you on a plane, or we can drive to Alice?'

'Alice,' Robbie said numbly.

It was a four-hour drive. Whenever a phone tower loomed close, she used the reception to work on booking a flight and send messages to Otis and her mother. At a petrol station Jack came back with coffee and a sandwich for her, a hot dog for Bullant. He looked at the clock as he turned the ignition. 'Don't worry,' he said, 'we'll get there. We're making good time.'

Robbie sipped the coffee, hot enough to burn her tongue, and stared out the window as they turned back onto the road and passed an enclosure of emus. 'Thanks, Jack,' she said. 'For doing this.'

Jack looked at her inquiringly. 'To be honest, I'd rather be here than there. It's a fucking shitstorm. Everyone's calling. Pollies, media, the whole lot.'

Robbie nodded. She thought about Viv and Jez and Rose, how they had lined up with the boys, as if they'd been expecting it, the yelling and the slapping. 'What's going to happen to them?' she asked.

'I don't know. That's their business. I wouldn't have a clue.'

Robbie could feel Jack looking at her, wanting to ask why she'd been there, but he didn't. She closed her eyes, her fingers in Bullant's fur, and fell asleep, a restless sleep, her head bumping against the window.

When Jack woke her up, they were at the airport. She stared out without moving.

'Robbie,' Jack said, 'you gotta go.' He made to lift Bullant off Robbie's lap. She snatched the pup close. 'Robbie,' he said, 'they won't let you take him on the plane.' She stared at him. 'I'll look after him for you,' he said gently. 'I promise.'

Robbie looked down at the dog in her arms. What if someone put a pink X on him?

'Robbie,' Jack said, his voice strained. 'You'll miss your flight.'

Robbie checked the clock on the dash. *12.05.* She felt her heart start to beat too fast again. She forced her breathing to slow. 'Okay,' she muttered. 'Okay.' She looked at Jack. His eyes were the smoky green of gum leaves. She passed Bullant to him. 'Please don't let anything happen to him.'

Jack smiled. 'I won't, I promise.'

Robbie nodded. 'Thank you.' She opened the door, the metal frame creaking as she leant over to pick up her bag.

'I hope he's okay,' Jack said quickly. Robbie nodded again, not looking at him, tears finally coming. She wiped them away with the back of her hand and headed towards the sliding glass doors, against the small tide of people coming out and recoiling at the heat.

*

Nasim met Robbie at the airport, and in a taxi they went straight to the nursing home. The manager met them out the front, giving Nasim a defensive look as she led them in through reception. 'The police have been,' she said in a tight, nervous voice. She tugged at her sleeves. Her clothes were wrinkled. 'We spent the whole night going over the surveillance footage to get a sense of what happened.'

Hearing this, Robbie snapped to attention. 'I'd like to see it too.'

The manager shook her head. 'No need. We identified when your father left his ward and the building. The police are looking for him.'

'I'd still like to see it,' Robbie said, a steeliness entering her voice.

The manager looked as though she was going to fight Robbie on it, then changed her mind. 'Okay,' she said. 'I can set it up in here for you to watch.' She looked pointedly at Nasim. 'And you too?'

Robbie nodded. 'Yes, my friend too.'

The manager showed the women to a desk, where they sat in front of three screens: one with footage from Danny's ward, one from the corridor, the last from the entrance.

'What the fuck?' Robbie said when she saw her father sit up in bed and look around before unlatching the cot side. He swung his legs out and lowered himself onto the floor, stretching out his hand to his walking frame. He went to the drawers and took out a pair of pants, wobbling as he lassoed a leg on each foot, pulling them over his pyjamas. He tugged a woollen jumper over his nightshirt, slipped on his moccasins and made for the open doorway, pushing the walking frame in front. Robbie shook her head in astonishment. 'You are fucking kidding me.' She tapped on the second screen to play.

He was in the corridor now, shuffling at an achingly slow pace towards the exit. On the third screen, the sliding glass doors were shut, the car park empty. Robbie watched the timer tick over. At 22.05 PM, the glass doors opened, and Danny emerged. He looked around the car park cautiously. Swinging the frame out in front, he lunged towards the street. He went under the camera and the women could see the top of his head, a small bald patch in the centre, like a bird's egg. He veered to the right. Then he was gone.

*

At the police station, Nasim waited outside. The officer at the desk asked Robbie to sit down, but she couldn't, pacing instead. When Otis arrived, she burst into tears. They hugged. 'You're kidding me?' Otis said when she told him about how Danny had walked himself out of there.

A policewoman came out to see them, ushering the siblings into a small room. 'We're taking it very seriously,' the woman said kindly. 'We've done numerous callouts, we've got every cop car on the road aware of it, foot patrol too. We'll call you if anything comes up.'

'Can you tell me where you've checked?' Robbie asked.

The woman looked tired. 'No, I'm sorry, I can't be exact. I can assure you we are looking – but to be clear, Ms O'Farrell, there are a lot of missing people out there. We'll need you to do some of the heavy lifting. Put a call out to your networks, check his old haunts.'

Robbie and Otis rang around and posted on Facebook. They went to the familiar locations. Nasim offered to come, but the siblings preferred to be on their own. Something about going back to those places; they didn't want to be observed. Plus, it was nice to be together, the two of them. In Otis's car, they drove to the school where Danny had been caretaker, and to their old townhouse. They even drove to Half Moon Bay, cursing the lycra-clad cyclists taking up the road.

On the beach, they were the only ones there, and sank into the sand in dismay.

That night she stayed in Claire and Nathan's flat, waiting for them to fly home. After Otis left, she lay on the couch, the television on, wondering where their father was right then, where he was sleeping.

She barely registered when the news began. But then a camera zoomed in on Uluru and Robbie sat up quickly, grabbing the remote, stabbing at the buttons to increase the volume. There was a close-up of the coiled chain on the ground, then archival footage of school groups in the 1950s and 1960s doing the climb, students' hands waving in that strange sped-up way of 8mm film. She started when Jack appeared in the frame. He looked wary, pausing before he spoke, considering the reporter's question. 'I think the community is pretty divided over this,' he said. 'I think people are scared.' He was cut off, the camera switching to another shot of Uluru.

Robbie changed the channel frantically. Jack reappeared on ABC News 24, unedited. 'I think the community is pretty divided over this. I think people are scared. You probably know this,' he said, looking directly at the reporter, 'but when Bob Hawke gave the title back to the Anangu in 1985, at the last minute he put in a protection so that Australians still had a right to climb Uluru, so it wasn't really a complete handback. Similarly,' he added, 'in 2007, the Howard government temporarily extinguished native title, obviously without the permission of the Anangu people.' Jack squinted. 'That was only seven years ago. So, I think many of the elders would have loved to kick that chain down, but I'm not sure they're entirely convinced they're out of chains yet themselves.' The reporter seemed pleased with that.

All night, Robbie watched the news broadcasts, switching between stations and searching the internet. Jack appeared again and again. Robbie smiled. He spoke so evenly, she thought, that he seemed untouched by anger. She felt a tug in her chest, seeing his green eyes and tangled red hair.

At one point she gave a yell and quickly paused the player on her laptop, then dragged the status bar back, stopping on a single frame. She leaned in closer and started to laugh. Jay was behind the reporters and all the others milling around. He was walking across the frame, his middle finger defiantly up, her orange speaker in his other hand.

*

The next day, Claire and Nathan arrived. Her mother was pale and worried, but also determined. She hugged Robbie. She already had a handful of flyers she'd printed in transit.

At the nursing home, they set out from the corner where Robbie had seen him disappear in the CCTV footage, with Claire in the lead.

They walked beside the road that split into three lanes and over a footbridge, alongside a sprawling golf course, then splintering off into streets. At each turn, Claire paused and then, as if finding his scent, strode on. They passed houses and blocks of flats and vacant blocks until they came to a shopping strip. The traffic lights were confusing, and people were walking across the middle of the road in front of oncoming trams.

'Mum,' Robbie called out as they crossed with a small crowd. 'Mum!' On the other side, Claire stopped. 'Mum,' said Robbie, 'there's no way he could've walked this far. How would he have even crossed here?'

Claire frowned. 'Honey, we didn't even know he could get out of bed by himself. Just a bit more. C'mon, Robbie.'

Claire moved quickly, in and out of shops, down alleys, looking in bus shelters, pausing to tape flyers on every pole. Nathan did the other side of the avenue, disappearing ahead of them. Then Claire stopped at a small street that had a park with a playground nudged against a fence, shielding it from the train tracks on the other side. A group of homeless people were sitting on benches, surrounded by striped bags, shopping trolleys and sleeping bags. 'There,' she said, almost calmly, pointing at Danny. He was sitting with his back to them, his walking frame on the tanbark nearby. A woman beside him was talking loudly, nattering into her chest. Robbie was about to lunge forward but Claire grabbed her jumper, holding her back. She had her phone out. 'No, Robbie,' she said. 'Sabeen should do it.'

Her mother was right. Danny had forgotten them, yes, but he couldn't ever shake them completely. There was always the possibility they might ignite something inside him.

Claire phoned the nursing home and it was Nasim who arrived in a taxi and said hello to Danny in the playground, who held his arm as he said goodbye to his new friends, who sat with him in the patient transport, calming him with her chatter and making him feel he was returning home. Robbie stood at a distance and felt a familiar bleakness. How many times had he died now, in her heart?

In her mother's flat, she showered, letting the hot water scald her. She slept for two nights and a day. Her mother urged her to return to Uluru, to her project, saying that she and Nathan would take care of things. They dropped her at the airport. Claire kissed her, trying not to make a fuss when Robbie let Nathan hug her goodbye.

This time, flying in, Uluru was blood red. When Robbie saw it, she felt something revive in her. Jack was on the footpath waiting, Bullant beside him. The puppy looked bigger, and he leapt all over her. Jack grinned, showing her the tricks he'd taught Bullant. 'Shake hands,' he said, and Bullant solemnly lifted a paw. 'Drop.' The dog dropped, black paws out, brown eyes on Robbie. 'Roll over,' said Jack. He rolled over, exposing his pink belly. 'Play dead?' Bullant sprang up, tail wagging. Robbie let the dog lick her as Jack shook his head. 'He refuses to do that one.'

In the car, he looked over at her as he drove. 'You okay?'

'Sort of,' she said. 'But I'll be okay.' She smiled bravely, expecting Jack to smile back, but he didn't. He nodded absently, his eyes nervous. He cleared his throat. Robbie felt a prickling on the back of her neck. 'What?' she asked. 'What is it?'

'I need to tell you something,' he said nervously.

'What?'

'The community. It's pretty quiet there at the moment.' Jack faltered. He looked straight ahead, at the road. Robbie dipped her head, waiting for the next sentence as if it were a wave she hadn't judged properly.

'Why? Because of the climb?'

Jack sighed. He shook his head. 'No. It's sorry business.' His knuckles were white on the steering wheel. Robbie felt her breath snag. Bullant whined thinly and she realised she had been gripping the pup too hard.

'Who?' she said softly, releasing her hands.

The radio crackled between them as a voice came on. 'Jack? You there?' the voice said. Jack threw Robbie an apologetic look and picked up the radio. 'Yep, here.'

'Can you come to the western flank, the waterhole section? We've got a walker down.'

Jack pressed the button. 'Yep, I can be there in ten. Serious?'

'Breathing but pulse is weak. Ambos are on their way too.'

'Okay.' Jack put the radio back in its holder. He avoided looking at her. 'Sorry.'

Robbie felt her blood thrashing, a roaring in her ears. 'It's okay,' she said. 'You can drop us at the road in on your way past. But tell me who?'

Jack shoved his hand through his hair, rubbing his forehead. 'I should have told you before. I'm sorry. I should have. But I didn't want you not to come back.'

Robbie watched him and felt a ribbon of warmth go through her. She reached over and put her hand on his cheek. 'It's okay. Just tell me now.'

'Charlie.'

Robbie jerked back. *Charlie*. The word was like a siren. 'Charlie?' Her voice sounded hollow in her ears, faraway. She saw that Jack was crying. Not heaving or gasping, just tears sliding down his cheeks, catching on his lip, a short drop to his chin and down again. Robbie thought of Uluru, how the rain curved down the rock's features. It was just there, out the window.

'How?'

Jack sniffed. He wiped his nose with his sleeve. 'Used the cord on a toaster. Viv found him.' The words were spooling out now. 'She tried to hold him up, to keep him breathing, but he was too heavy. You know how big he was.' *Was*. Jack looked at her, his eyes glassy. Robbie tried to nod. *Was*. She felt as though she were underwater, lying on her back, watching waves pass over her.

The radio crackled again. 'Jack? What's your ETA?'

Jack stared at the radio. 'Fuck!' he said, kicking the car above the accelerator. Bullant startled, triangle ears up.

Robbie willed herself to the surface. 'It's okay, Jack, it's okay.'

The turnoff was coming up. Jack pulled over. A vein throbbed furiously on his neck. Robbie put her palm on it, felt it twitch like a bug beneath the surface. 'Come back after? Soon as you can?' she said. He nodded, his lips pressed together. 'It's okay,' she said again.

Jack's shoulders dropped, his face softening a little. 'Right,' he said, trying to pull himself together. 'See you soon.'

Cracking open the door, she dropped her boots onto the shimmering bitumen and the heat threw itself over her.

It was quiet, walking in. She and Bullant turned a bend and saw a lizard poised in the middle of the road, neck up and long tail swishing. Bullant tore after it, and it scampered into the scrub, whipping its tail. When they got close to the community, Robbie saw a truck drive out from the gates. She stood to the side of the road to let it pass, whistling at Bullant to stay close. Two men, sitting high in the cabin, stared as they passed. An uneasy feeling came over her. She began to jog. She could only see a few cars – Bert's red Mazda, Eileen's ute and a couple of others up at the workers' quarters. Then she saw the cages, the wire doors flung open, the dogs gone.

'Bert!' Robbie yelled as she ran over to the cages.

He was lying in the dirt, his stockman's clothes dusty, his face bleeding. 'Oh fuck, Bert,' Robbie said, kneeling next to him. He moaned as Robbie patted him down to see if he was injured. 'What happened?'

Bert moaned again and sat up woozily. 'They came and got 'em,' he said. 'Knocked me over when I wouldn't let them.' Robbie balled the bottom of her T-shirt and dabbed at his face. She found a cut on his brow, just above his right eye. It was small, but bleeding a lot. She looked around for something better to stem the flow and spied a piece of mattress foam a few metres away.

'What are you doing here, Bert?' she asked when she returned.

'The dogs,' he mumbled. 'I couldn't leave the dogs.' He looked up then, gazing at the empty cages, the ground covered with dog shit. He put his palms on the dirt and pushed himself up, standing unsteadily. 'I've gotta go get 'em,' he said. He loped sideways, shuffling towards his car.

Robbie leapt to her feet. 'You're still bleeding, Bert.' He put his hand up, waving it over his shoulder, dismissing her. She beat him to the Mazda and stood in front of the driver's door, blocking it. 'I'll drive,' she said. He glared and started talking, words she couldn't understand. 'I'll drive,' she said again.

Bert narrowed his eyes, thinking. Then he shuffled to the other side of the car, Bullant pushing past him to the back seat, tongue out.

The keys were in the ignition. 'Where to?' Robbie asked.

'The tip.'

*

Bert sat forward, hands on the dash. His lips twitched, murmuring something to himself. The blood was drying, red creek beds now set-tled in the lines on his face. 'Faster,' he hissed, as Robbie sped down the road towards Yulara. Later, she had to remember everything, had to retell it to the police to the best of her ability: the cars they overtook; how she drove around the roundabout twice, not knowing which way to go; how they went past the campground and a building site, to the tip behind. She remembered each detail, but nothing of what was in her head, or how it switched from Bert to her, how he'd slumped when they pulled alongside the cyclone fence, seeing the men sitting on overturned milk crates next to a yawning hole, steadying the butts of their guns on their thighs, the truck's tray lowered. How Bert let it go and Robbie took it up, she couldn't remember. There were the dogs, their bodies tangled as they tumbled out, claws skidding on the metal slope, trying to get back into the truck, away from the stutter-ing gunshots.

It was Robbie who got out of the car. 'Stay,' she snapped at Bullant, the pup pining as she ran to the entrance, ducking under the boom gate. The men were cheering each hit, the dogs somersaulting, yelping, bending and twisting before landing with a thump. Robbie could see them in the pit as she got closer, some still alive and stuck underneath the others, periscope tails waving. A man stepped in front of her, a big guy with tatts on his arms, the Velcro on his orange work vest pressed together carelessly, the hems mismatched. 'Private prop-erty,' he said, the other men pausing their shooting. They stared at her while the dogs kept falling out of the truck, cowering in the pit, trying to climb up its sides. Robbie saw the men had beer cans in stubby holders next to their feet.

'I said,' the man growled, 'private property. Get out of here.'

Robbie moved to pass around him and he stepped to the side, blocking her. She went to go the other way and he followed. His eyes bulged. 'You want me to call the police?'

Robbie looked at him, at the red capillaries on his nose. In the hole the dogs were screaming. Sharp and constant, the sound scraped at her.

'Listen, bitch,' the man said, 'we got a contract to do this. So I'll say it one more time. Get the fuck off this property.'

Robbie was breathing fast, and the man's face swam. She couldn't focus on it all, only specific parts – an eye, a squarish tooth, the sunburnt cartilage of his ear.

A dog came up the side of the pit, its claws scrabbling to get a hold. It managed to pull itself up. It kept its eyes lowered and flattened itself onto the ground, trying for invisibility as it shimmied along the dirt. One of the men sitting on the milk crates got up and walked over. He kicked it back over the side with his boot. The dog disappeared with a yelp.

The sound flicked a switch deep inside her. She swung at the man in front of her, hearing a flabby *thwack* as she connected with his chest. He barely budged. He laughed, a grunting noise. Robbie looked past him into the pit. Dogs were writhing like maggots, their jaws fastened on one another, a swarm of pink Xs. 'Listen, you stupid bitch,' the man said, and she spat on him, a slag of white right on his face.

When he socked her, it was like being hit with a brick. She fell backwards into the dirt, away from the hole. Instinctively she twisted, hunching over and tucking her knees in under her ribs. She held the side of her face, the pain pulsing. There was screaming in her ears, and it was only later that she realised the sound was coming from her, a high-pitched yelping, short and sharp, just like one of the dogs.

Spirit Riders

Amos Bald Buzzard Homey lay on the ridge and lined up a shot next to the opening of the burrow. It was on dusk. The jackrabbit put its nose out, its enormous feathery ears flattening cautiously as it sniffed the air. As it hopped forward, Amos shot it clean through the head.

Back at the bus, he took out his flick-knife and cut a slit in the back of its neck, sinking his fingers in the pink. With his free hand he kneaded the hare's flesh, cracking its bones like knuckles as he shrugged the skin off. Squatting next to the fire, Gerry fed twigs into the flames and watched Amos intently, admiring the way he coaxed the hare into reverse, his hands swift, as though turning out a sweater. Amos's dark hair fell over his eyes as he worked. A thin silver chain rippled around his neck like a live creature. When he was done he dumped the hide in a bucket of water, which rose to splash Elliott, who had set up nearby in a plastic lounge chair.

'Watch it!' Elliott warned, as he lifted his sculpted, smooth legs off the ground.

Amos didn't say anything. He cut off the hare's head and feet, tossing them in the fire. The large ears caught alight first. Then he settled on the dirt next to Eva and slit open the hare's belly over a wooden chopping board.

'Ew,' Elliott moaned theatrically, as guts started to ooze out. 'Gross.'

Without looking up, Amos flicked the intestine out with the nib of his blade, the wet, stringy organ landing in Elliott's lap. Elliott screamed as he leapt up, shaking the skirt of his dress. ('It's not blue, Gerry darling,' he had corrected earlier in the day, 'it's cobalt.') 'That's disgusting!'

Gerry sniggered, unable to help himself. '*You!*' Elliott pointed a long black finger accusingly. 'Don't *you* dare.' Gerry held up his hands, trying to stop the laughter. He almost had it under control but suddenly snorted, which set him off again, and Eva too.

All the while Amos kept his head down, shuffling the innards, separating the heart, liver and kidneys, reddish brown and thick as menstrual blood. Finally, when Gerry and Eva stopped laughing, Eva leaned over to pluck the intestine out of the dirt, flinging it into the trees.

Elliott sat back down and pouted in the darkness. 'Tell your brother he's an asshole.'

Eva tilted her head slightly. 'You're an asshole, Amos.'

'Thanks, sis,' Amos replied.

Amos had no time for Elliott. From the first evening, there had been an inflexible dislike between them, owing mostly to Amos. Elliott had offered his hand, swan-like, but Amos refused to take it. Since then, Elliott had upped the ante, laying on the theatrics in an effort to get under Amos's skin.

'You know,' Elliott said now, swinging his ankle so that his sequined slipper dangled off his big toe, 'every man who doesn't like drag queens has a little boy inside of him who just wanted so badly to dress up in Mommy's things.'

After a long pause, Amos looked at Elliott, his black eyes unrevealing. 'I won't be in your show,' he said.

Elliott kicked off his slipper so that it thwacked against the chair. 'I'd never cast you, darling.'

Eva rolled her eyes and looked teasingly at Gerry. 'I wanna be in your play, babe,' she said, both of them laughing again. It was cruel, but Amos's arrival seemed to be shifting Eva and Gerry closer together, edging Elliott out of the tight trio they'd formed over the past three weeks.

Amos tossed the remaining innards into the fire. They sizzled, the guts sweating and crisping, smelling delicious. Cutting the meat into strips, Amos scraped it into a bowl with the heart, liver and kidneys. He held the bowl out to Elliott. 'Wash this in the river.'

Elliott folded his legs. 'No.'

Eva glanced at Gerry, the orange flames of the fire between them. He stood to take the bowl instead, but Amos snatched it away. 'No, Elliott can do it. I been with you three for, what, two days now, and I haven't seen *him* do a thing.'

'I do a lot, thank you very much,' Elliott said. 'I provide plenty.'

'What, pills and acid? Joints? You call that providing?'

Elliott fluttered his lashes, his teeth shining in the moonlight. 'Yes, I do, and I think you'll find, hairless birdman, I'm far more sought after than you, with your fiddly rodent.'

Gerry couldn't help but laugh. Amos glared at him. Gerry held up his palms. 'Don't get angry at me,' he said. He put out his hand and took the bowl before Amos could move it away again. 'I'll do it.'

Eva scrambled to her feet. 'I'll come too.'

She put her hand in Gerry's as they picked their way through the tall pines with rough, furrowed trunks. The moon cast a silvery light over the woods, the pine needles crushing underfoot. It smelled earthy. They could hear the slip of the river, where it slowed and wound its way around an ancient tumble of boulders.

Gerry stopped suddenly, and Eva bumped into him. 'Look,' he

whispered. On a low bough, a skunk was watching them. It had a thumbprint of white fur between its beady eyes.

'Oh, he's lovely,' whispered Eva. A noise snapped the dark and the skunk bounded away, its soft movement seamless, as if a marionette suspended on invisible strings.

They reached the riverbank and climbed down the round, smooth rocks. Gerry's hands went numb in the water as he washed the meat. 'You think Elliott will come with us?' he asked.

Eva sat down, propping her boots on another rock. She stared at the stars and was quiet for a time. 'No,' she said eventually. 'I don't think so.'

*

The instant he landed at LAX, Gerry knew that he had gotten it wrong. It hit him plain in the face. For a year and a half he'd worked three jobs to save up for this trip, and not once had he considered the moment he would actually land in the States. Not fucking once. It was as though he'd watched a rubber band as it was stretched further and further away from his face and hadn't thought, *that'll snap*. He'd figured he would get a car and head out to Joshua Tree. He knew the highways were meant to be a nightmare. But he'd never thought it would *feel* wrong, being there. He'd been so convinced the trip would be the answer, the solution, that he hadn't even thought, *what if it isn't?*

Still, he went through the motions. What else was he going to do? He took a taxi from the airport to a used-car yard with a white trailer on blocks surrounded by jeeps, sedans, SUVs and station wagons. Two dogs reared on their hind legs, slobbering and yanking on their chains, when Gerry walked by. A salesman sat in the trailer smoking a cigarillo and watched through the doorway as Gerry looked around. Several cars were parked on lengths of sloping plywood. Gerry ignored them. He remembered his dad saying to a salesman years ago,

'You trying to sell me a pregnant bitch?' Toohey had shown Gerry how the slope was disguising the car's sagging metal chassis. Most likely the suspension had gone to shit, he'd explained.

Gerry stood behind a Ford sedan, studying its lines for bends and warping. It had clearly been totalled and beaten back into shape. He moved on, stopping at a shiny black Honda. Its lines were straight. He walked around it, picturing the car in pieces, putting it back together. There was some rust, but he didn't plan on having it forever. He walked a few steps backwards to check that the tyres were aligned.

'You want to take a look inside?' The salesman, a wiry man in a blue-and-purple parachute tracksuit, had come over. He held out a squareish key. 'Where you headed?' he asked, when Gerry took it.

'Probably Palm Springs,' Gerry mumbled, opening the Honda. The interior stank of spearmint and cigarettes.

The engine fired easily. Gerry dropped the gears, pumped the brakes, and checked the wipers, indicator and lights.

'Happy for you to take it for a test drive,' the salesman said, as Gerry contemplated the bumper-to-bumper traffic. Gerry popped the bonnet instead. He put his hands in the engine and felt around like he'd watched his dad do, feeling along the saddle for grit, signs of welding. He checked the hoses for leaks and undid the caps, turning them over. Held the dipstick under his nose, sniffing. The salesman watched him shrewdly. 'Where you from?'

'Australia,' Gerry replied, keeping his eyes on the engine, slipping his hand under the belt and stretching it.

The salesman perked up. 'Australia, hey? You know Melboorne? I got a cousin there.'

Not wanting to chat, Gerry shook his head. 'It's a big place.'

It wasn't a great rig, but he could get in there, maintain it. The price, $1095, was written on the windscreen in white texta. 'I'll give you a thousand dollars, cash.'

The salesman grinned like it was too easy. 'Deal.' He held out his hand. Reluctantly, Gerry took it.

In the trailer, after counting the cash and signing the paperwork, the salesman looked at him before he slid the key over. 'Listen, kid, only advice I got for you is this. You get pulled over, you put your hands on the dash. You don't move them. If a cop asks for ID, you ask 'em if you're allowed to get it. I'm saying this because you're not from here.'

The rattle of the dog chains made Gerry flinch as he walked back to the Honda. Carefully he drove the car out and into the long centipede of traffic, inching past grimy bungalows with barred windows, convenience stores protected by metal grilles, boarded-up squats. The road was framed with billboards: the rectangles spun atop buildings, were lined up along walls. There were advertisements for lap-band surgery, coconut water, Burger King, libel lawyers – men with hammy moustaches and wide Texan hats – and churches: *Meet Reverend Steve. He Doesn't Have All the Answers But He Knows Who Does.*

Gerry furtively scanned the people in other cars, jaws flapping even when there was only the driver. Men with chests like Chesterfields, their flesh buttoned tightly into their shirts. Women with plastic talons glued to their fingers, driving with small dogs on their laps. Young guys who drove like they were wrestling an alligator, whipping out the back of their car like a tail, weaving forward. Gerry felt a fucking fool. How old was he when he got hooked on the idea of America? Eight, nine? He'd had this perfect image of the southwest, all Lone Star and hard men with good hearts. It wasn't as if he had his head in the sand; he had watched *The Wire*, Michael Moore, all that stuff, seen the endless school shootings on his feed, but his idea of the southwest, his cowboy country, had remained like a jewel lodged in his mind.

Gerry tried to restrain the panic as he drove in loops, spaghetti highways tossing him from one concrete strip to the next. He'd set his phone up at the airport but the wheel on his GPS turned lazily, refusing to focus. The square green signs announcing each turnoff only made sense to Gerry once he'd passed them.

What was he doing here? The question went around his head. His T-shirt was clammy with sweat. It was hard to breathe. The city seemed crushed into history already, a length of strata, thin as bible paper; a patina of dust, smog and concrete. In the flat grey sky, the orange sun dribbled like a split yolk. For fifteen seconds or so, Gerry took his foot off the accelerator, the other cars belting past as the Honda slowed. What if he just stopped? Would someone come to tow him? Would they tell him if he could take his hands off the dash?

Eventually the traffic began to spread out. Hummers, coupes and sedans were peeling off, and the Honda didn't feel so hemmed in. Behind him Los Angeles was a hazy glow, buildings pocked with window-shaped embers. Gerry swung out at the next exit, not even bothering to read the sign, and he was spat into the desert, the road blistered with truck lights. He drove, too scared to stop, and for two weeks he travelled like that. He shat out hard knots in gas-station toilets and drove grimly from campsite to campsite. Every day he raced the sun, desperate to arrive before it got dark.

At night he didn't bother with a fire. He didn't use his cooker, eating what he bought from the gas stations in his sleeping bag, shivering and listening, worrying about bears and worrying about people with guns. He wondered if he ought to buy one and shut his head up once for and all.

Gerry pictured his father's satisfaction if he came home early, his charade of perplexity. 'What, you couldn't do a little campervan trip in the *States*?' Gerry could hear it. 'I did three tours of the Middle East and you can't even stick out a few weeks in California?'

He took up smoking. Sucking on the white sticks for sustenance, like his father did. Days went by when he didn't speak to anyone.

His head felt like a nest of broken things. A couple of times he tried getting drunk, downing a bottle of bourbon in his tent, but his father's voice only got louder. *You fucking stupid, Gerry? What's your plan, Gerry? You look like a faggot, Gerry.* His father, knocking on his head like a door. *Knock, knock. Anyone home, Gerry?*

One night he punched himself. He rammed his fists into his face and his ears, boxed his own skull, searching out the soft parts and crushing his knuckles against them. Then he zipped his sleeping bag all the way up and sobbed, a muffled howling. In the morning his face was a bloodied mess.

A few times he stopped at tourist attractions. Took photos. He bought postcards and never sent them. He drove past a jail that had a neon *VACANCY* sign flashing out the front. And near the Mexican border he kept his hands on the dash while a policeman shone a torch in his face, another cop looking under the Honda.

'What you doing out here?'

'Camping.'

'Let me guess, you're a birdwatcher?'

'No.'

'A warning: you pick anyone up out here and we'll take you in too.'

'Okay, sir.'

How easily it came to him, this obligingness. He disgusted himself. 'Okay, sir,' he said as he drove on, mimicking himself. 'Okay, sir. May I lick your balls, sir?'

Gerry never saw anyone come out of the desert to flag him down. But then, he made a point of not looking. *You see what you want to see, and you don't see what you don't want to see.* One of his father's sayings.

So, did he want to see Eva? Even though all that was visible was her calves and lace-up boots sticking out from under the bus? God, yes.

The brightly painted vehicle was parked in a clearing on the side of the highway. A jack was wedged precariously underneath. Next to it a set of legs were twisted like liquorice, trying to dig the heels of their brown leather boots into the gravel. Gerry pulled over and parked a little way off. As he approached the bus, he could hear the person grunting and the *ping, ping, ping* of metal on metal. 'Fuck, shit, fuck!'

Gerry knelt. He glimpsed the back of the girl, much of her hidden in shadow as she cursed, her upper body, mostly shoulders and arms, trying to force a wrench downwards. She had a gold-and-brown cobra tattooed on one of her calves. The snake's hood flattened as it reared up behind her knee.

'Hey,' he called uncertainly, and the girl jumped, banging her head. 'Ow!'

'Sorry, I —' Gerry stopped talking as she scrambled out, holding the lug wrench aloft. She was so unexpected: her short dark hair flopping over grey eyes, her small ears rattling with silver jewellery, and a thin white scar running up the side of her neck like a single gill, luminous against her ruddy skin, mottled with freckles. Even her lips had a dusting of the tiny mud-brown spots. But it wasn't just her; his own reaction caught him off-guard, the way his breath snared in his throat. He had become so used to the loathing and the highway. The bone-dry deserts. The lakes in massive stone basins that looked like drained baths, rimmed with algae. He'd felt ugly and could only see ugly, but she was exquisite.

She looked at Gerry and he found it hard to return her gaze, his eyes slipping nervously to the side. After a pause, she seemed to relax, and loosened her grip on the wrench. She kicked an old tyre that was lying on the ground. 'I got the first one out fine, but the second is being a bitch.'

'You want me to try?' Gerry winced at his voice. His words felt lumpy, unused for so long.

'Sure,' the girl said. She handed him the wrench. 'If you do get them off,' she added, 'it's probably because I already loosened them for you.' Gerry nodded solemnly and she grinned. 'I'm kidding!' She wiped her greasy hands on her top, a faded turquoise Miami Dolphins T-shirt. Savaged into shorts, her black jeans stopped at the knees. Gerry felt himself blush. He crawled quickly under the hood of the wheel hub. In the oily darkness he breathed freely, gathering himself. He placed the wrench over a fat lug and tried to spin it downwards. His hand slipped.

'Fucking hell,' he said. 'Someone put them on tight.'

'It's those stupid machines,' the girl called back. 'The ones they use at mechanics. They put them on too tight.'

Gerry repositioned himself, coiling his body so he was inside the hub. Steadying the wrench around the lug nut, he put his weight on it and pushed down. He felt a small movement. He did it three more times, finally getting it, the bolt easing free. When he held it out, the girl whooped: 'Yes!'

It took twenty minutes to take out the rest of the bolts. Gerry was hot, aching from being bunched up, but he didn't want it to end. When he crawled out, handing her the last bolt, the girl did a victory dance and he felt like weeping. *Go back to the car, drive to Catalina, set up the tent, eat tuna from the tin, sleep.*

'You did it!' the girl said, clapping.

Gerry allowed himself a lopsided smile. 'Only because you loosened them,' he said.

The girl snorted and punched him playfully on the arm. They both looked at the tyre Gerry had rolled out. It was bald and tattered. Gerry shook his head at it. 'Where's your spare?'

'That is the spare.'

'Oh?' A small gust of hope picked up in Gerry's chest.

'It's okay. Elliott's gone to get a new one.'

'Oh.' The gust died. 'Well —'

'I'm Eva.' She stuck out her hand.

Gerry took her hand without looking at her. 'Hey.'

'And you are?'

'Gerry. Well, I better get going.' He started walking back to the Honda. He'd left the door wide open.

'Where are you going?'

Gerry felt a twinge of annoyance at the girl. 'Catalina,' he said, turning to answer her.

'Oh. Okay.' She shrugged. 'Well, thanks.'

Gerry nodded. 'No worries.'

In the Honda, Gerry tried not to feel revolted by the empty drink cans and chip packets. He put his hands on the wheel. They were streaked with grease. He sighed. Jumped when she tapped on the glass.

'Do you *have* to be in Catalina?' Eva asked, when he wound the window down. Gerry was barely able to answer. He shook his head. 'Then have a drink with me,' she said.

＊

The bus's original interior had been gutted and replaced with a small kitchen and a booth with yellow vinyl seats and a laminex table bolted to the floor. At the rear, where the back seat would have been, there was a double mattress piled with pillows, a ginger cat asleep in a wave of linen, curled like a croissant. A guitar was propped in the corner, and books spilled over the floor; the ceiling was strung with fake vines and flowers. Dozens of tiny cacti sat snug in eggcups on the table while streaks of flour and grains of rice were stuck to the kitchen bench. Brown bananas lay next to a sticky blender. Near the folding door, Gerry read the chalkboard leaned against the wall. *Pancakes! Freshly squeezed juice! Smoothies!*

Eva filled two metal cups with rum and squeezed a lime in, let-ting the juice run through her fist. 'Let's sit outside,' she said, grabbing a leather pouch on her way out. Gerry followed her across the red-dish earth, the cactuses cartoonish with their prickly arms sticking out like traffic wardens.

Eva stopped at a bunch of rocks and climbed to the tallest one, balancing the cups. Clumsily, Gerry followed. 'Cheers,' she said, when they were settled. They clinked cups. Opening the leather pouch, Eva chatted as she rolled a joint, Gerry eying it warily. She told Gerry that she and her friend Elliott had driven out from San Diego for the summer and were planning to finish up at Burning Man in Nevada.

'You've never heard of it?' She looked at Gerry in amazement. 'Oh my god, you'd love it.' She described a week-long party with thousands of people. 'No, not a party,' she corrected, 'a gathering. Everyone turns up in the middle of nowhere and builds a city in the desert. At the end of the week, everything is burnt.' She smiled wist-fully. 'Leave no trace.' She lit the joint, exhaling in a swirl. 'You should come with us,' she said, passing him the joint.

Gerry shrugged. He was pretty sure he wouldn't love it. Trying to seem casual, he took a toke. He'd only had a few joints in his life; a girl he'd been sleeping with for a few weeks had been into it, always bringing a spliff when they hooked up. They'd made him feel strange – not in a way to make him not like it, but not enough to enjoy it either. The girl, Tilley, would go all breathy and giggly. It had annoyed him. The joint didn't seem to alter Eva; she sat upright, humming as she took it, chatting seamlessly through the smoke.

She and Elliott, she continued, had gone out with the Border Angels near the Mexican border. 'We put out bottles of water for peo-ple crossing the desert.' She tilted her face enquiringly at Gerry. 'Do you think that's stupid? Elliott was a total bitch about it. He thought it was a dumb idea, that no one would find them.' She looked at Gerry intently. 'What do you think?'

Gerry tried to work out what to say, feeling an odd, faraway panic. The joint crackled between his fingers. A ripple of nausea passed through him, his hands suddenly clammy. 'I don't know,' he mumbled. 'How many people are crossing? I guess it depends on heaps of things.'

Eva nodded. 'Well, it felt better than doing nothing. And the people in the Border Angels, they'd heard from migrants who managed to cross that they found the water.'

'That's good,' Gerry managed to say. It was getting on. He stared at the Honda turning to shadow and leaned towards it like an animal keen to return to its den. He fumbled in his pocket for his cigarettes, tapping one out, hoping it would steel him. He sucked it weakly. He felt woozy. Eva's hands flitted as she spoke. He felt the colour drain from his face. 'I've gotta go,' he said abruptly, standing up. His cup slipped from his hand, clattering over the rocks. He sat back down, on his knees this time, hunched over.

'Gerry?' the girl said as he heaved. 'Jesus, are you okay?' She was not quite touching him, but too close. He felt queasy. He retched again. 'Shit,' she said. 'Gerry? Is there anything I should know?'

He squinted, the girl blurring in his vision. He shook his head. 'I'm okay,' he said. 'I'm just tired.' He stood up again, wobbling as he carefully climbed down. It was almost night, pink spooling out over the horizon. He began to shiver. 'I've got to go,' he said, fixing his eyes on the Honda, walking towards it.

Beside him, Eva put her hand under his armpit nervously, trying to help. 'Your shirt is soaking,' she exclaimed. Gerry nodded grimly. His teeth began to chatter. 'Come on,' Eva said as she steered him away from the Honda, 'you can sleep in the bus.'

*

On a length of foam, Gerry sweated and shivered. He dreamt his car had been stolen and became anxious. He mumbled and kicked a blanket off. His eyes snapped open when Eva pressed a wet cloth to his forehead. 'My car,' he said wildly.

'Shh,' she said. 'It's okay.' She rubbed the cool cloth down his arms and wrapped it around his feet. When he woke next, it was black outside, a moonless night, and quiet. He sat up, his bones weak as kindling. The girl was on the mattress, asleep, the cat on the pillow next to her head, licking itself.

He needed to piss. He got up stiffly. His sneakers and socks were set neatly at the end of the foam. She must have taken them off. He stumbled outside and felt the hot relief as he leaned out with his hips, smelt the curdled scent of urine. Stars winked at him. He climbed back up the steps and into the bus, spying a bottle of water, and gulped it, letting some dribble down his chin.

Eva woke up. She watched him drink. 'You okay?'

Gerry nodded sheepishly. 'Yeah, I think so.'

'You hungry?'

He was about to say no but realised he was starving. He looked through the window at his Honda. What was in there? A loaf of sliced bread, a half-eaten packet of pretzels, some Ritz crackers, a cheese spread that didn't seem to go off in the heat. He felt nauseous again.

'Do you have any fruit?' he asked. 'Just an apple?'

Eva climbed out of bed, the cat leaping from the pillow. She was still wearing the Miami Dolphins T-shirt and had switched her shorts for a baggy pair of men's boxers. 'I'll make you something,' she said firmly. 'You lie back down.'

Gerry crawled thankfully under the blanket. He put his knees up to his chest and wrapped his arms around them. Eva turned on a lantern and he listened as she busied herself, opening and closing an esky and putting things on the bench. The cat mewed, turning figure eights around her ankles. 'Oh, sorry, Pickle,' he heard her say quietly, 'I forgot to feed you.' Gerry began to feel sleepy. He heard a whisper of gas followed by a small sizzling.

'Hey.' Eva gently shook his arm. The smell of food opened his eyes. She was sitting cross-legged on the floor, a plate of fried flatbread and scrambled eggs with chunks of avocado and tomato beside her. He sat up in a rush, scooping the food into his mouth. She was smiling when he finally looked up, using the last bit of bread to clean the plate.

Gerry looked around the bus. 'Where's Elliott?' he asked.

Eva rolled her eyes. 'Waylaid, apparently,' she said sarcastically. 'I knew I should have gone instead.' She smiled again. 'But I'm not sure you would've been so lucky with Elliott. He is possibly the shittest cook I've ever met.' She laughed, revealing a crowded bottom row of teeth. 'Do you know what he did with the juicer? He put the oranges in *with the skin on* – and served it! People were gagging. It took me ages to work out what happened, and he was like, huh?'

Gerry thought a bit. He felt good, better than he'd felt in weeks. His face tingled as though he was being coloured back in. 'You have to cut the rind off before putting them in?'

Eva looked at him. '*Yes.*'

'That's annoying.'

Eva laughed. 'Oh, man,' she said, rising to put the plate on the bench, the cat leaping up to check for scraps. 'That's just great,' she continued. 'Another genius in the mix.'

*

'Hello, is this Toohey Colpitt?'

'Yes?'

'Father of Gerard Angus Colpitt?'

'Yes?'

'My name's Rory Hardwick, from the Department of Foreign Affairs.'

'Is he dead?'

'Dead? Ah, no.'

'Good.'

When Toohey put down the phone, he went to the cupboard. His uniform was bunched together on three thin wire hangers, a sheet of clear plastic from the dry-cleaner over the top. He took it out and laid it on the bed. From the top shelf, he took down a shoebox. In it was his passport. He checked it, flicking through the pages, and put it on top of the green military uniform. He punched a number into his phone. 'Pete? Listen, I'm going to have to disappear. A week, but maybe longer. Yeah. Yep. First thing. I should be back in time. You will need to prep the rosters. Correct. Make sure you keep an eye on Vihaan. Lazy-arse bastard will just stay in the car sitting in his own stinking farts all night if he can. Right. Correct. Good.' And that was it. He leaned over his bedside table and pulled his charger out of the wall, winding the white cord around it. Took two of everything from his drawers: underwear, shirts, socks, pants. A pair of leather shoes and a tin of polish. Affairs in order.

Behind the bedroom door, Melanie began to scratch. Pining for him already. He'd shut her out there when he got the call. Affairs not in order. He looked at his phone. She would call soon. She could look after the dog.

Sure enough, it began to ring. He waited. Six rings, then picked up. Put the phone to his ear as he pulled the small black suitcase from under the bed. There, affairs in order.

*

Gerry was in the fruit and vegetable section of a Colorado supermarket when it started to rain. There was the rumble of thunder and then a fine mist began to fall over the apple display. A little earlier, in aisle seven, a box of Cheerios had spoken to him, then Captain Crunch, the two boxes talking fast, bending in the middle like mouths, so Gerry was wary. He looked up at the ceiling for signs of clouds, seeing a subway network of pipes, chutes, air-conditioning units and fluorescent lights, all of it dotted with shiny CCTV eyes. He looked back at the suspiciously rosy apples, which had only become rosier with the mist. He put out his palm, watched the water bead on his skin. Suddenly two arms snuck around his waist, wrists chattering with bracelets, the left tattooed: triangles and circles in white and blue ink. He leaned back. Counted the kisses between his shoulderblades up to the nape of his neck. *One, two, three, four, five.*

The two of them lurched forward as another body barrelled into them. 'It's raining, it's fucking raining!' Elliott hollered, swinging a bag of hamburger rolls, his brown eyes popping. His lips were stained with plum juice and his wild Medusa hair writhed like a dozen coral-banded snakes, dreadlocks threaded with white and red clay beads.

As if to mock his own athletic godliness, Elliott wore dainty old-lady dresses, pearl buttons busting over his chest, hems riding up his inflated thighs. A few times Gerry had seen the muscles under Elliott's skin suddenly begin to twitch as if the sinew was being awoken. The tall man would pace, eyes darting until he'd found something physical to sate the itch, be it lifting a minor boulder, tilting a picnic table or levering a road sign out of the dirt.

On Gerry's first morning in the bus, he'd woken to the idling engine of a pick-up truck and a coquettish 'See you later, boys!' He'd propped himself on his elbows in time to see a man straddling a large tyre as he waved to a group in the open tray of the truck. Elliott, Gerry realised. He was wearing tiny pink shorts, a yellow blouse and bright yellow sandals.

'Yoo-hoo!' he sang, rolling the tyre adroitly down the escarpment. He paused at the parked Honda, peering through the window. 'I said, yoo-hoo!' he called, straightening up.

'Eva,' Gerry hissed, and sleepily the girl lifted her head, gazing at him before flopping back on the pillow and rolling over. The bus door banged open and there were noisy footsteps. For a moment he considered closing his eyes, pretending to be asleep, like when he was a kid and his father had come home. Instead, he sat up to watch Elliott enter his life.

Together, the three drove past straggly cornfields, Gerry's Honda sometimes in front, while the sea-green bus, with its painted mermaids, led the way around red mesas, tall and jagged contortions of time. Early on, Elliott had scrutinised Gerry solemnly, like a doctor, before prescribing a starter of pills, followed by a large dose of acid. 'No pot,' he advised, conferring with Eva, 'at least not to begin with.' And so, on MDMA Gerry sank into velvet nights and velvet streams. Waves of cloying, almost unbearable warmth rushed through him. The three of them danced, hips and hair flicking light around the bus, and Gerry fell in love with Eva's shoulders, the curve of her collarbone, the palimpsest of tiny warts under her knuckles. They got drunk in a bar decorated with gilt-framed portraits of men in sombreros, where in among the bottles of booze were jars containing scorpions and rattlesnakes suspended in piss-yellow formaldehyde. Behind the bar, an older woman in a strapless leather dress and pink lipstick served them tequila shots. A stuffed roadrunner stood next to a John Denver record, and in the toilets Gerry and Eva kissed, pressed up against the cistern.

He had come to the southwest looking for cowboys and instead he'd found Eva, with her shark-grey eyes, the long white gill on her neck, in her earlobes tiny dangly lightbulbs she'd fashioned into earrings. Eva, who took him to a peepshow in Tucson, his job to feed coins into the slot while she sketched the women dancing in the booths. He'd found Elliott, who wrote *Moses* on his forehead when they spied a group of evangelicals playing celebrity head elsewhere in the city; Elliott, who strode into the hall, shouting, 'I'm Moses, praise be! I'm Moses!' And every day, there was sunny reflection as they drove, music playing and the highway humming, when a fragment of the previous twenty-four hours came back to Gerry as if written on a postcard.

Eva holding Pickle to my ear so I could listen to her purr.

Elliott performing Nina Simone's 'See-Line Woman'.

Eva asking about the scar on my forehead, and telling her about the rock.

When we saw a gopher, Eva saying in an idiotic voice, 'Let's shoot it,' and how now it's a thing, whenever we see a creature, not hurting anyone, we say, 'Let's shoot it.'

Eva kissing me in the toilets.

And, unlike the touristy postcards he had bought and not sent, littering the floor of the Honda, these postcards, slips of memory, made his heart lift.

He got scared once. He was leading their mini-convoy, and a sort of cold entered his chest. He could see the other two in his rear-view mirror, Eva driving, Elliott gesturing, his palms pale and fluttering like two moths. He got annoyed looking at them. Anger took hold, his foot sinking heavier on the accelerator as he thought about how they laughed for ages at stupid things, how their voices crowded his head, how they took forever to make a decision. It was the sticky, quicksand nature of them, he told himself, as the bus receded to a speck – and then the speck was gone. It was like he'd driven over the edge of the world. In a freefall, Gerry felt released. He cheered himself on, still accelerating. The stretch yawned ever wider between the Honda and the bus. In his mind he had a bird's-eye view of them, the two dusty tumbleweeds, calling it quits.

He could hear himself again. *Yes*. He could make the decisions again. *Yes*.

He saw a gas station ahead and pulled in. Had trouble getting air in his chest suddenly. It had happened to him before, a long time ago. When the Department of Human Services showed up. He'd watched from a window as a woman parked in their driveway, Gary the policeman stopping his car behind hers. In the hallway, his mother and the woman spoke, while Gerry stood to the side, his backpack on.

The woman held out a plastic envelope to his mother. 'The number is in here if you need to get in touch with myself or Gerard, as well as the details for the hearing. There is Legal Aid information in there as well.' Jean dipped her head, taking the envelope, fixing her eyes on the floorboards. 'Let's get going then,' the woman said gently, to Gerry but also to Jean, indicating it was time to say goodbye. His mother nodded. She was polite. She put her lips on Gerry's cheek. 'Be good,' she said.

Gary didn't come into the house. He was there in case of Toohey, but Gerry's father never left the bedroom. He lay in the semi-darkness, the curtains drawn, the door half-open. After he'd checked and repacked his bag, Gerry padded down the hallway and stopped at his parents' room. He could make out the shape of his father on the mattress. Toohey slept violently, so Gerry knew he was awake. He stood for a while, just watching. In a way, it was the bravest thing he'd ever done. He got the sense his father was watching him too.

In the back of the woman's car, he had trouble breathing. 'Being removed', as the DHS woman had called it, was kind of the perfect description, he thought later. Like he was being rubbed out. The woman chatted as she drove, and he never let on that he couldn't breathe. 'On a scale of one to ten,' a doctor had asked him once, when his arm was fractured, 'what is the pain like?' Gerry had been bewildered. *You hide pain, you don't talk about it. You don't rate it.*

So he stared out of the window in silence, trying to find some air.

It was a fifty-minute drive to the foster home. In the yard was an old trampoline, its hinges rusty and cobwebbed. In the weeks that followed, he jumped on it most days. He jumped without pleasure, just up and down, side to side, backwards and forwards. He didn't try any tricks. He only jumped, willing his body to come into focus, to stop the feeling of being removed.

Now, at the gas station in America, Gerry felt it again, the filling up of his airways, like someone had gotten in there with a glue gun. He'd read a Steinbeck story once, as part of his cowboy obsession, about a colt that couldn't breathe. It had a sickness called the strangles, one of those words that sounds like what it is. In the story the stablehand had to cut a hole in the horse's neck. It worked, for a time. Syrupy blood gurgled out and then the horse took a huge gulp of air into its lungs. Gerry thought about that cut in the horse's throat as he sat wheezing in the Honda. It was empty, the highway, no sign of Eva and Elliott, and the kid in that story, it was his job to keep the hole clean and clear with a piece of cotton so the colt could keep getting air in. Gerry's breath was ragged just thinking about it. He pushed open the door to let the outside in. How many holes can you puncture a body with to keep it alive? He almost pissed himself with relief when the painted bus rattled into view.

*

After that, Eva and Elliott persuaded Gerry to pool in with them. At a town in southern New Mexico, he sold the Honda and they celebrated with lunch at a Native American restaurant across the road from a McDonald's. Local families sat at round tables eating frybread, strips of bacon and eggs sunny-side up, passing ramekins of cottage cheese. Women wore turquoise barrettes in their hair and some of the men had two long shiny plaits, silver hoops in their ears, and shirts with a length of leather under the collar, joined with a cat's-claw pendant. At one table a group of girls in white basketball uniforms with purple and black stripes, the words 'lady chiefs' emblazoned on their backs, joked rowdily, cheeks flushed and dark hair greasy with sweat.

Gerry looked around, amazed. 'I can't believe I was so dumb,' he said to Eva and Elliott, telling them how he'd come to the southwest with this naive idea, how he'd gotten it into his head that he would find this world of cowboys with ruddy faces and squinty eyes who broke in wild horses and said *whoa, whoa* under their breath, how he'd practically heard the voices, soothing him to sleep.

'And then what?' Eva asked.

'What do you mean?'

'What would happen after you found the cowboys? The guys who said "whoa, whoa"?'

Gerry spread his hands. 'I don't know. It was more a feeling than anything.'

'Let me guess,' Elliott interjected, 'in all your fantasies, not once did you imagine a black cowboy?'

Gerry shook his head. 'I never even heard of a black cowboy.'

Elliott sniffed. He stirred sugar into his coffee. 'You think the Lone Ranger built this country? No, siree,' he quipped, shaking his head. 'Hi-ho just branded his niggers before sending them out to brand his cattle.'

Gerry looked sheepish. 'Like I said, I was really dumb.'

Eva squeezed his shoulder. 'You were a kid.'

'There's an old poster out west,' Elliott said in a nasal drawl. He looked at Eva. 'You remember that?' She smiled dryly. 'There's an old poster out west,' he said again, 'that says *Wanted: dead or alive.*'

Eva rolled her eyes. 'What an idiot,' she said.

Elliott nodded. 'President Bush junior,' he explained to Gerry. 'One of your beloved cowboys.'

Eva pushed her plate away, folding her cutlery over it. 'It's a brand basically, the cowboy thing,' she said to Gerry. 'Marlboro did it, most of our presidents do it. Reagan wore a Stetson hat and said shit like, *Go ahead, make my day.*'

Gerry laughed in disbelief. Elliott and Eva bobbed their heads vigorously at him. 'It's true,' Elliott said. 'And even though the real cowboys were mostly black or Native American or Spanish or Mexican, that isn't what people think of when they think of cowboys. If they did, I bet they wouldn't be so popular. You know why people love cowboys?'

Gerry shook his head.

'Because their idea of a cowboy is a straight shooter, meaning a white man who gets things done —'

'— by sending the fodder in,' finished Eva.

Elliott's eyes were shining now. 'Exactly.' He looked around the restaurant. 'To these guys, white folk were like fucking zombies. Kill one and they'd come back tenfold. Now they send us in. White folk who don't have to send their own sons to war because why would you do that when you got my black brothers —'

'And rich people,' interrupted Eva, 'who say they shouldn't have to pay taxes because those on welfare are leeches who should be burnt off the teat. The same rich bigots who are leeching fucking oil out of the ground.'

'Right,' said Elliott.

Gerry looked at Elliott with interest. 'Your brothers went to Iraq?'

'Nope,' Elliott replied, shaking his head. 'Afghanistan. Jerome's still there in a million little pieces.'

Gerry recoiled. 'Really?'

Elliott looked at him coolly. 'Really.'

'My dad fought in Afghanistan. And Iraq.'

Elliott looked perplexed. 'I didn't even know Australia was in the war.'

'From 2001 to 2005, three tours,' Gerry said, reciting his father's mantra, adding, 'Came back with pieces of bone from a suicide bomber in his neck.'

Eva's nose crinkled. Elliott snorted, shaking his head as if appalled, then caught himself. He looked at Gerry, an unusual expression on his face. 'You mean, like shrapnel?'

'Yeah,' said Gerry.

Elliott stared at him for a minute. When he spoke, his face was changed, a layer of unexpected possibility in his eyes. 'I wonder if Jerome . . .' He stopped. It was like a leaf, this new idea, slowly detaching itself from its branch and falling, swaying on its way down, the air an invisible ocean of waves and currents. 'I wonder if,' Elliott began again, 'one of the guys in Jerome's unit . . .' He paused, then finished his thought, 'brought a piece of him home.'

After they left the restaurant, they parked near the Rio Grande, a silty brown river that funnelled its way through the long grass, and Elliott announced it was time to change gears. He held out in his palm three tiny balls, the size of poppy seeds. He looked pointedly at Gerry. 'I think it's time to drop these.'

Gerry peered at the specks. They didn't look so powerful. 'What are they?'

'Microdots. Acid. Kaboom.' Elliott made a cup with his other hand and launched it from his head like a mushroom cloud.

A tingling went up Gerry's spine and into his hair, each strand prickling like it had caught alight. Eva wet her index finger with her tongue and dabbed Elliott's palm. She picked up a dot and put it in her mouth. Gerry followed her lead.

Eva laid a rug on the grass and brought out a few cushions. Pickle tentatively picked her way down the steps, whiskers twitching. Elliott brought out a speaker and started doing stretches a little way off, near the water, while Eva carried her easel out of the bus, tightening the wingnuts under a canvas she was working on. Gerry watched them, trying to relax. He lay on the rug with the book Eva had tossed his way a couple of days earlier. He tried to focus on the type, but his eyes were restless. When Pickle started batting the pages with her paw, Gerry was grateful. He let the book go and played with the cat, pulling out a strand of grass, Pickle leaping and twisting for it. He laughed as the cat flattened herself on the grass and wriggled her back legs, getting ready to pounce.

When he looked up, the world had changed.

It was brighter, crisper. The blue sky was like a blown-glass dome and the grass crackled as if a kind of static ran through it. He sat up, to look through the whispering grass at the river. The water was amber, sunlit beer. A neon green dragonfly flitted across the surface and a strange feeling came over Gerry as he watched it, the needle body zipping about and hovering. He sensed an upward swell. *Something is going to happen*, he thought, and then a large fish jumped up out of the water, snatching the insect. Gerry looked around to check if the others had seen it. On a sandy patch at the river's edge Elliott had his arms stretched to the sky, his sequin dress shimmering. Eva had stopped painting. She was watching Gerry, the brush still in her hand. She smiled and mouthed 'hello' when their eyes connected, heat and light radiating from her to him.

'Want to go for a walk?' she asked, holding out her hand. Gerry let her pull him up. All around his sneakers were purple flowers like tiny mouths. 'Elliott?' Eva called. Elliott floated his arms down and seemed to swim over. Gerry laughed, then got caught up in the sound of his laugh, a series of differently shaped bells being rung, and the pleasurable act of it, the feeling of being lifted and bobbing in the waves.

'Do you see it?' Elliott swam up to him. 'Do you see it?'

Gerry nodded. He could see everything. He could even see his laughter, how it rippled out, like a bird flitting into a pond. *Air is water*, he thought, and it felt momentous. He wanted to tell the others, but they were laughing now too, the air splashing around them.

Eva led the way. Underneath them, the ground shifted, the earth a rich peat. Gerry's worn sneakers sank at each footfall, as if in snow. Eva floated her hands over the wheat-coloured cattails as she walked, and a bee, loud as a helicopter, passed Gerry's ear. At a large old tree, its trunk split, Eva stopped. The three of them studied it: the furrowed strips of bark; the zig-zag of ants. How each greeted the other with a caress of feelers before continuing their journey. Gerry glimpsed silky white bundles of spider's eggs tucked under the bark.

'Want to climb it?' Eva asked, not waiting for an answer, putting her boot in the tree's cleft, hauling herself up, then wriggling onto one of its long limbs. As Gerry climbed, the tree breathed, each ridge and groove the sinew and fold of skin. At the split where it sent out six or so arms, he peered into the trunk and saw a fragment of rings: years it had seen.

Elliott sprawled on the largest branch. Sunlight dappled them. They grew old there: Gerry watched them age, their skin catch the dust of time and roughen like the bark. 'You okay?' Eva called softly, and Gerry nodded. He wasn't scared; he felt safe in the ligaments of this cottonwood tree. But there was a warning in his bones of an unbearable sadness. Their scars, he saw, were shinier than ever. Eva's gill, the pocked craters on Elliott's cheeks, the notch on his own forehead, the skin white and hard, a coagulated embroidery.

How old had he been? Eight? The night had been punctured with stars and he could feel the scratchy bush he'd hidden behind, the chafing of his wet shorts. He had peed himself. He could hear his father pacing on the side of the road, yelling at him to come out. What came first – closing his eyes or the crack against his forehead? For a long time, Gerry had thought his father had somehow stretched his fist out all the way from the highway and into the desert to punch him.

It only dawned on him years later that his father must have thrown a rock. Now, a cowboy wouldn't do that. Perhaps that was what he'd been banking on. A cowboy would soothe a frightened animal. He would make it brave.

Gerry shut his eyes, uttering an anguished moan. He felt Eva climb close to him. She put her hand on his and seemed to hold him by a wire as his body detonated, each level crushing down into the next, as with a building. Every now and then, something extra burst, a tinderbox tucked away in some recess. It took forever, until finally it was done. He was rubble. Slowly he opened his eyes. Eva was beside him. He cautiously touched his face, his skin wet. He had been crying. He stared at Eva. 'Am I gone?'

She smiled and shook her head. 'No,' she said, turning over his hand and tracing the lines on his palm with a finger. 'You're here.' She had done this a lot, Gerry realised, this peculiar way of dying. He looked over at Elliott. He, too, was familiar with this. He wondered how many times they'd done it, this sloughing off of old skins.

'They even have scales over their eyes,' his mother explained once when he'd come home with a snakeskin, back when they lived on the side of the mountain. He had been hoping to scare her, but instead she became wistful, studying it. 'It must be an incredible feeling,' she said. 'Imagine being new again.'

*

They sat in a circle, sharing a joint. The smoke was soothing, softening the sharp edge that had snuck up on Gerry. When they finished, he and Eva lay back, their hair tangling, feeling the brief kisses of insects on their skin. Lacing their fingers, they watched the sky roll over them. It was impossible to determine the stretch of time before they heard feet. Elliott was breathless as he stood over them. 'You've got to see this!' he said, and they followed him, hurrying along the riverbank until Elliott stopped and split the tall grass with his hands. 'Look,' he whispered.

Eva's eyes went wide with surprise.

There, neatly folded on the grass, was a pair of faded blue jeans and a denim cowboy shirt, an old salt-stained brown felt hat on top. Beside the pile was a pair of snakeskin boots. Even with what they all knew about cowboys, Gerry so recently educated, the mystical appearance of cowboy clothes on the riverbank had them transfixed. Eva looked at Gerry. 'They're yours,' she whispered. 'I just know it.'

Elliott nodded, his dreadlocks like springs. 'I know,' he said. 'I know, right? That's what I thought.'

Gerry looked at them both, then back at the pile of clothes. He felt the world had stopped for him.

'Put them on,' Eva whispered.

Gerry looked around. 'You sure?'

'Yes!' they said, emphatic.

Gerry kicked off his sneakers, undid his pants and shrugged off his T-shirt. He pulled on the jeans, and clicked the pearly buttons on the shirt, and slid his socked feet into the boots. Elliott picked up the hat and put it on Gerry's head. It sat a little lopsided, but snug.

Eva clapped her hand over her mouth and Elliott whooped. 'Damn, man, you look amazing!'

Gerry grinned. 'Really?'

Eva shook her head, looking dazed. 'Gerry, it's perfect.'

Then a slurp came from the river as a naked man pulled himself out by the reeds, scrambling up the mud towards them. 'What the fuck are you kids doing?' he yelled, beard dripping, skinny arms shaking angrily, droopy dick swinging.

The three stared as he came at them, and then Elliott broke the spell: 'Run!' Gerry and Eva snapped to it, all of them scattering, and laughter burbled from Elliott first, then Eva, then Gerry, until it was almost impossible to run, they were laughing so hard. As Elliott led the way, he made a trumpet with his hands. '*D-d-dum, d-d-dum, d-d-d-d-dum, d-d-dum, d-d-dum, the Lone Ranger!*' he sang, and a stitch in Gerry's side almost grounded him, but at last they reached the bus, hurling their things in, the cat bolting inside, and Eva peeling off as Gerry and Elliott collapsed in giggles, shrieking at her to go faster.

It was only much later, after they'd driven north to another part of the Rio Grande and poured out trembly tumblers of rum, that Elliott wondered why the naked man hadn't caught up with them. 'After all, we were completely fucked.'

Gerry, in his cowboy get-up, slapped his forehead. 'The money!' he said. He pointed to the pocket of his new jeans. 'The Honda money was in my pocket. This,' and he gestured at his attire, 'is a six-hundred-dollar outfit.'

*

It was like that for a time, their life on the road. They played hide-and-seek in an outcrop of conical grey boulders like huge misshapen heads, while in a paddock of satellite dishes scanning the heavens they became paranoid and tetchy. They shared a picnic in the shade of a rock with petroglyphs of bighorn sheep, and walked alongside fences with odd lengths of wood nailed at strange angles as though they'd somehow gotten hitched there in a gust of wind. In San Acacia, Eva stared hard at the ground, turning over pieces of ancient clay pots. They followed signs pocked by bullets and stopped in boarded-up towns – abandoned railroad and trading outposts, dry water-soaks, exhausted mining settlements, and a few places just killed by the interstate. In disused trailers they found old newspapers and calendars open to the day of abandonment. Once, after crawling through a broken window at the back of a diner, Gerry pretended to be a waiter, passing Eva and Elliott out cups and saucers and wiping the counter.

In Santa Rosa, they drove to the Blue Hole, a luminous bell-shaped well in the desert. Stripping to underwear, they jumped in, the water cool, and washed off the dead towns. As the day drifted, they lay on warm rocks as other swimmers arrived, some kitted up in diving gear, waddling up to the well in their flippers and flopping in over the edge. A man told them that at the bottom lay skulls of steers from way-back Apache times. They parked on the sides of highways next to tourist attractions and outside strip malls, and sold pikelets, crepes and whatever other damn size pancake people wanted, and bought cheap boxes of overripe fruit, squeezing the life out of them, and Gerry had almost come around to Burning Man when Amos showed up.

*

'Navajo,' Eva said, as they waited for him. 'His mum, not mine.' Amos Bald Buzzard Homey was Eva's half-brother. They'd agreed to meet in a bar outside Santa Rosa.

'You just get out?' the bartender asked when they arrived, looking pointedly at Elliott and explaining that the first drink was on the house if he had papers showing he'd been discharged from the prison down the road.

'Nope,' Elliott said, adding, 'record's clean.'

The bartender shrugged, a doubtful look on his face. 'Bad luck for you,' he said, before swivelling to serve someone at the other end of the bar.

Elliott looked at Eva and Gerry, his eyebrow arched. 'Yeah, I guess so,' he said sarcastically. They slid into a booth with their drinks.

'You just get out?' they heard the bartender ask again.

'Sure.'

They turned around to see the speaker. The bartender looked cynical. 'Guadalupe Correctional?'

'Nope,' said the voice, 'Amazon warehouse.'

'Amos!' Eva leapt up and ran around the bar, launching herself at the wiry guy in a hoodie and baggy blue jeans standing at the counter. When he saw Eva, warmth cracked his scowl and he picked her up, spinning her around.

He sat down with them, and it was uncanny to see the two siblings, so different in looks: Amos with the cramped features of a boxer, his mouth, nose and new-moon eyes almost touching; Eva with her open face and wide-set irises. And yet, they had the same mannerisms. Gerry observed the way they tapped their fingers as they spoke, how their eyes flared when they had a point to make. Amos had a power, a charisma. He spoke and they listened, even Elliott – albeit reluctantly.

It seemed to Gerry that Amos had worked all over the country. He was a leak detector for a natural-gas company in Wisconsin, walking for miles along a buried conduit with a flame pack. He picked sugar beets in South Dakota. His last job was a stint at an Amazon in Nevada. 'I'm not doing it again,' he said.

Eva laughed. 'You said that last time!'

'Well, this time I mean it. The warehouse is the size of fucking Harlem and everyone shows up in their RVs and pick-up trucks converted into homes, or, if you're me, in your piece-of-shit sedan. It's fucking *Grapes of Wrath* in the twenty-first century.' He paused. Gerry hadn't read the book, but he nodded along with the others. 'Pickers and packers, that's what we are. Ten-hour shifts for eleven twenty-five an hour.'

Eva shook her head. Amos glanced at her. 'We can't all get scholarships to go to college.'

'Oh, shut up, Amos, not this again,' she replied.

Amos grinned at Gerry. 'You know Eva is a big-shot smarty-pants, right?'

Eva punched him. 'Shut up! Those two things don't even make sense together!'

Gerry smiled, eager to hear more, but Amos returned to his story. 'Each shift you walk, on average, about fifteen miles on concrete, the warehouse is that big.'

'Miles?' Gerry said, his eyes wide.

Amos nodded. 'Yeah, and heaps of workers think it's "*awe*-some!"' He said it in a high-pitched voice.

'No more, Amos,' Eva pleaded. 'Promise me you won't do another stint?'

He smiled. 'I promise.' He looked uncertain for a second, as though wrestling with something. 'I kind of lost it there anyway. Not sure they'd take me back.'

Eva sat up, alert. 'What happened?'

Amos glanced at Gerry and Elliott, as if wishing they weren't there. 'There's a thing on your scanner that starts a countdown when you scan something, showing how many seconds you've got to find the next item to scan.' He turned to Eva. 'I started to get strung out when the countdown started, and I fucked up after one scan, went down a wrong aisle, then another wrong aisle, and I tried to go back to where I'd been so I could start over.'

'Oh, Amos.' Eva said knowingly, and put her hand on his hand.

'Eight minutes and thirty-two seconds,' Amos continued. 'That was all I went over. Eight, thirty-two. It felt like forever. You know what I was meant to find?' Eva shook her head. 'An audiobook of *The Tibetan Book of Living and Dying*.' He stared at her. 'Can you fucking believe it?' His eyes became tight and angry. 'Can you two fucking believe it?' he said to Gerry and Elliott. Taken aback, they shook their heads. 'Fucking Americans, they tried to scorch us off the face of this country and some fucker orders in Buddhist bullshit from Tibet? I mean, *we* had men at the top of the mountain. We were fucking *there*.' Amos slapped his empty glass, sending it spinning across the table.

They were quiet. On a small stage with curtains and a disco ball, a band was setting up, checking *uno, dos, tres* into the microphone and tuning their guitars. Eva put her arms around Amos and he leaned gratefully into her. He had brought a new intensity, like the heat had been turned up.

They ordered more drinks. When the band began to play, they got up to dance, Amos slipping his hands around the hourglass waist of a honey-haired woman. Back at the table, Amos snorted when Eva told him they were heading to Burning Man. 'Not anymore,' he said. Elliott frowned. Amos tossed his head back so his straight black hair was out of his eyes and the woman snuggled into his neck. 'North Dakota,' he continued, 'Standing Rock. We're going to fight, little sister.'

*

'No drugs or alcohol allowed in the camp,' Amos told them. 'It's not fucking Burning Man.' And so, instead of gathering in a temporary desert city with a thousand glitterheads, Gerry found himself heading north. In his beat-up sedan, Amos led the way on a highway that cut through rusted cliffs and jagged escarpments marbled with various eras. They drove past feedlots, adobes with turquoise doors, and unfinished Earthships, the solar-earth shelters tiered into the sides of thirsty hills.

In Denver, Elliott announced he was out. He'd go to Burning Man without them.

At the railway station, he was dressed for departure in mauve, wearing a boxy, cropped jacket and a pencil skirt. Jackie Onassis–style sunglasses added to his wounded look. Eva and Gerry waited with him on the platform. 'You don't have to,' he said huffily, sober heels clipping on the terrazzo. Eva rolled her eyes. Gerry felt bad. He stood a little to the side to give Eva and Elliott some space, but Eva kept drawing him in.

When the train arrived, the doors wheezed open to let people off, then sat idle.

'So, see you later, Skippy,' Elliott said, propping his sunglasses up on his hair. His lashes, thickened with mascara, hung like awnings over his brown eyes. Gerry looked at the ground, at his cowboy boots. He couldn't say anything.

'Don't be a cock,' Elliott scolded, loud and haughty. Gerry blushed. People were watching them, corners of their mouths turned down in disgust. He felt it then, the menace and malice, a barely contained tolerance, how it seeped towards Elliott. He hadn't noticed it before, how Elliott deflected it. 'Eyes and teeth,' he often said, tapping the side of his brow near his eyes and the enamel on his teeth as if turning them on, his eyes instantly sparkling, lips wide. Gerry felt ashamed. His loyalty was thin. He had sniffed the air and fallen in line without even realising it. Elliott had sensed it, too.

Don't be a cock. Gerry took a breath and looked at Elliott. He laughed, seeing himself suddenly. A kid dressed up as a cowboy.

'What?' demanded Elliott. 'What's so funny?'

Gerry shook his head. He felt a bolt of love for Elliott and put his hand on the man's cheek. 'Nothing,' he said, smiling. Amos, he thought, was a prick for not playing along. His father would have done the same. Maybe worse. Gerry felt a tiny burst of bravery. So fucking what? Who cared what his father or Amos would do, would think? He pulled Elliott close, clutching his mauve waist, and put his lips on his. He felt the surprise in Elliott and the ripple of disgust around them. Elliott closed his silvery, powdered eyes, and when they separated, he opened them, throwing his head back, his laugh filling the station. Gerry grinned. Elliott looked at Eva before pulling her in for a hug. 'We brought him up good,' he said teasingly.

The loudspeaker gave the final boarding call. 'I love you, Elliott,' Eva said, easily and simply. And with that, Elliott cut a swathe through the crowd and boarded the train. Eva and Gerry watched as he strode down the carriage. After he chose his seat, his suitcase in the over-head, Elliott waved out the window as the doors slid shut and the train went out the same way it came in.

*

'Good morning, Staaannnding Rock,' called a voice on the PA. 'Wake up, water protectors. Remember why you are here.'

Eva stretched her arms above her head and rolled over to kiss Gerry, her lips warm on his skin. They could hear the camp stirring: zips on sleeping bags, muffled voices, the thud of mud banged from soles. She reached out and pulled back the corner of the woollen blan-ket they had pegged over the window. The light was golden. A dance of dust played around Eva's wrist. She was naked except for a pair of thick knitted socks. Gerry pulled her back under the covers, kissing the pale curve of her breast. Eva giggled as she escaped from his grip, pulling on an oversized jumper that covered her triangle of pubic hair. 'Wake up,' the voice intoned. 'Wake up, water protectors.'

Eva scooped up Pickle as she walked to the gas cooker, rubbing her nose to his in an Eskimo kiss. Gerry watched, already missing the shape of her. A hunger had built between them once Elliott left, and now there was the privacy to sate it.

Amos had changed things. Gerry found himself drawing back, steadying the parts of himself he'd let run loose and wild with Eva and Elliott, like winding in a kite.

'Keep your shit to yourself,' his father had said, when they had met for dinner before Gerry flew out. 'Everything you do – talking, walking, everything – hold yourself like a fighter. Tuck your head in, fists up. Leave no way in.' It was hardly wisdom for a fun holiday, but then his father didn't believe in holidays. The irony of advice from a shithouse father; Gerry had loathed it, of course, but it had lodged for a time. He'd been coiled up tight as a prison screw before he met Eva and Elliott. It wasn't like that now. It was a more watchful, welcome stillness, a chance to take stock. Gerry had started to write, sitting in a slant of sunlight on the bus with a notebook. Not stories; just describing places they drove past, and people, recording snapshots and snippets of talk. He'd enjoyed it as a kid, writing, but had forgotten it. He found pleasure working on the cars too, lying under Amos's sedan and the bus. Enjoyed the ground under his back, grease to his wrists, dirt in his hair. When he ran the engine, he listened, seeking out the clunks, rattles and drags, and took to hustling up spare parts in wreckers' yards. Eva and Amos admired it, looking at him with new eyes. Eva especially.

He loved watching Eva frown with concentration when they fucked, her bottom lip tucked behind her teeth, eyes shut, grinding her hips, intent on making it up the staircase to wherever it was that women felt things. Afterwards, she would sink her teeth in his skin and sometimes she'd come again, an extra wave of pleasure, her fists tight. They could have turned into moles under the bedcovers, the way they sought each other out in the darkness. Each night they fucked, and in the morning too, if they could, pink feathering the sky beyond the covers, though Amos was relentless, banging on the bus at eight sharp to get a move on.

The land got sparse near Cannon Ball, North Dakota, plains turning to crops. It was cooler, too. The road was patched with new bitumen like a quilt. A casino came out of nowhere on the prairie, tour buses with grasshopper mirrors parked out front. A few stubby trees, like the heads of broccoli, and some low-slung buildings marked the reservation. Three white crosses were staked next to the road, and over a hill lay the Missouri River, wide and flat.

Earlier, Amos had shown them the proposed route of the oil pipe-line on their roadmap. 'So,' Gerry said, putting his finger on a blue blot and trying to get it straight in his head, 'they want to put it here' – he squinted to read the print – 'under Lake Oahe.'

'It's not a lake,' Amos said.

'Huh?'

'It's not a lake.' Amos tapped his teeth. 'It's a dam. Government did it in the fifties, flooded land belonging to the northern tribes.'

'Oh.' Gerry rubbed his brow. He began again, starting at the Bakken oil fields, tracing his finger downwards, around the city of Bismarck and halting at the Missouri River. 'So, the pipeline will come from here ...'

'And another one is being built this way,' added Eva, tracing her finger from Illinois. 'And they're planning to connect it somewhere here.' She stubbed her finger in South Dakota.

They were leaning in, peering at the map, when Amos suddenly whipped it away. He scrunched it into a ball and threw it against the wall of the bus. 'Fucking stupid map!' he snapped. Gerry stared at him, mouth open, his stupid look seeming to enrage Amos even more. 'You believe in that map?' Amos asked, his tone poisonous. Gerry looked at Eva helplessly and she gave him a tiny shake of the head, as if prompting him on a test.

'I don't know,' Gerry answered weakly.

Amos stalked to the paper ball and unfolded it, pressing it flat with his fists. 'This map is bullshit. Look at Missouri River. You think that's really how the river goes? No,' he said, answering for Gerry. 'That river has been drained, narrowed, dredged, diverted. It had fake riverbanks put in so folk can keep their riverfront houses, and boul-ders blown up for smooth passage.'

'Jesus.' Gerry stared at the pale thread that writhed on the paper. He would never have thought to question it.

Amos stabbed at the roadmap with his finger. 'There isn't a fucking honest map left in this country.'

Eva was nodding. 'You know how coal companies are taking off the tops of mountains in the Appalachians?' she said. 'It's the same thing. Something like five hundred mountains have been blown up and the government just changes the maps. Flattens out the contours and it's like they were never there.'

'See this?' Amos pointed to a shade of brown marking the Standing Rock reservation. 'It's bullshit.' He tapped the map, pointing out tiny wedges of brown, one after the other. 'All of them are bullshit. We respect the' – Amos held up his fingers and counted them off – '1851, 1858 and 1868 treaties, even if the government won't.'

Gerry was silent. He had no idea what to say. He'd studied the map and the names of places had jumped out at him. He knew them all: New York, Mississippi, Utah, Miami, New Orleans, California, Los Angeles, Detroit, Chicago, Arizona, Washington, Florida, Texas, Kansas. He knew the country better than his own – at least he thought he did.

'What's it like in Australia?' Amos was looking at him with curiosity now. 'Is it the same?'

Gerry frowned. 'How do you mean?'

Amos waved his hand at the map. 'As this.'

Gerry reddened. 'I don't know,' he said. He had a memory of his school assignments – how he would photocopy pictures from books, gluing them onto paper, colouring them, to distract teachers from the distinct lack of information. He'd been to so many different schools and managed to turn up just in time to study the gold rush at nearly every one. Five times he had to do an assignment on the gold rush, and he never got any better at it.

As though reading his mind, Amos pointed to a patch on the map. 'Black Hills,' he said. 'Ink was barely dry on the Sioux Treaty when the government changed their mind. Got to thinking there was gold in those hills. People starved, the reservations got small.' He scowled. 'Cunts.'

'Pricks,' Eva corrected.

Gerry felt sick. Five assignments and not once had he thought about the people who'd lived on that land. Fuck, he had mentioned the 'chinks', had even eked out some sympathy for them. But. Not. A. Single. Thought. How the hell had he missed this? He had a feeling his brain was a plant, its grey tendrils pushed against the inside of his skull. He felt an urge to dunk his head in some river, rerouted or not, and thump his skull, get the plant out, give it water.

*

'Good morning, Standing Rock!' There was gurgling and the rich smell of coffee as it spat up into the top half of the pot. When it finished, Eva used a sock to take it off the burner and poured it into two cups. Gerry got up, putting on the same pair of undies as the day before, jeans, shirt. He glanced at the map, etched with the creases of Amos's fury, as he picked up his mug. Eva had marked it up in pencil, including an X for where they were camped, next to Cannonball River, with the Missouri about a mile downstream. She thumped open the bus door and they sat on the steps watching people emerge from trailers, tents and tepees, crusty-eyed, tin cups in hand. Each person flicked their eyes across the water, a sun salute to the security guards and police who had spent the night watching them. Behind the guards, a temporary fence was guarding the Dakota Access Pipeline bulldozers and diggers, orange mouths open like cooling crocodiles. Floodlights mounted atop the enormous crooked arms had shone into the camp all night long, forcing the activists to squint and bury their heads under pillows, while a surveillance plane turned like clockwork above.

'Good morning!' called a protester on the riverbank, his hands cupped around his mouth. He was wearing moccasins that tied over his jeans and a coat with a woollen collar. The eyes on the hill opposite swivelled and settled on him without a word. 'I said,' he called, 'good morning!' There was laughter in the camp, and a few more people called out to the wordless mound. It was a kind of dance. Less than a week ago a black thread of snipers had lain draped there when activists had gathered at the riverbank. 'Rubber bullets,' one of the leaders explained to Eva and Gerry in an information session in the community yurt. 'But they can hurt like hell. Take an eye out if you're unlucky.' People had waded in across the icy water and the police had tear-gassed them.

'Coffee?' the protester yelled now, holding up a coffee pot. The grass was flecked with ice and he stamped his leather boots in it. Sometimes the protesters played frisbee where he was standing, exaggerating their squeals of delight and taking wild leaps, showing off. 'Want to play?' they'd call across the river to the security men. It was teasing, Gerry figured. Bear-baiting. Appealing to their humanity, Eva countered.

There was a crackle of static. *Remember why you're here*, the voice said. Eva flung the dregs of her coffee onto the dirt. There were mornings when it felt simultaneous, hundreds of brown splats, small rivers in the shape of lightning bolts on the ground. Eva went inside the bus to put more layers on. It was mid-November. They'd been in the camp for six weeks and had watched the lowlands change from pale green to a rusty hue, the grass moulting like a buffalo hide. Overnight, the creek had turned to ice. Amos had shifted into a tepee with people he'd grown up with. He had a glow about him. A lot of the protesters did.

'Out there,' Amos tried to explain one evening, 'we don't exist. You can't even imagine what that's like.' He laughed. 'Man,' he said to Gerry, 'you'd have to take your eyes out to even try.'

'Even then,' Eva interrupted, 'it would be impos—'

'I get it,' Gerry said hotly.

Amos laughed again. His face shone. 'But here,' he continued, 'we're fucking *here*. We exist!' He pointed to his eyes, shaking his head. 'Shit, I didn't even know it. I mean, I know our history – but my eyes, they may as well have been yours, man.' Gerry winced a little, annoyed. So, just because he was white and male, he was part of the problem?

Still, it was incredible, Gerry knew that. He had never seen anything like it. Their camp was a sprawl of yurts, pick-up trucks, wagons with tarps stretched over metal ribs, tents and caravans. Nailed placards read *WATER IS LIFE* and *WELCOME, WATER PROTECTORS*. People were busy. Men and women, hair plaited or in ponytails, waistcoats and shirts woven with tight stitches of beads. Dark-eyed kids from cities, jeans low on their hips. People had come from all over, crossed the invisible lines, and like a mercury instrument cracked open over a map and spattered across the continent, they kept coming, they eased down into the prairie, forming a single silver fist.

*

Toohey Colpitt surveyed the cream tiles of the airport floor, the people wrapping their bags in plastic, the bored queue. He stood behind a young couple already wearing their inflated peanut pillows around their necks. Toohey stared at them scornfully: idiots.

The queue shuffled forward a step at a time, but Toohey refused to move until there was enough space for a dignified stride or two. He ignored the clumps forming behind him. In the inside pocket of his coat he could feel the hard rectangle of his passport. Within it he had slotted a letter from DFAT, along with several names and numbers. The consulate had provided him with contacts and given a guarantee that he was cleared down the line in the States. 'However,' the consular official had warned, careful with his words, 'things have gotten a little unpredictable in immigration.' Toohey had snorted his approval of the new American president. 'And so they bloody well should.' *Not like this bullshit leftie country that betrays its own damn countrymen for the sake of a foreigner,* he'd thought.

It was Wedge who'd told him, fucking shit-stirring Wedge from his old unit, who had somehow made it up the ranks to officer. 'I just thought you should know, man,' Wedge said on the phone. 'The woman, she's here.' Toohey didn't catch on at first. 'She asked to come and they let her,' Wedge continued. Then Toohey clocked; he saw it, vivid as the frigging couch he was sitting on: the woman in the back of the car, wailing, blood everywhere. 'I just thought you should know, man,' Wedge said again.

'Where?' Toohey managed to ask.

'That's the thing, that's why I thought you should know. She's in Melbourne, same as you.'

Toohey started to shake then, his legs moving of their own accord, his hands trembling. 'Where in Melbourne?' he'd croaked, but Wedge clammed up, as though it was Toohey who had made the call, put in the enquiry.

'I can't say, mate, but I just thought you should know.'

At the airport, Toohey loosened the collar of his shirt to let some air in. His uniform was tight. But it still fit. Jean had looked admiringly at him when he tried it on and he'd showed off a little, punching his arms into the khaki jacket sleeves, dancing it over his shoulders with a jaunty shrug.

He hadn't expected his breath to catch when he'd opened the door to her. Five years since he'd seen his wife, and if anything, he had expected her to be a mess, not just because of the news about Gerry, but because she'd been without him. But her presence gave him a jolt.

Not once in all the time he'd withdrawn had he considered that Jean might be with another man, but looking at her, her cheeks pink, her eyes luminous and secret, he wondered. The dog was going crazy, jumping up on her, pawing her leggings, and he gaped as she knelt to scratch Melanie behind the ears. Jean's hair was curly, pinned up with bobby pins. A single brown tentacle escaped down the nape of her neck. Toohey's chest tightened in a wave of worry. Was she still his?

Melanie lurched at Jean's face, pink tongue out. Jean giggled and put her hand on the doormat to steady herself, her knees wobbling. Toohey ran his gaze to her fingers. Their wedding ring – she was still wearing it. Instantly his insides stopped their attack. Jean looked up shyly and he let a few seconds pass before he smiled. Then he opened the door wider and whistled for Melanie to come back in, nodding at Jean to follow.

'What the hell does Gerry care about some oil pipeline in America?' he asked, once the two of them were seated awkwardly in the lounge room. Jean shrugged. 'It's that school you sent him to,' Toohey continued. 'The hippy one.' Her brow creased. She was silent. It made Toohey nervous. He'd been used to her placating him, feeding him crumbs to go on with. 'Well?' he said pointedly. 'Do you have any idea why he's gone and done this?'

Jean shook her head. 'No, Toohey, I don't.' She took a sip of the tea he'd made; he'd put it in front of her like a gift. She sighed, and Toohey got an uncomfortable feeling that she was looking right through him. 'Do you know they pulled your father's house down?' she said suddenly.

Toohey frowned, confused. 'I assumed they would,' he replied curtly. 'What's that got to do with Gerry?'

Jean didn't answer. Instead she continued, her voice tired and dreamy. 'I went and saw it. A big ugly house is there now. All grey. Pulled the nectarine tree out too.'

Toohey snorted. 'Of course they did, the thing was half-dead.'

Jean smiled. 'It was half-alive too,' she said, and looked at him so directly Toohey felt that jolt again. He wondered if she knew about the Iraqi woman. If Wedge had somehow called her up, told her too, just to get something going. He looked away.

Melanie was sitting on her cushion, watching them both with interest. 'Get down from there,' he said, pretending she wasn't allowed up. He felt strangely unsure of himself. 'So, I'm going,' he continued.

Jean nodded.

'I got the red-eye flight tomorrow.'

'Good,' Jean said.

'It was very expensive,' he added.

Jean didn't say anything.

'I'll need someone to look after Melanie.'

The corners of Jean's lips turned up slightly. She looked at the dog and patted her lap. Melanie jumped up neatly and Jean ran her fingers through the white fur. 'Okay,' she said. She tilted her head and smiled. He missed her then. All that time, and he missed her then. Abruptly he reached across and touched her cheek. 'Jean,' he said hoarsely. He pressed his thumb gently just below her eye.

He wasn't wearing his ring. He'd taken it off years ago, storing it in the jar where he kept the shrapnel. They had all come out now. The last fleck, half a head of a nail, had popped out with its usual stink of pus a year ago. For a week or two his neck was red and the skin around the hole stung. He cleaned it with antiseptic, but as always he got a fever, his dreams vivid and lurching. Yet when Toohey came out of it, it was the strangest thing. He didn't want a cigarette. Out of habit he lit one up anyway, but it tasted bitter. He gagged in disgust and stopped smoking. Just like that. Which, he figured, explained the extra weight. Like his uniform, the ring was a little tight when he tried it on after Jean went to collect her things. It would be best, they had decided, if she moved into his flat to look after Melanie. But he pushed the ring down and spun it stiffly around under his knuckle, and found himself glancing at it in a way he'd never done before, not even when Jean put it on him all those years before.

*

'TIGHTEN UP!' yelled one of the marchers. 'TIGHTEN UP!' Everyone drew close, linking arms as they walked along the bitumen towards a bridge. A pounding of hooves came down the line, and Gerry turned to watch the spirit riders go past. The sleek black hair of the men lashed the air as the horses thrust forward, galloping in tune to the tightness of the legs slung over their backs. A chorus of trilling rang in the riders' wake. 'Stay strong!' people sang out. 'Stay strong, water protectors!' Up ahead, past the burnt-out cars wedged on the bridge, three rows of riot police stiffened, the sun catching the plastic windows of their helmets. Everyone could see how the cops paused as the riders came close, uncertain, glancing at their commander. Perhaps they were just being shrewd, knowing they could not beat such an image should it run in the press. Spirit rider against machine. 'Poor bastards,' Eva often said of the cops. 'I bet some of them don't want to be here.'

Amos hated it when she said that. He didn't think they deserved sympathy. 'No one's fucking forcing them,' he retorted.

'CLOSER! GET TIGHTER!' The linked arms tightened. Gerry twisted his neck until he spotted Eva, two rows from the front. She was wearing a red bandana over her face, only her eyes visible. Her backpack was bulky. In it, Gerry knew, was a first-aid kit and a few plastic bottles of milk to squirt into people's eyes. He looked behind him. The vast highway was gone, a river of people in its place. A lump swelled in Gerry's throat at their unexpected magnificence. There were six hundred at least, most of them were wearing red – red shawls and shirts; red beanies and bandanas over their faces. 'Water is life!' people yelled.

Gerry swung back to face the front. They were close now, the sour smell of burnt rubber filling his nostrils. He could just see the metal wires fanning off the tyres of an overturned wreck. Behind it, the police had put up slabs of concrete and coils of barbed wire, and behind that they were lined up. Beyond them were four army tanks, the hatches open and enforcement poking out, clad in black and homing in on the marchers through eye-pieces.

'STAY THERE,' a voice ordered over a megaphone. 'DO NOT COME ANY CLOSER.'

Adrenaline coursed down the line. 'Stay strong!' someone yelled, and the marchers pushed up against the wrecks.

'I REPEAT, DO NOT COME ANY CLOSER.' Gerry could see the speaker now, a large man with a sheriff's hat. 'STAY WHERE YOU ARE,' he ordered, and there it was, the line between violence and nonviolence.

Eva had taken to it easily, this nonviolent direct action. Amos and Gerry, less so. 'Is it even possible?' Gerry had asked one evening, after the three of them spent the day in a training session. 'Confrontation without violence?'

'Of course it is,' Eva had replied impatiently. 'How else can you have civilised debate?'

Amos shook his head. 'I don't think confrontation and debate are the same thing, Eva,' he said, and Gerry smiled, knowing she'd take his opinion more seriously now.

'Exactly,' Gerry continued, enjoying the new certainty in his voice. 'Surely,' he added, just a little pompously, 'the very act of confrontation is violent.'

But Eva was sharp, choosing her words like a seasoned debater. 'Well, it depends on which definition of violence you are thinking of.

In this case, the *correct* version would be the *legal* definition of violence and nonviolence.' Gerry narrowed his eyes at Eva for a second before breaking into a sheepish grin. Eva smiled back. They looked at Amos, who was quiet. 'What do you think, Amos?' Eva asked.

He didn't answer immediately, pressing his finger to scattered grains of salt on the table and making a pile. 'I don't know,' he said. 'It's clever, I'll give it that.' He listed the things they had been taught, how they could all play a role: be a PRA (person risking arrest), support crew or a jail contact, a police liaison, get trained in deployment, diversion, maybe become a media spokesperson. How he'd felt a thrill, just as they had, when they saw the nerve centre of the campaign, a busy hub set up almost like an army tent, with maps and laptops, the seesaw of red and green lights of various chargers and the static of multiple UV channels. 'But,' Amos began, then shook his head. 'No, nothing.' He tried to smile. 'I've just gotten so used to losing that I've forgotten how to win, that's all.'

Amos did a lot of healing sessions over the next few weeks. He did smoking ceremonies with elders and stayed close to his old friends, speaking in dialect. He seemed quieter, less angry, lighter. Eva thought it was great. It was like watching her brother bloom, she said, and she sat close as he repeated stories he'd been told.

Gerry was wary. 'I don't know if it's all good,' he said carefully to Eva one day, and for the first time she got properly angry with him.

'What would you know?' she snapped, those shark eyes of hers going cold. Gerry lifted his shoulders. 'I don't know,' he replied a little shrilly. 'But.' He took a deep breath. 'It's not as if he can stay here. It's temporary, right? He can't ...' He struggled to find the word.

'Can't what?' Eva was bristling.

'I don't know,' Gerry muttered. 'Forget it.'

But Eva wouldn't. 'Well, it's not as if you can stay here either,' she said nastily. 'Have you thought about that?'

Gerry bit his lip. He looked away, hurt. He had thought about it, and he tried not to think about it. His visa had already expired. He hadn't told Eva this.

Eva softened and rushed to him. 'I'm sorry,' she said, kissing his mouth and eyelids and neck. 'I'm sorry, I didn't mean that. It's just so nice to see Amos happy. At peace.' Gerry nodded. Let her kiss him, wrapping his arms around her. But he wasn't so sure it was peace Amos had found.

*

The protesters in the front row held up homemade shields: garbage-bin lids and chipboard. Two elders stepped forward and positioned themselves between the car wrecks. One produced two bundles of sage, and all down the line, at least a kilometre in, a singing started up – a low, deep humming at first, then words Gerry didn't understand. People beat on skin drums. The elders lit the sage, waving the bundles so the scented smoke lifted and swirled over the bridge, towards the police. The spirit riders came back, making a wide arc over the field, the hooves digging up clods of mud and ice, the riders trilling. The police flexed behind their shields, metal canisters and shotguns like sashes over their chests.

'Remember, this is peaceful!' a voice called. Gerry nodded as if it had been directed at him only. He loosened his grip, realising that he had been clenching the wrists of the people on either side of him. He strained a little, trying to find Amos. They'd seen him before they'd started on the march. He was tense, drenched in red. 'He's focused,' Eva said when Gerry commented on it. He didn't say, but he knew something was wrong. He knew because he could feel it himself, a jittery sensation like a pinball in his chest.

It wasn't going well.

Three weeks ago, they'd tried to stop a raid on the Treaty camp.

There were armoured vehicles and Humvees and three hundred riot police on foot. They started slashing the tents and tepees and a group of protesters was cornered. People were yelling to get out, that they needed to move quickly to stop police sweeping south to the other camps, but Gerry had seen Amos stuck in that corner, and he ran through the protesters towards him.

'Shut up!' a cop was shouting at a woman, the group pulling her back. 'You bastards!' she hollered. 'You bastards. This is OUR land!' Her face was streaked with tears, and a few people tried to talk softly to her. 'No! No, no, no,' she screamed.

Amos was standing a little apart, his face blank. 'Now, now,' another cop said, wagging his finger, 'listen here, no bows and arrows.' At this, a current of fury went through Amos; Gerry could see it. He moved quickly through the group and put his hand on Amos's shoulder. At first, Amos couldn't even see him – there was no recognition – and then his face shifted.

'Now, now,' Gerry whispered, wagging his finger. Amos smiled.

Then, close behind them, a boy on a horse appeared from between two tents, just a kid walking the animal slowly, and the cops shot at him. *Pop, pop, pop.* The horse reared up; the kid came off and landed, his arm bent the wrong way, as the horse tap-danced beside him, hooves jumping as the dirt kept popping with rubber bullets. Its legs seem so fragile, Gerry found himself thinking. It began to trot backwards and Gerry could see it twitching, burrs matted in its coat.

'Stop it!' the woman screamed at the cops. Amos caught the horse's reins so the kid could roll out. *Whoa, whoa,* Amos said softly in all the noise, calming the scared animal. That day, at the Treaty camp, the police used pepper spray and stun grenades; sound cannons perforated eardrums, the barbed hooks of tasers snared skin like fish, and rubber bullets rained.

*

'It's naive,' Gerry had said to Eva after that day. A bunch of protesters had split from the chain of command and driven two vehicles
onto the bridge, setting them alight to stop the police raids going any
further. There was division after that – the NVDA people condemned
the act while others got angrier, agitating. Thing was, they could all
see it. Winter was near. It was going to get harder to hold the line.
Then news broke about the Oregon mob, white ranchers who'd holed
up in a declared wildlife refuge, armed to the hilt. The main guy, it
was said, had trained an assault rifle on police, but the cops just let
him come and go as he pleased.

'It's not the same,' Eva said to Gerry. 'First of all, they're white,
and they're protesting against environment legislation. This is about
oil, Gerry. Oil.'

*

'Stay strong!' a voice yelled. Gerry closed his eyes, nodding again.
'Pray!' another intoned. 'Stay peaceful!' *No violence, no violence.* The
urgent, almost pleading message went up and down the line, and
Gerry tried. But honestly, it was difficult. It was like being told to
dance but to resist the beats of a song and move your body to the
silent parts.

'Water is life!' the woman beside Gerry yelled. He opened his
eyes. She smiled at him. 'Water is life!' Gerry joined in, his voice
trembling at first, getting stronger. 'Water is life!' For six hours they
stood like that, dancing and jumping to stay warm. More bundles of
sage came out, elders using convenience-store lighters to ignite them
while others fanned the smoke with bits of cardboard, sending it over
the barricade. *Pray,* went the signal down the line. *Pray. Remember,
this is peaceful.*

*

'Business or holiday, sir?' The officer held Toohey's passport open at his photo, eyes efficiently moving back and forth between subject and image.

Toohey straightened and cleared his throat. 'Business,' he said.

*

'Fuck!' A man swung out, clutching his wrist, his red bandana loose around his neck. 'My hand!' His eyes were wild. His hand was bleeding, fingers sticking out at odd angles.

A woman ran through the crowd and crouched beside him. 'Move,' she ordered the others, 'make some room!'

Another man spun backwards, gurgling as he ground his palms in his eye sockets. 'My eyes,' he screamed. 'Ow, my fucking eyes.'

The woman helping the first man looked over at him. 'Don't touch your eyes,' she hollered. 'Help! Someone stop him rubbing his eyes!'

Gerry stepped forward, pulling the man's hands away. 'Blink,' he commanded.

The man was thrashing, trying to free his hands. 'It's fucking burning!' he screamed. 'Oh god, make it stop!'

Gerry grabbed hold of the man's hands and looked around for help. The man started coughing, a rasping sound. He toppled over, bringing Gerry with him. Gerry saw blood leaking from a gash on the back of the man's head. 'Shit,' he said, kneeling. 'Okay, mate, you've got to breathe, you've got to get some air in.'

The man started to suck in short, shallow breaths. Gerry scanned the crowd over his bloody head. It was chaos. The plains were dark, while the road was bright as a supermarket from floodlights the cops had set up, halogen heads like Arabic amulets. The march that had been ordered and united was in disarray, protesters bent over, huddling, a few loners straying onto the grass, yelling into the darkness, dancing like unhinged marionettes near the wire. A helicopter was roaring over them. It was freezing.

'Eva!' Gerry yelled, seeing her at last with another medic off to the side, both squatting next to a woman on the ground, her head between her knees. 'Eva!' he yelled again, and she looked up at the sound. 'Over here!' She spied him, and he pointed to the man he was holding up.

Eva said something to the other medic and started weaving her way to Gerry.

'Tear gas,' he said, when she got near, 'and this.' He pointed to the blood on the man's head.

Eva took a bottle out of her bag. 'Okay,' she said to the man. 'I need you to tilt your head back. I'm going to pour this onto your eyes. It'll stop the burning.' Trembling, the man arched his neck, his face caught in a grimace as Eva poured the milk over his eyes. 'You need to open your eyes,' she commanded.

'Argh,' he moaned. 'It stings.' But after thirty seconds or so his breathing began to ease, his body relaxing.

Gerry loosened his hold. He searched through Eva's bag and took out the wipes, patting the back of the man's head, trying to locate the cut.

There was a rise of cries, a flare of fire to their left. The tear-gas canisters were igniting patches of the prairie. Protesters rushed to stamp out the spot fires.

'Where's Amos?' Gerry yelled.

Eva looked around, worried. 'I don't know.'

A burst canister smashed on the ground nearby, and they jumped. Gas began to seep out. A woman ran over and kicked it away. It skidded off the road and into the dark. 'The cops are fucking aggro!' Gerry shouted.

Eva nodded, her eyes searching the back of the man's head. 'Let's do this, then move him,' she said. She found the cut and dabbed at it. Gerry moved to shield her and the man so people wouldn't trip over them. Eva put a wad of cloth over the gash and it soaked through almost immediately. Gerry got a fresh wad out of the kit for her and peered at the man's face. 'You okay?'

The guy took a shivery breath, his eyes shut. 'Yeah, yeah, I'm okay.'

'Your eyes?'

'Yeah, they feel better.'

'Can you open them?'

The man sucked in his cheeks and carefully opened them.

'Can you see?' asked Gerry.

'I think so. Fuck, they sting.'

'We'll move you after Eva does the bandage, okay? Then we'll put more milk in your eyes. Okay?' The man nodded, clamping his eyes shut again.

'Gerry?' Eva asked. 'Gerry, can you put two fingers here?'

He straightened, and kept the end of a bandage firm against the man's head as she wound it around a few times like a headband, then looped it under the man's chin. 'Okay,' she said. 'Let's move him.'

They got on either side of the man, slinging his arms over their shoulders, and half-dragged, half-walked him away from the frontline. 'There,' Eva yelled, pointing ahead at a van.

A massive force punched the three of them in the back, lifting them off the ground, skittling them forward a few metres. 'Water cannons!' a man screamed, and everyone began to run. Gerry and Eva tried to get up, Gerry bending to help the man, and the stream of water came back, the force of it slamming Eva in the face, yanking her neck back in whiplash.

'Eva!' Gerry scrambled past the man to where she'd fallen. 'Fuck! Eva! You okay?' She had her head down and her elbows tucked in under her. He could see her back rising and falling. After a moment she eased herself up, looking dazed. Gerry was beginning to panic.

'It's coming back!' someone yelled, and he looked, the thick jet of water heading towards them, like the cop was watering his garden. Gerry pulled Eva up by the hand and clutched at the man. He legged it, dragging them both. Water whipped the backs of his legs, the push of it propelling him. Arms grabbed him and the three were hurried out of the maelstrom to a group of people building up a fire, two women trying to protect it with tarp. Everyone was soaked. Teeth started chattering. Eva looked at Gerry, wide-eyed.

'This is dangerous,' she said. 'This is bad.' He tried to warm her, willing the fire to take. Her hair iced over under his lips. She shook him away and shrugged her backpack off. 'We need to do the milk again,' she said, gesturing to the man she'd bandaged up.

He was huddled in close to the fire and another man was swearing, piling on things to burn with superhuman strength. 'They're using water!' he kept saying. 'They're using water against us!'

His words sank in as they watched the flame tentatively lick the fuel and grow. A woman started to cry. 'What water are they using?' she asked between gasps. 'Is it from the river?' She looked around at everyone. 'Is it from the river?' No one answered her. They watched the fire. In front of them the barricade was misty with frost and tear gas. They could hear the *pop, pop, pop* of rubber bullets and the whistling of concussion grenades.

'Amos?' Eva asked softly, looking at Gerry. He looked back at her grimly. He took off her fingerless gloves and squeezed the water from them. His jacket crunched as he moved.

A few more fires had been lit and people were huddling around them, trying to get warm. 'You bastards!' someone would suddenly yell, peeling off from the fire and running at the barricade, and then *pop*, down they'd go. Still, near the wire, some protesters hopped and spun like dancing bears.

'We need to get out of here,' a woman said. 'Everyone needs to get as dry as possible and then we need to go.' People stared at her numbly. She pointed at Eva, who was holding the plastic bottle of milk. 'You can do that later. We've got to get out of here. I'll tell the others,' she said and started to walk over to another group around a fire.

There was a *pop* and the woman dropped.

'Fuck!' Gerry said, running over to her. Then came a roar of water again, and everyone screamed as the tarps were torn away, the spray knocking them backwards, fires sizzling to black.

Gerry got the woman up and ran with her. 'Eva?' he shouted, finding her and pulling her along with them. She was soaked again. 'Come on,' he said, and around them people were yelling. 'We gotta go! Everyone! We'll die of hypothermia!' But Eva wouldn't move. Gerry knew why, but he pretended not to. He took off her jacket and his, removed his thermal shirt and put it on her. 'Come on,' he said.

'No,' she murmured.

He looked at her, pleading.

'You know I can't,' she said quietly. 'He'll still be here.'

Gerry sighed. He squinted at the bridge, trying to see through the debris and smoke. 'I'll go,' he said, giving her a gentle push. 'Okay?'

Eva laughed. They were both shivering, the wind biting. 'Don't be a dick,' she said simply. He loved her, he realised, watching as she went back into the fray. He hurried to catch up. Everyone was running the other way, telling them to turn around, until the road emptied, leaving only an eerie feeling. All their paraphernalia of protest – bin lids, discarded placards, crushed water bottles, red cardigans curled up like dead foxes – lay as rubble. And through the haze, the marble-eyed cops watched them from the other side of the bridge.

'Amos!' Eva yelled. They saw him. He was lying under one of the wrecks. He turned, hearing her voice. 'Amos!' she called again and began to run.

Gerry followed. *He's got something*, Gerry thought. *Something's not right.* He craned to see as they ran towards the wrecks.

Amos waved them away. 'Get back!' he yelled. 'Get back!' He had rigged something up, Gerry could see now.

It was Eva who pulled up first. Her hand shot out to Gerry. 'Stop,' she croaked. Under the wreck, a white, fizzing light lit up Amos's face. *Magnesium*, Gerry thought, instantly recalling the thin ribbon he'd held in metal forceps over a flame at school. 'Don't look at it directly,' he remembered the teacher saying. *So you did learn something*, he mused as he looked away, to the police on the other side of the bridge. They levelled their guns. *It's just rubber*, he thought, reaching out to catch Eva's hand. And then there was a bright explosion.

Pop, pop, pop.

Shh, I Can Hear the Sea

'Put it on speaker,' instructed Robbie, as she drove too fast along the narrow suburban streets, taking a shortcut to the highway.

Nasim was in the back seat, next to the baby capsule. She frowned at Robbie's phone. 'I don't know how,' she said finally. Robbie stretched her arm back, opening her palm like a clam. Nasim put the phone in her hand and Robbie flicked her eyes from the road to her lap, tapping the screen with her index finger. A static ringtone filled the car.

'Hello, Robbie?' said a voice.

Robbie tossed the phone onto the empty seat next to her. 'Mum?' she asked loudly. 'Can you hear me?'

'Yes, dear?' the voice said.

'Hi, Mum,' Robbie said, putting her indicator on and creeping forward on a red light.

'Hello, dear. How are you? How's little Sid?'

Robbie instinctively glanced over her shoulder. Sidney was gazing at Nasim with wide, happy eyes. 'He's good. Sabeen's here, too.'

'Oh, hi Sabeen!'

'Hello, Claire,' the Iraqi woman replied, leaning forward. 'How are you?'

'Mum,' interrupted Robbie. 'You've got to get in your car.'

'Why? Is something wrong?'

'No, nothing's wrong. It's great. They're putting it up, on the West Gate Bridge.'

'Putting wha—' Claire began, then stopped. 'Really? Today? I thought it was suspended.'

'The premier overruled it. They're going ahead!'

'That's fantastic!'

'Yeah. But you've got to get moving, Mum, otherwise you'll miss it.'

'Nathan's in the bathroom.'

'Well, tell him to get out!'

The station wagon was on the highway now, Robbie weaving across the lanes. From Robbie's phone came the muffled sound of her mother's footsteps, then knocking and murmuring.

'Okay, Nathan's ready,' Claire said at last, her voice clear. 'We're walking out now.'

*

It was Nasim's job to entertain Sidney, to keep the boy from crying, as he often did in the car, but she allowed herself an amused smile as they passed the strange, vacuous structures dotting the highway. 'Public art,' Robbie had told her once, listing their colloquial names. 'Here's the cheese sticks ... this is a whale's ribcage ... they're the pick-up sticks.'

Nasim had chuckled, feeling a rare spark of love for this peculiar country with its unusual shape, alone at the bottom of the world. There was a newness here that sometimes made her feel as though she were in a toy city: the toy boats on the bay, toy people with their toy concerns. 'You're so young,' she'd clucked when stopping at a building in the city to read a brass plaque. *1854*, it said, as if the sandstone structure – underwhelming, she might add – had seen enough history to merit recognition. This dumb-headedness gave her an odd sensation of superiority. And relief. Her main concern was that more of her kind would come, and bring their ancient feuds with them. Nasim and Robbie often clashed over that. 'But you're a refugee,' Robbie would insist in disbelief whenever Nasim complained that Australia was letting in too many migrants.

'Yes,' the older woman nodded, as if it was merely a query. How to trust stories of forced exile? Nasim's own claim to sanctuary was based on a lie. Even Robbie, whom she'd come to love as a daughter, did not know her real name. To the girl, to the landlord, she was Sabeen. To the authorities, she was a Baghdad mother who had found herself on the receiving end of the Australian army, her mewling baby lost, their compensation an act of grace. She knew her real past was horrific, perhaps even worse than her stolen one, but she also knew that her actions in Baghdad would cancel out the sympathy of this docile, clumsy country. Here, a victim must be pure to stay a victim.

In Baghdad, the only 'public art' had been the looming spectre of Saddam. His regime had built four enormous bronze heads, so that his face glowered over the sprawling city, his gaze criss-crossing with his own, his blank metal eyes all-seeing. Massive statues of the man rose out of wedding cake–style plinths, and in the centre of the ancient Arab metropolis were the two huge fists of the Swords of Qādisīyah. They towered over the road, and in each fist Saddam held a stainless-steel sword, the blade extending forty-three metres into the sky. When Nasim was young, they'd driven under this arch, and her mother had shuddered at the sight of the arms coming out of the ground. 'It is like he is underneath us,' she muttered.

'Shh,' Nasim's father had said, his two-fingered hand on the wheel of their boxy Renault. Saddam was everywhere. He even resided in their pockets, a statesman on greasy dinar notes. Nasim was unable to shake Nhour's vision after that. The entire city was his skin, stretched over monuments and domes, houses, apartments and bunkers; when he yawned, he made graves for people to fall into. In his time, Saddam had rebuilt the ancient city. He'd changed the faces of past rulers to resemble his own. He even banned surnames, so no one could accuse him of starting a dynasty.

The Americans had pulled down the statues and melted the bronze heads – but found they couldn't bring themselves to destroy the sword-clenching fists. Instead they positioned their headquarters just beyond them, as if to say that some things would stay the same.

'Why didn't they just disarm him?' Robbie asked, when Nasim told the girl about 'public art' in Baghdad. 'Leave the hands, and remove the swords?' It was ideas like this that made the older woman adore Robbie. Since Sidney was born, Nasim had taken two days a week away from her salon to look after him so Robbie could keep working. The girl was a talent; she had a studio in Collingwood, and several younger artists helped her create large-scale projects. For a moment, Nasim yearned for the youth and ambition to remake herself, to return home and demand they remove the blades. But then, in her mind's eye, she saw what would remain: a martyr, his hands reaching upwards, like a drowning man begging for help. Like so many boys of Iraq buried in the desert, their bones crushed to grit by British tanks, ignoring the scraps of white material in their surrendering hands.

They passed the Melbourne Star, a bulky Ferris wheel, its glass capsules dangling like baubles. Nasim sniffed. What does this country think it is – a carnival? Billboards flickered past, with smirking breakfast-radio hosts. The highway was about to split in two, and Robbie shifted to the right lane, which would take them towards the bay. In the distance, over the shipping yards with giraffe-like cranes, where the sky and sea compared blues, was the West Gate.

Robbie leaned forward, hunching over the wheel to squint at the bridge. 'I can't see it,' she said. The sun was bright, pinching at the horizon, and she put her hand above her eyes like a visor. Nasim moved forward, trying to see, but her sight had long since failed her at a distance. Up close, though, her vision was crisp, and in the oblong of Robbie's mirror she caught sight of herself and was startled to see, looking back at her, the uncannily combined features of her mother and father.

It was happening more often, this reappearance – be it genes or ghosts, for who was Nasim to distinguish? – of her parents. And again, it was Robbie who had given her the words for it. For when Robbie's father died, she spoke of how she kept seeing him in others: the shape of his head; his frame, shoulders hunched; the familiar incline of a stranger's chin. It was as if, Robbie said, in the long space of her father's dying, he had vanished, only to reappear after his death in the guise of other people. She had to stop herself from calling out when she thought she saw him.

These strange recognitions didn't always pain Nasim as they did Robbie. It was easy to brush off the unkinder qualities, like detecting her mother's sharp tongue in her own voice, or catching her mother's unflinching, critical gaze in the mirror. The gentler glimpses caused more pain: the crinkle of her father's eyes, say, and Nasim would remember his teasing smile. She would see the fullness of her mother's lips in her own, the fuzz of bleached hairs, and she would remember the strangeness of her mother's kisses, how she pressed her lips to people, her love bruising, rather than puckering and pulling back.

Sidney began to mewl, preparing to wind up to a wail. Nasim shook herself to attention as Robbie bent sideways to search through her bag on the floor. The car wobbled as she tugged free a sachet of baby puree and flung it onto the back seat. Diligently, Nasim twisted off the cap and offered the nozzle to the baby, who clamped his lips around it and began to suck.

Steadying the car, Robbie fixed her eyes on Nasim in the mirror. The older woman's skin prickled. Robbie had a 'look'; Nasim had seen it turned on others, but rarely was it trained on her. It was an almost surgical gaze in which the girl peeled layers off a person's being until there was only a bare truth. Nasim started to hum to the baby, but Robbie was undeterred.

'So,' she said, 'who were those two men in the mall?'

*

That morning, Robbie had pinched her nose before peering inside the nail salon. 'Sabeen here?' she'd asked, nasally, cupping her other hand over Sidney's mouth and nose.

The girls in the salon smiled and Aisha leapt up from her table, abandoning her customer. The baby was strapped to Robbie's front, fat legs dangling in a cotton jumpsuit. Often when she walked, she'd hold a foot in each hand. 'Ooh, baby Sidney,' Aisha cooed, coming close and pulling down her white mask. Robbie shifted so Aisha could see him better, watching Sidney's eyes bulge a little as he took in the girl. She was wearing a crimson hijab, and her oval face was thick with make-up, lashes fanning outwards. Extensions, Robbie had learned the previous year, the salon girls laughing at her incredulous expression. Aisha tickled Sidney's chin with a magenta acrylic talon. Robbie tried not to gag. She hated the things. Yet, despite this, the Oushk Nail Salon, tucked between a carwash and a Lebanese sweet shop, had become part of her mid-morning Friday routine, even if she didn't dare inhale.

'Robbie's here!' one of the girls called up the stairs at the back.

There was a muffled reply and Nasim emerged, carrying a plastic bag. 'My darlings,' she sang, swinging the bag. She was dressed elegantly in a silk blouse, wide-legged black pants, embroidered slippers and a headscarf of sophisticated pale blue. 'I finished it!' she said, removing a crocheted bundle from the bag. She shook out a blanket, stretching it between her hands. Robbie gasped as she took in the vivid colours and shapes.

'Do you like it? I did it in the style of Hundertwasser for you. Very ugly, I think – but you like ugly things.'

'Sabeen!' Robbie said, throwing her arms around the older woman, Sidney squished between them. 'It's amazing!'

Nasim smiled proudly. She took a swift step back to gaze at Sidney. 'Hello, my darling boy,' she murmured. Sidney gave her a wet gooey smile and tried to lurch forward for a hug. Nasim touched his cheek, then busily wrapped the blanket around him, tucking the corners into the straps of Robbie's carrier. 'There,' she said. 'Perfect for winter.'

'I really love it,' Robbie said, running her hand over the wool.

Nasim nodded. 'Good.' She looked around at her clientele then, and moved to one of the pedicure chairs, where a thin blonde woman was sitting with her feet in a girl's lap, the bony knobs of her ankles on show. 'Ah, Mrs Pearce,' Nasim said with a smile, 'you getting ready for the big day?'

'Oh, yes,' the woman replied in an excited, girlish voice. She picked up the phone in her lap. 'The dress was finished just in time. Would you like to see?'

'Of course!' said Nasim, looking over the woman's shoulder. She sucked in her breath theatrically. 'My goodness, Mrs Pearce,' she exclaimed. 'What an exquisite dress.' The woman nodded avidly. Nasim inspected the varnish on the woman's toenails. 'Wonderful choice,' she said. 'They will go together splendidly. Aisha?'

Aisha looked up from her table, where she was buffing a woman's nails.

'When you do Mrs Pearce's hands, be sure to add some diamantes – free of charge.' Nasim looked at Mrs Pearce. 'A wedding gift for the mother of the groom.'

Mrs Pearce beamed.

Robbie retreated to the footpath to breathe fresh air, and rocked Sidney as she watched her friend through the window. She considered the way the older Iraqi woman charmed her customers, the confident manner with which she moved around the salon. Robbie was proud of her friend, thinking how far she had come from the voiceless and fearful woman of six years earlier. How cleverly she'd landed on her feet. But recently there had been something else, something that made Robbie less sure about her friend. She had always assumed the Iraqi woman's story was too painful to tell in full, not that she was hiding something. But now Robbie wondered.

It was the piano that did it. A garish purple instrument had appeared in the Coburg Mall where, since Sidney was born, the women had a weekly routine, strolling to the area where people sat on metal chairs around wobbly tables. Here, the two would have morning tea, drinking sweet coffee and sharing pink cubes of Turkish delight.

'Oh!' Robbie had said last month when they saw the piano placed under a dusty stunted tree, the painted instrument flecked with pigeon droppings. *Play me,* read the words scrawled on its front. Nasim had paused. Robbie leaned over to sound a few notes, with Sidney gurgling in delight, immediately stretching out his hands to the source. And then Nasim sat down. Not once had the older woman mentioned being a pianist. But the moment she sat on the rickety stool and held her hands over the keys, even in the seconds of silence before her fingers touched the notes, Robbie suddenly had a feeling that she'd been naive.

*

It was the piano that did it, Nasim was certain. It was, how do the Australians say, a moment of weakness. Less than a week after she had played the piano in the mottled sunshine of the mall, the two men came to the salon. It was true, there were other ways Nasim might have been recognised. Oushk Nail Salon was a success; no doubt she'd raised the ire of the Chinese-owned salon up the road. Who knew what connections they had? And she had dropped her guard, become too involved, both in the lives of her girls and in those of her customers. Since opening the salon, Nasim had attended many weddings – big, loud affairs in reception centres with meringue wedding dresses. All the nails done by Oushk, of course.

Nasim had taught the girls. She had demonstrated how to work the nail drills with foot pedals and attachments. They learned to apply gel and acrylic, and effects like marbling, practising on rubber fingers, hands and feet. She showed them how to organise the work trays, dipping ointments and powders, and at the back of the salon, the sterilising equipment that hummed like a dishwasher in the evenings.

It was inevitable, considering Nasim's history, that the girls became 'her girls'. Her seven employees were a mix of Turkish, Syrian and Lebanese, as well as Laila, a shy and lovely Afghan girl. After a period of good revenue, Nasim had negotiated to rent the upstairs as well, and she decorated her new flat with rugs, wall hangings and cushions with wispy golden threads, her girls sometimes joining her for bubbly smoke and sticky baklava. She created a sanctuary for these unusual Aussie Arab girls, many of whom lived under the watchful eyes of their fathers and brothers. In this, Oushk was a kind of penance, an atonement for the forced labours Nasim had had to inflict on her girls at Nostalgia – and for that she slept better, even in the fog of acetone. Sometimes she even forgot, albeit briefly, that she'd taken the name of a dead prostitute who had once been in her care.

And now there were the two men.

The bell above the door tinkled as they pushed it open. The shorter, stocky man stood in front, in a brown leather jacket and beige pants, while the other, lankier, in a long-sleeved shirt and jeans, hung back. All the girls had left for the evening, except for Laila, who was mopping the floor. Both she and Nasim froze.

'We're closed,' Nasim said, trying to sound stern, though her heart was hammering. The men smirked at her. Then the short man in the leather jacket nodded at Laila.

'Is that even halal?' he said. He returned his gaze to Nasim, watching as she paled and put her hands on the counter to steady herself. He smiled.

'No,' she murmured.

'Yes,' he said.

Nasim's head spun and for a few seconds she could only picture the piano, stupid and ugly in the mall.

'It's a street piano,' Robbie had explained that day. *A street piano*, Nasim now thought viciously. *You stupid people with your stupid ideas.* And then self-loathing coursed through her: she recalled how she'd sat on the stool like a princess, and held up her hands, silently counting herself in. What had she been thinking? That she could start afresh?

Is that even halal? It was Salima's saying. Now, in the salon, Nasim did not dare look at Laila for fear the girl might be able to see her ugly truth.

'Go upstairs,' Nasim said, keeping her eyes on the men, and Laila ran across the wet floor, feet light on the wooden steps. Nasim waited for the girl's footfall to end, then said quietly, 'What do you want?'

*

It was a curious thing to be comforted for the death of a father by that same father, and yet this is how it was for Robbie. She was pregnant, baby Sidney sprouting inside her like a mung bean, although at the time she did not know it.

Robbie had already performed the repetitive dance with the dementia patients when she'd arrived that morning. In reception: What day is it? *Tuesday*. Near the dining room: When is the milkman coming? *Very soon*. In the hall: What time is my son arriving? *I'll find out*. Outside Banksia Ward: I've misplaced my keys. *Here they are*, Robbie said, handing them a set of pretend keys from a bowl on the sideboard. It's my birthday. *Happy birthday*, she recited. Once she brought the birthday woman a present, a little painted box she'd found in an op shop with a brooch inside it. The woman's eyes lit up when she saw it. 'You remembered!' she exclaimed, hugging herself.

Robbie stood in the doorway of her father's room, a chain strung across it to stop the walkers. They were prone to stealing things while the bedridden patients watched in despair. Sometimes the walkers would pee in a corner, women raising their nighties to squat. But the flimsy chain seemed to deter them from entering.

Robbie looked in. Her father was sitting up in bed, hitting himself monotonously in the face. It was a new thing, this hitting – the nurses said that towards the end, the disease would progress quickly, and sometimes when the patient briefly stabilised he or she could develop strange ticks. It's a self-soothing thing, said one, suggesting the family could try rocking him instead. Robbie did this now, approaching him carefully and bundling her father's hands in her own, holding them down. He tried to wrench himself away but she put her other arm around him firmly. 'Shh,' she said, the white dandelion fuzz of his hair against her cheek. 'Shh.'

Dementia, she had learned, was as much about training your own brain as it was accepting the patient's feckless ways. You had to, in a way, mimic them, make your thinking similarly slippery, eel-like; a habitual, amnesiac way of living. It was theatre, she'd once told Jack, a weekly role she had been playing for a very long time. 'I'm like Alf in

Home and Away,' Robbie said. 'I've been in this show so long people can't even remember how I started off.'

Jack laughed lovingly, reaching out to draw her to him. 'Maybe there'll be a big reveal in a later episode,' he said, 'and you'll go back to being his daughter.'

Robbie remembered Jack's words as she rocked her father, and perhaps it was this that set her off, or maybe it was the hormonal shift taking place in her body, or a premonition that it wouldn't be long now, but she began to cry. Her tears fell fat and slow, landing on her father's hair, and she felt him stiffen. She could sense without looking the stricken expression on his face, feel the pull of his hand under hers, wanting to find his buzzer. But she couldn't stop. She let him go, waiting for the electronic beep to summon the staff. But instead she felt the tentative tips of his fingers, his touch wary on her arms, and then braver, his hands on hers.

'My dad,' she said suddenly, her voice thin, and it came out of her, unplanned, a truth and a big terrible lie. 'I'm sorry. It's my dad,' she said. 'He died.' And her father put his arms around her, shyly, giving a light pat on her back. 'He's dead,' Robbie said again, a warble of hysteria in her voice.

He began to rock her, his hands firm now, his chin gentle on her head. 'Shh,' he said. His fingers were in her hair and he whispered, just like she'd done, 'Shh, shh,' holding her like she was a child, as though he remembered how.

He died five months later. He was ragged by then. He had lost his voice, could only rasp a breathy 'ha, ha, ha', eyes milky with blindness.

Beverley came to see him towards the end. To say goodbye would be a stretch, as she'd never had the opportunity to say a proper hello, having only met him in his demented state, but it was a farewell of sorts. Her daughters were with her, walking either side of the large, dignified woman. Beverley greeted Robbie, Otis and Claire, clasping their hands, and chuckled to see Robbie's inflated belly. Then her daughters, as if choreographed, located a chair, slipping it under the older woman's bottom next to Danny's bed, placing their hands beneath her arms to ease her descent. Beverley spoke softly to her brother and sat for a long time, holding his hand. Finally, she said something in language, a rugged rolling of vowels.

'What did you say?' Robbie asked when the woman stood up, the daughters solemn sentries at her side.

'Sleep well, big brother,' Beverley answered. Tears sprang to Robbie's and Claire's eyes. Otis looked away. Beverley cleared her throat, looking steadily at Claire, her eyes piercing. The woman was going to ask something of them, Robbie could sense it. Something that would hurt.

'Can we bury him?' the woman said. Robbie sucked in her breath as Otis looked up, startled. Beverley showed no sign of noticing, continuing to look at Claire. 'We would like to return him to his mother,' she said.

There was a heavy silence, and Robbie felt suddenly woozy. She put her hands on her belly, and Claire put her hand out too, her arm stretching across Robbie and Otis, as she would do in the car if she had to brake quickly and one of them was in the front passenger seat. Claire's eyes searched her children's.

'No,' she said at last to Beverley. 'He's ours.'

There was another silence as Beverley shifted her gaze to consider the siblings. Otis looked at the floor, but Robbie returned the woman's stare.

After a moment Beverley nodded. She swept her eyes over them and back to Danny, then led with her chin, footsteps slow and deliberate, to the doorway. But one of the daughters would not move. She stood, her expression resolute. Beverley stopped. 'Come on, Penny,' she said, looking back, but the girl shook her head. She sharpened her gaze on Robbie. 'No, Mum.' They were likely the same or a similar age, the girl and Robbie. Cousins, if they willed it.

The girl sized Robbie up, widening her stance, and Robbie felt a tiny shock. *She's like him*, she realised. When Danny had shadow-boxed in the courtyard of their old house, he'd showed Robbie and Otis his stance and made them stand in front of him, giving a surprise shove to see which foot they would put out to save themselves from falling. 'You're goofy,' he'd said with a laugh to Robbie, when she put out her left. Then he showed them how he tucked in his chin, pinning his elbows to his sides to protect his ribs, and put his right fist up to guard his face. 'Your strong arm stays in the rear,' he said, 'unless you want to fight like a mud crab.' Then he danced – at least, that is how it seemed to Robbie. She loved watching him, his left fist in front, popping it out and back, seeking out pockets of air as he hopped on his feet, his right fist glancing like a shadow of the former. He seemed to repel light and flatten shade, and in spring she would shadowbox with him, geranium on the breeze and new butterflies unfurling, their wings setting before flying off on ribbon routes, and her father would seem briefly happy. There was a similar steely insouciance to the girl, her father's niece, as she glared at Robbie.

'Our grandma loved him,' the girl said, her fists clenching. 'They took him away. They made sure she had nothing, then said she couldn't care for him.' Robbie tried to look away but the girl shifted, finding Robbie's gaze. 'She said it was like a piece of her had been carved off, like they had pulled out a hunk of her flesh. She didn't know where he was, if they made him work or just fed him to the dogs, or what.' The girl paused, her eyes angry, the irises a stormy grey. 'Every time someone died she would study the pictures in the papers to make sure it wasn't her son. My grandma had a hole in her – she had it every day of her life after losing him – and we can put him back. It shouldn't be up to you.'

Robbie frowned. She hated the girl. She stared at her, then at Beverley. *Fuck you*, she wanted to say. *Fuck you. He* is *ours.* She didn't say anything. She looked down, glaring at the vinyl floor until they left.

*

'Shh, I can hear the sea,' a child had said to his mother on the day the purple piano appeared. Nasim and Robbie had overheard him as they walked past, smiling when the boy flattened his palm over his mother's mouth, cocking his head at her to listen. Above them, the pale green gum trees whispered. There was no sea; it was a hazy, hot suburb of concrete in the north with a bluish-grey graph of skyscrapers jutting out of the horizon like a crystal growth. The boy was hearing the whoosh of the wind, leaves rubbing together like dry skin, but the mother didn't say so. She shared an amused look with the two passing women.

There was such sweetness in the day. It had rained in the night and everything felt washed clean, the quartz in the bitumen sparkling in the sunshine. Beneath the footpath, it was almost possible to feel the roots of the stunted shrubs stretching and drinking. It all seemed to mesh: the slow turn of lamb spits, rugs with Arabic books laid out on them, men crouched easy on their heels, cigarettes parked on their lips as they fingered the pages. When Nasim had arrived in Australia she'd missed Baghdad so much, the feeling had coiled up inside her like a sickness. There were times she had been wracked with a pain so physical that she was convinced she was dying. It was the girl who had brought her here, persuaded her to get on a rattling tram, travel through the city and out the other side, where the appearance of Arabic shop signage made Nasim's chest start to flutter.

It had been a mistake. But how was the girl to know?

The existence of such a place was no surprise to Nasim – of course she was not the only one here – but her reaction? This was a shock. Her eyes shone as clusters of veiled women got on and off the tram. *It's the language*, she thought. The humming haggle, the voluptuous voices that swung out, vowels elongating like swaying hips, the tap of *q*s like teacups to saucers. Getting off the tram, Robbie led Nasim through an arcade, past a boy feeding coins into a mechanical horse, and into a market. A tangle of voices had washed over her. Guttural rich Arabic, words cantering outwards, queries never left hanging, always finding a response. Standing on the concrete floor that sloped towards various drains, Nasim had closed her eyes. What could she hear? There was some Syrian; Turkish, too. Some Zazaki, Pashto, Kurdish; there was Farsi, Urdu, and oh! It was Iraq! She peered into the marketplace, trying to place the speaker – from the north, Mosul perhaps. Then she heard a word – *Baghdad* – and it was like gold running through her veins.

'Are you okay?' came Robbie's voice.

Nasim shook herself from reminiscence. 'Yes,' she replied, trying not to stammer. 'I just remembered something.'

Robbie grinned. 'How long had you forgotten it?'

Nasim stared at the girl, puzzling over her youthful wisdom. It seemed so unearned, which was a mean thing to think, perhaps, but Nasim did not intend it like that. 'It feels like forever,' she answered finally.

The two women walked around the market and Nasim breathed in the men, their familiar odour of sweat, thumbed newsprint, fermented vinegar and chickpeas. She took in the women, their woody perfume, with notes of rose. At stalls, people were selling dimpled copper bowls, ladles; in nut and legume shops, there were plastic containers of Bahārāt, baskets of Babylon dates, tall bottles of rosewater and cranberry molasses. One shopkeeper had placed a halved pomegranate on his counter, its red jewels glinting. Nasim felt her chest split, not unlike the pomegranate; she could feel all the honey-comb chambers of her heart burst.

When she saw men and women lay their cheeks on watermelons like children about to fall asleep, gently drumming the thick rind with their palms, the recollection was sharp. Several years after Nasim received her mother's body from Abu Ghraib, she had managed to source some of her mother's chapbooks. In souks she crouched with men, poring over piles of books, searching for her mother's name. It was in one of her earlier collections: *In the marketplace*, Nhour Amin had written, *we listen to watermelons like lovers, a husband's ear pressed to his wife's pregnant stomach.*

Nasim put her hand in Robbie's and squeezed it. 'Thank you,' she said, for, like most animals would if given the chance, Nasim had decided to stay in this northern suburb, a tiny pocket of home. For all its reckonings, this was the only habitat she knew.

Shh, I can hear the sea.

A long time ago, in Baghdad, Nhour Amin had told her daughter she played piano without heart. She was cruel like that. Nhour loathed pretence, did not believe one ought to feel one's way around the truth. 'If truth is a bomb, then let it explode!' she'd say. Her mother was right: as a girl, Nasim, while technically brilliant, lacked a depth that could not be taught. She could coerce everything from a piano – obedience, timing, tricks, glory – except life. Perhaps it was this blandness that ensured she kept her extremities under the regime, while her father had his fingers amputated and her mother lost her tongue. And so it was curious, after so many pianos Nasim could not coax into life, that it was a purple street instrument, with its damp, out-of-tune innards and birdshit tableau, that ultimately yielded.

Nasim played the pedals first, levering them in and out to quicken the action, the keys flinching at the mechanism. She pressed a single note then, the sound shivering out of the creaking wooden box. She glanced around the mall nervously, but no one was listening, groups of old men dipping sweetbread into their coffee, women kissing the powdery remnants of cakes from their fingers. Only Robbie was paying attention, a surprised look on her face. Nasim's hands hovered, fingers dangling. She saw the notes in her head, tapping out a classical composition – Bach perhaps, or Gershwin, as she'd practised over and over for the academy. Then she saw another kind of song: the folk songs she'd played at Nostalgia, women undulating like sand vipers as the men clapped their thighs. *Does it even exist*, she thought, *the music I want to play?* Then she recalled Nhour, her mother who could not read music but marked the piano keys so as to remember her made-up melodies. It did exist.

Nasim lowered her hands and remembered.

At first it was the simple patter of rain, the notes sparse, and slowly people in the mall began to look up, some at the sky. Then the notes fell heavier, shiny droplets of sound, and over the top came the twisting melodies, Arabic maqams, those scales the teachers at the academy had openly scorned, and then hidden their scorn for fear of being butchered. There had always been a severity to Nasim's playing, and in Coburg this had not changed. She felled each note, sometimes letting it linger for a moment, other times deftly flicking the key upwards with the underside of her index finger, cutting it short. But she was whirling, dancing, and at times her fingers slipped in her sweat, stumbling to another note, strangling a chord. When this had happened in her youth, a brief shame would bloom in her chest each time. *Play on*, her mother would say to her in the days she listened to her daughter practise, and Nasim wouldn't; she'd start from the beginning, as a composition ought to be flawless. Yet here, she played on. Was this playing with heart? For Nasim ached; she leaned into the piano, her feet paddling the pedals, and she wanted to kick the instrument hollow, she wanted to punish it and she wanted to drown in it, swallow the notes.

And she played on.

She played for her father's amputated fingers and her mother's razored-off tongue. She played for the girls she broke in, for the rank brownish blood each of them found in their underpants from whoring. She played for her concertinaed city, its olive-eyed citizens and dreams made of silt and clay. And into the melodies of her mother, she played her own history.

Nasim knew everyone in the mall was listening. She'd long learned how to feel an audience's attentiveness. It was an energy in the air. A woman, her blonde hair tied back, came near the piano with her child, and in the incongruous way of so many of these Australians, encouraged her daughter to dance, but the girl couldn't find the beat. When the mother tried, nor could she. It was as though the Arabic rhythm was a Western misfit, putting sound where there should be silence, and vice versa.

*

Not long into the occupation, the Iraqi Symphony began to rehearse again. They passed through security, opening their cello and violin cases for the American soldiers, then moving into the theatre Saddam had used for his Ba'ath Party functions. Nasim had gone, braving the street-by-street warfare, hurrying along the blocks, telling children not to play in the debris, their legs dusted in the powder of fallen buildings. She stood outside the convention centre gates, near the razor-wire and sandbags, watching the musicians enter. It was here that Saddam had held loyalty meetings, reading out the names of traitors, weeping as if filled with sorrow at their treachery, watching them being led away.

The musicians were thin. Decades of persecution wore at the corners of their mouths. Nasim feared for them. The theatre was safe now, as safe as one could expect – she knew this – but she could not shake the feeling. It was as though they were filing into the jaws of a lion. She also, desperately, wanted to join them. She had come all this way in the hope that one of them would recognise her. She clutched to her chest a book of Chopin's nocturnes she had found in the rubble of a music shop targeted by Shi'a militia.

Nasim took a step closer to the musicians as they lined up. One of the soldiers noticed, lifted his weapon and came over. A few of the musicians turned to see what the problem was. Nasim held her breath. *Please remember me.* Their eyes washed over her and swivelled back to the front as she was ordered to move away. 'You want to be searched?' the soldier asked.

It was December 2003, the same month the bronze heads of Saddam were removed from the skyline. By then the American-led occupation had unleashed a catastrophe.

'Damn place is a fucking hornet's nest,' a Marine had said to Nasim during a visit he and others from his unit paid to Nostalgia. There were more of them than there were girls, so they took turns, playing poker in the kitchen with cards bearing the faces of their most-wanted Iraqi enemies. 'You got the Ace of Spades for Saddam,' explained the Marine, laying the card face up on the table next to a decorative ashtray. Nasim peered cautiously at it and he laughed at her. 'Don't be nervous. Bastard can't get you now,' he said with pride. He flipped over another card. 'Uuuu-day,' he said, exaggerating his American drawl, not noticing how Nasim shrank back. 'Ace of Hearts,' he said, 'because he was a lover, right? A *real* ladies' man.'

*

'Are you going to play again?' Robbie asked Nasim. She'd gathered up the crocheted rug; it was too hot for Sidney to be wrapped up. Nasim stiffened at the question. She was hoping the piano would no longer be there, disappearing as seamlessly as it had appeared. She shrugged, trying to appear casual.

But the girl didn't let it go. 'I can't believe you can play like that,' she said. 'Why didn't you tell me?' Nasim detected a needling in the girl's tone. She glanced at Robbie's face as they walked and saw her instinct was right. Robbie looked put out, suspicious even.

'It is not important,' Nasim said.

Robbie arched her eyebrows. 'Really? You were playing like a proper, I don't know, a proper musician.' Nasim shrugged again and strode ahead. 'I mean,' Robbie continued, catching up, 'if I could play like that it would be pretty important to me.'

Nasim was silent.

'Sabeen?' said Robbie. 'I'm just wondering —'

'Enough!' Nasim snapped, turning on the girl furiously. 'It is none of your business! Enough.' She made a motion as if to zip her mouth.

The girl stared back, eyes wide. 'O-kay,' she said slowly.

They walked in silence after that. Nasim's heart was racing. It was falling apart again, she worried. She'd become comfortable, even happy; how was she going to start over? What new incarnation was even possible from here?

'No Yasemin today?' Robbie asked after a time.

'Not feeling well,' Nasim said, not looking at Robbie.

'Sharon, too?'

'Yes,' Nasim said, 'Sharon, too.'

In truth, the girls were gone. It was the first thing Nasim had decided after the men came to see her. Yasemin and Sharon were her favourites; they were regulars at the upstairs soirees, lively young women whose company and sharp jibes delighted her. But Nasim had learned this lesson long ago: the first to go must be the oldest and most assured, and most importantly of all, the confidantes. She told the two women the instant they arrived, in front of the other girls, handing them their pay and asking them to leave. Then she informed the others they would no longer be paid minimum wage and their earnings would be commission-based. If any of them were unhappy with this new arrangement, they too should leave.

The men wanted money, of course. Their 'cut', they said, as if they had earned it. They did not say how much they knew. They demanded to see her books, and attributed seventy per cent of her earnings to themselves.

'How do I explain it?' Nasim asked numbly, though she knew the answer. 'To the tax office?'

The men smiled. 'Insurance,' the shorter one said.

'In case of fire,' added the taller man, his timing flawless.

*

The purple piano was still there. A girl was sitting on the stool, two plaits sprouting from her head like handlebars, her fingers slow and clumsy. Nasim recognised the Minuet in G Major. Robbie went into a café to order while Nasim sat down, jiggling Sidney on her lap. She watched the girl with growing irritation. The minuet was tiresome. Her head hurt, a thump just behind her brow increasing as the mall's cups, saucers and small spoons clattered, and the beep and whir of the pedestrian crossing pressed in on her.

Near her feet, a male pigeon puffed his feathers, bobbing furiously as he pursued a female, cooing and rolling his Rs. 'Why doesn't she just fly away?' Robbie said, as she appeared with a plate of falafel and dip. She still wore the baby carrier, its straps hanging loose near her thighs. Sidney wriggled on Nasim's lap and reached for Robbie. Nasim passed him over, both women chuckling at the female pigeon walking in circles. Nasim felt ashamed for being nasty earlier. She wanted to give Robbie something, a story, to draw her close again.

'You ever seen a baby pigeon?' she asked.

Robbie shook her head as she broke open the hot falafel balls, releasing the steam. 'Wait, Sid,' she warned, as he reached for them.

'Ugliest things you ever saw,' Nasim said. 'Big hooked grey beak with,' she held a hand above her nose and pinched her fingers upwards as if tugging on the skin, 'a hump on them. Very ugly, like your Hundertwasser.' Robbie looked up, catching Nasim's eye, and grinned.

'A man kept a flock on the roof of my apartment building in Baghdad,' she continued, as Robbie delicately picked up a piece of falafel, bringing it to her lips to cool. 'A funny man. We' – she caught herself – 'I used to think he looked like a baby pigeon himself. He had a nose just like them.'

'What was his name?' Robbie asked.

Nasim frowned. 'I don't know. I can't remember. Maybe S'aid?' She shrugged. 'It stank up there. All these cages and roosting boxes, pegged shut with twisted wire. He let them out in the afternoons. It was too dangerous at dawn or dusk because the bigger birds, like the shikra, would be out hunting.'

'Was it beautiful?'

'What?'

'The flock. When they got out to fly?'

Nasim thought a moment and nodded. It was. Before the fighting, the sky had filled with flocks of pigeons swooping and arcing in tight, ever-shifting circles. With the cloying heat and the distant hum of traffic, the muezzin's call to prayer, it was beautiful. It was the place between skin and city, when it was all, ever so briefly, inseparable.

'I used to go up to the roof to watch them,' Nasim said, though this was only partly true. She had been on the roof just twice, the last time in the evening, and it had not been beautiful. She climbed the five sets of stairs, only remembering the pigeons when she opened the hatch, a sharp stink of rotting meat coiling in her nostrils. She had contemplated going back down to the apartment, but that was a ridiculous thought. Dead birds were the least of her worries. When she climbed up through the hatch, there was a scrambling in the boxes. A few of the birds were still alive. Nasim untwisted the wire and opened the cages. 'Come on,' she murmured, propping open the doors with empty water containers and bowls. The birds looked out; they were mostly naked, the white spines of their remaining feathers showing like ribs. Then, with a weak flutter of wings, the pigeons rose up as one, wheeling over the city, and immediately the shikra came out of their hiding places, beaks hooked, brown wings out like blades, talons ready. Nasim had unrolled her blanket and tried to sleep.

'It was very nice,' she told Robbie.

*

Robbie's phone chirruped and she walked a distance away to take the call. Nasim bounced the boy on her knees, singing softly. Sidney gurgled happily, with a gummy smile, his blue eyes slightly lolling. '*Ya'aburnee*,' she whispered close to his ear. The boy giggled at the touch of her breath, his ear twitching like a horse's might. '*Ya'aburnee*,' she said again. *You bury me.* 'You bury your mother, too. All us old people.' He gurgled and grabbed her nose.

Then, catching movement from the corner of her eye, she sensed them. She turned and saw the two men. They were in the café where Robbie had bought the falafel, at the counter. The shorter one was wearing the same brown leather jacket, tapping out a beat with his fingers. The café owner was busily shaving lamb off the spit. Nasim studied him carefully, watching for signs of stress. He turned back and filled two pitas with meat, tabouli and lettuce. When he finished, he wrapped the souvlakis and passed them to the men. They turned and left. The owner flicked his eyes up then, as if he could feel Nasim's gaze through the window. He was Turkish, tall and good-looking, with coffee-brown eyes. Robbie thought he was handsome, was always flirting with him. He gave Nasim a slight nod, and she returned it.

'Why hello, Nasim,' said a voice, and Nasim jumped, her hands tightening around Sidney's waist. The two men were standing next to her table with their souvlakis. A thin dribble of white sauce ran down the short one's wrist from the paper bag. He held up his arm so the sleeve of his jacket fell away and slurped it off his skin. Nasim gritted her teeth, not saying anything. 'Who's this?' the taller one asked, leaning forward as if to tickle Sidney's chin. Nasim jerked the boy away.

'Sabeen?' Robbie was back, standing next to her with a quizzical expression. The two men nodded at the girl and then at Nasim before making their way out to the street. Robbie watched them, then began to gather up her things. 'Sabeen?' she said again. Her voice was excited now. She reached out for Sidney. 'Can you do me a favour? Come with us?'

*

Danny died when he forgot how to swallow. 'Have you ever heard of a death so determined to come full circle?' Robbie had asked.

'Listen,' Claire told them after the day Beverley came to see Danny. 'I'm not sure what I want when I die. I don't know if I want to be buried, and I also have Nathan to think of. I'm not sure your father would appreciate having his wife's boyfriend buried with him.' She paused. 'So,' she said slowly, 'I'm afraid this is on you two. It's your decision, and I'll do whatever you want.' Claire put her hands in Robbie's and Otis's. 'And I promise I'll only say this once, but if anyone ever took either of you away from me, I don't know if I'd have been able to survive.' Her eyes brimmed with tears and she shook them loose. 'That's not true. I would have survived, because that's just what you do. But that girl of Bev's is right. I would have always felt as if you had been cut out of me. I don't even know if I could be dead peacefully.'

Robbie glared at her mother. 'Jesus Christ,' she said. 'That is a hell of a thing to only say once.' She looked at Otis and saw he'd already decided. It was up to her.

And so, Danny O'Farrell was buried with his mother, Betsy Carol. They were Christians, Beverley and her family, Robbie learned with surprise. She wasn't sure her father would have been so keen on a church service, but by then it was too late to object.

'We're letting go,' Claire liked to say to her, and annoying as it was, Robbie didn't mind hearing it. It was stupid, too, she had begun to realise, to go on about what Danny wanted, because since when did he ever get what he wanted? And maybe if things had been left well alone, a church service in Geelong would have been the natural way of things.

At the cemetery, the small crowd clustered around the pastor, who stood next to a hole in the ground in his black robe and white collar, a shiny granite marker for Betsy Carol already in place. On one side of the grave stood Beverley and her daughters, their arms linked, their clan clustered around them, while Robbie, Otis, Claire, Nathan, Jack and Nasim stood on the other side. People fidgeted in the heat. A mosquito landed on the pastor's cheek. 'There is reason to rejoice,' the pastor said solemnly, brushing the mosquito away only for it to land on his brow. 'There is reason to rejoice,' the pastor repeated – flinching as the mosquito sank its black proboscis in – 'for Danny O'Farrell is returning to God.'

There was a cough. It was Beverley's daughter, Penny. 'Um, to his mother actually,' Penny said loudly, and across the grave, the families grinned.

*

Robbie took the slip road and turned the corner into a highway thick with traffic. There were crammed cars and minibuses, vans flying the

Aboriginal flag from their windows, speakers belting out tunes – a mix of Archie Roach, Thelma Plum, Ruby Hunter, Dan Sultan and Baker Boy floated on the breeze. Robbie heard the tinny sound of the Warumpi Band. She laughed. There was the ordinary traffic, too, cars with just a driver staring ahead, cabs and petrol tankers, trucks hauling sheep, woolly bums pressed against the sidings. Up ahead, the service station was buzzing with television crews and vans with satellite dishes, and further on, flanking the highway, was a long line of police, some on horseback, others in vehicles parked at an angle, blue lights flashing. At the beginning of the bridge, police in hi-vis vests waved traffic wands, funnelling the vehicles in and upwards.

Robbie peered at the sky. 'I can see them!'

Nasim leaned forward. 'Oh, yes,' she said. 'So can I.'

The West Gate Bridge was like a sauropod, a long grey tail of concrete and steel arching up into the sky, its back stretching over the water, and then, lazily, a neck curving its way to the ground. At some time in the night, workers had received the go-ahead from the government to climb the two concrete towers jutting from the bridge. They had hauled down the tattered Australian flags and clipped on the black, yellow and red flags the size of houses. Then up and up the flags went, bold against the skyline.

'They must have wanted to do it without any warning,' Robbie said out loud, though more to herself. 'In case,' she added over her shoulder, 'there were any protests.' Nasim nodded. It was beyond her, this fixation of Robbie's on whose country this was. Small-minded, too, for surely it was a mere cigarette paper of sediment in the history of the earth. 'All countries are the inheritance of murderers,' she had said once to Robbie.

'And all history is inscribed by the inheritors,' she had replied.

Nasim had nodded. At least they agreed on this.

From there, they differed. 'Fifty thousand years of culture before the Brits came,' said Robbie. To which Nasim would think, *lucky them*. Once, she'd countered that it was unlikely that those fifty thousand years had been peaceful. To this, Robbie had snorted impatiently. 'Of course not. But they didn't fuck up the country in the process.' Nasim said nothing in reply. How could she? As the flotsam of history herself, it was hardly her place.

Robbie inched the car forward. She'd wound down the windows, waving at people in adjoining lanes. 'Treaty now!' someone yelled, and Robbie cheered. Behind them a policeman on a motorbike was weaving, making his way through the maze of traffic, when he paused alongside their car. He peered in at them. Robbie scowled as he gestured at them to pull over. Nasim felt worry build in her stomach.

On the side of the road, he put his hands on either side of his helmet, lifted it off and placed it on the bike's seat. Then, with a purposeful stride, he went to Nasim's window. 'What's your name, ma'am?'

Heat rushed into Nasim's face. Robbie was livid. She twisted in her seat to glare at the cop. 'What the hell is this for? It's because she's wearing a hijab, isn't it?'

The cop looked at her coldly. 'Just a random check,' he answered.

'Bullshit,' Robbie said. 'It's racial profiling, that's what it is.'

'Nasim Amin,' Nasim said quickly, to quell Robbie's anger, and immediately a sick feeling took hold in her throat. Never before had she made this mistake. Robbie fell silent, looking at her, confused. 'I mean, Sabeen,' she stammered. 'S-Sabeen Tahir.'

The policeman cocked his head. 'So which is it, ma'am?' he enquired.

Nasim felt her skin prickle with sweat. 'Sabeen,' she said again. 'Sabeen Tahir.'

'May I see your ID, ma'am?'

Nasim nodded, reaching for her handbag at her feet, wishing she could somehow disappear.

'Slowly, ma'am,' the policeman warned.

Nasim held out her licence. Her hand was trembling, the little plastic card already wet with her sweaty fingerprints.

The policeman took it. He looked at Nasim and at the licence, back and forth. Nasim could feel Robbie watching her.

'Where are you from, Sabeen?' said the officer.

'Iraq, sir.'

'How long you been in Australia?'

'Six years.'

'You like it here, Sabeen?'

Nasim nodded, trying to make her eyes shine with gratitude as if it were he who had built the country and let her in. 'Oh yes, very much so.'

Robbie snorted. 'Excuse me, officer, do you think I could see your ID?'

The policeman looked at her. 'Your licence, too,' he said.

Robbie glared back, thinking on it, then Sidney made a sound and she relented. She rifled through her bag, pulling out her licence. The policeman took it, along with Nasim's, and returned to his bike. Robbie stared after him. 'Fucking cunt,' she muttered.

'Shh,' Nasim whispered.

Robbie looked at her again, suspicion growing. 'What's going on, Sabeen? Or should I call you Nasim? Those men back in the mall called you that too,' she said.

Nasim could feel her hair beneath the hijab becoming damp. A lump formed in her throat. She opened her mouth to say something, but didn't know what to say. Then the policeman was back beside the car, and she was almost relieved to see him. He handed over Robbie's licence without fanfare and looked in again. He had her licence in his hand. 'Can I ask why you are here, Sabeen?'

Nasim's head began to thump. Why was she here in Australia?

Was that on the computer? Was he checking her story? Her eyes widened with fear and she felt snared by the cop, his inscrutable gaze on her. 'Why are you here?' he asked again, but then pointed at the bridge up ahead.

'Today?' Nasim breathed.

'Yes,' the cop said impatiently. '*Today*.'

Nasim looked helplessly at Robbie, pleading with the girl to speak for her.

'She's helping me,' said Robbie. 'With the baby.'

The policeman looked at Sidney, then back at Nasim. 'Okay,' he said. 'Well, I've made a formal note of both of you being here, so if there's any trouble . . .' He let the sentence trail off, the meaning clear. He passed Nasim's ID to her and straightened, so the women were gazing at his stiff leather jacket. Then, bow-legged, he returned to his motorbike, revved it and took off.

Nasim sank into the seat, drooping with relief. She tried to smile weakly at Robbie.

'It's the hijab,' Robbie said.

Nasim nodded.

There was a strange look in Robbie's eyes, as though she were no longer looking at her but studying her. 'What's going on, Sabeen?' she asked, perfectly to the point. The girl's directness had been what drew Nasim to her in the first place. But not now.

'I think I should get out,' Nasim said quietly. She pointed at the service station. 'I can get out there.' She waited for Robbie to say no, to shrug and say it was no big deal, but the girl didn't. Nasim spoke to fill the silence. 'It's my first name, Sabeen. Nasim is my second name. Many people go by their second name in Iraq.'

Robbie continued to stare at Nasim. 'Okay,' she said coolly. She turned back to the front, starting the engine again. There was more space between the cars and they made some headway, slowing again alongside the service station. 'You can jump out here if you want,' Robbie said, gazing at her in the mirror.

Nasim looked away, suddenly angry. She was subject to someone's whim again, this time a girl almost half her age, a girl who thought she knew so much, but knew nothing. *Nothing*. Nothing of surviving, of war. This girl – she was just like her mother had been, Nasim realised. Unforgiving and unyielding. Obsessed with truth as if it were the only important thing. Nasim set her jaw, unclipping her seatbelt. Then she looked at Sidney and wanted to cry. She put her finger on his puckered lips and softly strummed the bottom lip, smiling as he gurgled. She didn't want to leave them.

Robbie had turned around in her seat, the car stopped in the emergency lane, indicator ticking.

'It's this,' Nasim said, tugging on her hijab.

'I know,' Robbie replied. 'That's what I said.'

She spoke impatiently, and it made Nasim feel old. She blinked and looked down at her hands.

'You could take it off.'

Nasim winced. Robbie had never said that before. She knew Nasim was not Muslim, that she wore it for some other reason, a reason the older woman could not or would not explain. But Robbie would often see Nasim without the hijab. In each other's homes, the headscarf lay on a dresser or draped over the back of a kitchen chair. Nasim never felt the need to put it back on when Jack came home. It wasn't like that.

She hung her head now, the scarf shielding her face. 'Yes,' she said quietly. 'I could.' She put her hand on the door. 'Here?'

Robbie nodded, softening a little. 'You could get a taxi from the service station?'

Nasim did not want to lose Robbie. She had crocheted that rug for the baby in that awful ugly fashion, deeply in love with the girl, her lover and their child. There were times on weekends when she would see Jack wearing the baby carrier, Sidney knitted to his chest, and she would feel as though she might break at the beauty of it. 'In Iraq,' she often said to them, 'you would never see a man doing this,' waving her hand at Jack. But the girl knew. Not the truth, but that there was a lie, and Nasim knew the girl. It would not go away. She would have to know. They had reached an impasse.

'Okay,' Robbie said quietly. Nasim gathered her handbag and leaned over Sidney, kissing his warm mossy head, breathing him in. Then she wriggled between the two front seats to the girl. Their lips grazed, and their eyes met, and she said goodbye.

*

Robbie edged back into the traffic. She fiddled with the stereo until thick hip-hop rolled out, and almost involuntarily, her fingers began dancing on the lip of the open window. The road started to lift. Again, Robbie had to slow down, the police waving her into the two lanes they'd left open. From here, Robbie could see the artificial islands and clay-coloured treatment ponds beneath the bridge, a vast car park where brand-new vehicles were unloaded from carrier ships. The mouth of the wide river flushed boats in and out of the bay, while on the horizon a queue of ships had anchored. To the west were the markers of the industrial age built atop coastal tussock and saltpans: lime burners and oil refineries, smokestacks puffing next to wheat silos and tallow works. She came to a standstill, a few rows from the front, waiting her turn to drive onto the bridge. Her chest hummed with excitement. *Just say you're Italian*, her father had said to her before he got properly sick. Now Robbie winced, felt a familiar, habitual hurt in her heart. *You poor, poor bastard.* She thought of him, how beautiful he'd been, and complicated, too. As though he'd worried himself into knots. 'A Wurundjeri Wathaurung man', the priest had been instructed to say at the funeral, 'also of Scottish and English heritage'. But he wasn't. He was the man only she, Otis and their mother knew. And they'd loved him.

Robbie's phone beeped. Jack. *You on the bridge?*

Almost, she typed back.

Sid okay?

Robbie turned to look. *Sleeping*, she typed.

That'll be right. Sleeping through history.

The policeman waved his wand at her to pass. She lifted her foot off the brake and eased the station wagon onto the bridge.

Up she went, up, and Robbie sat tall. Not proud, as this, it wasn't hers to be proud of, but tall, in that she was part of it.

*

A couple of ruined jetties stuck out from the brown water, mangroves growing around them. Nasim had given up waiting for a taxi and walked past the service station, around the slip road, hugging the concrete barrier, and found a gravel side road that doglegged off the arterial. She walked down it, hot and thirsty, until she emerged into a squally suburb tucked under the bridge, wedged right up to the water's edge. She'd never been this way, taking in a row of tiny houses among the factories. In the little front gardens were blooms of geranium, groups of gaudy gnomes, a wishing well. Inside a pair of old boots someone had planted powdery white succulents with pink flowers. She looked up and saw the underside of the bridge, its ribbed belly like a snake. She could see the police gathered on their horses, cars compressed, then released, two by two, onto the bridge. All of them were small as Lego.

Nasim unclicked a rusty gate and bent over a tap, twisting it on and drinking, letting the water run down her chin and inside the neckline of her headscarf. Her thirst quenched, she walked on. At the end of the road, an uneven path of quarry rocks extended into the water and Nasim followed it out, sometimes having to jump between stones. She passed Asian fishermen with bells on the ends of their rods. Another finger of quarry rocks came out, and further along she could see more lone fishermen, each on a solitary perch, stranded by the tide.

That's one way to get away from the missus, Nasim thought, smiling at herself in surprise. Maybe she was becoming an Australian after all. At the end of the trail of rocks, she sat on the flat curve and looked out at the sea. She ran her shoes over the mussels and barnacles, trying to lever the limpets off with her acrylic nails. A movement startled her and Nasim looked up to see a grey heron beside her, two long legs coming out of the water, neck folded like a U-pipe. It had frozen, pretending to be a statue, or perhaps a rock. Nasim wagged her finger at it. 'I can see you,' she said. She admired the bird, its eye on her. Then she turned around to the bridge, wondering if Robbie had driven over it yet. She hoped Sidney was asleep and not wailing.

On the breeze, there was a tinkling. A fisherman moved quickly to wind in his line and Nasim watched the water break, a silver fish emerging, twisting on the hook. The angler reached out to catch it, detach it from the tiny barb and throw it back in. Nasim leaned back on the warm rock and closed her eyes. She was tired. The sun glowed red behind her eyelids. In her quiet, crabs edged forward, out of their cracks. Sleepily, she reached up to loosen her scarf, letting it spread out around her. Beside her, the heron lifted its skinny leg, then the other, its beak poised to pierce the water, deciding to trust the woman on the rock.

For Fuck's Sake

'Argh, for fuck's sake,' Toohey growled, slowing. Ahead was bumper-to-bumper traffic, winding all the way down from the Bolte Bridge and into the slip road. He leaned forward, peering at the West Gate, the next bridge along. It too was jammed with cars. 'What the fuck's going on?' He threw a sideways look at his son, trying to coax something out of him, but Gerry said nothing. The kid sitting in the passenger seat was not a kid anymore, that was obvious, and Toohey was oddly pissed off that he hadn't been the one to spur his son to manhood. Instead, a bunch of fucking American leftie freaks grew him up. So much for Gerry's little campervan trip.

'Your mum will be pleased to see you,' he'd said gruffly on the plane, when they'd finally negotiated their way out of the States, and Gerry had looked at him with interest. Toohey thought he'd finally connected with his son.

'Are you and Mum back together?' the kid asked, and Toohey, he'd no idea where he got this line from, because it most certainly wasn't his own, replied, 'How would you feel if we were, son?'

Gerry drew back in surprise, then collected himself. 'I honestly wouldn't care,' he said, and Toohey's temper quickened.

'Well, you can drop the attitude, Gerry,' he snapped.

The kid didn't quail. He looked out the port window, then

squeezed the side button on his armrest, tilting his seat back. They had an empty seat between them. Toohey was antsy; he got up and paced regularly. He'd got the fright of his life, seeing Gerry in that cell – seriously. It was more frightening than that time with the woman with the baby in Baghdad, and then tracking her down in Melbourne, sitting in the car outside that ugly nail shop, seeing her falute around the joint with stupid airs. He didn't recognise her. He doubted he'd ever known what she looked like – all he'd seen was the wetness of her open mouth and the bloody blouse. He had a letter drafted, was planning on sending it to a bunch of departments, demanding an answer to why she was here. For fuck's sake, whose side were they on? He'd held off on emailing it when the Gerry stuff happened, figuring he'd better lie low with immigration until he got the kid home.

But still, he hadn't expected the emotion, seeing his son in a standard-issue tracksuit sitting on the floor with an al-foil blanket over his lap, playing cards, a lone white guy among the Mexicans. It was the disrespect, mostly. He'd fucking fought an American war and they put his son in here with god knows what kind of scum. Then there was the steely way his son appraised him. It wasn't that Toohey had thought of himself going in as the saviour, that Gerry would be overcome with gratitude – it wasn't that. But there could have been at least a bit of grovelling. Of ingratiating. Not that he would have respected that. When Toohey said Gerry was lucky he wasn't up on terrorism charges like the Indian kid, his son looked at him with contempt, and Toohey had almost left the boy then and there. But then Toohey got this uneasy feeling the kid wouldn't care. That it was him who was cornered. And there it was: the fucking to-ing and fro-ing in his head, the not knowing what he wanted from his son.

'For fuck's sake,' Toohey said again, fiddling with the car radio dials, flipping past snippets of music and ads until he got to talkback, the host taking calls from outraged drivers.

'You know, if they want us to feel the least bit sympathetic for them, then this is the wrong way to go about it,' a woman sniped, the host cutting her off.

'That's Cathy's point of view. How about you, Chris, what are your thoughts?'

'Well, Dayno, next election this government is going to seriously regret today.'

Toohey turned the dial again, stopping at the next station along. 'The Victorian premier says today is a momentous day for treaty negotiations as Melbourne's most famous bridge, the West Gate, is flying the Aboriginal flag on *both* towers for the first time since its erection. Lucy, a member of the Kulin nation, is on the bridge right now. Lucy, how —'

Toohey snapped off the radio. 'You're fucking kidding me!'

Beside him, Gerry shifted, staring hard out his window. 'I can see them,' he said. 'There's two of them, two flags.' He looked at Toohey. 'Can you see them?'

Toohey didn't look; instead he shook his head furiously. 'What a fucking joke this government is! Look at the pile-up. They've stopped the entire city, for what? A fucking flag?'

Gerry unwound his window and held out his phone to take a photo, pinching the screen with his fingers so he could zoom in on the bridge. Then he brought the phone back and started tapping on it.

'What are you doing?' Toohey said fiercely.

Gerry didn't reply, just kept tapping.

It overtook Toohey, the anger, and he jerked his hand out, whacking the phone from Gerry's hand. It fell on the floor at the kid's feet, and for a second, Gerry just looked at it. Briefly it pleased Toohey, seeing the tautness of his son, the rope of rage uncoiling. *You little fucking prick,* he thought, *welcome to the real world. What, you think you're some Red Indian chief now, all zen on your mountain?*

Well, fuck you. Welcome, fucking welcome.

But it all drained out of him when his son leaned down to pick up the phone. Gerry sat up and unclicked his belt. 'You're still living at the same place, Dad?'

'What are you doing, Gerry?'

'Mum's there too?'

Gerry opened the car door and Toohey rolled the car forward but there was nowhere to go, the car in front wedged tight. 'Same place, Dad?' Gerry asked again, and he did that thing kids do, kind of nodding in reverse, like a seal pushing a ball up to the surface; smooth, sort of jazzy. It shat Toohey to no end. He clenched the wheel.

'Well,' Gerry said, getting out of the car. 'I'll make my own way there, I reckon.' He reached into the back seat and pulled out his pack, swinging it over his shoulder and shutting the door. He popped his head back in the open window. Toohey saw all the different faces in the kid then, bits of Jean, bits of him, bits of his own mother. The kid smiled and Toohey wasn't so dumb that he thought Gerry was smiling at him, more for the impending escape, but still, he suddenly wanted it. He wanted that smile for himself.

'Thanks, Dad,' Gerry said.

Then the kid walked, between the cars, people looking from their windows at him, irritated and envious. He walked down the Bolte Bridge, and paused at the slip road that led to all the fuss at the West Gate. Gerry took it, the road, disappearing around the bend, Toohey watching until he lost him.

Acknowledgements

The author is indebted to the reporting, research and analysis of many – in particular, war reporters Paul McGeough and Jon Lee Anderson, and authors Said K. Aburish for *Saddam Hussein: The Politics of Revenge*, Jessica Bruder for *Nomadland: Surviving America in the Twenty-First Century* and Geraldine Brooks for *Nine Parts of Desire*.

'Sorry Rocks' is inspired by the lived experience of the Anangu, traditional owners of Uluru, and rangers at the Uluru-Kata Tjuta National Park, and draws on the work of Jasmine Foxlee, who documented the 'sorry rocks phenomenon' in her work *Cultural Landscape Interpretation: The Case of the Sorry Rock Story at Uluru-Kata Tjuta National Park*.

The author acknowledges the timely and generous assistance of the Australia Council for the Arts, Deakin University and the Sidney Myer Fund.